WHITE
WORLD

WHITE WORLD

SAAD T. FAROOQI

Cormorant Books

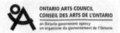

We acknowledge financial support for our publishing activities: the
Government of Canada, through the Canada Book Fund and The Canada
Council for the Arts; the Government of Ontario, through the Ontario Arts
Council, Ontario Creates, and the Ontario Book Publishing Tax Credit.

LIBRARY AND ARCHIVES CANADA CATALOGUING IN PUBLICATION

Title: White world / Saad T. Farooqi.
Names: Farooqi, Saad T., author.
Identifiers: Canadiana (print) 20240364252 | Canadiana (ebook) 20240364260 |
ISBN 9781770867451 (softcover) | ISBN 9781770867468 (EPUB)
Subjects: LCGFT: Novels.
Classification: LCC PS8611.A77 W45 2024 | DDC C813/.6—dc23

United States Library of Congress Control Number: 2024934031

Cover and interior design: Marijke Friesen
Author photo: Michelle Elliott
Manufactured by Friesens in Altona, Manitoba in August 2024.

Printed using paper from a responsible and sustainable resource,
including a mix of virgin fibres and recycled materials.

Printed and bound in Canada.

CORMORANT BOOKS INC.
260 ISHPADINAA (SPADINA) AVENUE, SUITE 502,
TKARONTO (TORONTO), ON M5T 2E4

SUITE 110, 7068 PORTAL WAY, FERNDALE, WA 98248, USA
www.cormorantbooks.com

To Paul Auster

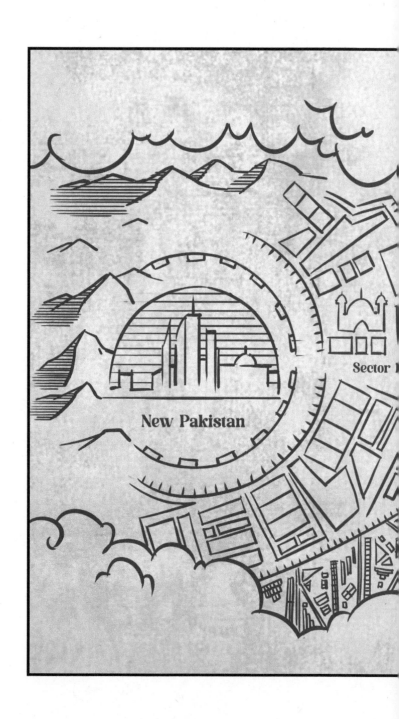

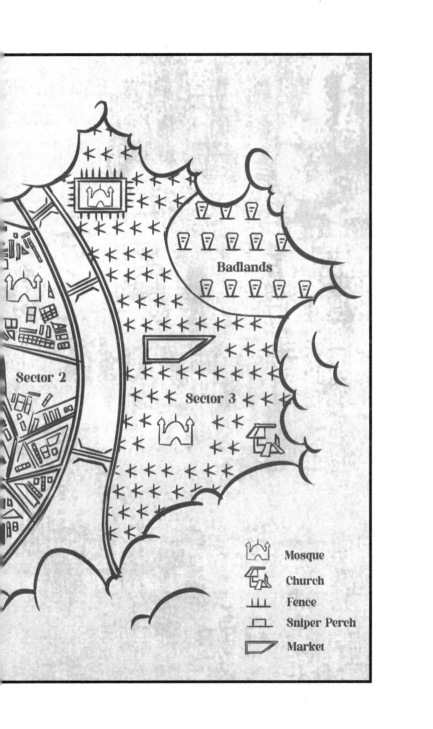

Badlands

Sector 2

Sector 3

Mosque
Church
Fence
Sniper Perch
Market

PART I
THE LAND OF GHOSTS

Episode 1: Untouchable

Avaan

July 31, 2083

Three years ago, I sold my kidney for a few cans of beans.

I did it to save my brother, to save my family. To save Doua. But they died anyway. Killed by soldiers like the one standing in front of me now with the Lee-Enfield rifle slung over his shoulder. As languid under this gelid snow as the rest of us, he's like a shadow given sentience. Black camo uniform, black ski mask, and black gloves reveal nothing of the human underneath, only the belligerence in his eyes.

There's a sign above me on the razor wire fence: Old Pakistan: Sector 2 Bridge, Checkpoint 3.

Hands clasped behind my head, my shawl pulled apart in the cold morning, I try to keep my heartbeat steady. I'm failing miserably. My thoughts keep looping over the thin stack of rupees crumpled in my right fist and the contingent of soldiers guarding this checkpoint.

My ID card in his hand, the soldier squints at my black clothes. "Name?"

Avaan. "Salaba."

"Father's name?" the soldier inquires, his voice muffled.

Don't know. My eyes trace his bolt-action .303 rifle. "Hatteb."

He studies the ID card and stares at my face.

"Can I cover my mouth now?" I ask. My long hair and scraggly beard do little against the cold and snow.

Nothing.

Pale veins of dawn pulse through the grey clouds. The light illuminates my city, Old Pakistan, with a halo of colours rarely seen around here. For a moment, the world is reborn with blues, pinks, and purples.

Then the clouds blot out the sun. The world grows white again as the snow falls. It falls over the soldier standing before me. It falls over the hundreds of Pakistanis queued behind me, and over the three sagging bridges that connect Sectors 2 and 3. It falls over the four military jeeps mounted with belt-fed RPD machine guns guarding this checkpoint.

But this isn't snow.

"What's your business in Sector 2?" the soldier asks.

"Cleaning."

He returns my ID card. "You know the rules. If we find any weapons on you, you'll be shot on the spot."

"Yup."

He pats me down, his hands slapping their way over my arms, back, shoulders, armpits, and waist. And over Baadal's Colt 1911 .45 in the back of my jeans.

Our eyes meet.

Nodding to my right, I flash him the stack of rupees in my fist. "Is there a problem?"

He pats down my arms again, and the money disappears from my hand.

"No," he replies, looking away. "Let him through."

As the fenced gate crawls open, I wrap the thick brown shawl around myself and over my mouth and nose. I slip my shades on and stare behind me at Sector 3. The snow speckles the cracked, half-sunken dirt roads, the rusty metal roofs, the squalid mud-brick homes and shanties.

But this isn't snow.

Walking through Checkpoint 3, I move briskly along the bridge. It feels unsteady under my feet. Year after year, there are renovations to stabilize these bridges, and year after year, they sag lower toward the river below. Across from me, there's a welcome party of even more RPD-equipped jeeps and armed soldiers. They watch me with disgust as I pass through, their guns converged on me.

In Sector 2, narrow, cracked buildings spike the air like the rib cage of a whale carcass. The faint smell of decay and filth in the air is a not-so-gentle reminder that Sector 3 is just a flimsy bridge away.

I walk along the riverbank.

Dark-skinned, red-clad Christian children use layered cloth to filter the polluted river water. Rags tied up to their noses, their *shalwar-kameez* drenched, the children perch the large earthen pots on their heads and toddle behind Sunnis and Shiites.

"Don't spill the water, *kafir*!" a Sunni woman hisses at a little water boy. Her green abaya and surgical mask are immaculate amidst the squalor.

"Sorry, *bibi*." The boy's big brown eyes grow bigger still as he struggles under the pot. There's a grimy silver crucifix around his neck.

As the duo walks past me, the boy stumbles, and the pot crashes to the ground, water splashing everywhere.

"You idiot!" she screeches, her face bright pink.

People stare. They notice that it's a green-clad person doing all the shouting and look away. Some shake their heads, but no one says a word.

The woman stomps up to the boy menacingly — right up until the moment I stand behind him and place both hands on his shoulders.

"Leave him alone." My voice is a low growl. The boy trembles under me, probably from fear as much as the cold.

The woman scoffs at me. "How dare you talk to me, *paleet*?"

Paleet. Abhorrent, detestable. Untouchable.

"He's a little kid," I point out. "He can't carry such a huge pot to Sector 1. It's hours away."

"It's what I'm paying him for," she snaps. "The little kafir chose this."

Technically, he isn't a kafir, but that's never stopped Pakistanis before. "Nobody chooses this."

"I just want water for my family."

"Collect it yourself then."

"I'll call those soldiers," she says, pointing at three soldiers approaching us from a distance. "I'll tell them you're harassing me."

Under the shawl, my hand settles on the .45. Two bullets. I keep the other hand on the boy's shoulder. "Go ahead."

"It'll be my word against yours," she reminds me.

The boy looks up at me. "*Sahib*?"

I tighten my grip on his shoulder and shrug at the woman. "Go ahead. We're still here."

People begin whispering among themselves. Most of them wear blue clothes, some green. They all look at my black clothes with that odd mix of disdain and pity. I shut myself off to it, the way I have my entire life.

Glaring at me, she tightens the hijab around her bright pink face. "Go to hell. Both of you."

And she's gone.

"Thank you, sahib," the boy mumbles.

I pat his head. "Don't let these bastards put you down, Baadal."

"Baadal?" the boy asks, puzzled.

Shit.

Pushing my shades back, draping myself in the shawl, I rush into the nearest alley. The boy stares after me, his big brown eyes shining in the morning light. Just like Baadal's.

———

I pause next to a decrepit two-storey building, yet another cracked tooth in the decaying mouth of this city. Most windows are shattered. The rest are barred or covered with duct tape, newspaper, cardboard, and strips of wood.

At the entrance, a paleet woman haggles with a couple of Shiite proprietors for a room, any room, even the tiniest room, as long as it means not spending another day in the Badlands. Two little boys cluster behind her. The paleet pops open a suitcase full of her family's government-issued black clothes and some utensils. The Shiite proprietors look everywhere except at the paleet and her sons.

That's the end of it. Post-apocalyptic real estate at its finest.

Dejected, she notices me, a fellow Untouchable. I shrug. As I walk away, she remains standing with her arms around her sons, sheltering them from the falling snow.

But this isn't snow.

In a secluded cluster of buildings, I study the pencil sketch Humayun handed me in the dark hours before dawn. It's of a man a little younger than me. Early twenties. A lifetime. Maybe it's the sketch, but he's got too many earrings, a whole row of them going down his right ear like the spine of a notebook. There's an address on the back of the sketch — *use second alley, near Blue Mosque; tin roof house, low pale walls; opposite street cobbler* — and a circled name.

Maseeh.

"He dies today," Humayun whispered, his pale blue eyes eerily playful.

Tapping the gun in the back of my jeans, I keep walking.

In a courtyard, paleet women in black shalwar-kameez pick cardboard strips, bottles, and plastic bags off the ground. Several Hindu women work with them, dressed in orange sarees. They all coil their shawls around their mouths as they work, the large garbage bags tied to their waists already full. Mother did this kind of work to support us. For the eight years I knew her.

Approaching them, my ears catch some disjointed words.

"Loyalists are still fighting —"

"They're calling them terrorists even though —"

"— smuggled all the food and the medicine."

"Another civil war is coming, isn't it?"

"They're not terrorists. Yaqzan is giving us a choice. He's our —"

"Quiet —"

"The snow falls over it all."

"Quiet. Someone is coming."

The group disperses into the mist as I keep walking.

When I look up, the buildings around me seem taller and narrower, looming like a scorched forest. The Blue Mosque glints a few miles ahead. I follow the bending, forking, twisting pathways weaving toward it. It's a wonder people get to their destinations in Sector 2. Especially at these early hours of the morning when load-shedding is long and the snowfall is heavy.

Turning another corner leads me to an alley littered with whitener addicts, muttering and moaning in their collective heap. The pungent, acrid smell is all too familiar.

A handful of them gawk semi-lucidly as they huff white stains on rags or plastic bags. The unconscious ones are already hours deep in the forever-seeming dreams of the white poison. Dreams worth a coat or a can of food or pieces of your liver or a kidney or a family member you could live without. The market is always fluid.

I manoeuvre through the misty snowfall, trying not to step on any of the vague, dark shapes under me.

Bony fingers clutch my arm.

"Whitener," gasps a junkie. His jaundiced eyes peer out from a crusty, sallow face. "I need whitener."

Prying my arm away, I tuck my head low and walk past him.

He sidles along, unkempt and unsteady. "G-give me some rupees, p-please," he stutters. "Hey, you listening to m-me?"

More shapes spawn from the black ground and walls, surrounding me.

"Help me." Someone gets in my face. He pulls his lips down with both hands, exposing blue-grey flesh. "Sky Sickness."

I keep walking, hand cupped at the side of my face.

A talon-like hand grabs my shoulder, tearing my shawl.

"You're not from here, are you?" It's a different voice this time. A woman, her face weathered and battered into a masculine scowl. Her nails dig into my skin. "Remove the shawl. Show us your clothes."

"Leave me alone," I whisper, trying to walk past her.

"Look at his skin. So dark," someone says behind me, his face hidden behind a surgical mask. "Are you a Hindu? Why are *you* in Sector 2?"

"He's no Hindu," the woman snarls, yanking at my shawl. The fabric tears at the edges as she pulls away enough to unveil my shirt. Enough for the ensuing gasps. Gasps that let me know this is going to be one of those days. "He's a paleet."

"Disgusting. Don't touch him."

"Go back to where you came from, paleet. Go back to the Badlands." The woman points above. "Allah burned the sky because of you. Godless piece of shit."

"Get lost," I snap, pushing past them. I grip Baadal's 1911. The Big Heat, he used to call it.

They mob me again.

"Is th-that a weapon, p-paleet?" The first guy grabs my arm. A bottle shimmers green in his other hand. Three more junkies stand behind him now.

"It's a gun." The woman blocks my path. The stench of her rotting gums makes its way to my face. "Burned the fucking sky. Brought diseases. Now you bring guns?"

I don't draw the .45. Only two bullets. One for Maseeh. One for me.

"PFM!" someone shouts. "PFM!"

The Blue Mosque peekaboos at me from the left, between two collapsed buildings. Still miles away. I make a mental note of it and shuffle in its direction.

"Go back to the Badlands," the woman snaps.

Someone pushes me.

"Look at her when she talks to you," growls another man, blocking my way.

I turn around, keep my chin tucked.

There's the *sssnik* of a brandished knife. Furtive and deadly. "Fucking paleet."

Can't pin down where the sound came from. Everywhere I look, there are sinister faces. In a flash of panic, I realize the Blue Mosque isn't to my left anymore.

The Blue Mosque isn't anywhere.

"PFM!" The woman spits at me. "PFM!"

I shove her away. Hard.

Rookie mistake.

Something hard shatters across the back of my head. An instant later, breaking glass echoes inside my skull.

"F-fucking paleet."

I nearly fall but manage to gather my legs under me.

Head's ringing. Spinning. Warm blood oozes down the back

of my skull and neck.

I dart toward a wall to brace myself.

They run after me.

"*Maaro isko!*" someone yells. Strong, scabbed, cold, clammy hands yank and tear at me. "*Saala paleet.*"

I start punching, swinging wild and blind.

It doesn't get me very far.

Muscle and bone crush into me from all sides. This time, I tumble to the ground, my bleeding hands crossed over me. Angry faces cram into my vision, more hands clawing and punching at whatever inch of me they find.

"P-paleet."

I turtle up, arms like pillars around my head and neck. The gun. Two bullets. One for Maseeh. One for me.

"Allah burned the sky because of you."

Grunts and growls surround me. Fists and feet rain over me. No one has stabbed me so far. Silver linings.

One of the dozen hands grabs my hair. Another hoists me by the collar. They drag me deeper into the alley as I struggle and slip and slide on the wet ground.

I break free and scramble away. The mist cloaks them, only to reveal them a second later, a sick joke.

"You're going to die here, paleet."

I draw the .45, the silver slide gleaming in the faint morning light. The black wooden grips settle into my hand, all too familiar.

Two bullets. For Maseeh. For me.

They back off.

I stumble back, my feet unsteady, my head heavy. My face and arms are peppered with bruises. The .45 rattles in my hand. I try to navigate my way out of the maze of pathways and dead ends. The sudden silence feels disconcerting against the shrill violence from seconds ago. The pounding in my chest doesn't let up.

I look back. Dark, grainy shapes slouch after me in the snow, utterly silent. "Get back!" I yell.

They take another step.

I cock the hammer. That gets their attention. "Take a step — one more fucking step. Come on! Try me."

They don't move.

The wetness at the back of my skull grows colder. Turning the corner unsteadily, I dash into the street that led me here. I pass more unfamiliar faces staring glibly at me. My feet pound the wet pavement, rubber squelches echoing in the still morning. The pounding in my chest echoes in my rib cage.

Leaning against the wall for support, I glance back at the alley. I'm alone.

The snow plays hide-and-seek. A red traffic light reflects on the wet tarmac. I step into a puddle. Icy water sloshes into my duct-taped shoes. The realization that my feet are soaking prods my mind — a nagging indignation that seems worse than everything else that's happened this morning.

Despite the snow and the scattered morning light, I catch the little sapphire glint ahead of me. The Blue Mosque.

Gun still cocked, I gingerly pat the back of my skull with my other hand, the skin electric where I touch it.

Something sails past my ear. Glass shatters behind me.

"Die, paleet."

It's the junkies again, materializing out of thin air. They hurl whatever they can find at me. Bottles. Cans. Bricks. I'm still too far away for them to aim properly, but it's only a matter of time.

The option of shooting them presents itself again, and again I ignore it. I run instead, as fast as I can. I keep running as the voices and footsteps echo distantly. Miles ahead, almost too far away, the mosque is a blue-eyed wink in the misty snow.

But this isn't snow.

———

"Get the fuck out of the way, idiot!"

A supply truck zooms by, blaring its horn, the scream of swerving tires deafening. Its rich blue chassis is about the only solid stretch of colour underneath all the fangled bells, chains, mirrors, mosaics, ribbons, and plastic flowers. I'm surprised the driver didn't plow through me when I ran into the dirt road.

Clutching my sides, I try to regroup. Each breath sandblasts my lungs. I ran too fast for too long. The back of my head stings.

I'm here. At the Blue Mosque. Silver linings. This city offers no respite. In Old Pakistan, you get tiny lucky breaks once in a lifetime. The long-abandoned shops are a vision of decay and neglect, their rusting shutters closed like the eyelids of some sleepy iron titan. The alleys on either side of the mosque are empty.

Mostly empty.

Mangled, malnourished women and men count their wares. They hail the occasional vibrant rickshaw. All of them — kafirs, Hindus, hookers, fornicators — are winding down for the day, beginning their three-hour ride back to the Badlands before the soldiers chase them away.

Passionate haggling ensues. Resources are pooled. Curses tossed around.

Madarchod. Motherfucker. *Bhenchod.* Sisterfucker — because why leave out the sisters? *Gandu.* Faggot.

The language only gets more colourful from there.

Bhosdi-ka. Chuut, chuutya, or *chuutye,* which have been embellishing the Urdu language for centuries.

Once the haggling is over, they cram into the rickshaws, three or four at a time. Those with enough strength or limbs hang from the side as the little rickshaws trundle toward Sector 3 and the Badlands, their undersides dangerously close to the tarmac. Come the late hours of the night, they'll be back again for another shift of begging and whoring.

A Hindu girl, disfigured and desiccated, limps down the street. There's a black rubber cap around her right arm, her wrist and hand gone.

"P—p—p," she pants through toothless gums. *Paisay*, she's trying to say. If she still had a tongue. I walk past her quickly, trying to keep myself from being hurled down a kaleidoscope of past horrors.

Under the shawl, I grab Baadal's 1911 and make my way into the second alley left of the Blue Mosque. The pathway grows narrower, heaps of newspaper and plastic constricting it. Washing lines criss-cross the walls above me, damp blue clothes and white undergarments identical at each turn. Black power lines wind and bind, a nest of vipers.

Allah burned the sky! some chuutya has spray-painted in blue over a wall. It's barely visible, courtesy of a pink *Quran 9:5* splotched over it, as well as a purple PFM. There's more, of course, a collage of bigotry that's plagued Pakistan since 1947.

All these street artists and not one of them drew breasts. That's art that'd truly unite all men.

A white cat hops out of a trash can, a tiny mouse squeaking in its jaws. She stares at me, her one eye amber, the other green. I walk past.

The pale, cracked wall appears exactly where Humayun said it would be. I don't see a cobbler anywhere, but this is the place.

The wall is barely taller than me. A layer of broken glass glued to its top side makes a convincing argument against hopping over.

I do what a postman would: I ring the bell twice.

No sound. Load-shedding is still in effect.

I knock, the metal door clanging. There's no sound from the house. If someone were inside, everything would've come to a standstill. That's how you know someone is hiding: that sudden, unnatural silence of people flash-frozen in fear, too scared to breathe.

I nearly knock again when light, quick footsteps approach from the alley behind me. Maybe a woman. Maybe Maseeh. But behind me? Am I in the wrong place?

I disengage the .45's safety as quietly as I can. But this still morning is bent on revealing all secrets. The soft click echoes.

The footsteps stop. Everything becomes quiet. Unnaturally quiet. Maseeh is here.

The footsteps start again, quick, panicked. I follow the sound.

The pathways twist in a blur of snow and bricks and trash. Tattered newspapers and plastic bags flutter around me. Each corner I turn throws me off. The footsteps become fainter.

There's a cry for help. From the right? Behind me? Left?

Left.

I dash into the street to my left, knocking over a trash can. It rattles violently. The street grows narrower. There's an alley on either side. I pause, trying to pin down the sounds.

Footsteps. Same as the ones before. Light, soft. They're mixed with two more sets of footsteps, loud and plodding.

Things grow quieter. Faint voices. Words exchanged too fast to make sense.

I hear a name. Yaqzan. The name that's only whispered in this city.

Gunshots erupt. Sounds I recognize instantly: 9mm and .38 Special. Muzzle flashes light up the alley to my right.

I sneak forward. My breath rasps against the air like a blade. The snow spirals down, dazzlingly white and eternal.

Muffled voices. More gunshots.

The cold lick of anticipation travels down my spine as Maseeh runs onto the road. He's a few metres away, his bright red *kurta* striking in all the gloom. The row of earrings in his ear is exactly as the sketch. He's short and reedy, the black Walther P38 looking massive in his hand.

He fires into the alley he just ran out of. There's a faint groan of a man falling dead. A sound as ubiquitous and unnoticed in Old Pakistan as torn newspapers.

Maseeh still hasn't spotted me.

Sidling along the wall, I aim the .45 at his right temple. "For Humayun," I whisper.

Closer to him now, I realize there's a problem. A big one.

Maseeh isn't a man in his early twenties. He's a lot younger. Eighteen, if that.

I don't kill women and children. That's been my deal with Humayun. A deal he's honoured for the last three years.

I hesitate, lower the gun, then hesitate some more.

Humayun doesn't tolerate loose ends. He doesn't kill women and children. He also doesn't send multiple people for one job.

What the fuck is going on?

"For Humayun," an angry voice echoes. A man dashes onto the road, Model 10 revolver in hand. There's a sharp snarl and a muzzle flash.

An instant later, Maseeh yelps like a terrified animal and falls backward, his red kurta becoming redder where the .38 Special punctured his ribs.

The man squeezes the trigger again.

He's out. Humayun only gives two bullets for a job.

Sprawled on the ground, Maseeh screams something — a curse, a cry for help. It's a boy's scream. He shoots his P38 several times.

The man doesn't grunt or shout. He makes short sounds: a gasp cut short. One minute he twitches, the next he thuds on the ground as if the earth just yanked him down. He's no more.

My .45 still cocked, I have no idea what to do.

Maseeh struggles to his feet and immediately hunches over in the middle of the narrow road. He whimpers when he looks at his wound. I see his busted nose and lip. A crisp, unsullied white rag around his right bicep is out of place. I can't focus on anything else.

Inevitably, his P38 reclaims my attention. At that exact moment, he spots me, gun in hand.

He points his gun at me, hand unsteady.

"Get back. I mean it," Maseeh says in a voice that breaks and warbles.

"Put the gun away, kid." I point the .45 down into the tarmac. "You don't want to do this."

"By God, I'll shoot. I'll blow your fucking head off."

"I'm not going to hurt y—"

"You're working for Humayun, aren't you?" Maseeh asks.

The gun in my hand. "Walk away, kid."

"Why? So you can shoot me in the back?"

"I don't kill women and children."

Doua's voice seeps into my ear. *Is that what you said three years ago too, Avaan?*

Maseeh cocks the hammer. "Yaqzan has given me my orders, and by God, I'm going to see them through."

Yaqzan? This kid is a Loyalist? "Look, I'm not going to hurt y—"

He shoots. Misses.

The P38 isn't for children. Between its bulk and the heavy trigger, the recoil is unpredictably harsh if you're not ready for it. Especially if you're a scrawny, terrified kid who's been shot already.

Maseeh grits his teeth as he grabs the gun with both hands. As he should've done earlier. "The snow falls over it all," he says.

"Don't," I plead.

He cocks the hammer again.

Bang. The big full stop.

My ears ring. An unending squeal ricochets off the cluttered walls and tears into my brain.

A thin trail of smoke rises from the gun in my hand.

One bullet left. One bullet for me.

A pool of blood cradles Maseeh's body. I inspect the hole in his chest where the .45 ACP hollow-point tore mercilessly through meat and marrow.

I look around at the windows and doors. Peeking eyes. Staring figures. Low whispers.

"For Humayun," I say. Loud enough that the windows and doors shut, and all whispers grow quiet.

Lowering the hood over my face, I gather the guns littered around and, one by one, drag the bodies deep into an alley.

I search their pockets. The novice assassin has nothing. Maseeh has a small loaf of bread wrapped in plastic and a stack of a hundred ration cards. A thousand rupees.

Gathering the loot, I lean against a wall. A large snowflake lilts down before me, and I hold up my hand to —

"Don't look at me like that," I sigh.

Doua appears, leaning against the wall opposite me. Her glass bangles tinkle. Her fingers brush her collarbone, her neck, her earlobe. Long, wavy black hair and dusky skin offset her white saree. No *dupatta*. No shawl. She's a ghost bride haunting the rubbles of her wedding church. Doua. My Doua. Her liquid black eyes antagonize me.

White ghosts rise from my lips. "He was going to kill me."

Is that always going to be your excuse?

"Doua —"

She presses her lips into a thin line. The light acne scars across her right cheek dimple. *What now, Avaan? What do you want?*

"You. I need to find out what happened to you."

I died three long years ago.

It takes me a moment to exhale. "I need to be sure. I need to tell you what happened that day."

I watch her walk in the falling snow. Her spectre-like steps, the silhouette of her legs, the gracious curve of her hips, the slight outline of her panties against the fabric. I follow her and accept the true extent of my desolation.

As she walks, Doua holds her hand out under the burned sky. *It is getting heavy. They keep telling us that it will disappear, but it only grows heavier and heavier.* She lets the snowflakes pile in her hand and blows them at me. A kiss. *The snow falls over it all.*

"The snow falls over it all," I whisper.

But this isn't snow.

Episode 2: The Snow Falls Over It All

Rahee

January 13, 2043

"The snow falls over it all," said an old man with long hair, walking under my window. "The snow falls over it all."

Peeking through the white curtains, now turning yellow, I watched the old man walk through the crowd. People stepped out of his way, showing him the same veneration they showed the Mullah-sahibs. He continued to walk until he disappeared into the falling snow, somewhere between the road and the burned sky.

Standing by the window, I reached out to catch one of the flakes. It slipped through my fingers, settled on the pavement, and became a white speck among the rest.

The next day, I smoked my first cigarette by the window. I was almost eight. I blew the smoke out of my lungs, a strange kin to the snowflakes. That was when I noticed it: the snowfall seemed heavy. Heavier than I remembered.

"The snow falls over it all," I whispered, just as the old man had. Words that have since become the terrorist rallying cry.

"What are you doing, Rahee?" My father startled me. His hazel eyes were alive with fear.

"Sorry, Father." I tossed the cigarette away. "I'll never —"

"Never say those words, son. Those are Yaqzan's words." He shut the window and pulled me close. "Promise me."

I never did.

When it came to the snow, the Mullah-sahibs said it wasn't mentioned in Islamic eschatology. They said it was blasphemy to mention it because our enemies would point to it as evidence that Islam doesn't have all the answers. All we were promised was that the snow would disappear soon and those who said otherwise were our enemies. When it came to old man Yaqzan, the Mullah-sahibs said he was our enemy.

No matter how much they promised and prohibited, there remained a voice inside me. A voice low and disquieting. Yaqzan's voice.

The snow falls over it all.

May 31, 2043
Before Allah burned the sky away, my father was a history teacher. He said that every generation of Pakistanis is united by memories of either a martial law beginning or a martial law ending.

Mere weeks after Yaqzan's words, violence tore through Pakistan, talons and fangs dividing this nation once more. This time, between Yaqzan loyalists and Yaqzan opponents.

Before long, the army promised to save us.

In the beginning, we didn't recognize it for the horror story it was. Months passed, and the violence got worse. When the army began to storm homes and arrest Loyalists, it was simply another vestige of the martial law most Pakistanis had known or their fathers had known. Per Section 298 of the Pakistani Penal Code, repeating Yaqzan's words was punishable by a year in prison.

Before long, it was no longer just about Loyalists. There were flyers in the streets warning of mass displacements and executions.

Flyers informing us of mandatory dress codes: blue for Shiites, red for Christians, and orange for Hindus. Black for all the despicable, the Untouchables. The apostates and trannies, the faggots and fornicators. When stories spread of how soldiers were lashing fornicators and faggots, to most Pakistanis it was the army imposing *Sharia* law as it had during the martial law of 1977. When stories spread of how soldiers were executing atheists and apostates, to most it was simply Section 295 of the Pakistani Penal Code being used as a cudgel against blasphemers yet again.

Doors were smeared with symbols to brand those who lived behind them. I began to hear words like *kafir* and *paleet*. They became common. For the first time in my life, there were Sunni doors and Shiite doors and Christian doors and Hindu doors. There were black doors.

Before long, the army promised a New Pakistan.

New Pakistan was our future. Our independence. It was what we Muslims were to fight for, son against father, brother against brother, friend against friend. It's the reason why today, Pakistan is carved into sectors where nothing changes, where entire generations live and die. Once, all sectors were united as one city called Pakistan. A city that, an even longer time before — before the Fifth Indo-Pak War, before Allah burned the sky away — was a country of over 300 million people. New Pakistan was our refuge from violence and madness.

In the beginning, we didn't recognize it for the horror story it was.

———

June 3, 2043
Before long, PFM entered our language. Painted on walls, etched on gates, scraped over rusting cars. It was everywhere. *Pakistan for Muslims.*

My father warned anyone who'd listen that the army would soon come after Christians and Hindus. After them, we Shiites were next. He'd remind anyone who'd listen that he had lived through the cataclysmic Fifth Indo-Pak War, and he had watched the sky burn away. He'd warn anyone who'd listen that the only way we'd survive was by staying united as Pakistanis.

No one listened.

———

July 29, 2043

"It had to be done." Pakistani Muslims nod after a slight pause. Then they stick their chests out. "PFM."

Meet someone old enough and there's a brief hint of dread when they talk about Operation Searchlight II — *II* because something like it had happened once before, back in 1971, when West Pakistan had waged war against East Pakistan, fracturing forever into Pakistan and Bangladesh. A war in which Pakistani soldiers had committed the genocidal rape of over three hundred thousand Muslim women — a horrendous act, yet one condoned by most Muslim religious scholars at the time. Because those women had sided with the enemy, and so they were kafir.

What your right hand possesses.

Before long, the first military jeeps began rolling into our neighbourhoods. This time, the soldiers dragged Hindus out of their homes, tore their clothes, raped their women and girls, broke and burned their belongings. They drove them into the outermost parts of this city, into a barren land with little water, little food, and no energy.

"It had to be done. PFM."

Pakistani Hindus could only collect water from the river at night. They could not sell food to Muslims, because they were kafirs and food made by their hands wasn't considered clean.

Months later, Pakistani Hindus were showing up to scrub the houses they had lived in for generations. People would only see Hindus late at night or in the Christian neighbourhoods of Pakistan, where they would beg on street corners. Where their women would sell their bodies.

This horror was still not Operation Searchlight II.

On July 29, 2043, two days before my mother's birthday, I woke up to the sound of screaming.

My mother stood by the window, the mouldy yellow curtains parted. An orange glow seeped through thick black clouds in the distance. *This must be what dawn looks like*, I wondered, standing next to her. It was the most beautiful thing this world had lost.

My mother put her arm around me, and I realized that this wasn't dawn. The broken moon hung in the burned sky like a cracked dinner plate, a shimmering, swirling trail of celestial debris forever tumbling toward us. Even today, far away in the horizon, we hear giant moon rocks hit the world in awful shudders.

What struck me then was not the wall of fire in the distance. It was not the giant pillars of smoke rising into the night like shadowy hands. It was not the military jeeps, whose gunfire sent shivers down my spine to my toes. It was not the people standing in the neighbourhoods, their faces blank as the wall of fire grew higher and brighter.

What struck me was how I could hear the Hindus screaming from so far away. Before long, the snow began to fall heavily in thick, greyish-white puffs. It wouldn't relent.

Meet someone old enough and there's a brief hint of dread in their eyes when they talk about Operation Searchlight II. It was a period of three burning nights when the military attempted to eradicate Pakistani Hindus.

It had to be done. PFM.

———

September 2, 2043
Before long, our lives became harder, more violent. Pakistan became bloodier. Fear slithered its way around every corner, inside every house, into our hearts.

I saw my younger brother die first. On a quiet, cold September evening, that horrible fever came and never left. Sky Sickness, they called it. As Radhi coughed and cried for three nights, my father remained steadfast. When the illness took him from us, my father didn't cry, he didn't break. My mother didn't cry either, but all sounds left her that snowy evening.

For Radhi's funeral, my father said only that he was gone and would never come home again. He said I was only eight, too young to understand that all this was a test from Allah. My father made me promise that I would never let my faith be broken.

"'Allah does not burden a soul more than it can bear,'" my father would recite from the Quran. "'Pardon us and forgive us and have mercy on us.' *Ameen.*"

We would all say *Ameen*, except for my mother.

December 4, 2043
Before September 2043, whenever my mother walked into the room, my father would smile, a young man in love. She was a few inches taller than him, an elegant creature who glided. Vivacious, with light-brown eyes, she would fill the house with laughter. The rooms would echo with the soft jingle of her silver anklet, the smell of jasmine. My mother's favourite flowers.

There would be fresh *pakoras* and tea in the afternoon.

Before September 2043, before the Sky Sickness took Radhi, my father's hazel eyes would grow slightly wide when he looked at my mother. In those days, she played classic English songs on a little radio she had salvaged from Old Market. Anytime she was distracted or lost in whatever she was doing, she would hum this one song that always made my father smile, no matter how violent or cruel the city had become: "Anyone Who Knows What Love Is."

After September 2043. The days after Radhi's death. All songs spilled out of my mother, along with the colours and smells that were my childhood. There were no songs, no pakoras, no tea. No smell of jasmine. She became the sombre, faded woman in the window who spoke so little that I forgot the sound of her voice.

Somewhere between these two versions of my mother is perhaps the reason my life has turned out the way it has.

———

March 7, 2044
I was nine when little Roshni was born. There were voices in our home again. It mattered not to me that the voices were crying and shouting. Quiet sobs and broken plates as my mother swore she'd never forgive my father for Roshni's birth. I was content that the silence, the stillness that hung over our home, was broken.

My father, my mother, Roshni, and I endured the worst shortages Pakistan experienced. Hunger kept us awake. Pakistan showed us little mercy in those days. Before long, people — our neighbours, our friends — began to die of starvation. My family continued to survive. What starvation spared, the violence took care of. My father said that this was the worst year in Pakistan's history since the Fifth Indo-Pak War.

"We are enduring." My father would beam. "We will continue to endure by Allah's will."

My mother would not say Ameen.

———

October 14, 2044

Before long, Roshni was seven months. My father was out almost all day in Old Market, shoulder to shoulder with countless others, waiting to be picked up for menial labour. The furniture disappeared from our home, one chair at a time, replaced with cans of food and pink ration cards that bought little.

At home, my mother and I moved in and out of each other's worlds like silent ghosts. The sparseness of the rooms made it difficult not to notice each other. In those days, I was an adult in a nine-year-old's body, with adult chores, cleaning up after my little Roshni, bathing and feeding her. Roshni had me as her mother, and the only thing I knew about motherhood was the silence.

————

April 8, 2045
Why would Allah do this to me, Ra-Ra?

I was thinking about my father's words as I turned a corner to avoid the group of four teenagers huddled by a trash can bonfire. They wore green.

The streetlamp had been vandalized. The light flickered, hurling my shadow at the walls around me. Unable to see clearly, I stepped into a puddle. The slosh echoed in the night.

The boys spotted me, pointing at my blue kurta. They pointed at the food I carried: *samosas*, still hot and fresh. A bottle of milk for Roshni. She needed strength to fight the sickness that had left her lips blue.

"Are you a Shiite?" they growled at me.

I grabbed the switchblade in my pocket. I was ten. "Yes."

Moments later, I was clutching at a long cut across my arm. The puddle I had stepped in minutes ago was now deeper. All four of my assailants lay dead at my feet. Scattered among them were the broken samosas and the shattered bottle.

As the streetlamp flickered, I saw a white speck above me. A snowflake. Except it wasn't an intricate lattice of icy lines but a delicate, faintly shimmering clump. More snowflakes, more ghosts, fell from the sky and into the puddle. They became sullied with blood and grime.

"The snow falls over it all," I whispered.

Blasphemy. If someone heard me, I could be reported to the army.

Biting my lip, I cupped my hands before me and begged Allah to not punish my sister for my transgression. I begged Him to spare Roshni. My family had suffered enough. I begged Him not to break my father's faith for the sins of his child.

I came home empty-handed. Together with my father, I prayed the entire night. My mother stood in a daze by the window, the yellow-brown curtains blowing in the cold wind.

"'Truly distress has seized me.'" My father recited the verse over and over. "'But You are Most Merciful of those that are merciful.'"

My sister, my little Roshni, died the following evening. I realized I was the only one in my family who would survive. I had already outlived Radhi and Roshni. Before long, I would outlive my father and mother.

I was ten, old enough for all the burdens on my soul.

Episode 3: A Quiet Evening in Old Pakistan

Avaan

July 31, 2083

I wake up from a recurring dream: standing in a white grass field, my bare feet bruised and bloodied. Behind me, Old Pakistan is on fire. There's a white door before me, ajar. No walls. No support. There's no snow in this dream. Only an endless white grass field. And the door that I need to walk through. Or lock shut forever.

Small wonder I'm an insomniac.

I sit up and look to my left. A glass bottle perches on the doorknob, perfectly balanced. Safe at home. Colours from the billboard stream in through the barred window. Neon blues, pinks, and purples.

Cold air thieves through the barred window and threads the glass in a frozen cobweb. Staring outside, I watch New Pakistan's crystalline white buildings pierce the evening sky. Against the shadowy mountains, that walled city remains incandescent while Old Pakistan curls around it in dark supplication.

We've all heard the stories of New Pakistan — more food and water than a person could consume in a lifetime, electricity with no load-shedding, safety and protection, zero crimes, clean air. No snow. A slice of heaven.

Three years ago, I stood at its gates and came closer to that slice of heaven than I ever will again. It was the day I died.

Bells chime via the PSA system. They reverberate from New Pakistan, sector by sector, drawing closer and closer. It happens again in spaced-out intervals, the feedback in the three microphones searing the evening air.

Any time I move my battered body, the thin, dumpy mattress coughs up polystyrene and foam. On the floor beside it, there's a paper bag with the Model 10 and Maseeh's P38. It's a reminder that I must see Humayun. I can't stomach it. Not after what happened this morning.

Sketches of Doua litter the floor. Doua smiling. Doua cupping her face. Doua lying naked on her stomach, asleep and at peace. Doua pensive. Doua peering at me, teasing and daring. Doua laughing at something. This is what I've been reduced to these last three years. I'm Majnun composing mad-love poems in the wilderness, seeing Layla everywhere. I'm Orpheus on his lyre, mourning, surrounded by indolent wild beasts. I'm Devdas craving solace in bottle after bottle, reliving loss with every drop.

I hum that old song of Doua's. Our song. A song of pieces and abrupt ends, because she only knew parts of it. "Anyone Who Knows What Love Is".

The bells stop ringing. The lone orange bulb dangling from the ceiling dims.

Like a strained breath, the power goes out in Old Pakistan. The only light left is New Pakistan's immaculate skyline farther away than mere distance.

———

The bottle falls from the doorknob and shatters.

My heart plummets to the pit of my stomach. Baadal's 1911 in hand, I wonder who it is. Soldiers? Has Evergreen arrived to put me down?

I allow myself to dream. "Doua?"

Oil lantern in one hand, Kanz limps past the glass shards in the doorway. In his other hand, he holds a bowl of cornflakes, soggy with booze. Booze-flakes, he calls them, breakfast of champions. His woollen coat hangs on him loosely, even if he wears it with the same swagger as the day he peeled it off one of our targets. In those days, he wasn't setting off his gun in its holster.

Underneath the brown coat, the whiteness of his underwear is garish. He's wearing nothing else.

"Sorry." He's sheepish. He should be. "Got to the rendezvous point, but you'd already left."

I wasn't expecting him to be there. Haven't for a while now.

I hold out my hand for a shake. "Just get your shit together, man."

"Yeah, yeah." Kanz shakes my hand and collects half the stack of rupees I got off Maseeh. He slips it into his coat in a hurry. "Thanks."

"Don't worry about it." I scoot over as Kanz settles next to me, spilling booze-flakes onto the mattress. I notice how pink his eyes are. "What were you watching?"

"*The Terminator.* Can't go wrong with Aaanold."

Normally, Kanz is a regular hard-ass, ready to duke it out with people twice his size. Bum knee and all. With enough alcohol in his system, the little girl clawing inside every macho man breaks free. He watches old action movies and cries at the happy endings.

"Flyers came in today," he tells me. "No load-shedding later. Got any plans?"

Try to sleep. Sketch Doua. Count the rupees stashed inside the mattress. Try to sleep. "The usual."

"Movie night?"

"Sure."

"*Terminator 2* or *Lethal Weapon 2*?"

"*Lethal Weapon 2*. Action, great characters, and comedy."

"And a bummer ending. Fuck that. *Terminator 2* has Aaanold."

Can't argue.

Kanz reaches down to scratch the wound near his knee. It looks less like a scar and more like an over-fried egg. A .45 ACP will do that.

"Humayun sent the new guy over when you were on the job," he says. "Ponytailed one who's always looking at you funny."

"Slick Bastard?"

"Yeah, him. Asked me why I wasn't out with you, and, well, I had nothing."

"Shit."

"Said Humayun wants to see us both tonight." Kanz sticks out his index finger and thumb. "Did you …?"

I nod.

"Who was it?"

"Some kid."

"A kid?" Slurping a spoonful of booze-flakes, he shakes his head. "Humayun never did that before. Something's made him snap."

"Don't know."

"Think it's got to do with Yaqzan? Heard the terrorists looted another supply truck today."

There's that name again. "I don't know what's going on with Humayun."

Anytime I try to figure out what he's thinking, what he's planning, I end up remembering how Baadal got his Colt 1911 in the first place. How he died. And how Humayun is linked to it all.

"Humayun asking to see us both." Kanz stares at New Pakistan. "Can't be good, Sal."

"It'll be fine."

There's a fleeting, exhausted smile on his lips. "How many

jobs have I done for him since — you know?"

Since we began working together. Since he saved me from six scavengers on a hit. That was three years ago, and the man has always done right by me. Except for making me watch *Terminator 3*.

Or maybe Kanz is talking about his other reference point in life. That one rainy day three years ago when he returned home to find Jahangir standing with a bag full of Kanz's rupees in one hand. In his other hand? Kanz's Hardballer Longslide.

As if reading my thoughts, Kanz exhales. "How does he even look in the mirror? Leaving me like that. Taking my rupees."

"Jahangir shot you too."

"Thanks for the reminder." He deflates, spilling more booze-flakes onto my mattress. "True love."

True love made Kanz believe Jahangir was or would've been or should've been his *the one*. Then again, true love for him began with cheap booze and a blow job on a street corner. All Kanz has to show for true love today is a bum knee and this two-storey, two-room mudbrick house in Sector 3 that Humayun let him move in to.

"If the fat bastard fires me," Kanz starts after a long stretch of silence, "I won't have anything to donate to the Red Mosque."

"Forget the mosque. You barely have enough for —"

"This is for my soul."

Fuck. Here we go.

He points at the window. "This is the end, my only friend. Everything was foretold by Prophet Mohammad: the senseless violence, the darkening of the sky, the sun being close to the earth —"

"The sun isn't close to the earth," I interrupt. "It's where it's always been."

"Metaphor. Allah burned the sky away and —"

"The war burned the sky away, Kanz. Whatever was left was

then fucked over by the celestial debris that's still falling."

"Who started the Fifth Indo-Pak War? It was those kafirs in India."

When it's not kafirs and paleets in Old Pakistan, they blame India for Allah burning the sky away. If there's an Old India out there, they're probably blaming Pakistanis for the same.

I shrug. "All I know? No one wins a nuclear war."

"We did, by Allah's grace."

"Really? Because we didn't win in 1948. Or 1965. Or 1971. Or 1999. By Allah's grace."

"Don't blaspheme."

Several trucks trundle by. A stench lingers in the air. The smell of nearly expired food and medicine that hardly anyone wanted in the other sectors and hardly anyone can afford in Sector 3. Or the Badlands.

"Signs are here, Sal. Murder, greed, fornicators, faggots who —"

"Faggots? You mean people like you?"

"If I don't act on my impure desires, imam-sahib said I'm not sinning. Islam isn't unfair."

"That's not fair."

"Everything out there," he snaps, "was prophesized, Sal. Wake the hell up."

"Everything but the snow."

"You sound like Yaqzan."

Round and round we go. "It wasn't foretold. Why is it here?"

"This is the end. I'm sure of it." Underneath all the fatalism, there's relief in his voice. I believe every holy person has already condemned humanity to ruin. Piety is just their way of pretending otherwise. "Why do you deny the signs, Sal?"

"I deny anything to do with religion."

"Don't blaspheme, apostate."

"You didn't say paleet. How progressive."

"'Deaf, dumb, and blind, they will not return to the path.'" Quran 2:18. A classic. "Think it's a coincidence that all of humanity ends up in one location? That was foretold."

"Tens of thousands of people is not all of humanity. For all you know, the rest of the world is still intact. The twenty-first century rolling on by while we're stuck in the seventh."

"No one has met anyone from outside the city in almost fifty years." He sinks deeper into the mattress, making it burp foam and polystyrene. "This is the end."

"You know what I see?" This time I look him straight in the eyes. "Muslims, kafirs, and paleets freezing our balls off in the snow. Snow that's been growing heavier despite what the Mullahs say."

"The snow will disappear."

"It's growing heavier, Kanz. You know it is."

"It'll disappear."

I hear Doua. *Let him be, my love. Few have had it worse than him.*

I sigh quietly. "How much have you donated to the Red Mosque?"

"Most of whatever you've split with me," he replies. There's so little left in him. Just a body holding out for something better. "Isn't much."

Whatever appetite I had for theological debates dissipates. Kanz doesn't deserve any of this. True love broke this man but left just enough for the Mullahs to peck at. An alcoholic, crippled assassin; a heartbroken gay man holding on to faith in a faithless land of ghosts. He's as much a victim of religion as I am.

"You think Jahangir will ever come back?" Kanz asks after another long bout of silence.

Glass bangles ting. In the window, there's the reflection of a ghost. Doua's soft pink saree glows in the fogged-up glass. She's standing next to the mattress, watching Kanz without expression.

Her right hand brushes her neck and ear before resting over her exposed belly. When she looks at me, her mirror-like world shatters.

"Come on, put some clothes on." I pat his clammy thigh. "Let's go see Humayun."

———

Downstairs, I triple-check the .45. One bullet between me and the world.

I slide off the heavy wood plank barricading the door and push it open. Sector 3 stretches before me. Miles and miles of boxy mudbrick houses amidst a mess of wooden walls and tin-roof shanties. Without electricity, oil lanterns cast lonely yellow flickers inside these tiny homes. A cat's cradle of washing lines connects the houses on all sides, red and orange clothes fluttering in the shining snow. Military jeeps go by on filthy dirt roads, the faint hum of machinery echoing in the mulberry sky.

"You forgot this." Kanz stumbles next to me in a dark-green kurta and passes me the paper bag with the two guns inside. "Let's go."

Despite the late hour, three red-clad girls sit by the corner with a small collection of white-beaded *tasbihs* on a sheet. A bright pink rickshaw zooms by in the direction of the Badlands, carrying a nervous-looking Mullah. The smell of diesel streaks the air long after it's gone.

Kanz burps, loud and proud. The kafir girls giggle. Then they notice the carved *H* in the top-right corner of our door next to the green crescent and look away.

"Let's go, Sal."

I take a deep breath, the chilled air rushing inside my lungs. Going out into Sector 3 takes some psyching up. No matter how long you've lived here, some part of you can't quite believe that this is happening. Like getting shot. Or being raped.

"Anytime now, Sal."

I check the .45 again. One bullet. "Let's go."

―――

Rows of icicles line the arched canopy over the heavy red door of Humayun's Diner. The Ashraf-ul-Makhlooqat sign jangles as I hold the door open for Kanz.

Inside, candles line the tables, windowsills, and counter. Their light dances off the bottles and reflects throughout the diner. The regulars are here for the legendary *daal paratha*. Sunni Mullahs from Sector 1 cluck among themselves, tossing Arabic words into the conversation for extra piety points. Shiite proprietors from Sector 2 cluster together, ensuring no one touches them or their high-end Christian and Hindu hookers. Last, and certainly least, a gaggle of paleets whisper among themselves in the farthest corner of the diner.

"What do you want?" asks a waiter in a blue button-up, top buttons unbuttoned. He looks sidelong at me, his grin as slick as his oiled ponytail.

Slick Bastard in the flesh.

I hand him the paper bag with the two guns in it. "Give this bag to Humayun."

He sneers at the black armband around his right arm and then at my black clothes. He doesn't take the bag.

I push it into his chest. "Give Humayun the bag, errand boy."

Slick Bastard takes the bag and fucks off to I-don't-care-where.

An auspicious start to the evening.

I spot Humayun wedged behind the counter. He bulges out of his blue kameez, his man-boobs shaking with each movement. Several *taweez* coil around what's either his neck or a third chin. The fat bastard fussily wipes the counter, talking intently with someone I haven't seen before.

He's a long-haired, lanky old man. Even sitting, I'm pinning Lanky Bastard to be around six foot four. He wears black sunglasses. Reclined in his chair, sipping *karak chai*, he barely acknowledges Humayun. His grey hair falls over broad shoulders. A neatly trimmed grey beard rolls down his angular face like a waterfall of ashes. A leathery taweez digs into his veiny neck. His wrinkled greenish-grey suit somehow retains its dignity. He's dressed like a Sunni, but the bulk of his story is contained in the deep blue armband around his right arm. He's an ex-Shiite.

As if feeling my eyes on him, Lanky Bastard turns and spots me. He does a double take. Something jolts him, the slightest twitch at the corner of his nose and mouth. A snarl. I feel his gaze on me from behind those rectangular shades. My guts start to gnaw on themselves.

Pushing my sunglasses down, I join Kanz on the far side of the counter.

A cracked overhead TV hangs precariously over where we sit, flanked by a green flag with a white crescent and star. There's no white stripe, distinguishing this PFM flag from the standard Pakistani one.

On TV, a cartoon coyote chases a roadrunner past a cliff, only to realize it too late. Defeated, he waves goodbye as gravity plummets him into a ravine.

Kanz scoffs. "Hate that fucking roadrunner."

I glance over at Humayun. Lanky Bastard is saying something to him and pointing in my general direction. Whatever he's saying, the fat bastard isn't liking it.

"Yup."

Humayun motions for us to join him.

"The job done?" he inquires, a bushy steel-wool eyebrow raised. He points at the two chairs beside Lanky Bastard, who hasn't stopped eyeballing me.

"Yup." I take a seat. So does Kanz. "You wanted to see us?"

Humayun pokes all three of his chins at me. "Your gun empty?"

"One bullet," I reply.

"Let me see."

I eject the magazine, push the slide back, and snatch the fat hollow-point as it pops out. I place the gun and bullet on the table.

"Nicely done, golden-eyes."

I push the shades back. "What about my pay?"

"Thought you forgot." Something's off with Humayun. Not the slightest trace of merriment in his pale blue eyes. He's studying me, dissecting me. He's had that look ever since Lanky Bastard started talking to him.

He slides me ten stacks of ration cards, one stack at a time, his dark pink lips twisted. Ten thousand rupees of pink, New Pakistan–issued scratchy paper that buys less and less every year.

"What about my pay?" Kanz asks nervously.

Lanky Bastard snickers.

"There's no pay," Humayun replies. "You are fired."

Kanz, predictably, isn't taking early retirement well. "Humayun, I've been shot in the leg. I can't even walk straight."

"So fucking what?" Humayun doesn't bother looking at him. "I warned you. Warned you repeatedly. Sal needs backup. You are backup. You keep failing. You get fired."

Kanz looks at me, his mouth wide open. An SOS if I ever saw one.

"Maseeh is dead, isn't he?" I blurt out. "Wasn't that the job?"

Humayun isn't impressed.

I try the loyalty card. "Come on, me and Kanz —"

Humayun scoffs. "Kanz and I."

"We've been working our asses off for you. You can't do this."

"Humayun, it's me," Kanz pleads. "Your number one shooter."

Lanky Bastard snickers again, louder.

"No, not anymore." Humayun holds out his hand. "Your gun, now."

"Not happening."

About a dozen waiters quickly surround us, fingers sliding inside their aprons or the backs of their shalwars. Slick Bastard is among them, leering at me instead of Kanz.

"Your gun, Kanz."

"No!"

Before anyone else can even twitch, Kanz draws his Hardballer, the silver machine cocked and ready to spit fire.

The waiters draw their guns: not .38 revolvers or Colt 1911 clones. P38s. The same 9mm as the soldiers. And Maseeh.

The Mullahs and proprietors rush toward the exit, pushing and shoving each other. The high-end hookers tiptoe out under the icy sky, stilettos in hand as the snow falls over them. Only the paleets stay behind, munching their food, the violence so pedestrian it barely registers.

Kanz stands in the middle of the guns, brave and bold.

In the periphery, I spot Lanky Bastard reaching into his coat. I can't see his hand, but I know he's packing heat.

"Do something," Kanz snaps at me. "The fuck are you just standing there for?"

I'm stuck in the middle of both parties, trying to figure out why everyone is carrying military-grade guns suddenly.

"I'm not asking." Humayun is running out of professional courtesy. "Tell him, Sal."

"Kanz, listen to me." I stand between my best friend and a potential wall of 9mms. "I'll talk to Humayun. Just go home."

"He's not taking my gun."

"He's not." I look back at Humayun, who takes way too long to nod. "See? No one's taking your gun."

"Fine. And we're watching *Terminator 3*."

For the love of — "Go home."

Kanz uncocks his gun, pushes past the waiters, and limps out of the diner.

With Kanz gone, everyone's bowels return to normal. The waiters go back to working the diner as if nothing happened. Humayun cleans a shot glass in his hand while Lanky Bastard fondles his steaming cup of tea.

I lean back in the chair. "You could've been more delicate with Kanz."

"That ungrateful faggot," Humayun mutters. He sounds — dare I say — hurt. "I sheltered him. Brought him here. From the Badlands. Gave him everything. A good house. A good life."

He's too kind. "Look, I think you should give him another chance. Bum knee or not, you know there's no one faster than Kanz."

Lanky Bastard scoffs.

"You're faster, Sal." Humayun winks at me. "Don't be sly. Not with me."

There's that look again: the eerie glint in his eyes. *You die today*, it says with no equivocation.

Slick Bastard brings someone's tab to the counter. While there, he peeks at the P38 nestled in his apron and nods at me. I scratch my chin with a middle finger.

I'm reminded of something that's been bugging me. "Since when did your boys start carrying P38s?"

Humayun shrugs. "A new deal."

"With whom? The army?"

The fat bastard laughs. "Don't be ridiculous."

Lanky Bastard finds it funny too.

I spin my chair to face him. "You got something to say to me, madarchod?"

Lanky Bastard sips his tea and uncoils to his full height. Like a scarecrow amidst a murder of crows.

I stand too, kicking the chair back.

Everything goes quiet.

Toe to toe, he seems even taller. His coat is loose and baggy; even so, I can make out his coiled shoulders ready to explode. Feet firmly planted, he balls up his callused fists and smirks. Lanky Bastard is going to put up a hell of a fight. Fine by me. I haven't lost many fights. If it comes down to it, stomping his bony ass into the ground just might be the pick-me-up I need.

"Cut it out," Humayun hisses. "Both of you."

I step away, hands raised.

Lanky Bastard glares at Humayun. Yes, glares. Shades or no shades, Lanky Bastard's thin lips contort into such a nasty scowl that Humayun flinches briefly.

Humayun holds his hand out to me, not letting Lanky Bastard out of sight. "Sal, your gun."

"It's on the table, Humayun."

He slams his hand on the table, making everyone shudder. Everybody but Lanky Bastard.

Baadal's 1911 looks tiny in Humayun's doughy paw. He loads the hollow-point, pulls the slide back, and points the gun at Lanky Bastard.

Hell on earth.

A few gasps fill the room, followed by sharp murmurs, the sizzling hiss from the kitchen where the cooking oil has begun to sputter.

Lanky Bastard remains motionless, his lips taut.

Humayun eases the hammer, clicks the safety into place, and holds the .45 before me.

"Salaba, meet Sarv." He smiles. "Your new partner."

Episode 4: Burdens

Rahee

November 3, 2046

Nothing was unique about that night. Like all nights after Radhi's death, my father was out at work while my mother stood by the window, trying to catch snowflakes. The only difference was the silver anklet. She wore it that night. She was also holding on to something, I couldn't see what.

I was eleven.

"What are you doing, Mother?" I asked, sitting on the floor far away from her. It was the first time I had asked her that. Sometimes, I imagine doing it sooner. In that dream world, she cries as she confides everything in me and pets my hair as I fall asleep in her arms. Before long, though, no matter how much I dream, I wake up to the immutable reality of a motherless world. "Mother? What are you doing?"

"Ghosts," she whispered without looking at me. She hadn't looked at me in so long. "I'm trying to catch them."

Ghosts. It struck me how quickly people had begun calling the snowfall *ghosts*. Pakistan had become a nation of ghosts — a nation of men, women, and children trying to find everything they had lost in these ashes. My father told me that Pakistan was a nation chasing many, many ghosts. Men and women talked only of the old days when they used to be free, when food was cheap, when the air was clean, and when everyone pretended to care. No one talked of the present. Even before the Fifth Indo-Pak War, before Allah burned the sky away, Pakistanis always remembered old lives they longed to live again.

As she stood by the snow-kissed window, I saw what my mother was clutching: the once-blue baby shoes that had belonged to Radhi.

"The snow falls over it all," she said.

There was a *chnnn* from my mother's anklet as she climbed the windowsill and, an instant later, joined the wordless, soundless ghosts on the pavement below.

———

November 7, 2046

At my mother's funeral, my father stood still, holding my hand in his. He trembled now and then. I watched the faces of the handful at the funeral. Everyone we knew had only agreed to attend if we buried her in a remote corner of the huge graveyard. She was an Ahmadi Muslim, and my father explained that as per the 1974 Second Amendment and 1984 Ordinance xx, Pakistanis would never recognize her as a Muslim.

No tombstone or marker was laid over my mother's grave. We couldn't afford one. All that separated her from any other patch of dirt was an obscure mound that, for years, my father adorned with a leafy twig. He explained that every leaf, even one that's plucked, praises Allah until it dries out. My father made me promise that when he died, even if I forgot he'd ever existed, I must continue to leave a twig on my mother's grave.

"I am at peace now," he said to me as we walked back home. "Your mother is with Allah now, and it fills me with peace. I hope you understand."

"I do, Father."

At home, my father gathered her belongings, keeping the ones he felt we might need. He piled the rest and gave them away. People came and collected what they wanted. He didn't say anything when people told him how sorry they were for his loss while plucking away at my mother's shawls, sarees, and bangles. My father only made a sound — a short gasp — when someone took away her silver anklet.

The next day, we went to the graveyard again to pay our respects.

My father stood behind me, resting his hands on my shoulders. He didn't say a word for a long time. Unaware of what to do, I watched others standing sombrely over their dead loved ones, hands held together piously. I emulated them. But I didn't know what they were saying, so I held my hands and stared into the distance.

I felt a tremble. A more vigorous tremble made me look up at my father.

Tears were streaming down his face, his body convulsing with each breath. It was the only time I saw him cry. His hands weren't held together. He wasn't murmuring anything. The light gleaming in his tears said more.

Closing my eyes, I spoke to my mother, not in mantras and prayers but in simple words. I dreamed her alive but without pain, materialized not as a drifting shadow but as body and flesh. I dreamed of asking her why she'd stopped talking to me, looking at me. And though she had no answer, I forgave her without needing her to say anything at all. I dreamed of asking my mother why she'd tried to catch the ghosts falling from the burned sky.

Before long, I returned to the feel of my father's hands clutching my shoulders and the cold earth under my feet.

———

May 20, 2048

I was thirteen. Repeating Yaqzan's words was now punishable by life imprisonment. Every week, there were flyers imploring us to report Loyalists and blasphemers to the army. Fathers, brothers, sons, and friends were turned in. Before long, those of us still alive had mastered the art of mistrust.

New Pakistan was now a large walled city. A blossoming fantasy for many. A prosperous, shining city that would be a bastion where true Islam flourished. We began hearing stories about how safe that walled city was, how there was no crime, how there was no load-shedding, how there was clean water flowing from the taps. We heard stories of how no one had to fight for a loaf of bread because Allah had provided New Pakistanis with more food and water than they could consume in one lifetime. We heard that the snow didn't fall over that walled city.

My father said New Pakistan was a pipe dream fed to every generation of Pakistanis, even before the Fifth Indo-Pak War, before Allah burned the sky away.

"The only thing we have is each other," my father said in those last years of his life, his faith in Allah broken.

I feared the world was aching to take him from me. I prayed against this deprivation five times a day, my heart thumping in my chest.

"Do not take my father away from me," I whispered, my face and forehead pressed into the dusty prayer mats in the Blue Mosque. "Fill his heart with your love, your mercy."

Allah answered my prayers, but not in the way I wanted.

———

July 10, 2049

When I was fourteen, my father told me about how I got my name. We were walking back from my mother's grave.

"Did I ever tell you that I wanted to name you Ismail?" my father asked.

"No, Father."

"I like the story of Hazrat Ibrahim and Hazrat Ismail. The sacrifice."

"I know the story, Father," I said. We continued to walk in an uncomfortable silence, which I broke. "So, why didn't you?"

"Your mother." He smiled. "She refused to give you a traditional Muslim name. You know how she was when she got an idea stuck in her mind. You're just like her. Stubborn. So, she named you Rahee."

"What does it mean?"

"It's Arabic for *spring*. And Urdu for *wanderer*."

I wondered which one she'd had in mind.

_____

May 2, 2051

My father was among the several dozen men who were left crippled in a construction accident during the Green Mosque's renovation. Eyewitnesses said a rock from the celestial debris crashed into the mosque. Then the army came along, with Mullahs in tow, and anyone who spoke of the moon rock was accused of blasphemy under Section 298.

I began to work at the mosque after that. No burden was too heavy for my soul. Working with stones and bricks and hammers came naturally.

I was sixteen. Repeating Yaqzan's words was now punishable by death.

Before long, I began hearing about what was happening in Sector 1. I heard of soldiers violating Shiite homes. Just as my father had predicted. They dragged the families from their homes, raped their women, broke and burned their belongings. Those who resisted were shot. It didn't take much to get shot. Within days, only a handful of Shiite families were left in neighbourhoods that once had several dozen living alongside Sunnis.

Some Shiites fought back. They did not die quietly. It's not in our nature to lie down and die. Not in Karbala. Certainly not after.

Sameer Uncle was among those who revolted. He had worked with my father during the ill-fated construction of the Green Mosque and, miraculously, escaped with only minor injuries. Since then, Sameer Uncle had come every week to give us ration cards. He did this furtively, with a handshake at the end of his visit. People had begun calling these ration cards *rupees*.

To keep us going, he would say.

Sameer Uncle would talk about his three little boys who wanted to grow tall and strong like me, so they too could work with stones and bricks and hammers.

That week, when soldiers arrived in their jeeps, Sameer Uncle fought back. A gunfight erupted. It lasted an hour. My father and I pressed ourselves against the floor and prayed. When it ended, three soldiers were dead, and the remaining Shiites in our neighbourhood stood in defiance.

In retaliation, the army set Sameer Uncle's house on fire. For what felt like hours, Sameer Uncle and his three sons screamed through the flames. Soldiers formed a ring around the house, and anyone who stepped forward with water or ropes was shot dead or crippled.

Sameer Uncle's screams kept me awake for days.

When the army returned to our neighbourhood, they found my father and me sitting by our home with our belongings packed. The remaining Shiites in our neighbourhood were also there. Soldiers pushed us into the back of jeeps and threw most of our belongings to the floor. My father protested when they wouldn't let an old woman bring three heavy bags. She was shot. My father sat back down in the jeep.

Utterly powerless, we didn't look back as the jeep drove us to what we call Sector 2 today.

———

February 17, 2052
Toward the end of his life, my father was a sickly carapace sunk in the maroon armchair that seemed to grow around him. Like my mother, there was no voice left in him — just his indignity at being robbed of his children and the love of his life. A deep-seated hatred crusted inside him. Hatred for his country, his people. And for Allah.

"Why would He do this to me, Ra-Ra?" he asked, gazing distantly. He had begun calling me Ra-Ra, as he had when I was just a boy. This was my seventeenth birthday.

He had asked me this question only once before. When he'd still held on to his faith. The night our little Roshni had begun to cough and cry. My father had just come back with what medicine he could find, but Roshni was too weak, too emaciated.

My father had looked at me and said for the first time what he would spend his old age saying: "Why would Allah do this to me, Ra-Ra?"

Even now, years later, when I visit my parents' grave, I'm left distraught at the thought of hell and the horrors my parents face for their transgressions. How much they let the burdens on their souls break them. I pray I remain steadfast in ways their fragile souls couldn't.

Episode 5: DBE

Avaan

July 31, 2083

I have a new partner now. Sarv, the lanky bastard I nearly stomped into the floor a few minutes back. He nods at Humayun and bumps past me.

Chuutya.

"Let it go," Humayun mutters from the counter.

"I'm not working with that prick," I say, sitting down.

"Yeah, you are."

Choices.

An on-duty squad of soldiers barges in, two dozen boisterous rent-a-thugs drunk on power and prejudice. Humayun motions to Slick Bastard, who quickly greets them at the entrance and leads them to the special corner with the jukebox.

One of the soldiers, unsteady and way too loud, begins kicking it. "Which song do you want to hear?" she asks, voice muffled by the thick ski mask. "'The End'? Or 'Ankhon ko ankhon ne'?"

As they laugh and jeer, she pops in a coin, and it starts: the song I hate more than anything else in the world. "Ankhon ko ankhon ne" by Junaid Jamshed.

Might as well ruin someone else's evening. "Humayun, can I ask you something?"

"Go ahead, golden-eyes."

I push the shades back. "Who's Yaqzan? Where did he come from?"

"Why're you asking?"

"I overheard some women gossiping about him and the Loyalists."

His face reddens. "*Loyalists*, is it?"

"Terrorists, then."

"What'd they say?"

"They were talking about Yaqzan —" I start, but lower my voice when Humayun holds a finger to his lips. "Something about how he's some hero."

"He's a terrorist. They all are. Heroes don't smuggle."

"Smuggle? You mean they really did hit the supply trucks?"

"They did."

"But that's army territory," I point out, much to Humayun's chagrin. "That's some fucking balls Yaqzan has. For as long as he has them."

Humayun scoffs. "He's a fool. Arrogant old thug."

I feel cool fingers caress the nape of my neck, glass bangles clinking. Doua, ablaze in a red saree. She kisses my neck as her small, firm breasts press into my side.

Some days, I wonder why you trust this filth. Is Baadal not dead because of him?

"Not now."

Humayun raises a thick, bushy eyebrow. "You said something?"

I need to stop zoning out. "Just mumbling. The usual."

"Try mutton *korma*."

"Is it mutton?"

There's a pause. "Sure it is."

"Huh. Just get me the *lassi*."

Humayun reaches into a small fridge and puts a steel mug full of frothy lassi on the counter. Dumping a thin cube of brown sugar into it, he plops the mug before me, spilling some of the precious white liquid.

I take a sip. "Put some more sugar in it, you cheap bastard."

Humayun winks and drops a half-cube of sugar into my drink. For a moment, he's back to the old cheeky fat bastard I've hated forever.

As I take a generous gulp, an exhausted woman squeezes next to me, making me spill more of the lassi into my beard and shirt. Her rough beige shawl envelops her body and head but not her round, worried face.

"I'm Rosa. We spoke earlier," she says to Humayun. "This is all I could find."

"Let me see."

She pulls the shawl away to reach into her red shalwar, and as she does so, I notice — for the tiniest of moments — a white rag tied around her right arm. She's quick to drape the shawl back over herself again, but if I caught it there's no way Humayun missed it.

The woman gives him a peek at something silver in her hand. It's a pocket watch. It still works. The second hand is moving.

Humayun paws at the metal and pockets it with an unenthusiastic nod. "That's not enough."

Without hesitation, the woman breaks off a shiny gold crucifix from around her neck. She drops it into his pink palm.

He pockets that too. "What'll it be?"

"Please, I need information. About my boy." She holds her hand to her shoulder. "This tall. Had a row of piercings in his right ear. Please."

I focus on the foamy lassi, stirring it with my finger.

"He was killed," Humayun says, his indifference inhumane. "Early this morning. Near Blue Mosque. Claim the body."

The woman's throat lurches. "Who killed my boy?"

The fat bastard holds out his hand, palm facing up.

"Please," she croaks. "That was all I had."

"Then get lost."

The woman runs out, hand smothering her mouth.

That's Humayun for you. A turgid octopus buried in a murk of hidden agendas, dead bodies, and ulterior motives. A piggy bank of secrets for those who can pay. The only reason I work for him is that if ever there is information on Doua, this fat bastard will be the one to have it.

"You're a real bastard," I say.

He grins. "You too, Sal. A genuine bastard."

No arguments there. I'm Abu Lahab. I'm the Wandering Jew. I'm Lut's wife, a pillar of salt endlessly looking back in horror.

Humayun's mouth moves, but I barely hear anything. I'm drowning inside myself.

"Oy, Salaba Hatteb."

"What?"

"We've got company."

He's a big bastard, whoever he is. Standing at the entrance, he glowers at us like he's walked in on us taking turns on his wife. A plastic-bag poncho covers his body but not his scabbed hands, his weathered face, or the black shalwar he's tucked into oversized boots. When he plods over to the counter next to me, I notice a hollowness in his gaze. A tower of courage made of twigs.

Humayun regards him cautiously. "You want something?"

"I want the special," Big Bastard replies, his voice like footsteps on gravel. "Get me the DBE special."

Humayun looks up. I look up. Everyone within earshot looks up.

Hell on earth, Big Bastard. Just when the evening was getting quiet.

Doua speaks to me. *You are thinking about him again, are you not? About Baadal?*

Three years ago. One gunshot. The soldiers carried Baadal's corpse away. I was bound and gagged, kneeling beside the wreckage I'd once called home. It was Ground Zero, the day the soldiers took everything from me.

"Got a gun?" Humayun asks Big Bastard. "You'll need one."

Big Bastard shakes his head.

Humayun turns to the soldier squad and runs his index finger across his throat. Officer Loudmouth, with her penchant for kicking jukeboxes, chugs her drink and joins us at the counter. She bumps into me, making me spill even more lassi.

Fuck it, let's have everyone hover over me.

She slurs into her radio. Despite the ski mask and the cluttered feedback, I pick up Officer Loudmouth's requests for tightened security, snipers, and dogs. Standard DBE protocol. There's some grainy chatter on the other side that I can't make out.

Big Bastard slumps into the barstool next to me, staring up at the ceiling with his lost yellow eyes. Officer Loudmouth approaches him, reaching into her uniform.

Out comes a three-page contract.

Big Bastard flips through it, grimacing.

"Oh, you can't read?" Officer Loudmouth chortles and produces a thumb stamp. "That's fine. Just put your thumbprints here." She points it out to him. "And here. Oh, and here too. No need to worry about anything else."

"Is everything good?" Humayun asks.

"Yes," replies Officer Loudmouth.

Humayun enters a small, dark room behind the counter. I've seen him enter that room once before.

Folding the contract, Officer Loudmouth says something into her radio that makes my skin crawl. "Acknowledged. Alerting

Colonel Evergreen. Over."

Evergreen. The Butcher of the Badlands. A haunted relic from the civil war that carved this city into its many pieces.

Humayun returns with a large black briefcase. Murmurs puncture the stillness. I don't blame them. It's been years since anyone has seen that legendary briefcase. He places it before Big Bastard and pops it open.

Everyone gasps.

It's full of money. The physical embodiment of what separates Humayun from the rest of us: one hundred million rupees. All of it in stacks of crisp notes with more zeroes at the end than I've ever seen. All of it blood money.

Humayun grins. "Oh, wrong briefcase."

It's no mistake. The fat bastard wanted everyone to see it. With a dozen fully armed assassins ever present at the diner and nearly a hundred novice hitmen at his command, the briefcase is the crown jewel of Humayun's power. Only Evergreen is above him in the food chain.

And now, after all these years of fighting from within the shadows, maybe so is Yaqzan.

Shuffling back into the room, Humayun gets the other legendary briefcase and pops it open.

Inside? A gold-plated Colt Python. A six-shot revolver, the Python is a gorgeous killing machine. You point its fluted six-inch barrel at whatever is bothering you and pull the deliciously smooth trigger to make it stop bothering you. Big Bastard wraps his huge paw around it and holds it up. The diner explodes with applause.

Humayun raises a steel-wool brow, glib as always. "Make your peace. And good luck."

Big Bastard marches outside. The Ashraf-ul-Makhlooqat sign jangles and swings. His footsteps grow faint, echo, and disappear.

One by one, the patrons hurry out of the diner after him. No one wants to miss tonight's show. It's been three years since the last one.

Me? I pour the remaining lassi into my ungrateful system and bask in the silence.

You are not going? Doua asks in that smoky voice of hers. She enunciates her words, but with a kind of impatience. As if she can't wait for one word to end so she can savour the next.

"Nope. My legs are killing me."

It has been three long years.

"Doesn't matter. DBE will always be around as long as there's some poor bastard ready to risk it all."

Resting my feverish head on the cold counter, I deflate. The smooth wood feels like it's steaming against my temples.

"You should go," Humayun drones, wiping a glass in his pink hands. "See what's up."

"Is that an order?"

"I make requests?"

Choices.

I also think you should go. Doua leans into me. *Because you are going to find out if I really am alive. And maybe you will finally get to tell me your big little secret.*

———

August 1, 2083
"DBE," chants the crowd, hundreds of us headed in the same direction. "DBE."

Someone pulls my arm, trying to sell me *jalebi* for a hundred rupees. I wrestle myself from him and bump into a scrawny woman who blows *bidi* smoke in my face. I compose myself, and a mother clutches my shirt, begging me to buy her stale samosas. The bilious stench of burning rubber and sweat and gasoline and dirty laundry and rotting food clings to the air.

"DBE," the crowd chants. "DBE."

Walking for the last eight hours in the dark has left my legs feeling like charred meat. Black military jeeps, blockades, barricades, and black-clad soldiers funnel the crowd through the penumbra of Sector 2 and toward Sector 1's Checkpoint 1. Even at this distance, New Pakistan's shimmering white light leaves these spindly buildings almost translucent, like fingers held up to the sun. Or a night sky that has begun to burn and fall.

"Keep moving calmly," a joyless female voice orders through the PSA system. "Keep moving calmly."

Floodlights illuminate the crowd — several hundred paleets and kafirs with nothing better to do. Searchlights flash over miles of the razor wire fence along the border. Soldiers patrol the perimeters, their AK-47s aimed at us like the snouts of black hounds.

Despite the guns and itchy trigger fingers, for Pakistanis, this is all pedestrian. Since Pakistan's inception in 1947, not a single prime minister has served a complete term. If they weren't ousted or assassinated by political rivals, the army generously staged a coup. This is simply the fourth one, a forty-year martial law that shows no sign of ending.

Today, there's a nervousness in the way the soldiers scan us.

Yaqzan. It has to be.

———

Sector 1, Checkpoint 1.

The sun is a hazy red semicircle on the horizon. Most of the sky is blotted out and black, the celestial debris sparkling distantly through the clouds. I move slowly away from the middle of the crowd, my eyes peeled for what I know is doomed to happen.

After a few minutes of studying the crowd, I spot my prey. The one guy who's been watching a particular spot along the razor wire fence.

He's noticed the same thing I have: the searchlights seem to ignore that patch, leaving it in the dark the longest. Scratching his patchy beard, he rolls up the sleeves of his light-blue kameez and gestures at someone behind him.

Two men and a woman break off from the crowd and follow him. I do too, from a distance. Out of the soldiers' line of vision, they scurry over the barren dirt road along the fence, staying clear of the searchlights. Trailing them, I stay low in the shadow of collapsed walls that form Sector 2's boundaries.

After several minutes of walking, the Fearless Four make it to the spot. There's only one smart play here.

Climb over? Not with the razor wire on the fence.

Cut it? Not without the right tools — and even then, not enough time. And not with this many soldiers patrolling the area.

Dig? Same problem.

The men deliberate among themselves and seem to settle for Option C: digging. With their hands.

The lookout lady — I assume that's what she is — stays focused on the soldiers at the checkpoint we snuck away from. It's a considerable distance.

"Keep going," I hear her say. "Hurry."

Except all four of them are oblivious to the two soldiers sneaking up behind them.

I sink lower into the shadows and the rubble.

The searchlight illuminates them. Lookout Lady raises her hands and drops to her knees. The men leg it. At this distance, the soldiers barely need to aim. They just level their AK-47s and open fire.

There are snaps, crackles. Squelchy pops.

By the time the gunshots die down, three of the four idiots are mounds of redundant flesh and bone. Howling in agony, the only one still alive tries to crawl away. One soldier calls it in while the other walks up to the poor bastard and aims the AK-47 at his head. I look away but still see enough to haunt me for a few nights.

Let it be known: sneaking into Sector 1 is frowned upon.

The early morning is unnervingly quiet.

I stay hidden in the shadows as the soldiers frisk the bodies. They cover the little ditch the three idiots managed to dig and continue patrolling the fence. They leave the bodies.

The coast is clear now. Silver linings.

I slip the .45 into a plastic bag I find lying around. Staying low, I tiptoe past the dismembered pieces of those poor bastards. Using my hands, I re-dig the ditch, the earth much softer now, and drop the plastic bag in it. I manage to cover it up just as a white disk of searchlight skims the ground near me.

Returning to Sector 1's checkpoint, I stand in line and wait my turn. I show the soldiers my ID, answer the same questions as the morning before, raise my hands as two of them brush the metal detector over me, endure the hateful daggers in their eyes, and saunter through the checkpoint with my head still intact.

This was the smart play.

Past the checkpoint, it's smooth sailing. Relatively. The Sector 2 border may be a confounding maze of thistle-like buildings, but Sector 1 is miles and miles of generally intact villas and townhouses that the Sunnis were more than happy to usurp after the Civil War.

Most houses are sequestered behind high walls and metal gates. The mostly intact asphalt under my feet, the huge Green Mosque, which keeps getting expanded and renovated despite all the construction accidents, the old Lollywood posters on billboards — all of this evokes a bygone age.

I traverse a long semicircle that takes me through rows of idyllic homes and back to the hole I dug under the fence. I hang back and time how long it takes the patrolling soldiers to pass. I observe the searchlight patterns, time their movements, and eventually exhume the .45 — the only memento I have of my little brother and his ill-fated quest to help us survive.

A gaggle of kafirs and paleets traipse the Sector 1 streets, all of us heading in the same direction.

Most Sunnis know better than to come out on such volatile occasions. Now and then, I catch a glimpse of them gawking at me from behind windows. They have that expression that only piety begets. That eyebrow-raised, lopsided smirk that blends patronizing pity, disgust, and disdain. A primordial revulsion punctuated by the all-green PFM flags planted by their homes. Some even took the time to etch the entire Section 298 on placards.

Every few streets, there are tiny pathways strewn with black garbage bags and bottles.

Military jeeps drone along the tarmac, ensuring that this small crowd of untouchable, godless heathens marches straight for the vast field of scorched earth past Sector 1 and nowhere else. As I walk forward, the sound of tires on the tarmac is a constant.

Farther down the street, the white light grows brighter than the dull reddish sun still crawling toward its perch in the sky. The snow, dancing and dappled in the light, is like a flight of fireflies.

Finally, I see it: New Pakistan and its giant walls, cradled in the lap of five mountains. *Dust-e-ilahi*, the Hand of God. It's these mountains that give this slice of heaven its unique circular shape.

No longer boisterous or festive, there's a pensiveness in the air as we walk the field surrounding New Pakistan. Sandbag revetments reinforce the razor wire fence at its perimeters. Countless hands latch on to the fence, their bloody fingers groping for the pristine white buildings that look like pillars of light.

Sandwiched between the fence and New Pakistan's tall white walls is a vast marble courtyard. An entire regiment of the army either stands guard or marches along this area.

Standing by the fence, I can see the gigantic Iron Gate, the only breach in the sturdy walls. A V-shaped pathway leads up to the gate, but the abundance of RPD-wielding sentries, snipers, and floodlights converging over it would dissuade even the staunchest Loyalist.

This is the New Pakistan Checkpoint. The final one.

This is where I stood three years ago when there was nothing more for me to lose.

Today, I'm not one of the two men standing on that V-shaped pathway, the snow falling around them.

One is Big Bastard, without the plastic-bag poncho. Panting, sweaty, he lets his hand flex over the golden Colt Python.

The other is tall and tranquil. His left hand extends an inch above the pearl grips of his Peacemaker. Nothing distinguishes him from other masked soldiers except for the black duster reaching his knees and the mantis-like PAK10 gas mask that hides his face.

Hushed and stagnant, he is Death Itself. This is Evergreen.

———

August 21, 2080

I was twenty-five. A week after Ground Zero.

I lay in the army's infirmary, covered in bandages. The Sector 1 Precinct. Evergreen stood next to me. He parted the white curtains and glanced out into the city, standing upright and dignified.

"If it were up to me, you'd be dead by now. You're fortunate things played out the way they have." His voice was an unearthly hum because of the PAK10 mask. The red eyepieces and the protruding canister on the left side of the mask rendered him more alien, almost insectoid. "Considering the circumstances of your brother's death, my superiors think it earns you the right to live. Luck of the devil, if you ask me."

I stared at the ceiling, rubbing my hand over my cropped hair. "Who tipped you off about Baadal?"

"Huh. Things happen the way they do for a reason, boy. Maybe Allah has a plan for you after all." Evergreen exhaled long and hard before continuing. "As a final courtesy, we have cremated Baadal. I know you would've wanted to be there, but all I can do is present you with his ashes."

I heard the metallic urn being placed on the table. I didn't look at it.

"I saw to it that his funeral was anonymous but respectful."

I sat up, holding my head in my hands. "Where is Doua?"

"She's dead, boy. Everyone in that library is dead. You aren't. Consider yourself lucky."

The pain that I felt wasn't sharp. It wasn't like being skinned or stabbed or struck or shot. It wasn't dizzying or debilitating. It wasn't like drowning. When I found out that I'd lost Doua, I finally saw it: the hole in the world. A yawning emptiness at the centre of everything. Whatever was full of colour, whatever was warm and soft, had begun circling this hole. And I was circling with it, sinking deeper and darker. Circling endlessly.

———

Bang.

It's over.

Big Bastard is left sprawled on the ground, the right side of his forehead and skull smeared over the marble.

Evergreen eases the hammer of his Peacemaker and holsters it without theatrics.

Pulling out a piece of white cloth, he kneels beside Big Bastard and drops it over what's left of the man's face. He remains like that for a while, head lowered. When he stands, he cups his hands before him, and all those present join in, ruminatively reciting a prayer.

"And cleanse him with water, snow, and ice. And purify him of sin. As a white robe is purified of filth."

I don't join in the prayers. I look at Big Bastard. Under the white cloth, I imagine him as calm and beautiful as I wish I will be when it's my time. It's what Big Bastard wanted, after all: Death by Evergreen.

Evergreen picks up the Python and places it in his pocket. The army always returns the gun to Humayun, a tradition carried over from a time when countless women and men would ask for the DBE, all for a chance to take out this nightmare of a man.

Two soldiers carry Big Bastard's corpse to the V-shaped entrance where I'm standing. Evergreen follows, head bowed, hands crossed behind him.

The soldiers place the body at the entrance and stand guard behind Evergreen, their AK-47s and Remington 31s pointed at the crowd.

I slip my shades back, cover my face with the shawl, and try sneaking away. The sheer number of people leaves me with little wriggle room.

Panic cracks open inside me, seeping down the pit of my stomach.

"Is there anyone here to claim him?" I hear Evergreen ask, his voice cold.

No one does.

"Fine. Take him away," Evergreen says, his voice closer than I'd ever want. "Take him away and see to it that his funeral is respectful."

Doua's small hand on my shoulder gives me more courage than the steel of the .45. *I am sorry you have to see this man again. All this because of me.*

I accept my fate.

"Hello, Avaan." I hear Evergreen's voice directly behind me. "And here I thought you were a dead man."

Episode 6: Conviction

Rahee

July 25, 2052

Glassiness had begun to form in my father's eyes. My mother had been dead for six years by then. Grey and wizened, my father was in his late forties but looked decades older. He would ask me where Radhi was, where Roshni was. He would tell me to go ask my mother for tea. He would call me Ra-Ra. Like he had when I was a boy.

One evening, the glassiness disappeared as he watched the falling snow. Those ghosts that had stolen his love from him.

"What do you want, son?"

"Power."

"Power?"

"So we can live a good life, Father."

"We do live a good life."

Sameer Uncle was no longer there to give us ration cards. "Yes, Father."

"You are earning for the family through hard work," my father said, a thick blanket folded over his dark, skinny legs.

It was true. I'd been working on the roads for a year, breaking rocks and stones with a sledgehammer twelve hours a day. I'd earn seven cans of food for a week's work, and enough money to squeeze by. In the evenings, I cleaned homes that had once belonged to Shiites, in neighbourhoods we had been displaced from.

"It's not a lot, but it's an honest living, son," he said again. "That's good enough for me, and that should be good enough for you."

I almost said, *It was not good enough for my mother. It was not good enough for Radhi and Roshni.*

Instead, I asked a question. "Why are you talking about this now, Father?"

"Because of this." He pulled out a leaflet. A large white sheet of paper. A green circle sat at the centre with a crescent and star inside. It was one of the leaflets the army had been distributing in all neighbourhoods. New Pakistan, a walled haven for true Muslims. "You promised you understood, son."

"I do understand."

"Do you?"

"I do, Father."

"No matter what you do, you're always going to be a Shiite to them."

When I didn't look up at him, when I didn't speak, my father said something that haunts me to this day. "You're too much like me, son. And you're not enough like your mother."

I don't want to be like my mother. I'm not an Ahmadi kafir, I wanted to say, but I kept silent, becoming more like her in the process. So I said it out loud. My father said nothing for a long time.

When he finally spoke, he called me Ra-Ra and asked me where my brother and sister were. He said he wanted my mother to make him a cup of tea because it was snowing outside.

———

October 26, 2052

"I need you to promise me something, Rahee."

My father had my mother's picture folded in his lap as he held his leg out for me to massage. He could barely move his legs on his own anymore. The cold would soak into his bones, and the only respite was massaging his legs with warm oil.

"What is it, Father?"

"New Pakistan." My father was in one of his moods, as he often was in that last year of his life. It was either this or him staring ahead with glassy hazel eyes, unsure of where he was. I cannot say which version of him I preferred. "It's all a bloody lie, son."

"Things can change, Father."

My father wriggled his leg out of my grasp and sank farther back into his armchair.

"Do you know how often I've heard the expression? *New Pakistan*? Even before the Fifth Indo-Pak War, before Allah burned away the sky. Your grandfather and his father before him, all heard this expression. Every generation of Pakistanis has heard it, son."

"Yes, Father."

"We are Shiites, son. Never forget that, because this country never has. Not since 1947. You remember what happened on August 14, 1947?"

"Pakistan's independence."

"Yes. Pakistan became a nation for Muslims. Do you feel independent as a Pakistani Shiite?"

"No, Father."

"A Shiite isn't a true Muslim. Not for Pakistanis. It begins with *not a true Muslim*, becomes *not a Muslim*, and ends with *not a human*."

I massaged the warm oil over my father's legs. They were covered with sores and brittle veins.

"It's what happened to the Ahmadi Muslims with the 1979 Amendment and Ordinance xx. To Pakistani Jews. It happened to Pakistani Hindus, Sikhs, and Parsis. Even before Allah burned the sky away. What the army is doing today — the displacements, the killings — it's always happened before in Pakistan in one form or another."

"Yes, Father."

My father snickered. It was a snicker I had begun to loathe. The dryness in it, the resignation. His shattered illusions given a voice.

"Remember what happened when they pushed the Hindus out of our neighbourhoods? And the Christians? Remember how all the Muslims celebrated?"

"They were kafirs."

My father's lips twisted into a scowl. "Christians are not kafirs, Rahee. They're *Ahle Kitab*, People of the Book."

"Mullah-sahib said that anyone who isn't a Muslim is —"

"You forget the bloody Mullahs."

"Yes, Father."

He didn't say anything for a while. I was content with long silences.

"A country for true Muslims." He snickered again. "Do you know the name of the man who founded Pakistan?"

"Muhammad Ali Jinnah."

"Did you know Jinnah was a Shiite?"

"Yes, Father. You told me."

"When he died, his family said he had converted to Sunni Islam. Did you know that?"

"No, Father." I massaged his legs, but they remained cool and cracked.

"Imagine that. Even the man who created Pakistan was not Muslim enough for Pakistanis."

"Father, don't. You never know who might be listening. Why do you —"

"The snow falls over it all, son."

"Stop it." I wanted to break this bitter, brittle old man in half. "It was a test. All hardships are His test, Father."

"Your mother was right."

"Don't blaspheme, old man. I'm warning you. You've seen the flyers."

My father stared at me the way my mother used to look at him. "The snow falls over it all."

———

January 6, 2053

In the last weeks of his life, my father held my hand for support as he bent down to put a leafy twig on my mother's grave. He couldn't walk or stand for too long. After praying to a God he had lost faith in, my father told me about a dream he'd had.

"I saw her, Rahee. As she used to be before Radhi. You were there too. But older, as I've always imagined you as an adult: tall and proud. Like your mother."

I don't want to be like Mother, I almost said. "What happened in your dream?"

"You two were arguing in an old house. You wore black as if you had just come back from a Christian funeral. You were so angry, Rahee. I don't think I've ever seen you so angry. So full of hatred."

A flutter of white feathers caught my attention, circling over me. A bird swooped down, grabbed a rat in its claw, and perched on a tree near us. It was a crow. An albino crow, without family or friends. It cawed softly and stabbed its beak into the powerless rat's abdomen. Its beak bloody, the lonely, ashy bird stared at me with red orbs.

"What happened then, old man?"

"Your mother listened. She didn't say anything, even as you hissed and spat like some venomous snake."

"Just like in real life."

"Stop it. She watched her children die. It broke her heart."

"Not all of them."

"Stop it."

"I was still alive, Father."

"You don't understand what she went through, son. Her losses broke her. But she loved you. You have to believe me. She loved you dearly."

I glanced at the tree. The white crow was gone.

"What happened then?" I asked, wrapping my arm around his stooping shoulders. This old man was my father, I reminded myself.

He made a sound. *Huh.* As if surprised and not surprised at once.

"Take this." My father reached into his breast pocket and pulled out another leafy twig. He slipped it into my hand and looked at the grave of the woman we both had lost. "Give your heart some peace."

I placed the twig over my mother's grave. When I stood back up, my father held my hand.

"I don't hate you," he said quietly.

"What?"

"That's what she said in the dream. After everything you said to her. After all the shouting and screaming. That's what your mother said to you: 'I don't hate you.'"

———

January 24, 2053

"What is your name, boy?"

The Mullah-sahib's tiny black eyes regarded me across the long, white table. He had the same black uniform as the soldiers, although they didn't wear masks back then. His orange-dyed beard and thinning white hair made his complexion seem that much darker. There were murmurs about how he'd fought during the Fifth Indo-Pak War.

I cleared my throat. "My name is Rahee. Sir."

A soldier sat next to him, shorter, stockier. Scribbling over a form, he barely looked at me. A small Pakistani flag blocked my view of what he was jotting down.

"Rahee." The Mullah-sahib did his best to beam at me, but no wrinkles formed around his cheeks. It made his yellow, cracked teeth look unnaturally large. He reached up and scratched the scaly black *zabiba* at the bridge of his forehead. "Just go over why you are here."

"Sir, I —"

"Speak up, boy. If you're here to report theft, then know that we have too many cases already. We will do what we can, of course, but I wouldn't get my hopes —"

"It's not theft, sir."

"The same goes for missing persons."

"I'm not reporting a missing person."

The soldier looked up for the first time. "Then what is it?"

"I am registered as a Shiite Muslim." I sank my chin into my chest. "I have decided to convert to Sunni Islam. I want to serve New Pakistan, sir. I want to serve my new faith."

The soldier scribbled something on the form.

"*Mashallah, mashallah.*" The Mullah-sahib smiled. Again, no wrinkles formed. "You are doing the right thing."

"Yes, sir. Thank you."

"Thank Allah, boy. Not me."

"Of course."

The soldier stopped scribbling and put his pen down.

"You are aware that we still require evidence for your sincerity," the Mullah-sahib said a little too quickly. "We have to be sure that your faith is genuine. Understand?"

"Yes, sir."

"Not that I do not believe you, boy," he said with his hands raised, again a little too quickly. "Those are just the rules in place. It's too easy for you people to pretend, understand? For all we know, you want access to New Pakistan. Like so many others."

"I am here to serve New Pakistan. I am here to report a blasphemer."

"This person will have to confess to his crimes, as per the Pakistani Penal Code."

"Yes, sir."

The Mullah-sahib scrutinized the expression on my face. Whatever it was. "Two soldiers will be there to bear witness to this person's confession and your deed. Understand?"

"Yes, sir."

"This person cannot be a stranger. It cannot be a friend. It has to be family."

"I am aware, sir."

"Good," the Mullah-sahib said, smiling joylessly. He nodded at the soldier.

The soldier spoke again. "Who are you reporting?"

"Ayyub Sarv, sir." I spoke the words with such conviction. "He is my father."

February 1, 2053

"Why are you doing this, Rahee?"

I was almost eighteen. I hadn't seen my father in two weeks. In those two weeks, the whiteness of his sparse hair, the wrinkles over his face, had made him look more withered. Swallowed by his maroon armchair, my father looked like a hapless chick in the jaws of a monster.

Glancing behind me, I could tell that the soldiers bearing witness were growing impatient.

"Why are you doing this?" the old man who was my father asked again, his voice louder — so loud, it struck me that it came from the emaciated husk before me. He wasn't looking at me anymore. He was looking at the worn-out Model 10 revolver in my hand. Yet, there was no hatred in his hazel eyes. No malice. Just a deep sense of longing. As when he'd held on to my mother's anklet. "Why, Rahee?"

"Power," I replied and shot the old man in the heart.

Episode 7: The Good, the Bad, and the Chuutya

Avaan

August 1, 2083

"Come on, Avaan. Aren't you going to say hello?"

How the fuck did Evergreen recognize me?

Purple saree. It's a welcome flash of colour in this dreary rainbow of greys and browns. Doua squeezes my hand tightly.

I turn around and face the man in the red-eyed gas mask. Evergreen. The man who burned my world to the ground three years ago. The soldiers behind him form a ring of gun muzzles. Green canisters hang from their belts.

"Avaan Maya, in the flesh." His voice. It cuts like frostbite. Or maybe it's hearing that name again. My old name. "How many years has it been? Five?"

Three. "How did you —?"

"Golden eyes." He snatches the sunglasses from my face. Without them, the actuality of the world, the dull colour, feels like an indictment. He crushes my shades in his hand and drops them at my feet. Chuutya. "Why are you here? What do you want?"

"Nothing you can give me."

A chime goes off inside the white walls. The bells. They ring across the PSA system throughout Old Pakistan, sector by sector, each echo more lonesome and distant than the previous one.

The crowd dissipates rapidly. Only a handful of protesters remain, vociferously demanding clean water, power, and basic human dignity.

"More load-shedding?" I ask. "How long do you think you can keep doing this to us?"

"You sound like Yaqzan." He minces the name between his teeth. "Or Baadal."

"My brother was trying to help them at the library-shelter."

"And now they're all dead. Because of him."

A snowflake falls between us, breaking open in glinting crumbs.

"They're dead because of you." I feel my temples throb. "Keep this up and another civil war is inevitable. You think New Pakistan has enough bullets for that?"

"You'd be surprised how many bullets we have. Allah burned the sky away, but this land still needs cleansing."

"The sky burned for the just and the unjust alike, Evergreen."

Behind me, I hear whispers. They're faint, but I hear them — words that have always meant more to me than anything I've heard from Muslims or Christians or Hindus.

The snow falls over it all.

"It'll disappear before long." Evergreen's voice drowns them out. "The snow will disappear. Yaqzan continues to lead you all astray with blasphemy. With his lies and propaganda."

"The snow falls over it all." I grin.

"Don't blaspheme, boy. Don't press your luck any more than you already have."

Echoes of the final chimes reverberate throughout the city. The few remaining pariahs hurry back to Old Pakistan before the soldiers start roughing up the stragglers.

The bells stop.

An instant later, all the bustling, all the humming machines — it all comes to a halt as Old Pakistan's monstrous heart enters cardiac arrest. Section by section, the city plunges into shadows and silence. Only the New Pakistan glow remains, eternal and incandescent, illuminating us at the fences.

Evergreen points behind him at the haloed city. "You remember that light, Avaan? You came so close to being one of us that day."

Doua's voice. *Avaan, please. Do not let him goad you. You cannot defeat him.*

"Us?" I snicker. "You still pretending you're New Pakistani?"

His fingers twitch over the pearl grips of the Peacemaker. "Only a matter of time, boy."

"You're a glorified watchdog, Evergreen. Always have been."

"Huh. You always did have a mouth on you." Behind the red orbs, his eyes are like some horrible spell that's sealed away from the world. "Just like that little paleet whore, Doua."

———

November 6, 2080

I was twenty-five.

Illuminated under New Pakistan's floodlights, I stared at this tall, motionless shadow of a man before me. The one who had taken everything from me. Evergreen.

The golden Colt Python dug into my palm.

I aimed, saw him in my sights.

Evergreen shot first.

The .45 Long Colt tore into my stomach.

My legs buckled.

A dull, cold pain flooded inside me as the Python slipped from my hand. The marble floor rushed up and struck me in the face.

The whiteness of the snow, the whiteness of New Pakistan, all faded to blacks and reds.

That is the day Avaan Maya died.

————

I draw the .45. See him in my sights.

One bullet. One bullet for Evergreen.

But the six-inch barrel of his Peacemaker is already prodding at my heart.

He's faster. All these years later, he's still faster.

"Drop the gun!" the soldiers behind him shout. A dozen rifles point at my torso.

Evergreen raises his hand, and the soldiers stand down.

"Doua was here earlier, Avaan," he stabs. "She's alive."

Blood rushes to my face. The only thing my brain processes is the .45 in my hand and the slight squeeze required to blast this smug bastard away.

I take my finger off the trigger. "Where is she?"

The PSA system sizzles and pops with static. A dour female voice orders the stragglers to disperse and return to their sectors immediately.

They don't budge.

Evergreen's voice is acid in my ears. "She doesn't know you're alive, does she?"

"Where is she?"

"I imagine she has questions of her own. About why Baadal and everyone in the library is dead but not you. About who tipped us off."

"Where. Is. She?"

Evergreen turns around and snaps his fingers.

Without warning, the soldiers toss those green canisters at the crowd. Purple smoke smothers and blinds me. I press the shawl over my face and retreat along with everyone else. My breath rasping, lungs aching, eyes watering painfully, I stagger in the snow that isn't snow and feel Baadal's 1911 rattling in my hand.

Doua is alive.

———

I twist my way through the Sector 1 streets.

Doua is alive.

There's a fog of voices and footsteps around me. Near? Far? I can't tell anymore. The opaque sun still refuses to illuminate the world. The load-shedding and the snow make it even more difficult to see. The slimy, stinging tears lacing my eyes don't help.

Doua. If she's alive, then Humayun must be privy to that information. If he knows about her, then it's only a matter of time before he figures out who I am. That I'm not Salaba but Avaan. The way he was staring at me yesterday — does he already know? Was he waiting for me to confess?

The wide street strangles into a smaller alley. The houses here are dingier, by Sector 1 standards. I pause next to a spavined house, an uneven brown mess of four walls leaning into one another. A wide shit-brown metal gate protects it. Weak room lights shine in a couple of windows, the generator buzzing.

I prop myself against one of the walls to rest and gather my thoughts.

Everything I've gleaned for the past three years, everyone I've spoken to, bribed, and threatened — every lead I've chased has painted the same picture. Even my extremely veiled questions to Humayun have led to the same scratch notes: Doua died three years ago when Evergreen destroyed the two-storey library she had converted into a shelter. The only home I've ever known.

In the week that followed, almost a dozen bodies were recovered. Doua was declared to be among them. That was the day she vanished from the face of this earth. As if the moment her shelter was destroyed, every thread binding her to this world snapped as well. The soldiers wouldn't give me her body. Nothing for me to cremate, place in the colourful paper boats, and set free over the river toward the Misty Wasteland, where no one goes and no one returns.

And so it was always there, the shadow of a doubt. A singular thought, whittling and scraping against the surface of my brain: *What if she's still alive?*

Doua is alive.

All this time — three years — she was alive, she was breathing, she was smiling her sad smile. I hate myself for losing her. I hate her for not knowing why I've become who I am.

A weak orb of light approaches. It's a bright pink rickshaw. A Mullah reclines in the back, head lolling and hanging out the side. Somewhere in my hazy mind, I remember seeing him before.

The rickshaw stops. The driver steps out, a dark-skinned, emaciated old man in a red shalwar-kameez. He's wearing a black armband. He helps the inebriated Mullah to the shit-brown gate of the house I'm leaning against. He props the Mullah by the gate, knocks loudly, and drives off.

Hardly a minute goes by before the Mullah pukes out a white-yellow slurry and face-plants on the ground. The sound of flesh and bone hitting the asphalt makes me cringe.

He isn't moving.

I walk up to him, glancing around me. No one.

"Hey." I shake him. "Hey, wake up, sahib."

He groans but remains face down, gasping for breath as more slurry streams out of him.

I look around again. No one.

Forcing him to his side, I keep him from rolling back into whatever the fuck it is that's spewing out of his mouth.

That stacked wallet in his side pocket? He probably wants me to keep it. As thanks for saving his life.

"*Ya Allah*, what are you doing?" A Sunni girl stands wide-eyed at the gate. She gapes at me, at my disheveled hair and beard, at my black clothes. At the Sunni at my feet. At his fat wallet in my hand.

I deserve this. Whatever is about to happen, it's exactly what I deserve for being this fucking stupid.

I drop the wallet, but she pulls down her surgical mask and screams. Her parents storm out and recoil at the very sight of me.

"Why are you doing this?" the father asks, hand shielding his mouth in the snow. "What do you want?"

I raise my hands to try and convince him that I mean no harm.

The father isn't looking at me anymore. He's looking instead at the two soldiers heading our way, a female and a male. Remington 31s on both of them.

"Help!" the father cries. "Help us, please."

I rush to the far end of the street. The soldiers follow me.

They don't call out. They don't ask me to stop. They just follow me, street after street, faceless black wraiths watching me in that truculent, all-knowing way I imagine our demons do.

Doesn't take a genius to understand that the only thing stopping them from obliterating me is the short range of their shotguns.

Tiny passageways creep between the houses. I run in to one of them. I need to maintain this distance, make sure I don't end up stuck.

Shit. A dead end.

It's them or me now.

Impenetrable grey walls cradle small hills of cans, cardboard, plastic, paper, and trash bags. Only one way out of this: through the two soldiers.

The passageway is dark enough. My first break.

I draw the .45, but it's pointless. Any gunshot and more soldiers will converge on this point. Need to make this quiet.

The amount of trash around means there's got to be a bottle. I find one quickly and pick it up. My second break.

Pressing my back against a wall, I make sure they don't spot me.

The chatter of their radios gets louder. They're close. There's that unmistakable *shuck-shuck* of the shotgun.

Footsteps, one set of them — light but quick. It's the female. She's taking point.

I fight every impulse to run or surrender.

She steps past me into the alley. She hasn't spotted me.

My shoulder judders with the impact of the bottle breaking across her head. Springing from the wall, I strike the gun out of her fingers and kick it away when she lunges for it.

The broken bottle pressed against her throat, I force her out into the street. She'll make a human shield in case her partner is trigger-happy.

Her hand slips down to her P38.

"Don't," I whisper, the bottle puncturing a bit of skin over her jugular. She gets the idea.

Her partner aims the Remington at me. The sight of my human shield leaves him hesitant.

"Get the —" the dumb bastard mutters, but the broken bottle splinters into his throat. He sinks to the ground, clutching his neck, blood spattering.

I barely register the odds of making such a good throw when the female soldier smacks my jaw with the palm of her hand and elbows me in the head. A kick to the gut makes me stagger back.

She draws her sidearm. She's fast.

But I'm stronger, heavier. And I've got something to fight for. Doua is out there, and I'm going to find her. I'm going to tell her what happened. My side of it.

I swat her shooting arm away. The P38 still goes off, the sound so loud that a screeching static trembles between my ears. I can't hear anything else.

So much for keeping this quiet.

She tries to shoot again, but this time I grab her wrist and knock the gun out of her hand.

Her head grows too wide, too quickly. She headbutts me. Square in the nose.

My eyes water instantly.

I swing wildly. I hit nothing. She sweeps my legs from under me, and I thud against the asphalt.

The P38. She scrambles for it.

I trip her with my hands. She tumbles to the cold tarmac. I pin her under me. She pushes my chin up with both hands so hard my neck cricks and pops.

I can't hear a thing.

Just this monstrous hiss inside my head. I feel the feverish pulsing in my temples and her hot, throbbing neck in my hands. I feel cuts and bruises over my arms. I feel something scratch my face. I feel her jolt violently. And then I see her, the soldier lurching on the ground. Her clawing hands fall lifelessly next to her as her eyes roll back in her head. She stops moving.

I can't hear a fucking thing.

———

Sarv reclines over the steps outside Kanz's house. A steaming paper cup of tea in hand, he's wearing a rumpled dark green suit with a blue armband. A white cat sniffs his leg curiously, like she knows him. He pets her gently, but the cat remains ambivalent, the edge of her tail twitching.

"What're you doing here, Sarv?"

Long bars of afternoon light imprison him where he sits. I can't help but feel some kind of pity for him.

And then he opens his fucking mouth. "What happened to your face?"

"Had a rough night." It's been hours since I ran into Evergreen. Since I found out Doua is alive. Since I — since that soldier duo died. This isn't going to end well. Someone will know. Evergreen will know. And that'll be the end of me. "Why are you here?"

He takes one last sip of his tea and throws the cup away. His rectangular shades make him impossible to read. "Humayun has a job for us."

"I'm not working with you."

He walks past me. "You've been given your orders. Stop pretending you have a choice."

"I don't give a —"

He turns around and gets in my face. "Look here. We can pretend that there's some level we won't sink to. That we have a code. The truth is, there's no line I won't cross as long as it means I get there." He points a long, bony finger at the glorious white skyline. New Pakistan. The slice of heaven. "Stop pretending you're not what I know you are."

I don't give a fuck what you know, I almost say, but the words remain stuck inside my throat.

He passes me two pencil sketches with names and an address.

I recognize the woman from yesterday. Rosa. Maseeh's mother. The other target — the other victim — is a girl barely in her teens. Inayah. She has large, curious eyes and short, curly hair.

"Are you coming?" Sarv inquires, a lurid expanse of shanty homes heaving around us.

"She's just a kid. Thirteen, tops."

"Thirteen?" His back to me, I hear his dry leaf rustle of a sigh. "A lifetime."

I was thirteen, older than I should've been.

Mother and Father were long gone — a bitter, broken creature and a coward, respectively. It was just me and Baadal then. Two more abandoned children in the Badlands, working in a tea shop until late at night, pickpocketing, getting into fights, and being slick. The main clientele at the shop were truck drivers who'd stop by at all hours.

Most of the drivers were Sunnis and Shiites, with long beards and zabiba on their foreheads. They coiled ornate tasbihs around their wrists and rolled their pants or shalwars far above their ankles.

Baadal helped in the kitchen, his hands scrubbing greasy, grubby steel plates and cups. I served tea and snacks, wriggling through a cramped patio brimming with drivers. They'd try to chat with me as I took their orders, their sweaty hands always finding their way to my shoulders, my arms, my hips. They'd jabber about this merciful creator, Allah, and how everything in my life was a part of His grand scheme. About heaven, where everyone He loved went. About hellfire for those He loathed. For those who worshipped anyone but Him, for those who turned their backs on Him. For the faggots. For the abominations. For women who said no to their husbands.

Later in the evening, they'd quietly request the alcohol I'd slip in their teacups. And the promises would start. Promises of easy work as their conductor, of doing that for a year, tops, before getting my start in the business with a rickshaw to work the hours I wanted. There'd be promises of a place — *Laari Adda*, the truck stop — where I could sleep and get free food. Where I'd be protected. There'd be promises of sharing whitener too if I'd take extra care of them.

I was thirteen, older than I should've been. Baadal — poor, sweet, innocent Baadal — was too young. Too naive.

One morning, I came into the kitchen, and the crusty old bastard who ran the place told me that Baadal had gone with one of the drivers.

"Why didn't you stop them?" I yelled.

He shrugged.

I grabbed a cricket bat and ran. I ran like never before, like never since. I ran so hard, so fast. I have no memory of anything else. In the murk of that memory, one moment, I heard the crusty old bastard's words; the next, I was inside one of the sleeping quarters at Laari Adda, bat in hand.

Baadal sat on a man's lap. He was demonstrating how he'd make the taped tennis ball spin when bowling. The man, an orange-bearded driver with a splotchy zabiba on his head, wasn't listening to a word my brother said. His mouth wet, his leg bouncing excitedly, the man leered at Baadal.

"Baadal." My voice was hoarse. "Run. Now."

One look at me and Baadal knew I wasn't going to say it again. He ran out without looking back. Just as I'd taught him.

The driver snapped upright, his shirt greasy with sweat. "Who the fuck are you?"

The sound of the bat smacking the driver's side — that wooden crack of the bat against his ribs, the impact quivering up my arms and shoulders — I'd have given anything to hear that sound again, to feel the impact again. To watch his face wracked with pain.

I didn't.

I was thirteen. He was a full-grown man. Fuelled with rage, he struck me down. Blood washed into my mouth, like I was kissing a piece of rusty iron.

"You paleet piece of shit." He punched me again, hard, as if fighting someone his size. "You piece of shit."

I cried out as the driver grabbed my hair and slammed my face into the damp floor. The dark room, the faint orange bulb swinging, the sound of my face hitting the cold floor — all of it felt distant, farther and farther away from me.

He pinned me under him, suffocating me, his breath hot and caustic.

Everything after that is murky, distant. It happened to someone else, observed from miles away. As if I was immured behind a window and had traded places with my reflection.

———

"Salaba?"

My past. It's a storm of shattered mirrors. Every time I look back, every time I see myself, I'm left bruised and bloodied.

"What?" I ask, snapping out of it. "We're hitting them today?"

"Is that a problem?"

"Humayun never puts out hits this quick." Kanz was right. Something has forced the fat bastard's hand.

Sarv reaches into the pocket of his green suit and drops two hollow-points into my hand. Three bullets. One for Rosa, one for Inayah. One for me.

"No loose ends."

———

Sarv follows me. I try to make my stomach stop chewing itself, but anytime I look back, there he is, steady and silent, following me like a suicidal thought.

The river is silver and sibilant in the morning light.

"Sector 1, twenty-five hundred. Sector 2, one thousand." Young boys lean out of their bright rickshaws and zigzag through the crowd. They bark their wares anytime a Sunni or Shiite is within earshot. "Sector 1, twenty-five hundred. Sector 2, one thousand."

Every first Sunday of the month, like today, Sector 3 is brimming with kafirs and paleets bumping and pushing their way toward New Market. There, Sunnis and Shiites pick them out, a few dozen on a good day, for all manner of menial labour. From cleaning homes, picking trash, carrying water and luggage to removing dead bodies off the streets. Everything is on the table.

Remington-armed soldiers accompany the Sunnis and Shiites, responsible for dragging out the lucky kafirs and paleets from the masses.

We pass a cart with clothes piled in greens, blues, reds, oranges, and blacks. A soldier stands next to the colour-coded shawls, button-up shirts, kameez, kurtas, shalwars, and sarees. A Hindu man walks up to the stall and hands the soldier an ID card. The soldier studies it, collects the rupees, and tosses him three orange shirts.

A teenage girl holds a bunch of balloons before me, numerous strings tied around each finger. She can't be more than fourteen, diminutive in her blue kurta.

She shivers as I grab her left hand. "Sahib, what are you doing?"

"Did they hurt you, Asha-Eksha?" I ask, rolling up her sleeve, inspecting her hand, which is pink from the fierceness of my grip. Three balloons break from the cluster and fly into the air, their blue, pink, and purple vibrant in the dull sky.

There are tiny cuts on her fingers from handling the coarse strings, but beyond that she's fine.

"What's wrong with you?" Sarv seizes my wrist and twists it. I can almost hear his teeth grind over each other. "You will let her go. Now."

I let her go.

The girl scurries between the countless wooden carts and stalls and disappears.

I'm spiralling.

Another mile of walking later, our feet crunch over white gravel. The farther we walk up the winding road, the larger the stones, until we find ourselves before a crumbled white structure. The White Church. At the entrance, my eyes linger over a defaced statue of a woman, her eyes, nose, and cheeks gashed.

Inside, shattered statues of saints and sinners litter the roofless hall. Some still have nooses around their torsos where Sunnis and Shiites toppled them from the walls and pedestals. The way Mohammad did when he conquered Mecca and smashed all idols inside the Kaaba.

A large, heavy door blocks our path farther inside the church.

Sarv sniffs the air. I do too. Something acrid stings my nose despite the open roof.

"Drugs?" I ask. It's nothing I've smelled before.

"Explosives." He sighs. "All wars begin and end inside a home."

Something breaks behind the door.

He motions me to circle back.

I rush outside, .45 drawn. In a dark alley to my right, I notice a red-eyed shadow. A woman in red sunglasses. But when I turn to stare, there's no one there.

A scream lacerates the air.

Someone shoots inside the church. Twice. 9mms.

I dash toward the back exit just as a woman bolts, Walther P38 in hand. She's wearing a red shalwar-kameez.

Rosa.

She opens fire. Three 9mms punch into the wall where my head was.

"Inayah!" Rosa shouts into the church. "Hurry!"

She fires once more at me. Two bullets left. Assuming she had a full magazine.

Rosa shoots. "Come on, Inayah!"

A gunshot goes off somewhere inside the church. A revolver.

"Inayah!" Rosa screams. She shoots once more. "Inayah?"

She's out.

Popping out from my cover, I take my shot. "For Humayun."

The hollow-point erupts in the bleak afternoon air. Two bullets. One for Inayah. One for me.

Rosa sinks to the ground. Pieces of the P38 scatter around her. Slivers and needles of bone tear out from where her thumb and finger ought to be. But it's the smoking hole in her chest that's done her in. She knows it too, and she looks at me with pure hatred as I stand over her.

"Why?" She presses her left hand into the wound, coughing, applying pressure that means little. "W-what do you want from us?"

I say nothing.

"Avaan!" Sarv yells from inside the church. "She's coming your way."

At the doorway, frozen mid-dash, is Inayah. Her big brown eyes watch me through her wild hair. Big brown eyes.

"Please, don't hurt her," Rosa croaks.

For a second, I don't know what to do.

The second becomes two, then three. I still don't know what to do.

Tears roll down Inayah's cheeks as she watches her dying mother. When she looks at me again, she's no longer a child.

I lower my gun. Tiny lucky breaks.

Inayah bolts past me into the unforgiving snow and doesn't look back. Good habit.

In Rosa's expression, hatred gives way to what only the world's biggest madarchod would call gratitude. She fades away soon after, still kneeling on the floor.

Now, for my solo act.

Balling my fist, I punch myself as hard as I can, busting my nose and lip open.

Ouch.

Flat on the ground, I watch the darkening sky. Hot blood congeals in my nose. Snowflakes fall around me. I almost forget this isn't snow.

———

Like a piece of the sky, still and serene, Doua stands over me. Her small brown lips pressed in a straight line, her wavy hair dancing in the breeze, her light-grey saree — she is solace, she is distant. I hate myself for losing her. I hate her for not knowing what really happened that day.

Someday, you will tell me why you keep hurting yourself, Avaan.

———

Sarv stands over me, ephemeral as the snow itself. He holds out his hand. I take it, startled at the untamed vigour with which he pulls me up. A part of me is glad we didn't get into fisticuffs back at the diner.

"Where's the girl?"

"She blindsided me while I was dealing with —" I nod at Rosa, who's now heaped on the ground.

He kneels beside Rosa and pockets her destroyed P38. "You got punched out by a girl?"

"Blindsided. She hit me with something."

"Right."

"Didn't see her coming."

A sneer cuts across his scarecrow face. "Right."

Chuutya.

He inspects the wound in Rosa's chest. "The bullet went through her gun, her hand, and her chest. You're either really good or really bad."

"What now?"

He uncoils to his full height. "We go after the girl."

"Why? What could she have possibly done?"

Peering in the direction Inayah ran off, he scratches his chin. "She has ties to Yaqzan. She's a terrorist."

"She's a little girl," I remind him, standing to his right.

He exhales. "Age hardly matters. It's not about what she's done. It's about what she could do."

"So what? You're going to kill every child who might know Yaqzan?"

"Loose ends. I don't like them. Humayun doesn't either."

"Except there's always going to be a loose end. Always." I watch the right side of his face as my hand sneaks to the .45. "I've had to live with loose ends for three years. No matter what I do or where I go, there's always someone who knows more than me. Some madarchod who thinks he can play me. And you know what?" I press the .45 to his temple before he can move. Before his left hand can reach his Peacemaker. "I'm fucking sick of loose ends as well, *Evergreen*."

Episode 8: Monster

Rahee

February 17, 2053

I was eighteen. My father had left me. Like my mother, like Radhi, like my little Roshni. The house that was once a home, the window that had been my lens on the world, the maroon armchair where the old man had sat as I massaged his legs — it was all gone now. My childhood. My history. My story. I left it all behind and walked. I walked until I stood in a station full of soldiers and drafted myself into the Civil War.

———

February 14, 2054

"What are you waiting for?"

"Sir, I —"

"Boy, they are calling you a hero, understand? All those men you killed, all the bullets you've braved. The war is over. By Allah's grace, we have won."

"Yes, sir. But she's married. She's a Muslim."

I stood in the doorway, blocking the exit. The woman before me had large amber eyes. She called out after her husband, who had been beaten and dragged outside into the street. Try as I might, I couldn't bring myself to set foot in her room. She was alone and scared.

"This woman is one of them, boy," the Mullah-sahib hissed in my ear, grabbing my shoulder. "She is our enemy. She married a kafir. Understand? How many of our brothers died today?"

"But sir, I can't. This — this is wrong."

There are days when no amount of prayer, no amount of reciting *Surah Tawbah* can calm my mind. All these years later, after the hundreds of people I have killed, there remains one memory, one indelible stain on everything I have achieved. There are days when I look in the mirror and I know, without a shadow of a doubt, that though Allah is Most Merciful, Most Benevolent, I do not deserve His forgiveness.

"Look at her. She is our enemy. She brought this upon herself when she married a Christian man. When she sided with our enemies."

"But sir, she isn't a —"

The Mullah-sahib shook me violently. "This is your reward for what you've accomplished today, boy. A gift. Understand? You're going to reject Allah's gifts?"

"No, sir."

In my most private moments, when I'm alone, when I can't sleep, when I'm waiting for the *adhan*, when the last bullet has been fired in a gunfight, when I realize I'm not dead and I have the rest of my life to go on thinking and feeling — those are the moments when I remember that woman. The one with amber eyes who froze in terror as I stood with my revolver in hand.

"She is a kafir, boy," the Mullah-sahib said, patting me on the shoulder as my father once had and pushing me into the room. "You have earned it. Your right hand possesses her."

She is a kafir, I told myself as she pleaded with me, as she begged me to spare her.

She is a kafir, I told myself as I slapped her, hard, leaving her mouth bloodied.

She is a kafir, I told myself as I slowly closed the door behind me and became the monster I am.

———

August 3, 2058
"Excuse me, sahib, what song is that?"

A little girl with shining black eyes looked up at me, a large earthen pot balanced on her head. She couldn't have been older than eight.

Clouds weaved and wreathed in the night sky like incense smoke in the early hours of the morning, the only hours when my mother and I had collected water. In the days when music and voices had still been a part of my life. I no longer needed to collect water this way. Not since I'd joined the army. I didn't need to be there. Something about this night — something about the broken moon with its stream of sparkling pieces — made me remember my childhood. It made me remember my first cigarette and the woman who used to stand by the window. It made me remember the human being I had been before.

As I held the pot against the idyllic current, the girl's voice surprised me. Surprised, because she had been able to sneak up on me. Surprised, because she thought I was human enough to speak to.

"Huh. I didn't realize I was singing," I said, looking away when I noticed her blue shalwar-kameez. It was the same colour as the armband I'm forced to wear even now. "How long were you standing there, girl?"

"I heard you singing," she said. "You were singing some parts, humming others. It was really pretty."

"Pretty, was it?"

"Yes. It made me happy but also a little sad. Because you looked sad."

"Did I?"

"Yes," she replied, her eight-year-old fingers wiping the hair away from her face. She smiled, and her starlit-night eyes made me smile for the first time in a very long time. "What is the name of the song?"

"'Anyone Who Knows What Love Is'. My mother —" I took a deep breath, realizing that I was speaking louder than I wanted to. "My mother used to sing it."

"Sahib?"

"Yes?"

"Is your mama dead?"

I felt my worn-out Model 10 in its holster under my left armpit. "Yes."

"My papa died a few days ago. I really miss him. Do you miss your mama?"

I closed the water pot's lid and held it in my arms.

"Sahib?"

"Yes?"

"Can you sing the song again? The whole song? Please?"

"That's all I remember," I said and walked away.

———

December 31, 2058

"Come on in, Lieutenant Sarv. Mashallah, it's great to see you. How long has it been?"

"Almost six years, sir."

I sat at the same table as when I'd converted to Sunni Islam. This time, a PFM flag hung limply between us.

"Six years? Hazrat Mohammad said time will pass too quickly near the End of Days. May Allah have mercy on us all. Ameen."

The bright white light from the window made me squint. "Ameen."

There was a polished wooden box on the table. A white envelope rested over it.

The Mullah-sahib nodded slowly, mechanically. "I received your New Pakistan Pass request."

I smiled and looked at the envelope. "Yes, sir."

He grabbed a stick of *miswak* and began brushing his teeth. "Your reports on Old Pakistan are illuminating. Sector 3 and the Badlands continue to see increased crime rates?"

"Yes, sir."

"You don't seem happy."

"The plight of apostates and faggots is of no consequence to me, sir. My concern is only that our withdrawal might embolden them. Even as we speak, there are whispers of insurrection."

"You're talking about Yaqzan, yes? Seems he's still out there."

"Yes, sir. I think we should stay and root them all out. Scorched earth." I took a deep breath as the memory of my mother's arm around my shoulders crept inside my mind. "Removing our presence in the Badlands now might dull our advantage."

"If crime keeps ramping up, then it's only a matter of time before it collapses. Let them suffer."

"Yes, sir. But this may prove costly in the future. Desperation makes people —"

"Dangerous?" He laughed. "Banning and confiscating firearms across all sectors has effectively neutered them. Old Pakistan has no unison and no weapons. Let them tear themselves apart."

"Pakistan does have a long history of fracturing into smaller pieces: 1947; 1971," I said. "Like the Fifth Indo-Pak War."

He ignored my comment, smiling the same joyless smile. "Let me say again how proud I am of you, Lieutenant. You are a damn fine example to young Muslims. Mashallah."

"Thank you, sir."

"Your bravery on the battlefield is why New Pakistan is a reality." He lifted his wrinkled hand and pointed at the white lights shining through the pristine curtains. "That glorious city wouldn't be standing without you."

"Thank you, sir. You are very kind."

"The soldiers who fought alongside you can't stop talking about the things you did. Especially the fellow whose throat you ripped with your —"

"I was there. Sir."

The Mullah-sahib tapped the envelope. "You were like a divine sword. It was something to behold."

"Is there a reason you're not giving me the NPP, sir?"

He tapped the envelope some more. "This is not an NPP."

The ability to be shocked or disappointed had become alien to me. My soul could endure burdens on top of burdens. I expected nothing else from Allah. I was twenty-three. Repeating Yaqzan's words was now punishable by my hands. I was a Civil War hero. I was the Butcher of the Badlands.

"It's a promotion, Lieutenant."

I didn't say a word.

"I recommended you myself. You'll make a damn fine captain. I know you will."

"Huh."

"Captain Rahee Sarv. Keep this up and you'll be overseeing the perimeter guard in a few years. It's a high honour. One of the highest honours there is for someone like …" He paused. "You'll also get a house in Sector 1. With all the amenities possible."

"And the NPP?"

"I'm doing the best I can, understand? There are so many factors in your —"

"I'm not a Shiite anymore, sir. Nor an Ahmadi kafir."

"Of course, of course. This has nothing to do with that."

"Then?"

"It's red tape. So far, most of the people being awarded the NPP are" — he nibbled at the end of the miswak — "families and friends. Nepotism. It's the bane of this nation. But I vow to you that this time next year, you'll be in New Pakistan. Understand?"

"Thank you. Sir."

New Pakistan's white lights continued to shine into the room. The Mullah-sahib pushed the box near me. Inside was a glossy black revolver with pearl grips.

"Consider this a token of our promise. You prefer revolvers, correct?"

I took hold of the large gun. My expression must have encouraged him to speak.

"That's a Colt Single Action Army. Six-inch barrel. What you're holding in your hand is a relic. American-made. Designed in the nineteenth century, if you can believe that."

"It's gorgeous, sir."

"It certainly is. You can tell how legendary a firearm is based on the nicknames it's been given. This one has been called the Equalizer, the Frontier, and the Peacemaker. That's why I'm gifting it to you. Because you, *Captain* Rahee Sarv, are all three of those things. It suits you perfectly."

"Thank you. Sir."

I holstered the gun that has been with me in more killings than I can count. That has helped me become the monster I am today.

"One last thing," the Mullah-sahib said as I stood up to leave. "Starting next month, all soldiers will respond only to their call signs. It's a security measure. In recognition of your services, I'm allowing you to pick your call sign. What do you have in mind?"

"Evergreen," I said after a pause, then closed the door behind me.

Episode 9: The Glass Woman

Avaan

August 1, 2083

"Are you going to shoot me, Avaan?" asks Sarv. *Ever-fucking-green.*

Gun pointed at his temple, I speak as calmly as possible. "Yeah."

Hands clasped behind his head, he faces me with a nonchalant smirk. He might as well be getting ready for a blow job. "What gave me away?"

"You called me Avaan," I reply, staring into those black rectangles where his eyes ought to be. Instinctively, I step back. "When you were yelling inside the church."

"Huh."

"You're the one who's been supplying Humayun with those P38s, right?"

"Yes. We have a deal."

"A deal?" I remind myself of the gun in my hand. Two bullets, both for Evergreen. "The legendary soldier working for a Sector 3 hustler and supplying him with guns? What am I missing here?"

"You think I work for him? Humayun has been trying to clear his name for the last three years."

"Why?"

"Don't you remember, Avaan?" He nods at the gun in my hand. "There were almost no guns in Old Pakistan since the Civil War. But three years ago, suddenly everyone had 1911s. People like your brother. Once the army traced them back to Humayun — well, you can imagine how willing he was to cooperate. And now, with the terrorists running amok, he's been very eager to help."

My stomach sinks deep inside me. "So, everyone I've killed for Humayun —"

"Was at the army's behest, yes."

"So why let me live this long?"

"You? I thought you were dead all these years. Humayun didn't know who you really were until last night. As far as he knew, you were some paleet thug. Just your luck that I decided to pay him a visit when you were there."

The gun rattles in my hand. "You told him about me, about my past."

His sneer widens, cracks over a frozen lake. "Yes."

Three years. That's how long I've kept my past hidden. Faked my death, changed my name, changed my look, and breathed life into a lie named Salaba Hatteb. An illusion so pure that it fooled Humayun.

Evergreen smashed that illusion with a few words.

"You got sloppy, Avaan. You killed two soldiers in Sector 1 around the same time Humayun found out that you'd been lying to him for three years. Come on." He lowers his hands. "Do you think he wants that kind of attention on himself? Again?"

I keep the .45 trained on him. "You were supposed to kill me after Inayah and Rosa?"

"No. Humayun wanted you dead last night."

He nearly put me down three years ago and could've done it again last night. He's faster. No doubt about it. I've got the scar to prove it. "So why didn't you?"

"Doua."

Hearing her name from his lips twists me up inside. It's a violation. Like laughter in a graveyard. "What do you mean?"

His smirk turns to a scowl. "She keeps coming up in connection to the terrorists. And Yaqzan specifically."

I have the pieces but no idea what the puzzle is. "Who's Yaqzan?"

He shrugs, hands still raised. "All I know is that he's an old paleet with some history with Doua. And a marked interest in you."

"Me?"

"You don't think it has something to do with Baadal, do you?"

This road I've been walking leads back to that day three years ago. A road that begins with the library-shelter's rubble and my brother's corpse. The day Evergreen set fire to my life. Ground Zero.

I hold the .45 with both hands. "What's Yaqzan after?"

"Same thing I am. A second civil war."

Those whispers I've been hearing. Wistful murmurs, soft convictions. That certitude in mutual destruction that's been echoing throughout this city. The shiver in your heart before a fight.

"The snow falls over it all," I say, almost proudly.

"The snow —" His shoulders stooped, his face hidden by long grey hair, he sounds tired and old. "Do it."

"What?"

"Do it. This is the only chance you'll ever get."

I almost forget how much I hate him.

I am reminded of exactly how much when someone digs a gun barrel into the back of my neck.

Hell on earth.

Raising my hands, I find myself face to face with a pair of pissed-off soldiers who snuck up on me.

Officer 1 trains her .303 in my face.

"Sir, are you all right?" she asks Evergreen.

He takes a few seconds to reply. "Yes."

Officer 2 twists Baadal's 1911 out of my hands and whips it against my head, sending me to my knees. Blood trickles down my face, my neck.

Officer 1, not to be outdone, jabs the rifle into my chest, into the scar from three years ago.

"Let me kill him, sir."

"No," Evergreen responds.

"Sir, with all due respect, if he got the drop on you, then he's more dangerous than we anticipated."

Kneeling, my mouth filling with salt, I watch Evergreen loom over me, a hoary, malevolent spirit in the falling snow. He snatches the .303 from Officer 1 and rams it into the pit of my stomach. A hissed scream comes to a rolling boil in his throat as he plows the rifle into me again and again, the rectangular shades flying off his face. Writhing on the ground, my arms and hands taking the brunt of his rage, I catch a glimpse of the hatred in his large golden eyes. Eyes like a burning forest.

Silence creeps through the unsettling crunch of wood and bone and flesh.

Through murky strands of light, I watch Evergreen tower over me, his bony shoulders rising and falling. His face has reverted to a taut, joyless visage.

The thoughts in my head are so childish: *Why does he hate me so much?*

Doua drapes herself over me, shielding me from him. *Avaan?*

"Pick him up," Evergreen commands.

Officers 1 and 2 haul me to my feet.

Evergreen forces me to look at him.

"Doua," he says. He lets the name sink in. "I want you to find her, do you understand? Because there's a bounty on Yaqzan's head. Because catching that monster — putting his head on a bloody pike — is my ticket out of Old Pakistan. Do you hear me?"

I don't say a word. The last bit of defiance in me.

His voice is something out of a nightmare. "Look at me!"

Things spin out of focus. The world topples and blurs and fades.

Do not fall asleep. Please.

I look up, and what I see isn't Evergreen. It's big black eyes, shining and round. It's a dusky face with small, thin lips. It's the woman who cradles my head as I find the only solace I've ever known. I hate us both for what I've become.

———

Something stings my face. Cigarette smoke and sweat assail my nose. My mouth tastes of iron and salt. People cry and groan from multiple directions around me. A blanket envelops me completely, steam-cooking me in a stale, pungent odour of herbal medicine and sickness. Under me, a pile of damp cardboard sheets sticks to my back.

I wake up to a never-ending dream. Needles of light stipple my mind. A small canopy shelters me from the snow. A few paces ahead, a bunch of people gather around a trash can bonfire, murmuring away as they fondle tasbih beads in their hands. Collapsed blue walls keep the snowy night at bay.

Blue walls?

Strands of darkness collect over my view, my head spinning and growing heavy. And then nothing anchors me anymore.

———

The dilapidated blue walls greet me. They rise to the burned sky, the ones that are intact. The roof hasn't existed for decades — yet another remnant of the first civil war, the one that segregated Old Pakistan. Huge blue bricks and masonry are piled up in one corner of the fenced rectangle surrounding me and everyone else. There's a Pakistani flag towering proudly over us all. The real one, not that PFM bullshit.

Blue Haven. How the hell did I end up here?

A white cat sits on all fours near me, one ear pointing back. She's staring at the red-haired woman sitting to my right. She's pretty, and pretty tall for a woman, almost gawky the way her limbs poke out of her green kurta and ratty jeans. There are enough holes in both that I can make out her mismatched leggings and arm warmers. Her hair spills in lank, reddish-brown strands past her ears. Mid-twenties by my estimate. There's a black armband above her right elbow. An ex-Badlander.

Red. That's what I'm going to call her.

A half-extinguished cigarette hangs from Red's lips as she holds her hand close to her face. I try to see what she's looking at so intently. A small mirror. She smiles, her wide lips unnaturally pink. The light in her green eyes seems directionless, not radiating outward, as if confined by thick lines of *kajal*.

She catches me staring.

"Hey." Red flips the mirror shut, flicks the cigarette butt into a pyramid of others, and starts rubbing a damp rag over my face. It stings. "Still here?"

"Still here."

"What's your name, sahib?" Her voice is a little raspy, her cadence haphazard.

"Martin Frost."

"What?"

"Av — Salaba. Sal." I wipe my face, only to realize how much of it is covered in bandages. My hands are also wrapped in bandages, the skin peeking through in blue, pink, and purple bruises.

"You got some nasty gashes and cuts. A bruised rib too, from what I can tell." Her cheeks and lips pinch into a smile. "I'm no expert, but I think you got your ass kicked."

"You should've seen the other guys."

"Sure." She laughs. Quick and nervous. "Who were they?"

Evergreen and his thugs. "No idea."

A large, blackened trash can sputters ash and embers nearby. Naked and cold under the blanket, I wince at the thought of moving.

Red takes a deep gulp from a bottle in a paper bag, glances at me, and then pours me some in a plastic cup.

"Here. This'll help."

I hold it to my lips. "Is this medicine?"

She pauses. "Sure."

My lower lip burns as I take a sip. It's strong stuff, whatever it is. Exactly what I need.

"Thanks, Red."

"You're welcome. I have your piece." She extends her thumb and index finger. "Don't worry. I won't report it."

The subtle art of reminding me that I owe her now. Five minutes from now, she'll be asking me for a favour. And I'll tell her to fuck off.

"How did I end up in Blue Haven, Red?"

"No idea. You were here when I started my shift."

"Blue Haven." I say the name sardonically. "When I was growing up, they still called this place Yaqzan's Church."

She shushes me. "Please, don't say that so loudly. That name hasn't been said in decades."

"The snow falls over it all," I whisper, almost to myself.

I lick my lower lip. The saliva soothes the burning cut. It's been a few minutes, but I've managed to stay awake. Silver linings.

"Can I have my piece back?"

"I'll hand it to you when you're ready to leave." She leans forward to pat my arm. Her kurta parts, and I sneak a peek at her cleavage. "But don't worry. You're safe here. The patients have no past in Blue Haven."

She takes another gulp from the bottle. Her hand trembles. She flexes her long fingers and pours me another cup. "Those scars on your body — were they donations?"

"Food for my family."

"Kidney?"

"Yup." And a piece of my liver, as I found out much later.

"You've got other scars. Nasty ones. The one on your chest. I couldn't help but notice that gunshot wound."

I say nothing.

Her hand settles on my right side, tracing the scar. "Nobody deserves this."

"You don't know that."

"I know. Trust me. Selling pieces of yourself just to get by. Like we don't lose enough pieces of ourselves as it is. Our dignity, our pride, our happiness." Her voice is mostly quick puffs of breath. As if I'd startled her. As if she's resurfaced briefly from the depths and latched on to me for a sliver of breath. "Isn't that enough?"

She goes for another gulp, but I grab the bottle and hold it out of her reach. "You've had enough, Red. Come on."

I take a generous swig of it myself, and I hear Doua's admonishment. *Just drinking from her bottle has given you gonorrhea.*

"I know," she whispers, turning her head away quickly.

"What's wrong?"

Something about what I said makes her green eyes well up. "I lost a friend this morning."

"I'm sorry to hear."

She looks at me. Have I transgressed?

She begins to speak, stops herself, then says it. "Thank you, Sal. You're very kind."

In the name of all that's pure and holy, this woman is a mess. Her skin is lighter than mine, but that's probably because of the makeup she's wearing. Given the black armband, she's another byproduct of prostitution. Or rape. Despite the croaking voice and the tears, I sense a stronger woman buried somewhere under the glass rubble.

Too bad she is not older than you.

"You're going to pay for that, Doua."

"What did you say?"

"Nothing. Just mumbling."

"Oh." Her laugh again, fast and breathless.

"I'm going to head out, Red." Powering through the pain, I stand up. "Thanks for patching me up."

"Hang on," she says, reaching into a basket. She throws me a new shirt — a black button-up, most of the buttons missing.

As I put it on, she rubs her collarbone, flushed from the liquor. She looks up at me. From this angle, with such a gracious view of her cleavage, a part of me is glad I managed to straighten up.

"You can keep the blanket, sahib," Red says. "I'd stay here and get more rest if I were you, though. This place is safe."

Nice eye contact.

I should get out of here. Yet here I am, transfixed before this strange woman made of glass, struggling to keep herself from breaking apart.

"Why don't you come with me, Red?"

What?

"What?"

There's a pause as she squints up at me, and then her lips ease into a smile. "You sure?"

"Yup."

———

"Wow." Red steps inside the room, eyebrows raised. She tiptoes over the sketches on the floor and stops in front of the mattress. "You sure know how to make a lady feel special."

"Only the special ones see this room."

"Sure," she giggles. It's the laugh of someone still drunk.

"Sorry there are no fountains and marble floors."

"Fountains and marble floors? Is that what you think Sunni homes are like?"

"Aren't they? We've all heard the stories."

"Sure." She plops on the mattress. The polystyrene bursting out at the seams makes her laugh.

I sit next to her, and my bandaged hands caress her arm. I breathe in her scent as I kiss her neck and shoulder.

"Sal?" Her face grows dark, the mirth seeping out of it. "I need to tell you something. Before we do anything further."

I begin kissing my way closer to her lips. "Whatever it is, I already know."

"You do?"

"Yup."

Her already breathless voice grows huskier as my hands slip up her kurta. Unfastening her bra, I fondle her breasts. The lone bulb swings over us.

I flinch, my body tensing up. Something cold pools inside my chest.

Red grabs my face and kisses me. Her tongue meets mine, entwines with it.

My body feels like a stone.

She pauses. "Sorry, is something wrong?"

"No. No," I say, forcing my lips into a smile. "Keep going."

She kisses me again, and I close my eyes, focusing on her soft lips against my bruised lower lip, the pain sharp but delicious. The taste of tea and booze and cigarettes lingers between each kiss, between flicks of her tongue against mine.

But my heartbeat races.

"Sal?"

That floor. That damp, tepid floor reeking of sweat and dirt.

"What's wrong?"

Jaw clenched, I try to focus my dizzy brain on Red. "Keep going."

Red kisses me again, amazing me with how quickly she brushes aside what could easily be a deal-breaker. She pushes me down on the mattress, slithering on top of me. She kisses down my neck this time. Unbuttoning my shirt, she returns to my lips again as her fingers grab hold of my cock.

Helping her out of her kurta, I go back to kneading her breasts, her moans intoxicating. I roll her shredded jeans down her hips and legs. Grabbing a handful of her ass, I squeeze firmly and drink in more of her moans as we kiss deeper.

But there it is again: that faint chill in my heart. It won't go away.

In her white panties now, Red eases me out of my jeans and underwear. Climbing on top of me, she kisses the scars and wounds on my body. Waves of pain and pleasure sweep over me. She curls her tongue around my nipple; her finger traces the length of my cock.

I'm entombed in glass, destined to witness these moments as reflections of a world I can neither touch nor feel. A ghost, out of sync with reality.

My mind is yanked back to dark hands pinning me down.

My legs draw close together. "Stop. Please."

Red looks hurt. "Don't you …?"

What do I say? "This isn't a good time." I hold up my bandaged hands.

"Oh. I'm sorry."

"No. Don't be. You were wonderful."

She laughs. Too drunk to give a shit, I figure. Flat on the mattress, she watches me for a while before staring at the pale, cracked ceiling.

I walk into the bathroom and exhale.

I wipe the mirror's yellowing haze and find Salaba staring at me. His unkempt hair reaches down to his shoulders. The beard clumps and twists down his chin, strands of white streaking through it. Avaan and Salaba stand before each other, nothing linking them except their golden eyes. Evergreen's face flashes before me again. Golden eyes, like a burning forest.

When I come out, Red is smoking by the barred window in her white bra and panties, her back to me. She uses a cup as an ashtray. The billboard flickers on and off, shadows dancing over her in blues, pinks, and purples. I take in every bit of her frame. The flashing light from outside illuminates the smoke dancing from her lit cigarette. Her red hair is short. Her narrow, delicate back curves and flows down to the seams of her panties. She has a diagonal scar on the right side of her ribs, just like me. She too has sold a kidney.

I cough loudly, and when she looks back, I try to smile, managing only a grimace. I balance an empty bottle on the doorknob. Red nods in admiration. Lying down on the mattress, I stare at the ceiling as she continues to smoke.

Sirens blare outside as a military jeep zooms past, red and blue lights scattering through the room.

"That can't be good," Red sighs. "You think it's the terrorists?"

I remember Evergreen again. Large golden eyes. "Loyalists. And no."

Red stands at the foot of the mattress, imprisoned by the barred shadows. She folds her left arm across her belly and rests her right elbow over it. Her right hand and jaw glow orange from the small light of the cigarette in her lips.

"Can I ask you something?"

Stretching fully on the mattress, I clasp my arms behind my head. "Sure."

"How come you wear a shirt and jeans? Why not shalwar-kameez?"

"I like shirts and jeans. My turn: you got any family?"

She taps the ashes into the cup, her shoulders stiff. "Brothers. Three of them. I haven't seen them since I was fourteen."

"You ran away from home?"

"It was run or die."

"Was it the booze?"

"No, no. The booze came pretty soon after."

"That's horrible."

She shrugs. "It all happens as Allah says it should."

"That's what the Mullahs would tell us." I feel the old phantom pain where my childhood used to be. "When they weren't trying to fuck us."

She nibbles her lip. "Is that what happened to you?"

Takes me a few moments to respond. "You figured?"

"You're not the only one with horror stories, Sal."

I nod. "It happened at Laari Adda. It was a truck driver."

"I'm so sorry." Red looks away, eyebrows arched upward. "That's monstrous."

"It all happens as Allah says it should."

She shakes her head. "Come on. What that truck driver did to you, that's got nothing to do with Allah. Or Islam. Hell, it's a huge sin for a man to be with another —" She bites her tongue, slamming the brakes at the edge of the precipice. "Doesn't matter."

"Some All-loving Creator, isn't he?" I sit up and crawl to the edge of the mattress. Her cigarette is mostly a stick of ash now. "He'll abide one man killing another. For war. For punishment. For self-defence. Even revenge. But He won't abide one man loving another. Or not wanting to be a man at all."

"Stop it," she whispers. In the dim light, I can make out how red her ears are.

"It's why your brothers chased you out, right?"

Her eyes dart around the room, the light scattering in them like the first time I saw her. She extinguishes the cigarette in the cup and turns to leave.

Kneeling on the mattress, I take her hand gently. "Most people would've thought you swung both ways." I glance at the window, where there's a splash of yellow in the reflection. Doua. "Or they would've wondered if it was the booze. Or if you were ravaged by Sky Sickness."

She makes no sound, doesn't blink.

"I'm from the Badlands, Red, and I know it's none of those things. I've known people like you my whole life." I hold both her hands. "You weren't born a woman, right? That's why your brothers chased you out. Because you weren't always their sister."

"How did you —?"

"You're not the only one with horror stories."

When Red speaks, it's more to her reflection in the window. "I was the eldest *son*. Our parents were dead. It was all on me. Food, water, clothes, you name it. I scrounged, I fought for everything. I was so many things to them. A brother, a mother, a father, a friend. I had to be, right?"

I nod. I was all those things to Baadal too.

She continues. "All they had to do was let me be one more thing. It's all I asked."

Kissing her hands, I pull her into my arms. "I know."

"I've always felt like I'm being erased," she whispers into my chest. "Even now, I feel it inside me. This feeling that I'm slowly being extinguished."

"It isn't enough for them that we rot and die in a corner of this city," I say. "We must rot and die on the inside too."

"They want to kill me. Or fuck me. That's all they feel toward me." Hot tears fall onto my chest. "As if I'm insane for doing this to myself. Satanic. People like my brothers, people like these Mullahs, when they look at me — if they even look at me — all they see is a mutilated piece of meat. They think I chose this life. How could anyone choose this life, Sal?"

"Fuck your brothers," I say, holding her chin and making her look at me. "And fuck the Mullahs too."

That makes her laugh. "Yeah, fuck them."

A piece of chipped plaster sloughs off the ceiling and falls.

Red tangles her arms and legs around me on the mattress, snuggling tightly, as afraid of distance as I am.

"You live alone here?" she asks.

"It's me and another guy. You won't see him. He mostly stays in his room, drinking himself to death."

"Poor guy."

I hear her mouth open then close. When I look at her, a tight smile hangs on her wide lips. As if I caught her doing something she shouldn't.

"What's wrong, Red?"

"I'm sorry about earlier. I didn't know about — what happened to you. I would've done things differently."

"Don't be."

She kisses my shoulder, pressing her cheek to it. "Still, I can't imagine what it must've been like for you."

"Or you."

Time doesn't heal wounds. It makes you forget they're there. Right up until they tear open again. Like my wounds when I finally found Eksha and wished I never had.

"I'm glad we did what we did, Red."

She doesn't miss a beat. "Or tried to, at least."

I wince.

"Sorry," she giggles. "Too soon?"

I slap her ass.

Another piece of the ceiling crumbles to the floor.

Red reaches past me and picks up a half-crumpled sketch from the ground. Lying flat on her back, she studies it.

"Who taught you how to draw?"

"She did."

Picking up more sketches off the ground, she studies each of them with me. She goes through a handful, one at a time, letting the older ones fall. She holds up one. It's recent. One where Doua gazes to her left, her face cupped in her hands. I spent hours sketching it, the product of an especially Avaan-esque night.

"She's kinda pretty." Red's voice trembles. "Who is she?"

Doua sits with her legs tucked under her, sifting through the countless sketches littering the room. She picks up a sketch — the one of her naked under a thin shawl, with nothing else around her, as if floating in the sky. She slips onto the mattress and curls against me. The glass bangles jingle in the air where Red's question seems to echo.

Feeling her soft, warm body, hearing her light breaths, taking in the scent of strong, sweet black tea, the memory of her lips still fresh, I tighten my arms around her. Pieces of something beautiful. Something lost and found.

———

I was eighteen. She was twenty-three.

Doua stood before me, fingers touching her lips, bemused smile fading to bewilderment. I could still taste her lips, the heat of her breath, the scent of tea lingering over my lips and tongue. It was a moment I'd dreamt of ever since I first saw her. And yet, the moment it happened, something dark and leaden curdled inside my veins.

"Avaan?"

My breath was ragged. I mumbled an apology, an excuse. "I don't know why this — I didn't mean to —"

"Avaan?" she whispered, reaching out. "What is wrong?"

"I don't —" I managed to croak, my mind racing to memories that should've stayed lost. The truck driver. The cold, clammy floor.

The air I breathed felt like powdered glass. I bit the corner of my mouth, clenched my fists. It was no use. My breath, my heart-beat, my thoughts, my body — every inch of me was in mutiny. The world was smudged and narrow around a single point of light. Around the dusky, dark-haired woman before me.

"It is okay." She kneeled next to me. "Look at me, Avaan. Look at me. It is okay. Just breathe."

"Doua, I —" I grabbed my chest. I did everything I could to contain myself. But I shook in her arms. Tears flowed down my face. "I can't breathe."

"I am here." She pressed herself against me, her voice quivering slightly. "I am here. Everything is fine. Okay? I am here. Everything is going to be fine."

Her voice. Her touch. They buoyed me, a lifeline in the dark. She held me as you might a wounded bird. Gently, carefully. I couldn't break in her arms. She held me for a long time.

My breathing returned to normal. The tears dried up.

"You poor thing." She smiled, her eyes misty. "You poor thing."

Doua held my face. I tried to look away, my cheeks damp, but she didn't let me.

"May I?" she asked.

I nodded.

She kissed me, softly, gently. Waves of fear and panic and misery washed over me again, making my skin crawl, making my heart freeze, making me sink into myself. I held on to her. I held on to her voice as she whispered my name between hot, wet kisses. I held on to her soft, cool hands as they caressed me deeper into the kiss. And for the first time in I don't know how long, I wasn't alone in this world.

Episode 10: The Dot

Jahan

November 7, 2068

I never looked at myself in the mirror.

By the time I was ten, whatever I recognized as myself was a vague recollection. A familiar stranger. Never known intimately, never for too long.

What I knew about myself, I knew like a half-clouded memory. I knew my eyes were green. But whether they were the green of emeralds or the green of Pakistani flags or the green of the river when a rare sunbeam hits it just right — I could not tell you.

I knew I had short, reddish-brown hair. But if it was more rusty brown like some of the other Pathan children's or dark red like actresses' hairdos in old movie posters — I could never say.

I knew I was taller than most girls and some of the boys. I knew my shoulders were narrow and my hips broad because one of the children pointed it out as we bathed in the river. Everyone laughed at me.

By the time I was ten, the only part of myself that I recognized as me was in the centre of my mind. I existed in this inch-wide sphere, this dot. I breathed in this dot. I dreamed in this dot. No matter how many dreams I had, no matter how much I fantasized about being larger than this dot, about being the rest of myself, I was nothing outside this dot.

Mine were not the long, gangly, hairy arms; mine were not the thick, rough fingers that scraped against my nipples when I played with myself; mine was not the hard, flat belly; mine were not the plodding legs with ugly, squarish feet. I was not the erect, rigid thing between my legs that would bring a rude end to every fantasy.

Outside this dot, I was a dark, distorted shape I'd recognize during a forgetful glance in a window or a cup of water.

———

June 10, 2070
Our house looked like a scowling, grumpy old man. The heavy front door was misshapen. Two large windows were uneven. The bowed roof looked like a slouched hat. The walls were crusty and bulged outward.

I had just turned twelve when my parents moved here. My brothers were ten, eight, and seven. We were all excited because we were closer to the walled city, to the place where there was more food and water than you could eat in a lifetime, where there was no load-shedding, no crimes, and the air was free of the snow.

Pretty soon, though, all of us ended up hating this house. Aurangzeb hated the house because it was the last one in a street full of ugly houses and it was too far from all his friends. Salim hated the house because the windows weren't frosted blue like other homes, and we had to paste newspaper over them to keep New Pakistan's bright lights out. Zulfiqar hated the house because it was smaller, and that meant *Ammi* and *Abu* would fight more because there was less distance between them.

Why did I hate the grumpy old house?

I didn't. Not in the beginning. I loved it in the early months because it had an expansive, sunken rooftop where I could spend all day. Even as the rainwater pooled at its centre and turned into an unsettling green slime. Even as the bird droppings hardened against the walls. Even as the walls began to warp toward each other. I loved the house because of its rooftop.

It was where the pigeons flew from God knows how far away and cooed at me, unfussy as they ate everything I found for them. Up on the roof, I was free under the burned sky. I could breathe and sing and cry and laugh and read. It was where I had my first cigarette.

Up on the roof was the only place where I felt larger than this little dot. Up on the roof, I was more — I was larger, wider. I was uncontainable because I was the whole white world.

———

April 29, 2071
The first time I realized I was different was when I met a thirteen-year-old boy. He was Sunni like me. A wiry boy with curly black hair and surprisingly small arms for his stature. I don't remember anything else about his face except his dark pink lips. Between his lips and his curly hair, he might as well have been a featureless blur.

He lived by the Sector 1 border and would walk from far away just to play cricket with us. When forming teams, I'd be his first pick. If I grazed my elbows while diving on the tarmac to make a catch, he'd be the first to check on me, holding my arm in the most tender way. I'd catch him watching me while I was batting, and I'd catch him watching me when I was bowling or fielding. If I smiled, he'd smile. If I didn't smile, his ripe lips would become a small O. Every time I saw that smile, my stomach felt as if it were floating inside me, and my cheeks would become hot and puffy.

One day, he said he'd walk me home, as I had lost track of time and ended up playing cricket well into the night. As we approached my old-man home, his finger caressed the palm of my hand.

He looked at me, and those swollen pink lips pinched into a smile.

I looked at him and, with hot cheeks and my heart thumping in a frenzy, punched him in the side of his head. He stumbled backward and fell to the ground.

Dazed and confused, he watched me slam the door shut.

I never saw him again.

———

February 2, 2072
I sometimes wore lipstick.

My parents were dead, and the roof had been my living room under the sky for almost two years. I'd spend most of the day up there. My brothers had begun to distance themselves from me, and the few friends I'd played cricket with suddenly had no room for me on their teams.

At night, I'd leave my younger brothers in the care of Aurangzeb and spend hours cleaning other homes in Sector 1 or begging in Sector 2. Sometimes my brothers would join me as we scavenged a life for ourselves together. Most nights, though, I'd be alone. By the time I'd get home, my brothers would be asleep, and I'd go to the roof. On those nights, I'd put on the lipstick my mother had left behind — the only thing she'd left behind — and watch the falling snowflakes with my pigeons. Snowflakes that were so delicate that they'd crumble at the slightest touch.

The pigeons have been the only constant thing in my life. Before I understood why all of me was scrunched and locked inside an inch-wide dot, or what had happened to my parents, or why my brothers ignored me, there was my love for these gentle, sensitive birds. I loved everything from their curious stares to the faintest rustle of their talons as they waddled about to their almost feline purring when they were happy. I loved how they recognized and responded to human emotions. I loved how they could always find their way home, and how — unlike everyone else in Pakistan — they could fly into the horizon because they were free of the past. I loved them because they lived on rooftops where no one saw them, no one noticed them. It calmed me to know that although we had nothing in this world, my roof belonged to us.

———

May 30, 2072

"What are you doing?" Aurangzeb asked from the roof entrance.

I didn't have an answer. I was wearing Ammi's lipstick. I was wearing a kurta-shalwar that I had stolen from one of the washing lines. I had stolen it because of its turquoise-green fabric and the tiny, intricate hexagonal mirrors patterned on the sleeves and collar.

Aurangzeb balled up his fists. "What are you doing, you sick pervert?"

"Lower your voice," I hissed back, wiping the lipstick away with the back of my hand. "Do you want people to hear?"

"It's not bad enough that our parents are gone. It's not bad enough that we're fending for ourselves — you must bring us further misfortune?"

"Aurangzeb." My ears were hot with anger. "Shut up."

He glared at me from across the roof. The pigeons sensed the animosity and fluttered away. Snow and feathers floated in the air between my brother and me.

"Maybe it was you all along. Maybe you're the reason why Abu killed Ammi. Maybe you're the reason why our house is cursed."

Below us, we could hear Salim and Zulfiqar laughing as they played cricket indoors.

Aurangzeb's green eyes cut like broken glass.

I shook my head slowly. "Don't."

"Why not?"

I wiped more of the lipstick off my lips. "I'll leave quietly tonight. You'll never see me again. I promise. But don't tell them."

"Salim, Zulfiqar, come up here!" he yelled. "Bring the bat."

Footsteps rushed up the stairs leading to the roof. Salim and Zulfiqar stood on either side of Aurangzeb. They stared at me, their oldest brother. Confused, angered. Ashamed.

"What's wrong with him?" Salim asked Aurangzeb, bat in hand.

"Tell him," Aurangzeb snapped. "Tell him what's wrong with you."

"Nothing is wrong with me, Salim," I replied as calmly as I could.

Zulfiqar didn't say anything, staring at me in disgust.

"He's a *hijra*," Aurangzeb said, grabbing the bat from Salim. "He's a disgusting pervert!"

———

June 14, 2072

For years, I thought there was no one like me in this world.

If there's one thing I wish I could tell my fourteen-year-old self, it would be that I wasn't as alone as I thought. Even before Allah burned the sky away, there were Pakistanis like me who felt lost inside their skins, who felt and sensed the world around them as if they had been born inside a block of ice.

Oddly, I was glad that my brothers had chased me away into the Badlands. In that haunting, harrowed place, I met others like me. Some boys and girls were both at once. There were girls who found out they were boys when they reached puberty. Some men dressed as women, some women dressed as men. There were men who loved men, women who loved women. Some who loved both. There were boys and girls like me who felt trapped in the wrong body.

In Old Pakistan, the world seems a whisper away from ending. Even today, as I pass through Sectors 1 or 2 or 3, I'm overwhelmed by a sense that we can never ward off the end of the world because some part of us yearns for it, quietly and patiently.

But in the Badlands, as a lost fourteen-year-old, I felt it. It was unmistakable, like the smell of rain. Like the slight silver shimmer above the river.

Hope.

Despite its tents that look like a pile of dirty laundry, its broken windows smeared with bloody fingerprints, and its endless pilgrimage of black clothes, the Badlands is Pakistan's hope. It's the very edge of the world, a place where Pakistan pushed us away decades ago. We were supposed to die. And though we starve and suffer, we strive and continue to survive. Though they fly the PFM flags and blame us as the reason Allah burned the sky away, we're still here. We always will be.

Episode 11: Ghosts

Avaan

August 2, 2083

Humayun's Diner is closed for business at this early hour.

In the end, this was inevitable. There are too many players, too many people who have more answers than I have questions. Evergreen, Humayun, Yaqzan, Doua, Red.

Red.

My clothes smell different. Tea, cigarettes, and booze. She wasn't there this morning when I woke up. I remember her lips over mine, her body like warm dough in my hands, her scent, all of it lingering, a dream I didn't want to wake up from. Where did she go?

No. Not now.

Two bullets. I have two bullets.

Above me, the icicles lining the canopy appear longer, sharper. I push the dark red door open. The Ashraf-ul-Makhlooqat sign sways back and forth as I step inside. A sheen of detergent-smelling water makes my shoes squelch over the wooden floor.

I scan the diner. The upside-down chairs over the tables make it difficult to get a clear view of the place. Humayun, wiping the counter vigorously, pauses when he spots me. His mouth curls.

Squeegee in hand, Slick Bastard is startled at the sight of me. He goes for his gun. Or would've if Baadal's 1911 wasn't already pointed in his face.

"You want a shot at the title today, bhenchod?" I ask.

Slick Bastard holds his hands above his head and steps back.

Telltale clicks of gun safeties crackle in the ambience. Sure enough, a dozen waiters surround me, their 9mms cocked and ready.

"I just want to talk, Humayun," I say, the .45 still trained on Slick Bastard.

Humayun resumes cleaning the counter. "Let him through. It's only Avaan."

Hearing that name — my name — revolts me. It feels like an accusation. Or an incantation to resurrect the dead. Flipping a chair into place, I sit in front of Humayun. P38s in hand, the waiters surround us.

My face burns. My wrists, knuckles, and elbows feel like old furniture pieced back together in a hurry. Evergreen did a number on me. Despite the welts and bruises, I make it a point not to let my pain show. Not to let anything show. Whether I walk out of here or am discovered in a garbage ditch all depends on how this talk goes.

"You've got balls." Humayun smiles tightly. "Lying to me. All these years."

I lick my cut lower lip. There's the tiniest taste of iron. "And now you know, right? You've figured it out. So what does that change?"

"You tell me."

"Nothing." I lean forward. "Fucking nothing. Three years, Humayun. I've cleaned up every mess you sent me to clean, and for three years I came back without incident. So what does it matter if I did it under a fake name? What does it matter that it was Avaan who did that for you and not Salaba?"

"You lied, golden-eyes."

There's an unmistakable click of a P38's hammer being cocked.

Time to play another hand. "You already lost Kanz. You lose me and that's two of your best hitmen gone. Who's going to protect you then? These boys?"

Humayun shrugs. "Yeah, these boys."

"They're not ready."

"You think so?" He laughs.

"I waltzed into this place and had one dead to rights. So yeah, I think so."

Slick Bastard finds himself getting stared at.

"I've got Sarv." Humayun rebounds from the slight dip in his confidence. "I've got Evergreen." Like an animal on the prowl, Humayun senses my fear. "He'd kill Kanz. He'd kill you. He's Death Itself."

Slick Bastard places his P38 on the table, directly in my line of vision. Somewhere at the back of my mind, I promise myself to kill him.

I push through the fear. "You got Evergreen, Humayun? You sure?"

He tries to hide it. Almost succeeds too. But I notice the way Humayun's steel-wool brow twitches.

"You can't muscle him." I shake my head. "Push comes to shove, you know Evergreen would blast his way through these punks and put a bullet in your head. He wouldn't even break a sweat."

Humayun looks around at the waiters. "Bullshit he will."

"You said it yourself. He'd kill Kanz. He'd kill me too. Hell, he almost did it again yesterday. You think anyone here can stop Evergreen if it comes down to it?"

There it is. Arms crossed in front of him, his brows all knotted — that's the look I was waiting for.

"What's your point?" Humayun asks.

"We clear the air tonight. You and me. We go back to our original arrangement. You point me in the right direction, and I'll be your gun. Everything goes back to normal, and nobody gets hurt."

"What about Evergreen?"

"I'm still your best insurance policy."

"He'd kill you. You said so."

"Me versus him? Evergreen walks away the winner nine times out of ten. But I have that one chance."

His arms still folded, Humayun shrugs. "Not good enough."

"That's as good as it gets." I stick my finger in his face. "That's what happens when you try to put a leash on Death Itself."

The fat bastard scowls at me. I can almost hear the gears grinding in his brain.

"You know what?" Humayun chuckles, his belly jiggling. "You got me."

Finally.

The waiters break into nervous laughter. I smile tightly, stopping myself from lunging at the fat bastard and tearing him apart with my bare hands. No doubt the feeling is mutual.

Humayun pops open a bottle and lets me take a whiff. "Ever had any?"

"Nope." Not with the shit you pay me. "What is that?"

"A new kind of lassi. Made it myself. Let's celebrate together." He takes out more glasses and stacks them on the counter. "Come on, boys. Everyone gets some."

In any other world, it'd be alcohol. But Humayun doesn't drink, devout Muslim and all. I mean, lying, cheating, hustling, blackmailing, murdering, and being a grade A pile of shit? Sure. But booze? Nope. There are lines even he won't cross.

I tip the glass of lassi to my lips, but it slips from my fingers and spills all over the counter. As everyone laughs, Humayun eye-balls me in silence.

———

Humayun slides his glass away after his third helping and places a sheet of paper in my hand. I study the sketch.

Inayah.

"Looks familiar, right?" Humayun winks.

Time isn't a circle. It spirals, descending lower and lower. As the earth spins, you find yourself transfixed in a place you recognize from before — a home, a haven — but the earth has gone on spinning and you've sunk deeper into the ground. Before you realize it, you're buried where you once stood, every fading light a bad memory, every gasp of breath an apology.

"No loose ends. Not this time." Humayun smiles, a madman's mirth in his eyes. "You go there. To the Badlands. You stop her."

The Badlands. I swore I'd never return to that place, that grave ditch where everything I loved and loathed lies buried.

Humayun sneers. "She dies today. Promise me that. Then we're golden."

Doua is alive.

I fold the sketch. "She dies today."

———

I have her name and whereabouts. And Baadal's 1911, with two bullets.

One for Inayah. One for me.

Shoulders stooped, feet heavy, I pause before the vast stretch of rusted cars stacked on top of one another, spreading far on either side of me.

I sigh. "Doua?"

Nothing.

I pass through the giant wall of discoloured metal that lets me know that past this point is the very heartland of Decay.

The Badlands.

The squalid roads and mottled pathways grow narrower at every turn. Faded black clothes and white undergarments hang in tatters over sagging washing lines. Refuse and damp wood and plastic bags appear in lumps under my feet. There's the stench — a constant odour of sewage and rot that sticks in my gullet long after I've passed a dead rat or burning trash pile. Everything feels sickly. Like something you'd spit out after a coughing fit.

The true horror of this place is the look in people's eyes. That something-broken, something-sinister stare. It's a look that reminds you why you ran away, why you swore you'd never die in such a miserable place. It's a look that asks why you ever came back.

I came back here to kill a thirteen-year-old girl.

I came back here to find a woman so I can tell who I really am.

———

I was sixteen.

We were a dozen children in total, all of us subhumans discarded from the Land of the Pure. We ran around, picking pockets, selling crap that didn't work, and sweet-talking ourselves out of trouble. In that library-shelter, we felt like we were floating over the rest of the Badlands. Our house above the world, in its universe of half-torn books. Memories of my old life vacillate between two extremes: living something of a life with Doua and watching it all fall apart so easily.

All it took was two Hindu sisters.

They were twins. We called them Asha-Eksha because it was almost impossible to tell them apart. Whenever we'd see either of them, we'd call out *Asha-Eksha* and there'd be a smile as their

grey eyes shone. They were five, the youngest in our group, easy
to spot because of their orange sarees. They always arrived in
a rickshaw, waving at us, miniature royalty in our confederacy
of black-clad dunces. They'd bring leftover pakoras their mother
sold in New Market.

In the afternoon, we'd play cricket in front of the library-shelter.
Someone would always end up smashing a ball through one of its
many windows, and we'd have to leg it before Doua came out to
yell at us. Asha-Eksha would be among us, mouths open as they
ran. They'd umpire for us or squat behind the milk-carton wick-
ets, screaming *howzat?!* with their team and even the opposing
team, as loosely acquainted with the rules of the game as we were.
They were safe with us, they were free, they laughed openly and
loudly — things girls get to do little of in Pakistan.

Doua would let them sleep over on nights when their father
would come home drunk and beat them and their mother. Eventually, Baadal and I paid him a visit and described in detail what
repeated hits from a cricket bat do to a man's testicles. After that,
Asha-Eksha slept at the library-shelter only because they wanted
to, which was often.

One night, Asha-Eksha came to my room holding a silver tray
decorated with incense and *diyas*. Asha — I think — pointed to
the sky, where the broken moon glimmered through the cloudy
night and embers of celestial debris.

"*Shraavana*," she said. "Moon."

I had no idea what they were talking about. Neither did
Baadal.

We asked Doua what was going on.

"It is one of the months of the Hindu calendar," she said.
"Today is its full moon. Well, full-ish moon."

Asha-Eksha circled the tray in front of me and Baadal before
taking our hands. Asha tied bright, colourful threads around my

wrist. Eksha did the same for Baadal. They looked so happy; neither of us objected. We looked at Doua quizzically.

"It is the *Raksha Bandhan*," Doua explained. "You are their brothers now."

Asha-Eksha held sweets up to our lips. They said a word, *bhaiyya*, and from then on, that's all they ever called us.

———

The odd structures I pass by — half-collapsed homes, mouldy government buildings tilting toward the street, a huge reservoir pipe stretching for several hundred metres — are teeming with plastic-sheet tents that are tied, nailed, glued, or taped into place.

Quran 9:5 and PFM are spray-painted here too. I can't miss the haphazardly drawn mural on the side of a two-storey building: a heavily bearded old man in black, holding up his fist in defiance.

Yaqzan.

Pausing before it, I ask myself the same question I've been asking: what does he want from me? How am I connected to this man?

A few paces ahead, easily lost in the gyre of graffiti, is something I haven't seen before. Words anointed in black on a wall to my right, a child's handprint next to the message.

Death to Avaan Maya. Death to all traitors.

———

November 7, 2079
My twenty-fifth birthday.

Doua came to our room, panicked. Asha-Eksha, she said again and again. The kajal streaked down her cheeks, and her voice kept breaking. Had we seen Asha-Eksha, she asked.

We hadn't.

"Oh, no," she said. "Oh, no."

She organized a search party that lasted the whole day. Not a trace.

Then the whole week.

Then the whole month.

Asha-Eksha had disappeared. Deep down, I felt no one wanted to know what had happened to them. Doua, with all her persistence, would sob quietly in my arms at night.

But not me. I imagined everything, every scenario — and the more I imagined, the more desperately I sought the girls.

———

Now, navigating through the maze of memory, I end up before a wide clearing in the middle of the Badlands. It's a huge garbage ditch that has since encroached upon Old Market, leaving nothing of the ocean of wooden stalls and donkey carts it used to be. That forlorn sea of lost children, of mutilated women and men where everything began falling apart in my life.

———

Asha-Eksha had been missing for months. I was in Old Market again, traipsing along and scanning its large wooden carts of canned fruits and vegetables, dried meat, and eggs. A few tricksters performed acrobatics under the sparse snowflakes, while a handful played music or sold toys, haggling with their customers. Underneath all the pleasantries, that miasma of something sinister hung in the open air.

My instincts screamed at me to run and not look back.

Exhausted, I sat down on a bench, taking in the mulberry evening. The panorama turned ugly. Hookers preened, giving their tits and asses an extra jiggle. Emaciated women and men with cancerous wounds on their bodies cupped their hands before me. An otherwise healthy man showed me his shoulder, where a portion of his limb dangled like a half-eaten sausage, the pink of his flesh bright against the darkened skin. It was recent. No point asking what had happened. He couldn't answer even if he wanted to. I passed him a couple of pink ration cards, and he lumbered away, just one more in a sea of half-devoured Badlanders.

I held my face in my hands for a while.

Through parted fingers, I watched a scrawny girl walk up to me, several blue, pink, and purple balloons in her right hand. But it was her left hand that I couldn't look away from. It was a ghastly fist. As if her hand had been pinned over a table and hammered repeatedly until the ligaments and muscle and bone and fingernails mangled into each other. Whatever was left of her skin had been folded over it, holding everything in place.

Like a prize, she brought it close to me, as she'd been taught. Her work permit.

"P—p—p," she mumbled. *Paisay*, she was trying to say. Money.

"Asha?" I finally croaked, removing my hands from my face. "Eksha?"

Her grey eyes glittered in a face that was scaled over with hunger and thirst.

She bolted. I grabbed her arm.

"Asha-Eksha, stop!" I yelled. Some of the balloons broke free and floated skywards. "What happened to you? Who did this?"

She couldn't speak.

"Who did this to you?"

Her skinny arms strained in my grip, trying to break free. She looked around, tears flowing out of eyes that were black with fear. Incomprehensible whimpers escaped her lips.

She'd wanted to say *bhaiyya*.

But she couldn't. They had cut out her tongue.

Watching her tears, I loosened my grip. She broke free and

darted through the cluttered stalls, through the amputees and the diseased. She ran into an alley and disappeared. Above me, in blues and pinks and purples, her lost balloons scattered into the burned sky.

I'd spend years wishing I'd held on tighter.

Hours later, as I ran in circles, around corners, past rows of donkey carts and hookers and maimed beggars, I knew it was too late. There's always a spotter, always someone monitoring beggars, making sure they don't escape or scream or ask for help.

The next day, Doua told me that someone had found one of them. He had been sifting through a garbage ditch near Old Market and found Eksha's body torn open, missing its organs.

———

The bells ring from the PSA system, its three speakers yellowed and cracked where people have thrown stones at it in futile revolt.

I spot the landmark. A large, rusting graveyard of once-vibrant buses, now lying half sunken in the dirt. The structure next to it is a dilapidated bus stop where several dozen families live in tents. A girl sits cross-legged by the stairs, nibbling at a large white candy ball.

Inayah.

She's a wiry, morose little thing. Her tangled hair dances in the icy breeze. Her knotty shoulders do their best to hold up the red shalwar-kameez that she hasn't fully grown into. Probably belonged to her mother. Or Maseeh.

A woman sits by Inayah, patting her hand as she whispers. There's a white cane folded by her feet. Black square sunglasses cover most of her face. Thick lines of grey streak through dark hair combed over the right side of her face. She's wearing a black saree with embroidered foliage, most of it hidden behind a thick shawl. The intricacy of the saree keeps me pleasantly distracted from the toes poking through her heavily worn shoes and the dirt crusted at the bottom of her clothes.

The truth is, everything I've just described is stuff you'd hardly notice the first time you saw this woman. Maybe not even the second or third time.

Her hand trembles as she adjusts the black shades over an X of dark orange-brown skin and grisly scars where her right eye socket and cheekbone should be. Parts of the orange-brown skin travel down the right side of her cheek, jaw, and neck.

The woman hands Inayah a large paper bag and kisses her forehead. Unfolding her cane, she toddles down the steps; as if materializing from the shadows, a few tough-looking paleet children appear through the crowd and aid her. When she's fully descended, they disappear into the crowded street.

Covering my face with the shawl, I sidle along the narrow road out of Inayah's line of sight. I scan my surroundings. Clusters of hacking-coughing-wheezing men crawl back to whatever passes for a home around here.

Two pale, scrawny figures monitor Inayah. Under their shawls, they wear faded blue shalwar-kameez that must be hand-me-downs — courtesy of older siblings that outgrew their duds or failed to outlive them.

Little Inayah has connections.

One of the blue-clad youths has springy black hair that he pauses now and then to comb upward. The other is a scrawny twig of a man with almost out-of-place pristine teeth that are as startling as the ridiculous poke of his Adam's apple.

They're too young to be striding around this confidently in the Badlands.

Scrawny Bastard remains poised and quiet, nodding occasionally as the more animated Springy Bastard whispers and jabs his hands around at various angles. He pauses, reaches into his kameez, and pops a cigarette into his mouth. There are no shaking hands or fidgety fingers. As he fishes in his pockets for what I assume is a lighter, I spot a P38 bulging by his right hip.

Seemingly oblivious to it all, Inayah gobbles down the last of her candy and stands up. Across the street, Springy Bastard and Scrawny Bastard nod at her. She slips into the alley snaking around the bus stop. Her little hands clutch the paper bag to her chest. I hang back for a few seconds before following her.

I know where she's headed.

———

The click of the .45's hammer realigns everything to reality. To this mad white world.

Inayah turns around and gasps at the sight of me with the gun in my hand. "It's you. The man from the church."

A gust of wind pulls the shawl away from my face.

"You shot her," she whispers, shaking. "You killed my mother."

"I killed your brother too."

"You monster." She stares past me. "What do you want?"

Baadal's 1911 feels heavy, as it did when I shot Maseeh and Rosa. "There's something I must do. Someone I must find."

"I must do something too."

"I know where you're going, Inayah."

Her large brown eyes shine with conviction. "They took everything from me."

Me too. "You do this, and there's no coming back for any of us."

"You're here to stop me?"

"I have to."

"And if I don't go through with this — will you let me go?"

I hesitate.

She winces. "You're a coward."

"Where is Doua?"

That name gets her attention. "Why do you ask? Who is she to you?"

I'm unable to answer.

Inayah looks past me. To the passageway behind me. Her expression dares to become hopeful.

"I'm sorry," I say quietly. "But they won't save you."

Because nothing is getting in my way again. Nothing.

Everything that happens next is as natural to me as breathing and nightmares.

Scrawny Bastard hisses in pain as I jab the .45 into his throat. The hiss snaps into a choked groan when my heel digs into the front of his knee. The ligament and bone snap, squishy and audible.

Hunched and gasping, he flails his 9mm at me, trying desperately to get me in his sights. I don't let him. Yanking his face down, I slam my knee into his chin. A bony crunch later, Scrawny Bastard falls to the ground, his neck rolled unnaturally into his shoulder.

That's one handler down.

Springy Bastard.

Stupid, stupid Springy Bastard gapes in horror, finding himself at the business end of Baadal's 1911.

"No," he cries, hands raised in the air. The P38 slips from his hand and clatters on the road. He sinks to his knees, his face smothered in his hands. "Please spare me."

I kick his gun away. The .45 still trained on him, I look back.

Inayah. I spot her rushing into a street corner.

A millisecond later, something metallic gleams in the morning light. I lurch back as Springy Bastard nearly cuts me open from navel to nose.

He slashes wildly at me again, nicking my right arm. I grit my teeth. The .45 ACP hollow-point roars in the morning air, taking most of Springy Bastard's forehead with it.

Checking myself for blood, I realize Springy Bastard managed only a shallow cut.

Inayah.

I know where she's going. That two-storey, reddish-brown building where my brother was shot three years ago. The Badlands Precinct.

I need to stop her.

The alleys I run through are so narrow that the buildings on either side graze my shoulders. These alleys weren't built or designed, they accrued over time like fungus on days-old food. Running through them, nearly decapitating myself on the washing lines, I spot Inayah several metres ahead.

One hand inside the paper bag, she calmly walks toward the platoon of twenty soldiers playing cards and chatting by the precinct's entrance. The gunshot from earlier is just white noise to them. Two military jeeps are parked on either side of the wide metal gate. A single soldier mans the RPD on one jeep. The other jeep is unmanned.

The soldiers barely notice little Inayah approaching them.

"Inayah!" I call out, standing sideways against a wall, the gun in my hand hidden.

She turns around. Our eyes meet.

"Please don't," I say, shaking my head. I can't think of anything else to say. I need to know where Doua is.

There's no hesitation in her. Just hatred, the kind that can't be taught. It metastasizes for years, for decades, until something unleashes it. Or someone. She pulls her hand out of the paper bag and holds something above her head: three large cylinders taped together and sealed. It's an IED, a makeshift bomb.

There's no hesitation in her. So much like my brother.

The soldier manning the RPD aims at Inayah.

Bang.

I shoot him in the fucking head. That gets everyone's attention. As they scramble to their feet, they spot Inayah and the bomb in her hand. They can only howl in terror, ducking and dashing for cover. For all the good it'll do.

Inayah whispers something to herself. Even though I can't hear her, I know what she said.

The snow falls over it all.

The world flashes bright and loud. I'm slammed back several paces on the dirt road, the air gushing out of me. In the deafening darkness, I feel myself spinning. A screaming ache between my ears garottes my brain.

The stench of burning rubber and melting metal and seared human flesh sticks to the back of my throat. My heart beats painfully inside my chest.

I'm not dead.

Flat on the ground, I watch the dust and debris, the smoke and sparks. It all blends with the snow that falls over me, heavier than before. But this isn't snow; it's a mockery of something pure and beautiful.

Inayah is gone.

Sirens squeal in the chaotic air. Blues and reds flash in the distance. A numb, metallic pain spreads through the left side of my body. Holding up my left arm, I find it riddled with punctures and cuts and shrapnel, the sleeve tattered.

Gasping for air, I sit up and watch the fiery ashes dancing in the sky. Nothing will ever be the same again, I realize. I'm Majnun being refused Layla's hand in marriage. I'm Orpheus finding Eurydice dead in the field, the serpent still writhing around her leg. I'm

Devdas spurning Paro, not realizing that he's about to lose her forever.

A snowflake lilts before me and settles on my bloodied hand. A roundish, faintly glinting mound of dirt, it flakes apart in little whitish-grey chunks.

But this isn't snow.

There's a skeleton lying with a million others somewhere in this barren world, delicately held in place like cigarette ash on a windless day. A gale blows, and the balance shatters. The skeleton disperses into the sky in puffs of white. It travels over the world, and after years of aimless flight it finds its way into Old Pakistan. I try to hold it. But, like always, it flakes into a small clump of ashes in my hand.

No, this isn't snow.

PART II
THE LAND OF GLASS

PART II
THE LAND OF GLASS

Episode 12: Invisible

Doua

December 3, 2056

Whoever said opposites attract was lying.

Even as a six-year-old girl, I noticed how different my parents were. Where Papa's laughter filled the house, Mama was seething and silent. Papa was a paintbrush: tall and thin, with thick brown hair that had begun to grey. Mama was round and compact, an old teapot. Papa's face seemed to shine when he smiled, even when the Sky Sickness had left him starched and almost diaphanous, a forgotten shirt on a washing line. Mama never smiled. She smirked. A lot. That smirk came paired with a watching-you-down-the-length-of-her-nose stare that followed me, even after the last time I saw her.

Where Papa died young, Mama continued living and living — and for all I know, is still living.

It is strange how little I saw them together. My earliest memory is of Papa encouraging me to draw on blank squares of paper. Of Papa's starry blue eyes as his delicate hands guided the crayons in my fingers in abstract shapes that I thought were cats. Past his shoulder, I remember Mama sitting in her favourite green chair, her blue shalwar-kameez eternally pressed and immaculate, her dupatta coiled tightly around her head. I remember Mama sitting motionless as she smirked at me, her black eyes like a moonless, starless night.

———

June 18, 2057

"Say the words again," Mama said, her teeth clenched. "Slowly this time. What will people say when they hear you talk? That your mother raised a girl who clucks like a chicken?"

If I ever joined words together, she would tell me to repeat the same sentence ten times.

"Mama, please —"

"Do not *Mama* me. Who is running after you?"

"No one."

"Then? Why are you in such a hurry to get through the sentence? Are you a woman or a chicken?"

"Let her be, Sudduf," Papa said, his slender hands on my shoulders. As the years went by, Papa's protests grew softer and softer. But they were always there. Papa squeezed my shoulders gently as I stared at the floor. "She's just seven."

Mama turned her gaze to Papa, and his hands gripped my shoulders a little tighter.

"She needs to learn. I will not raise a girl who cannot speak like a woman."

"She's just a child."

Mama tightened the dupatta around her scalp. "She will not be a little girl forever. Mrs. Mirza's daughter is a year older than her, and she can recite Iqbal's poetry by heart."

"This isn't about Mrs. Mirza."

"If you keep spoiling her, she is going to stay a little girl. What will people say? Do you think I want that for her? I am her mother. She should know how much we sacrifice for her. Other people beat their children, and here I am who —"

"Enough, Sudduf."

"Fine." The smirk appeared on her lips. "We shall talk later."

Papa did not say anything.

———

August 3, 2058

When I was eight, I met a sad ghost near the river. He was singing because he thought he was alone. It was a song that was incomplete but beautiful. I memorized the words even though I heard them only once. I memorized the song because I wanted to sing it for the man I loved.

Some days, I feel our stories remain half-told for a reason. Society or death or the passage of time stops us from saying all the things we want to say. Like the sad ghost's song, beautiful things must remain incomplete.

Papa was gone, and there was so much I still wanted to say to him.

———

September 9, 2061

"Read it again. Carefully. And loudly this time."

"Mama —"

"Do not make me repeat myself, Doua. Your papa is not here anymore."

"I cannot."

"You are eleven now, but you still struggle with simple words like an idiot. What will people say?"

"Mama —"

"Is this what I have taught you? Is this why I work at the restaurant? So I can raise a girl no man will want?"

"No, Mama."

"Then read the passage again."

I was sitting at the table, my head clutched in my hands, the letters crawling and twisting on the page like frenzied ants.

"I cannot hear you, Doua."

Mama was cooking *roti* on the stove but had asked me to read aloud to her. It was a passage from *Moby Dick*. I was eleven years old — and even now, more than twenty years later, I know that one passage by heart.

Or is it, that as in essence whiteness is not so much a colour as the visible absence of colour, and at the same time the concrete of all colours; is it for these reasons that there is such a dumb blankness, full of meaning, in a wide landscape of snows — a colourless, all-colour of atheism from which we shrink?

"You stumbled again, Doua."

"I'm sorry, Mama."

"I *am* sorry."

"I am sorry, Mama."

"Better." There was a glimpse of silent heaven. It lasted a few seconds. "Start again."

I bit my lip, the words blurring into clouded black streaks. "'Or is it, that as in essence whiteness —'"

"Louder."

"'Or is it, that as in essence whiteness is not so much a colour as the visible apsence of colour —'"

"Absence."

"Yes, Mama." I started reading again. "'Or is it, that as in essence whiteness is not so much a colour as the visible absence of colour, and at the same time the concentrate of all colours —'"

"Are you an idiot? Tell me now that you are an idiot, so I stop working so hard. You can grow up like those paleet children, cleaning houses and begging. Do you want that? Do you belong in the Badlands? Tell me now."

"No, Mama."

"Then read it again. Focus. Stop dilly-dallying like your papa who kept forgetting to wear his mask."

The pages clouded up, growing smaller and murkier. "'Or is it, that as in essence whiteness is not so much a colour as the visible absence of colour, and at the same time the'" — I paused for the smallest of moments — "'concrete of all colours; is it for these reasons that there is such a dump blackness —'"

Something metallic clanged against the floor, spinning and spinning.

I heard Mama open a drawer, the sparse cutlery jangling. A breathy huff of flames came alive on the stove.

"Mama?"

For several minutes, I heard nothing but a sporadic popping sound.

She switched off the stove.

"Mama?"

Watching me down the length of her nose, she held a knife in her hand and approached me slowly, deliberately. The tip of the knife was red and smoking black.

"Doua," she whispered. Mama never whispered. "Read the passage again. And for your sake, I hope you make no mistake."

———

March 3, 2069

On my nineteenth birthday, I tried selling my paintings in New Market. My pieces. The covers had barely come off my art when the shocked disapproval scalded me like boiled milk.

"This is pornographic!" a man shouted at me. He pointed his finger at the image of a nude woman's back as she stood by a window watching the snow fall. "You should cover these. My children are here."

The female body. Nothing offends people of faith like a woman's body.

"They seem to like her," I said, nodding at his two little boys, who were giggling at another piece I had made of a nude woman floating in the sky, the clouds coiled over her breasts and between her legs.

Within an hour, a small crowd had gathered at my stall. Mullahs and proprietors, kafirs too. They all pointed, shook their heads, and glared at me.

"This is scandalous."

"This is indecent."

"This is not in our culture."

But they stood around, and they continued to stare. Women and men, girls and boys — they all crowded around my stall and kept ogling the bare skin, the curves, the breasts and vaginas. They crinkled their mouths, they shook their heads, but every one of them stared. Like the tall old man with long hair who stood before my piece of the woman staring out the window. He did not partake in the moral indignation. After what felt like forever, he turned around and walked away.

The only one who showed interest in my art was an eleven-year-old boy with curly red hair. He had been transfixed before my piece of a near-transparent naked woman standing by a bus stop. She was flaking away, pieces of her breaking off, pieces she held in her hands.

"What's this one called?" he asked.

"I do not name my art," I replied, standing next to it even as all the other people glowered at me. "But if you buy it, you can call it whatever you like."

He handed me a small stack of pink rupees. "*The Glass Woman*."

"*The Glass Woman*." I smiled and handed him the only art piece I have ever sold.

July 12, 2069

"Mama, I do not want to marry anyone. Not right now."

I had begun to sit as far away from Mama as I could at the table. I would fidget with the food even if I wanted to eat more because Mama would complain that I was becoming fat.

"Nonsense. You will marry Mrs. Mirza's son. You are getting older, and I have given your hand in marriage to Mohsin Mirza."

"Without asking me. I am nineteen, Mama."

Mama did not respond immediately. She stopped eating, placed her hands on the table, and smiled at me the way she would smile at Mrs. Mirza. "I am your mother, Doua. I know what is best for you. Everything I do, everything I have done, is for you."

"I do not want to marry anyone."

Her face turned pink and white like a closed fist. She was no longer smiling. "Do you want children when you are thirty?"

"I do not want children."

"Nonsense. You will marry and you will have many children because —"

"Because I am a woman?" I pushed my plate forward. "I do not want marriage or children. I want to paint."

"*Ya Allah.*" She inhaled sharply. "You would be lucky if you sell even one more painting."

"I will take my chances."

"With your dark skin?" Mama's black eyes slithered over my face and body like a serpent measuring its prey. "With those acne scars?"

"Mama, stop."

"Why do you insist on tormenting your mother who has done so much for you? Do I not deserve to be happy? After everything I have gone through?"

"Mama. Stop."

"Why must you insist on wasting His gifts?" She pressed her dupatta to her mouth, and tears began to stream down her cheeks. "Why must you insist on painting those naked whores?"

Younger me would have begun to weep. I would have wrapped my arms around her and kissed her damp cheeks. I would have promised that I would do whatever she wanted and that what made her happy would make me happy. Except now I could see her watching me, studying me, even as she cried. It was how she had cried at Papa's funeral.

———

October 26, 2069
Some days, I wish I could say that Mohsin was a bad man. That he ruined me, that he failed me. Some days, I wish I could say that Mohsin was a good man. That he loved me, that he tried to understand me.

Mama invited Mohsin and his family over to our home. He arrived with his mother and three sisters. I stayed in the kitchen as Mama had ordered. I wanted to hear his voice, but like me, he was invisible and without sound. Some days, I feel marriage is an agreement to lose your voice.

Mama called my name, and I came out of the kitchen with tea and sweets. I felt their stares on me — my face caked with makeup to make me as fair as possible, my steps smaller and slower, my eyes lined with kajal, my head covered because I was chaste, my gaze lowered because I was shy and docile. I served tea to Mohsin's mother, who smiled at Mama, not me. I served Mohsin his tea, and neither of us smiled. Some days, I feel smiles in Old Pakistan are only a sheath for fangs and forked tongues.

Our mothers did all the talking that day, and all days until the wedding. They laughed a lot, at times before the other even completed her story. Those same customs meant that I did not see Mohsin again until the wedding day. During the ceremony, I glanced at him, he glanced at me, and we stared back at the floor as stranger after stranger gave us their blessings. The only happy people at weddings are the guests.

That night, his mother gave him a necklace to place around my neck. He did, fidgeting with the clasp so much that I had to help him. I undressed and lay stiff on the mattress. We did not say a word. He kissed me but did not smile. I kissed him but did not smile.

The next morning, he had to help me out of bed because I was so sore. He apologized repeatedly. I wept all day. Mama took me aside and said new brides smile for the guests. I smiled and greeted the guests, who were strangers and gave the same blessings they had the night before. Mohsin apologized again as he held my hand. He swore that he would only touch me again when I asked him to. Some days, I feel I was raped that night. Some days, I feel there is no fair word to describe what happened that night.

Mohsin bought bags of coffee, though I liked tea. I cooked him *qeema*, though it gave him heartburn. Mohsin liked to nap in the afternoon and did not understand my art pieces. He told me they were a sin. I liked to listen to music in the afternoon and did not understand why a painting would offend Allah. Mohsin laughed when I was quiet and stayed quiet when I laughed. Mohsin wanted children, lots of children. I did not. I wanted to sing the sad ghost's song for him but could never bring myself to do it. I wanted so badly for him to touch me but could never bring myself to ask. I wept every day. Mohsin faded into the background. After six months, my marriage ended in the same silence that it had begun.

Some days, I hate Mohsin for agreeing to our marriage, for not standing up to his mother when he should have. Some days, I hate myself for agreeing to our marriage, for not standing up to Mama when I should have.

In the end, I could forgive neither of us.

Some days, rare as they are, I imagine a different life where I meet Mohsin by chance in a shop or by the river and we start talking. He is sensitive and sweet and thoughtful. He asks me about my art, of the story I am trying to tell, the names I would give the pieces if I could, and we talk about what they mean. Some days, I imagine that he kisses me, touches me, and does not need to ask for permission.

———

November 30, 2072
I wonder if my whole life has been a revolt against my mother. That for all my rebellion, I am fulfilling that bitter woman's predictions without realizing it. That no matter how far I have walked away from my home, no matter how much I steel my heart so as to never forgive her, my mother's black eyes still spear through me.

The library-shelter was my monument to motherhood. Not because I knew anything about being a mother or looking after children, but because in that cozy two-storey building, I did the opposite of everything Mama had done to me.

Children painted there. They laughed and played. Children read whatever books I could find for them. They cried and fought there, but by the end of the day, nothing bad lasted. Nothing bad lasted because the library-shelter was a place of you and me.

The library-shelter was also my monument to home. Not because I knew anything about housekeeping or family, but because it recreated a piece of my childhood home when Papa was alive. I lived with a man who was not my husband but to whom I sang. Though we maintained our distance in front of the others, our nights were full of kisses and whispered stories. The children watched me sing, they heard me read awkwardly to them, they learned to read and write, and our library-shelter swelled with stories. There were no PFM flags in this home.

All good homes have a story. All good mothers give their children a story. That story can be about loss and suffering, it can be about heartache and longing. But in the end, no matter how heartbreaking that story gets, it always has a happy ending, because the story is about love and family. It is a story of you and me.

———

July 10, 2072

"Do you have a husband?" he inquired in a voice that was softer than expected, but raspier toward the end. A voice that lost some of itself deep inside his chest.

"No, I do not, Avaan. Why do you ask?"

He was sitting on the windowsill, reclusive in his demeanour. He had been ever since that time a couple of months back when, out of nowhere, he had held my hand in his. When I'd slipped out of his grasp, he'd looked at me with apologetic, wounded eyes.

"Just curious." He dug his face back into the book he was reading. *The Plague.* Except he was holding it upside down. "But there was someone, right?"

His conviction startled me. I looked outside for a brief second and felt his big golden eyes on me.

"What makes you so sure?" I asked.

"I was reading this." He realized that the book was upside down. I pretended to look outside again as he flipped the book and pointed at a line that I had underlined a long time ago. "'A time came when I should have found the words to keep her with me, only I couldn't.'"

"Great line." I smiled.

"Yup."

"So? What about it?"

"Well, I read that and realized that sometimes words don't mean what I want them to mean. It's like the words aren't enough to explain what I feel, you know?"

"I know. If words were enough, there would be no art or music."

"Why?"

"Because I feel that the reason art exists at all is that someone looked at something, felt something, and did not have the words to explain what they truly felt. To draw it, to sing about it, to write about it — that is their way of filling the gaps left behind by words."

"So, why does anyone expect words at all?"

"I do not know," I said, smiling. "I suppose they are giving us a chance."

He pointed at the line again. "See, I kept thinking that this book is full of great lines. But you've only underlined this one part."

"Look at you, Mr. Detective."

He beamed. "So I thought that at some point, someone must've needed to find the right words to keep you? Or maybe the other way around, right? Which means that there's someone."

"Yes." I tried to smile — after all, that had been years ago — but I doubt I succeeded. "There was someone."

He grinned proudly, but his smile faded quickly. It must have been the look on my face. "I'm sorry, I didn't realize ..."

I folded my arms and shook my head. I looked up. The stupid tears began to roll down my cheeks, and I had no choice but to remember that I had married Mohsin. Just as Mama had said I would.

———

November 13, 2072

"You awake, Doua?"

"What are you doing here, Avaan?"

"Couldn't sleep."

"Again?"

"It happens from time to time. Are you painting again?"

"I am not sure what I am doing, honestly."

"It's — wow. I love how you've mixed blue with pink and purple. It makes me think of dawn. Not that I've ever seen one. But I imagine it'd be like this."

"Thank you."

"This is the most beautiful painting I've ever seen."

"Oh? How many paintings have you seen in Old Pakistan?"

"You're doing that thing again."

"What thing?"

"Can I sit with you?"

"Sure. What thing?"

"You paint these images, but you still hide this part of you from people."

"I —"

"Have you ever shown your pieces to anyone?"

"Of course."

"You had a stall? For like a day?"

"Ouch."

"How come you never show your pieces to anyone? The others don't know you still paint."

"You know."

"Yeah. Only because I barely sleep and noticed your lamp was on. It's like you're ashamed."

"I am not ashamed."

"Tell me about this piece, then. What's it called?"

"I do not name my pieces."

"Why?"

"I feel they should be unnamed. Because they are alone."

"Like you, you mean?"

"What?"

"Is that why you don't talk about your pieces? Because then they'd be apart from you?"

"Maybe."

"Except you're not alone, Doua. Not anymore."

"Thank you."

"Tell me about this piece. What would you call it?"

"This one? Hmm. *The End.*"

"Why?"

"Because of the colours of the sky. To you it is dawn, but for me, it is the approaching night. What else do you like about this piece?"

"Don't flip it on me."

"No, Avaan. I mean it. What do you think this piece is about? Because if I knew, I would not be painting. I would just know, and that would be enough."

"Okay."

"So, tell me. You find it beautiful. Why?"

"It's this part here, in the bottom half. These white lines — some long, some short, some thick, some thin. It makes me think of all the people in the streets when it's really busy. Like it's Eid and everyone is out in the streets, and it's been snowing. That's what I can't stop looking at. It's what makes this piece so — I don't know, I can't stop staring at it."

"Why?"

"Because even though all these lines are different shapes and sizes, they're all the same colour. The whole world is white, and everything is beautiful. Finally."

———

August 12, 2083

Ujala and Uzma had curly, stubborn hair that could never be tamed. The other children called them "negro" behind my back because of their dark skin and frizzy hair. They would cry to me when the kids were too mean. I would put oil on their hair to make it soft. Until the very end, I was the only person allowed to touch their hair. Ujala would have been twenty-three today. Uzma would have been twenty.

Sahil was the first child I decided to look after, the first who called me *didi* because I was a big sister to him and all the other children after him. Sahil was quiet and patient, and he remained quiet and patient when the Sky Sickness took him away just as it had taken Papa. He was also the first child we cremated by the river and set free in colourful paper boats. He would have been twenty-eight today, just like Salaba.

Ahmed and Ali were two brothers with the same birth defect. Their sight was disappearing, and they cried openly because, even in the Badlands, they wanted to see what the world was like. Back then, I was glad that they were spared all the ugliness. Ahmed and Ali's parents were first cousins. Ahmed would have been twenty-three today. Ali would have been twenty-one.

There was Nargis, whose long brown hair reached down to her waist. She was pretty, and all my boys loved her. Except Salaba. In the evenings, she would put flowers in her hair and stand at the second-floor window, where boys from the streets would whistle and hoot and promise to marry her. Sometimes, grown men would hoot at her and make the same promises, but she would look away and wave a middle finger. When I asked her why she did this to herself every evening, Nargis said that one day a man would come to make good on his promise, and on that day, she would leave the Badlands behind forever. She would have been twenty-six today, if the army had not destroyed my shelter.

Mary was the oldest. She was tall and big-boned. She wore sarees as I did, and in those sarees, Mary would play cricket with the boys outside. She was the best batsman of them all — even if she never said it out loud. Whenever Nargis was standing by the window and the boys and men became vulgar, Mary would march outside with a bat and chase them off, alongside Baadal. She would have been twenty-nine today.

There was Hameed who spoke so little and so softly, it took days for me to get a full sentence out of him. He was a scarred animal who sat in the corner away from everyone, watching. If he played cricket — and then only because the boys forced him — his hands shook when he batted. As a fielder, he would stand far away from everyone and refuse to join them as they celebrated. I never asked him how he'd gotten the scars on his arms and back. I doubt he would have told me. I never figured out how old he was.

Eksha was the sweet one, always smiling. She was gentle and curious. Her grey eyes had ripples of lighter greys in them, like the stones by the river. Asha was the fierce one. Her grey eyes were round and uniform and hard, like old Pakistani coins. Of all my children, I knew Asha would thrive in Old Pakistan because she was observant and defiant. She knew it too. When Asha-Eksha first showed up at the library, it was Asha who stormed inside and demanded that I let them stay. She was bruised and bloodied, but she looked me in the eye, and it would not have mattered if I had said no. Some days, I wonder if Asha knew that Eksha could not survive alone in Old Pakistan. Eksha would have been seventeen today.

There were two half-brothers; Baadal was the younger one. He was polite but hardened, charming but sharp. He was the one the others flocked to because he was impetuous and loud when he wanted to be. He was the older brother to all my children, though he was not the eldest. If they were playing cricket, he was the team captain. If anyone was out of line, he was the one they answered to. For all his good nature and best of intentions, he was the one who started the carnage. He would have been twenty-four today.

And there is his older half-brother. The one who fought Evergreen and died. Or so I believed. The one who loved me as no one before and no one since. The one who is alive now when all my children are dead. The one who killed Maseeh and Rosa. The one who razed my library-shelter to the ground.

Salaba, because I refuse to say his real name. The monster.

Yet, some days, no matter what they tell me he has become now, no matter how many times I remind myself of the people he has killed, in my heart he is not a monster. Some days, he is still the fragile boy who sat on the windowsill and read all the books I could find for him. The quiet one. The one who spent his first nights at my shelter blocking the door, as if ensuring that I would not abandon him or his brother. The fragile young man who stared at me with delicate eyes, who broke into pieces when I first kissed him.

Salaba.

Some days, he is still that half-erased sketch of a man, faded at the edges, blurred, with no colour to him as if it had all seeped away. Just a few desperate scratches separate him from the white world around.

Episode 13: The Fall

Avaan

August 2, 2083

There's darkness and a never-ending road. Sarah Connor soliloquizes over the uncertainty of the future, the battles fought to preserve it. You hear that a lot in old movies: fight for the future.

Me? I think the fight for Pakistan's future is a retreat in the face of our past. We march backward through time, from the present into the future, hoping to delay the inevitable massacre. But it comes sooner than later. There's no miraculous escape, no long goodbye full of forgiveness and understanding. It's all too late. Maybe that's why every Pakistani longs only for the past.

As the end credits roll, the last chimes of the PSA system echo in the evening sky. Moments later, load-shedding sets in, and the screen blinks to black.

"Marble," Kanz says. "Calling it now. And stop squirming."

He tries to tweeze out the last of the shrapnel from my left arm. It's a rolling thunder of torment.

Shirtless on the sofa, I hold up the oil lantern for Kanz. "Are you done?"

He finally squeezes out the shrapnel. "Got it!"

It's a tooth — a molar. We look at one another. He quickly tosses it onto a plate with several bits of bloody metal and marble pieces. Wordlessly, we agree to never bring this up again.

"Stitches?" I ask, not looking at the plate.

"No."

He tips a bottle of booze over the cloth and, without warning, presses it against the wound. It feels like I've been stapled several times at once. He's done that for every single wound, and each time he's insisted I'll get used to it. I haven't.

He scoffs. "Faggot."

My stomach rumbles. Pale fingers of light guide my eyes over corks, VHS covers, the foamless sofa, the once-red carpet, the once-beige curtains, and the bloody strips of gauze and cloth littering Kanz's room. My stomach rumbles again.

Kanz's stomach follows suit. "Check the fridge."

"Seriously? I was in an explosion."

"My knee hurts."

I get up and rummage through the frozen cardboard box outside on the window ledge. "Nothing."

He offers me a sip from the bottle as I crumple back into the sofa next to him. "Going to go see Humayun?"

"Yup." The brown liquid tastes like brake oil. I gulp more anyway. My head throbs; my arm feels uncomfortably hot. Pressing the perspiring bottle against my forehead is comforting. I pass the bottle back to him. "Just not now."

It's been a few hours since Inayah's death. So much has happened these past three days, I can barely think straight. Humayun and Evergreen are working together. They're both after Yaqzan. Yaqzan has a vendetta against me. And I'm on borrowed time with all three of them.

So much has been revealed, and yet I'm exactly where I started: still not with you, Doua.

Despite his thick coat, Kanz is cold. He rubs his hands together. "Any idea what he'll say?"

"Nothing good."

"Little girl playing suicide bomber — no way you could've seen it coming."

Neither of us says a word. Though he tries to hide it, Kanz's discomfort and pain are palpable.

"The army won't take this lying down," I point out.

"What are you going to do?"

"That explosion was Yaqzan's declaration of war. Him, Evergreen, they want another civil war." And Doua — is that what you want too? "I don't know what I'm doing here anymore, Kanz," I sigh. "Kanz?"

Kanz snores.

Snug in his coat, he looks even more fragile. His skin seems almost translucent against his sagging flesh. The lantern illuminates all the cuts and sores and rashes over his body, too many to count. Picking him up in my arms, his weightlessness striking, I place him on the mattress away from the window. I keep the lantern near him. Prying the bottle out of his hands, I bring it downstairs with me.

I open the door and watch the chilly night embrace my city.

There's more colour in Sector 3. The sombre rust-brown walls and shutters are caked over with blue, pink, and purple smears of *Quran 9:5* and PFM.

For the first time, there's a new colour. White. Whimsical, hoary, inert, tenuous, elusive white that partially conceals all other colours.

The snow falls over it all, it reads.

Still no breasts.

I don't psych myself up to face this city.

No shawl, no shades. No clues, no direction. No bullets in the Big Heat. No bullets between me and the world. And no Doua. Hiking my shirt up over my mouth and nose, I toss Kanz's booze far away, relishing the sound of breaking glass.

Shivering, my teeth chattering, I set off for Humayun's Diner. I feel it immediately — something new in the air. A latent, ambivalent buzz that tingles the tips of my fingers. Like a hunch. Anxiety? Anticipation? Good or bad, it's novel — and it's the closest I've come to being hopeful in three years.

———

The icicles under the arched canopy seem to have doubled in size. As I enter, that something in the air trembles inside Humayun's Diner as well. The place is thronged, courtesy of a buy-one-get-one-free deal on *parathas*. Cheap, oily food — it tempts the just and the unjust alike in Pakistan.

"You were sloppy," Humayun mutters as I sit before him.

"She's dead, isn't she?"

"Soldiers are dead. The precinct destroyed." He slams his hand on the table. "Evergreen is livid."

"Mention there might be a bomb next time."

Glaring at me for a second or two, he pokes his chins at my left arm. "How's the arm?"

"It's fine." Hurts like hell. Can't straighten it all the way. "What about my pay?"

He smiles. "Got something new."

"What? Humayun, I just —"

"You kill people. Who I say. When I say."

Slick Bastard saunters in from the kitchen, shirt half-buttoned, hair as glossy as the diner's floor. He stands next to Humayun, bending forward just enough so I get a good view of the Walther P38 holstered in his armpit. He looks at his gun then looks at me.

That's right, madarchod. You and me. Real soon.

Humayun pulls out an envelope from under the counter and slides it before me. "Here's the information."

There used to be a darkly playful twinkle in his eyes when he did this. Like I was being let in on a cruel joke. Before he found out that I'm the crazy bhosdi-ka who challenged Evergreen to a duel and died. Now? I feel like the main course at a cannibal wedding.

I don't open the envelope. "Where's the hit?"

"In Sector 1."

"That's army territory. Send Evergreen." I point at Slick Bastard. "Or this chuut."

"Evergreen will shadow," the fat bastard assures me. "I've asked him."

"You've *asked* him?"

Humayun extends his pink hand before me. "Your gun, Avaan."

"How many targets?" I ask.

He shakes his open hand. I comply.

Ejecting the empty magazine, he fishes out a small box of .45 ACP hollow-points from under the counter. It's half-empty.

He begins loading. One bullet, then another, then another.

Slick Bastard whistles.

Two targets in Sector 1? That's suicide.

Humayun continues loading until the magazine is full.

Seven bullets. Six for the targets. One for me.

Maybe Humayun feels it too, that something in the air. A faint crackle through it all. A feeling that it's all or nothing now. A war is coming.

Humayun snaps the magazine in and flips the gun for me to take. "They die tomorrow."

———

August 3, 2083
Stop staring at him, Avaan.

A teenage boy sits at the canopied entrance of this once-breathtaking two-storey villa. It retains most of its awe despite a cracked, blackened wall, no doubt courtesy of a Molotov cocktail. It's the house I need to be in. Six poor bastards are living their last moments on earth behind those floor-to-ceiling frosted blue windows. Out front, a PFM flag flutters in the snow.

"Hello?" An irate *tchhh* escapes the boy's lips. "Sahib? Hello?"

He's parcelled up neatly in a rich green shalwar-kameez and a black leather jacket. He spins a double-taped tennis ball and catches it with the same hand. The way he tosses the ball — rolling it with his index and middle fingers both wide apart — I know he's a spinner. Like Baadal.

It's neither the house nor the ball that holds my attention. It's the unnatural shortness of the boy's forehead, the sharp angle of the front of his face. As if some titan pinched his head into a teardrop shape. I'm a chuut for staring, and the way his wide-spaced, drooping eyes regard me, he seems to share that opinion. Pakistan is full of kids like him because of first-cousin marriages.

"What do you want?" the boy asks. His right eye — a piercing black one — studies me without flinching. His left one is an opaque blue dot.

"I'm looking for work."

"Why here?"

"Because ..." I pause. Because Humayun wants everyone in this house dead. Because war has been declared, and I've been ordered to return fire. Because you're one of the people Humayun wants dead, kid. "It's a big house. There's always work in a big house."

Again, I spot a red-eyed figure in a dark alley to my right. Spying, I notice a woman walk back into the dark alley, morphing into the shadows.

"Why come to Sector 1?" the boy inquires after a long pause. He spins the ball again and fumbles. The ball slips out of his hand and rolls to my feet. "Why not wait near New Market like everyone else?"

"I figured I'd have a better chance here."

"You people shouldn't be here at all."

"I passed through security. I'm clean."

The boy pulls out a bulky square of aluminum foil. I notice his pinkish, swollen left hand with six fingers. He unwraps the foil, and the aroma of buttered *naan* and garlic mutton tingles my nostrils.

I haven't had mutton in — what? Three years?

"You should leave." The boy folds the naan between his thumb and fingers. He rips off a piece of meat with it and chows down, oil drops falling into his six-digit dinner plate of a left hand. "You wouldn't want my uncle to see you."

"Is he here? I wouldn't mind talking to him."

"I doubt it."

My stomach grumbles, a whining old beast.

The boy breaks off a piece of the naan and mutton and holds it out for me.

"Eat," he says. "And then leave before my uncle finds you."

As I take the morsel, I make it a point to touch his skin, relishing the *tchhh* that escapes his lips.

"You're a paleet, right?" the boy asks as I chow down.

Holding my hand out under the canopy, I let the snow gather in my palm. "I'm Pakistani like you."

"You're no Pakistani." He shakes his teardrop head. "Go back to your sector."

"Sectors don't matter. Not anymore."

"Yes," says a voice behind me, heavy and deep. "Yes, they do."

Two sturdy pillar-like arms slam me into the door, bouncing my head off the hard, polished wood.

"Madarchod." I square up to the 18-wheeler of a man. He's tall, whoever he is. Pale-skinned, blue-eyed, red-haired.

Punching him in the jaw leaves him mildly dyspeptic. I punch him in the ribs a few times. He barely flinches. All I've achieved is tearing open the wounds in my left arm.

Almost in slow motion, I see him take a step back, and, an instant later, he kicks me in the chest like a howitzer, blasting me through the door.

Then, to really shit on my day, he unslings a Lee-Enfield .303 from his back and points it in my face.

Behind him, the boy shakes his pear-like head. "I told you to leave, didn't I?"

Still on the floor, I keep my hands where he can see them. 18-Wheeler's veiny forearms bulge out the sleeves of his green shalwar-kameez. He turns to the boy standing at the entrance.

"You okay, Rumi? He didn't touch you, did he?"

The boy, Rumi, shakes his head. "No, uncle."

"Bring me the radio. Hurry."

Rumi scampers off into the shadows. Nervous, sickly faces appear in the circular hall around me, watching silently. Almost a dozen of them, their stares vacuous, their lips unnaturally dark. Some cough, some wheeze, but they all watch me like drowned souls staring up from the depths.

With the huge barrel of his .303 pressed into my chest, 18-Wheeler pats my legs, arms, waist, and torso. He finds Baadal's 1911 at the back of my jeans. There's an audible gasp in the dim hall.

He holds up the .45. "What is this?"

"A gun."

He slips it into his shalwar. A second later, a fist, large and pale as the broken moon, cracks me in the mouth.

"You'll face the firing squad for this."

Rumi returns with a radio and hands it to 18-Wheeler. "The lines are dead, uncle. I tried, but there's no signal."

"Keep trying," 18-Wheeler insists before turning to me. "You. On your feet. Slowly."

I comply.

"Come on." He points the rifle at the stairs twining up to the second floor, where more wordless, emotionless women, men, and children watch us. "Up the steps."

"If you're going to shoot me, do it already."

"Not here." 18-Wheeler stands behind me and digs the rifle into my spine. "Up the steps. Move."

The pale-faced women and men shuffle after us up the steps, their dark lips unsettling against their already unsettling pallor. Rumi toddles behind us. There's some static and buzz as he fidgets with the radio.

"Is he a terrorist?" he asks 18-Wheeler.

"Yes."

I try to exhale, but my body has forgotten how.

We walk through a series of skinny plywood boards segmenting the hall into constricted rooms. There are no doors. The wobbly boards impart the barest sense of privacy. We pass by a family huddled in one of these rooms. Cardboard piles masquerade as furniture; thumb-sized cockroaches scurry freely. Four kids sit beside a mother who cooks on a rusty hot plate. The father lies sprawled in the corridor, a plastic bag in his hands as he drifts off in the euphoric fugue of whitener. A .303 leans against the wall next to him.

There are almost twenty people in this house, by my estimate. Most of them sick and fragile.

"There's Sky Sickness cases in Sector 1 too?" I ask Rumi.

Rumi nods. "It's really bad in Sector 1. We're suffering."

"Do not talk to this paleet." 18-Wheeler jams the barrel between my shoulder blades.

A tall woman in bloody overalls and gloves shuffles out of

another room. Her nose and mouth hidden behind a surgical mask, she carries a red-stained plastic box. There's a black armband above her right elbow. She pauses, startled at the sight of my gun-toting entourage, and moves aside to let us pass.

"Who are these people?" I ask.

"They're my family and friends," Rumi replies, still fidgeting with the radio. People in the hall smile at him the way people always smile at someone like him: a winsome scrunching of the cheeks that passes for a smile. Then they look at me, at my skin, at my clothes, and I'm reminded of how much lower I belong on the food chain.

"Rumi, don't talk to him," orders a new voice.

"He's dangerous," claims another, sharper voice.

Two new men have joined the entourage. They each hold a Walther P38. One of them is a thin, indifferent-looking bastard with permanently glazed eyes. The other is a rotund barrel of a man.

The sickly women and men who followed us up the steps? All gone, vanished like a whisper.

We approach a large, wide room at the far corner of the hall. 18-Wheeler escorts me inside with a slap to the back of the head.

Chuutya.

Dawn mingles with the frosted glass and imbues everything with a bluish-orange hue. Rumi sits behind a large oak table until Indifferent Bastard yanks him by the arm and takes the seat for himself.

Rotund Bastard stands next to him.

Another new guy — Nervous Bastard — leans against the window covering the whole wall to my right. He peeks outside, his wrinkled brow glistening with sweat. Compared to the others, he's jittery. His foot bobs constantly, his fingers twitching over his P38. It's inexperience. Or bloodlust. Odds are, when the inevitable lead storm erupts here, Nervous Bastard will be the one to watch.

Dumb Bastard sits on the table, regarding me cautiously. He's earned his moniker on the general principle that there must always be a dumb bastard in any room.

Rumi stands sheepishly in the corner, radio in hand.

18-Wheeler now aims the .303 at my throat. His shallow breathing is white noise in the room. Maybe that's my own.

They're all here now: the five men Humayun wants dead. And the kid.

Might as well be the first person to talk. "Boys, I'm just —"

A rifle butt to my solar plexus unseals the air in my lungs. 18-Wheeler grabs my collar and straightens me back to my feet again. I eye Baadal's 1911 poking out of his shalwar.

"You will only answer our questions," Indifferent Bastard says, fingers and thumbs connected before him. He barely blinks. His brows, his nose, his moustache — every inch of him is professionally glib. "You know who we are?"

I nod. The .303s made that clear. "You're soldiers."

"What is your name?"

"Martin Frost."

18-Wheeler punches me. A crisp, fleshy *thwack* echoes in the room.

Indifferent Bastard repeats his question, and I answer. "Salaba."

"Were you aware of who we are when you entered this house, Salaba?"

I shake my head.

He grunts. "Still, you came here armed. Even you must know the consequences."

I nod but keep my eyes focused on the .45 tucked inside 18-Wheeler's shalwar.

Indifferent Bastard holds up his hand. "You're a Loyalist, yes?"

"No."

A stiff blow to the kidney — the only one I've got — turns my legs to jelly.

Rumi winces.

Indifferent Bastard waits for me to catch my breath. "You're a Loyalist, yes?"

On my knees, I shake my head, my lips dry and salty. "Loyalists don't carry Colt 1911s. But you already knew that. Same way you know that only Humayun supplies 1911s in Pakistan."

Indifferent Bastard displays emotion: the slightest twitch in his chin. "What are you implying?"

"That I work for Humayun. And if I work for him, then that means I work for the army."

"Nonsense."

"Makes you think, doesn't it, boys?"

"This is ridiculous."

"You." I turn to Nervous Bastard, who's been looking out the window this whole time. "Seen any military jeeps patrolling the area?"

They all turn to him. Nervous Bastard doesn't look at them.

"Rumi?" I turn to the boy. "The radio still silent?"

He nods reluctantly.

I laugh. "This is a fall, boys. Humayun set me up the same way Evergreen set you up."

18-Wheeler digs the rifle into my cheek. "We should just kill him, sir."

"I agree," Nervous Bastard intones.

Rotund Bastard and Dumb Bastard seem hesitant.

Indifferent Bastard doesn't twitch.

Prodding your brain, aren't I?

"Come on." 18-Wheeler jabs the .303 deeper in my face. "Why would Colonel Evergreen do that to us? And for whom? Humayun?"

"It's loose ends," I sneer. "A paleet kills a Sunni family. That's me, doing my part. You? Your families? That's just a little tragedy Evergreen gets to spin as he wants."

Indifferent Bastard folds his arms on the table. "You're rambling."

"There's a war coming, boys," I say. "Evergreen, Yaqzan, they're fixing for a fight."

"Shut up!" 18-Wheeler screams, his cheeks erupting in reds and pinks.

Indifferent Bastard examines me, working on some dark arithmetic to decide my fate. Seconds bleed and breed into a minute. Seconds he doesn't realize he's run out of.

There's a scream downstairs.

Then a gunshot. A 9mm. Several more erupt.

Indifferent Bastard stands up, toppling the chair. "What's going on?"

Now or never. "For Humayun."

Bang.

There's no other sound after it. Just a squealing abyss. It doesn't grow louder or quieter. It's relentless, like the snow.

I'm still on my knees. Baadal's 1911 smokes in my hand as Rumi, Indifferent Bastard, Nervous Bastard, Rotund Bastard, and Dumb Bastard — hell, even me — watch 18-Wheeler thud on the floor next to me, a gaping hole under his chin. And through the crown of his head.

Six bullets.

There are scraps of sounds. Words. Stutters, stammers. *Click-clacks* of guns.

Still kneeling, I start shooting.

Rotund Bastard shields Indifferent Bastard and takes a hollow-point in the heart.

Five bullets.

Dumb Bastard ducks under the table and yanks Indifferent Bastard down with him. They flip over the massive table for cover. Someone's been watching Aaanold movies.

Nervous Bastard is finally ready to act, having spent the last few seconds staring dumbly at the carnage. Not that it does him much good now. A hollow-point punctures his head.

Four bullets.

A second later, Dumb Bastard takes a hollow-point in the neck and leaves this world behind.

Three bullets.

All sounds in my ears are static and screeches. As I stand, something rips into the left side of my belly.

The world spins as I fall backward. Things go blurry.

Who —?

A P38 looks massive in Rumi's shaking hand.

I still feel the steel of the gun in my hand. I'm not dead.

I train it on the poor, blubbering boy. He drops the gun and holds his face in his hands.

Flat on the ground, I shoot.

It's not Rumi that I shoot. It's Indifferent Bastard, who emerged from his hiding spot. A hollow-point inside his chest, he slumps over the table, P38 pinned under him.

Two bullets. For Rumi. For me.

Rumi whimpers something. Somewhere else, someone is crying.

Stumbling to my feet again, I press my left hand into my side, feel the warm blood ooze over it. A dull, stabbing ache radiates farther up my side, each hot-cold pulse more debilitating than the previous one. Things begin to slide out of focus. The static persists. It takes every bit of my strength to hold the .45.

A barrage of 9mms goes off downstairs in a smothered cacophony, as if underwater.

Rumi snivels as I press the .45 into his conical head.

"You monster," he whimpers.

I shoot.

But not him. I shoot the wall next to him, the sound so loud it makes him clutch his head and sink to his knees.

The carnage downstairs ceases just as abruptly as it began.

Footsteps. Near, far, I can't tell.

I ease the hammer back. Grabbing his arm, I guide Rumi behind the table and hold a bloodied finger to my lips.

With the gun in my hand, I face the door as the footsteps grow louder.

"Bloody hell," he whistles, P38 in hand. "You actually killed them all."

Everything is awash with blues and oranges as I face him — this menacing golden-eyed shadow that's haunted me for three years. Evergreen. He's wearing a black shalwar-kameez and a cap to hide his face. There's a white rag tied around his right arm. I can't see his mouth — a bandana half-conceals his face. But I know he's sneering.

Evergreen notices the bullet hole in my gut. "That looks familiar."

One bullet for Evergreen. "Loose ends?"

He nods.

"I thought you needed me alive."

"Not anymore."

He's located Doua. Hell on earth. "Last question."

"What?"

"Who tipped you off three years ago?" I dig my nails into the gunshot wound in my gut, relishing the pain, the anger, the hatred. I feed off it. "Who told you about Baadal?"

"Come now," Evergreen says, cocking his P38. "We all know it had to be you."

In a bright blue saree, Doua appears between Evergreen and me, her arms spread to shelter me from him. This is that moment,

the fall. The point of no return. I'm Majnun, ravaged and bloodied by the desert sands, all sanity drained away. I'm Orpheus, his
feet lacerated as he treads the Underworld in heady despair. I'm
Devdas, emaciated and decaying as the alcohol hollows him out
from the inside.

He aims.

I aim.

All sounds die.

Episode 14: Cleansed

Jahan

October 13, 2072

When I was fourteen and my brothers chased me away, my true dread was that I'd never see my pigeons again. As I scavenged something of a life for myself on a Badlands rooftop, my thoughts remained on my pigeons. For days, I'd fill small plates with seeds and bread, but the only birds who came to feed were squabbling, squawking black crows.

One day, as I crawled out of my tent, I saw a pigeon perched on a rusted TV antenna. He cooed happily at me as I gathered him in my hands. I was holding a cloud. The other pigeons came — and for the next few years, even in a place like the Badlands, I found my place in the world on a roof that belonged to us.

———

June 8, 2073

"Will this hurt?" I whispered in the dark room. It was my fifteenth birthday. I was the most scared I've been in my life. Only the Hindu transwomen in our community underwent *Nirvan*; but, by that point, I didn't care. I had to do this.

Bibi-ji, with her springy, coiled grey hair and amber eyes,

nodded at me. Though she was a Sunni, she had performed nearly twenty Nirvan in her life, and not a single woman or girl had lost her life in her care. Whether Muslim or Hindu or Christian, all the girls called her Bibi-ji because Allah always answered her prayers. Because for the last twenty years she'd prayed, fasted, and given alms to hijras and homeless children.

Bibi-ji began praying quietly. There was something squarish folded up in a green cloth before her.

I looked at the others: a semicircle of women sat around me, some teenagers, others old and grim and tough like stale bread. They watched me with dread and fascination, how a fly might watch a spider spin its web. All of them sat with diya in their hands.

After a few minutes of prayer, Bibi-ji held up a stone in her rough, calloused hand. With a swift crunch, she brought it down against whatever was folded up in the green cloth.

It was a mirror.

Carefully, she unfolded the cloth and began sifting through the broken pieces. She picked up a triangular shard the size of my hand and began heating it on a small silver stove. Panic and fear pierced my heart.

"Did you have sex?" Bibi-ji asked in a hushed voice.

"No, no," I said, the image of that boy's lips and curly hair flashing in my mind after so long.

"Did you eat anything spicy?"

"No, no." I had been fasting and praying for a month.

"Did you look into a mirror?"

"No, no." I hadn't looked at a mirror since I was ten, having seen a reflection that was nothing like me. It was the first time I'd noticed the block of ice I'd been born into.

"Good girl," Bibi-ji said gently, turning the glass shard over the blue flames.

My hair had already grown long. With my painted nails and lipstick and makeup, the girls here had helped me feel happier than I'd felt in years.

"Now," Bibi-ji ordered, firm but gentle, "pull your shalwar down and hold your legs apart."

I slid my shalwar and panties down past my knees, down past my ankles, and off my feet. Instinctively, in the dimly lit room full of people, I covered myself with both hands. The moment I did so, it was like touching something that wasn't a part of me.

"Remove your hands," Bibi-ji instructed. "Don't deny yourself the rebirth you have sought." She eased my hands away. "What is your name, girl?"

"Jahan." I trembled as she tied a thick string around the parts of me that I loathed most.

Gently, she made me look at her. "What is your name, girl?"

"Jahan."

Bibi-ji tightened the string and nodded at someone behind me. Two older women held my legs apart. I didn't flinch.

"Blood needs to flow from the wound. The more blood flows out of you, the less of your previous image shall remain." With a firm grip, she held those parts of me in her left hand. "Tell me again: what is your name, girl?"

"Jahan."

"Say it again."

"Jahan."

"Again," Bibi-ji said. The glass shard's hot tip seemed to glow.

"My name is Jahan!" I cried, hot tears rolling down my cheeks. I felt like I was made of wax. I was melting away. "My name is Jahan."

It was a second. A second that was burning and sharp.

I cried. Not in agony, though the pain crashed over me like a collapsing temple. Not in fear, though it fogged everything. As the blood flowed out of the fresh wound, the wound that used to be a knot that suffocated me, I felt my horizon widen. I felt larger than a dot. I watched the red pool grow wide between my legs. The burning, stinging pain grew hotter and hotter as the world throbbed in different shades of black. I cried with relief. I cried with some kind of joy.

———

February 7, 2074

"Just want to say," he said, glancing around, "not looking for anything serious."

"Me too." I pushed him against the wall and unzipped his pants. Cigarette between my lips, I moved into him as close as I could, breathing in his scent of booze. And cigarettes. He smelled like me. "I don't know about you, but I don't exactly go around looking for true love on street corners like these."

"Don't think I believe in true love." He scratched his head where his curly hair rumpled down his forehead. He was already a little tipsy, and something about his innocent smile made it impossible to look anywhere but at him.

"Wait." He wiped his hair back. "How old are you?"

"Me?" I slipped my hand into his unzipped pants and pulled out his thing. I had barely stroked it a few times before he was hard and out of breath. "Old enough to do this."

Eyes half-closed, he bucked his hips slightly to the rhythm of my hands. How happy must he have been that he'd asked me for a light?

Kissing down his neck, I kneeled before him and took all of him in my mouth. The things that came out of his lips then were all about true love, and all the things he was going to do to prove it to me.

"What was your name again?" he asked.

"Jahan."

When I took him home with me, I kept him up all night, then the next night and the night after that. Pretty soon, all we did was talk of true love. As if a nineteen-year-old boy and a fifteen-year-old girl would ever know anything about it. But it didn't stop us. For five years, we had laughter and many cigarettes and something like true love — all until I learned how fragile true love is.

———

September 11, 2077

I loved one pigeon in particular: J.J., whom I'd named after Junaid Jamshed. He was a tall, regal bird with a broad chest. Fluffy feathers covered his talons, as if he were permanently walking on clouds. The crown of his head, his back and wings, and even the first few feathers on the tip of his tail were silver, as if he'd dressed for a special occasion.

Every evening for nearly six years, J.J. would fly toward the horizon, and I'd be convinced that I'd never see my friend again. And every afternoon, he would return to me, like the other pigeons.

———

October 18, 2079

The Mullah-sahib sitting before me avoided my eyes. He was a sympathetic old man with a dark zabiba on his forehead. The shape reminded me of the chalk outline the soldiers had drawn around Ammi when I was thirteen. The day they took Abu away and hanged him.

I'd just asked the Mullah-sahib the same question I asked every single religious man who'd talk to me: Is it wrong that I love a man as a woman, though I wasn't born one?

This question had never left me since the first time the boy with beautiful lips and curly hair smiled at me. Even though I was twenty-one and living my happiest life, this question kept me up at night.

When the Mullah-sahib spoke, he probably thought he was being understanding.

"As long as you don't act on your unnatural desires, you are not sinning in Allah's eyes," he said, petting my arm. "I'll make *doua* for you, my son."

Unnatural. His answer meant nothing. His doua meant even less.

I'd been told he would be kind and open-minded. I'd been told that he'd fought during the Civil War and had spent his life helping young boys find purpose in life.

"Have you spoken to any other scholar about this?" he asked.

"Many."

"What did they say?"

"Different things." I had been called a hijra who wished to transgress against Allah. I had been laughed at. I had been called an abomination. I had been threatened. I had been chased and beaten.

"What about your parents?" the Mullah-sahib inquired. "Do they know of your thoughts? Your struggle? Do they know what you've done to yourself?"

"No, no." I do wonder at times. Ammi would've cried silently, big tears gushing out of her as they had when Abu struck her. Abu? He would've beaten me to death. And slept like a baby at night. "Why does Allah give me this body, these feelings, but call it a sin to act upon them?"

He began fidgeting with a green tasbih. "We cannot question Allah. I say the same thing to all homosexuals and transvestites who come to me."

"Is two men loving one another so bad that Allah had to destroy an entire city?"

"No, no, no. Allah does not hate people like you."

I ignore that like so many times before.

"He loves you like he loves all His children," the Mullah-sahib continued. "You will notice that the Quran doesn't explicitly say anything about homosexuality or transvestites. In the Quran, those men who came to Hazrat Lut's home were going to rape his guests. That's what the Quran means when it says, 'You approach men with lust.'"

"'Instead of women.'"

"What?"

"'You approach men with lust instead of women' is what the Quran says. You aren't going to say that raping women is okay, right?"

"No, no, no."

I sighed, long and hard. "Still, Hazrat Lut also says, 'Here are my daughters, they are purer for you.' Why was he offering his daughters to rapists?"

"No, no, no. He meant that they could marry his daughters. He didn't mean rape them."

"So, marrying rapists is fine, but men having consensual sex with one another is not?"

"No, no, no."

I shook my head, feeling empty. "If you insist that the Quran doesn't say anything about homosexuality, then why do you even call it a sin?"

The Mullah-sahib stopped fidgeting with his tasbih.

"These are all heavy questions, son. Look, you are far too young to understand such things. My advice is that you should read the Quran. Not with your mind but with your heart. It's the only way to see its true message. Its soul. When you do that, you'll feel healed and cleansed."

I went home and read the Quran. I read it until its pages were as wet as my eyes, and I kept on reading it into the early hours of the morning.

Episode 15: Illusions

Avaan

August 3, 2083

The P38 slips from Evergreen's bloodied left hand and clatters to the floor. He looks at me, an injured bird of prey.

I shoot again. Try to. I'm out of bullets.

An aura of violence wreathes him as he grows larger. A second later, he punches me in the gut, in the gunshot wound. Pure anguish that brings scorching acid to my throat.

Evergreen squeezes his fingers around my neck, his nails tearing the skin. He roars, his breath hot against my face. The walls become a blur. The room flips.

An instant later, the back of my head collides with something hard. Glass shatters. That sound — final and abrupt. I hold on to him, pulling him with me.

Shards of blue and orange. There's a rain of broken glass, cold and cutting. There's a shadow hovering over me, black and endless. Eyes like two burning stones.

Evergreen.

For a moment, I'm weightless in a rain of broken glass.

And then, the unforgiving cement slams into my back. The air blisters out of my lungs. Shards fall around me, the *clinks* echoing in the morning air. The tiniest of moments later, Evergreen thuds onto the cement next to me. Everything goes black.

———

You don't pass out for long.

That's something Aaanold movies never tell you. It's inevitable, the waking up. You're gone — maybe for a second or two — but then, like gravity, consciousness yanks you back. Like drops of water, one thing after another tingles your nerves. You become aware of the ungiving earth beneath you, the taste of old coins in your mouth. The burning-freezing bullet hole in your gut. You take a breath, sharp like paper cuts, and before you know it, the drops have become a flood and you're drowning.

Evergreen grunts next to me but doesn't move. The left side of his face is a battered, bloodied mess. I laugh, tearing the wound in my gut some more. Worth it.

Need to get to Blue Haven. Need to move.

Sitting up tears the wound further. I scream — no sound comes. I sink back into my cradle of broken glass.

Doua appears over me. *Why fight so desperately, Avaan?* Her blue saree is luminous against the blackening sky. She brushes back her wavy hair. *What do you want?*

Ah, what I want.

One day, I'll dream about what I want. It's a dream of golden sunshine scattered across a crystalline blue sky. About vivid paper boats sailing over the river and into the Misty Wasteland, where no one goes and no one returns. It's a dream about rich, creamy tea against my lips. About windows that are left open so laughter flitters into rooms, about summer-warm kisses, about skies without snow. But it's a dream that always ends in despair, because it's a dream that begins and ends with you, Doua.

A tall nurse stands over me, her white overalls bloody. There's a black armband above her right elbow. Her green eyes wide with fear, she pulls the surgical mask away as her short red hair dances in the breeze.

"You're going to be the death of me, Sal."

———

I have no idea when this is. Or where.

The sky is pink and glossy.

"Miss, he's bleeding all over the seat."

The wind — bitter, acrid — blows in my face, a cloud of diesel. This shadow woman, this wraith, appears in the long yellow-white strands of light.

Red.

"Sal? Don't sleep. Sal?"

"Miss, I can't be seen like this."

"Just keep driving, Chacha."

"What happened to him? He's bleeding too much. Is that — was he shot?"

I was shot. Evergreen? No. Rumi.

Miles below me, the world groans and cries like a giant mechanical infant. Deafening. Unending. You said I wouldn't stop crying, Mother. I wouldn't stop crying, and you nearly suffocated me — because every time I wailed, it made you remember what that monster had done to you.

"Sal?"

Why did you stay, Mother? You left when Baadal was too young to remember you. But not me. You stayed long enough that I'd pine after you forever. Is that all motherhood is? A severed connection? A lifelong yearning?

The shadow woman pats my face. "Wake up, Sal."

186 \ Saad T. Farooqi

There are no clouds, no celestial debris, no snow in this pink sky. The snow must fall over it all. If it stops, then the Mullahs were right. No. The snow can't stop. The snow falls over it all. Just as Yaqzan reminds us.

———

I'm standing in a hall of broken mirrors. The floor is littered with glass shards that cut and bruise my feet. Cuts and bruises criss-cross my naked body.

There's a narrow black hall behind me.

In front of me, a white cat nibbles at something on a plate. Something white and round and a bit too large for her mouth. A small ball? The white cat does her best to bite it, but it slips out of the plate and rolls to a stop at my feet.

It's not a ball. It's a bloody eyeball.

———

"Salaba? Sal?"

A name. It's not mine.

"Can you hear me?"

Painful bubbles of light pop against my eyes. I try to speak. Nothing happens. My throat is parched.

A damp, coarse cloth touches my lips. Water. My lips soak up the moisture. I try to speak again, but my throat feels clogged.

"Doua?"

"Sal?" Her voice is faint, coming from the sky. "Sal?"

Something dark and cold yanks me back down inside my mind. *When did you become this monster, Avaan?*

———

"You did it, Sal."

Kanz?

I lie on an endless field of grass. Tall, ash-coloured grass, soft to the touch. It goes on for as far as I can see, cushioning me under a lapis lazuli sky. Kanz lies on the grass next to me, a cigarette between his lips.

"First man to outshoot Evergreen. You're the lethal weapon. Not Riggs." He smiles, happier and healthier than I remember, as enthralled by this sky as I am. "You aren't afraid of death, are you?"

A long white cloth flutters in the air, casting a tenuous shadow over us. Its whiteness is blinding.

I turn to Kanz, try to speak.

He places a finger on my lips. "It's because you already died a long time ago, right?"

———

Water. It drips over my scalp and down my face. Trickling, tickling. I hear low, metallic snips. The world is a heady swirl of liquid lights and shapelessness.

I close my eyes. I'm safe behind closed eyes, right, Doua?

Metallic snips. Near? Far? I can't tell.

Someone grabs hold of my hair. *Snip*, quick and sharp. My scalp stings.

Who am I now?

———

Charred trees line a vast white field of overgrown grass, dead veins in a corpse-white horizon. I should be exhausted. I shouldn't be able to walk this much without my body giving out. Behind me, the monstrous walls of New Pakistan rise bleak and distant, brimming with fire and ash.

There's no snow.

The sun steams in the azure sky. Ashen twigs and roots snap under my bare feet. I'm dressed in black. Black *sherwani*, black slacks. My hair is tied neatly, my beard shaved. I have no idea who I am, and it relieves me for a reason I can't remember.

I push through the white grass; its blades reach up to my waist, stick to my cotton clothes. My feet are raw and bloodied, but I push forward. I keep walking in the hope the grass will begin to feel gentler. Looking down, I notice its blades bend into the ground.

When I look back up, there's a white door ahead of me. It's a little taller than I am, its width barely enough for my shoulders to fit. The frame is frail and cracked, but thick enough it doesn't topple over in the wind.

I twist and pull the doorknob. Nothing.

I push instead. It opens, echoing despite the whispering wind. I step through. A large circular patch of grass around me is bent flat, as if something heavy had rested on it. The bend of the grass is less intense for a few feet until it reaches five horizontal circles where the grass is pressed deeper again. Each circle is smaller than the next.

It's a footstep. I'm standing on a titan's footstep.

I hear something flutter above me. A long white cloth flies in the air, reaching the clouds. The wind twirls it round and round. Human skin and limbs bulge against the soft fabric. Coils of sheet cover portions of her legs, hips, and face. One arm shielding her breasts, the other covering the valley between her legs, Doua returns to me in folds of white and nakedness.

"Some days, I wonder if this is where the last titan collapsed, alone and godless."

"Is that all that's left of them, Doua? A footstep?"

"Most leave behind less."

"Seems pathetic."

"All is before Time."

"But a footstep?"

"What should it have been? A tablet? A tomb? A tower?"
The sheet continues to unfurl around her, leaving her suspended
between the grass and the clouds. I shield myself, the radiance of
the cloth and the sun painful. "Nothing quantifies our life, Avaan.
Time crashes forward, and you and I are branches in its wake."

I look back at the city I've spent nearly three decades in. The
fire and smoke seem like an epitaph for a lifetime of heartache,
gunshots, and lies. I miss the snow.

"What do you think the titan saw in the end, Doua?"

"A mad white world."

———

Cigarettes. The bitter smell of cigarettes mingles with the smells
around me. Musty paint, old, dusty furniture. Fresh laundry and
tea.

Someone is humming. A woman, her voice smoky and wistful.
She's humming that song I hate. "Ankhon ko ankhon ne." Humming it off-key, to make matters worse.

I look right. A flood of light brings small tears to my eyes.

I look left. I'm in a tiny apartment. The whiteness of the room
is startling. Cracked, mouldy, yellowing once-white walls and
tiles; a chipped, sagging white ceiling; an empty white chair next
to me with the brown of its wooden frame showing. Tattered
cloud-thin curtains do nothing against the light outside and even
less against the cold. A thick white blanket covers me as I lie on a
white, lint-specked mattress resting over a white pipe bed.

Yet the whiteness isn't the weird part.

Mirrors of every shape and size, every design and style, gleam
from the walls.

These mirrors, this white room — it's a temple of transience.

This transience hangs on Red too. Enveloped in a green button-
up shirt, her lower body naked except for her white panties, she's

completely unaware of me as she sits at the edge of the mattress. Teacup in hand, cigarette hanging from her lips, she gazes outside into the snow, or at the three pigeons cooing by the windowsill, or maybe at her reflection in the glass.

Is this what you do when you look in the mirror too, Red? Are you measuring how far you've fallen?

Reaching out to touch her shoulder, I spot the makeshift IV poking out of my hand. An X of tape keeps it in place. A new black button-up shirt and jeans are folded on a table next to me. Baadal's empty 1911 rests atop the pile. Peeking under the blanket, I realize I'm completely naked — save for the large sash of gauze around my stomach.

I sit up.

"Hey." Red looks at me and grins. "Still here?"

I hold up my hand against the light. "Still here."

"You really know how to show a lady a good time." She pulls the curtains together as the pigeons flutter away in a panic. "That better?"

"Yup." Light footsteps patter on the ceiling above me. A woman's. I'm in an apartment. "Sector 2? Is this your home?"

"This is where I live, sure." She squeezes my arm. "You're safe. Don't worry."

"How long was I out?"

"You were in and out for more than a week. It's August 11."

"Hell on earth."

"You probably got a concussion. Among other things. That happens when you jump out of windows."

"I didn't —" Evergreen. I shot him. I outshot Death Itself.

Red points a small flashlight in my face, studying my pupil dilation. "Hmm."

"What?"

"Nothing good. Not like it'll stop you. I bet you'll get into another gunfight before the evening is over. It's the other wounds that I'm more worried about. Especially your left arm. It's like you were in an ..." She pauses and squints at me. "You were there, weren't you? At that explosion in the Badlands?"

I don't say anything.

"Fuck. Please tell me you weren't behind it."

"Nope." The light from outside makes it hard to look at her. "You sure we're safe here, Red?"

"Relax." She holds up a mirror to my face. "I made sure you don't look the same anymore."

The man who stares back isn't Salaba Hatteb. This man has short, cropped hair and stubble. The eyes, the nose, the lips — everything feels larger somehow. I touch my face to make sure it belongs to Avaan Maya.

"I figured you'd need this." She hands me a plastic bag. "I picked one from the house you shot up."

The weight of the bag gives away what's inside. A Walther P38. Everyone seems to have one now. I never liked the 9mm rounds or guns that fire them. I always preferred the sombre metal-and-wood dignity of the Colt 1911 and the steadier recoil of the .45 ACP. Still, eight 9mms are better than no .45 ACPs.

"So." Red takes the bag from me. "Who did this to you this time? Terrorists?"

"Loyalists. And no."

"Oh." Her mouth opens wide. "Oh, fuck."

"Yup. Last time too." I skip the part where I shot Evergreen.

Red rolls herself a cigarette and inhales it almost halfway in one go. "You really fucked me this time, Sal."

There's a joke somewhere in there at my expense. "You'll be fine. You're a Sunni. Soldiers won't bother you too much."

"Oh, sure." She stomps over to a side table and pours two cups of tea. "Soldiers never trouble Sunnis in Old Pakistan, right?"

"I said too much."

"Sure," she says, handing me a cup.

The tea is sweet, soothing, with something of a kick toward the end. The aroma distracts from the smell of cigarettes hanging in the air.

"Great tea. Where did you get it?"

"It's a small shop in New Market. You buy the tea and get your fortune read for free."

What a load of shit.

Red tilts the cup to her wide lips. "Roll your eyes all you want, mister, but there's no harm in trying it. Her name is Ash."

Odd name. "What did she say about your fortune?"

"She saw a ring, an eye, horns. A triangle. And a cat."

"And that means ...?"

"Change is coming in my life. Something big. She also asked me to be wary of cats and broken mirrors."

I point at the mirrors littered about. "Is that why you keep looking at your reflection?"

"No, no." She coughs harshly, her lips pale. "I like looking at myself now."

"Now?"

Like some anxious animal, she steps away from me. "I used to hate seeing my reflection before. Anytime I saw myself in a mirror, in a window, in a glass of water, I wanted to punch a hole in it. It filled me with anger. Blind, directionless anger. Pretty soon ..." Her voice trails off.

"Pretty soon?"

She blows out a thin stream of smoke that mushrooms at the end. "You should rest."

"Oh, bullshit. Pretty soon what?"

She lets my question hang in the air. "Pretty soon that anger would go away. And I'd be left with this wave of — I don't know — pity? Regret? That always happened until my Nirvan."

"I thought only Hindu transwomen underwent Nirvan?"

"Sure. But I couldn't live with myself anymore. The Nirvan was when I felt it for the first time."

"Some kind of joy?"

She nods slowly, smiling. "Some kind of joy."

———

We eat roti in silence. Save for her coughing now and then.

Slumped at the edge of the bed, I fidget my feet on the uncarpeted white floor. Red sits next to me, her hip brushing against mine.

"Can I ask you something, Sal?"

"Yup."

She blows out a cloud of smoke, away from me. "Were your parents apostates too?"

"Mother was a devout Sunni."

"And your father?"

"Christian. He fell in love with my mother, married her against their parents' wishes. Got them both disowned and nearly killed. For honour."

"That's disgusting. Honour killing isn't part of Islam."

I nod. "Except, he wasn't my biological father. Explains why he barely ever said a word to me."

"Oh. And your real father?"

The hatred in his large golden eyes. "I only have clues. I'd hear my parents fight, the things they'd say — *not mine, what he did, that monster.*"

"Oh."

"There's also the fact that Mother wore black, even though she was a Sunni. And that I'm twenty-eight, which is around how long ago the Civil War was."

"Oh."

"Yup." I clear my throat. "I'm a rape bastard."

Red stays quiet for a while. "I'm so sorry, Sal."

"Don't be." Without even realizing it, I've devoured three rotis by myself. Red didn't protest.

"Is that why you disbelieve?"

The walls and roof tremble in my vision. "This city was always quick to remind me what I am. And that I'd pay for it. I was treated like a paleet long before I was an apostate."

"But you have a choice now, don't you? A lot of people come back to the fold. I did."

"And wear a black armband so that no one forgets what I used to be?"

She rolls with that punch. "I've done well for myself. You could too. It's not ideal, but you don't have to be a paleet your whole life. You don't have to live in such a hell anymore."

"It's a hell Pakistani Muslims made for me."

She snuffs out the cigarette in an ashtray. "Don't you think that's just you being hateful?"

"I don't hate them. They hate me." Again, the world wobbles. Red seems farther away from me than a few seconds ago. The gunshot wound throbs, but there's no pain. There's some medicine in the tea, I realize. "We get pushed to the edge of society. We're threatened, violated ..."

"You can't act like all Pakistani Muslims do that, Sal. Most of them are decent people."

"Didn't say they aren't. But tell me: anytime a gay Muslim is banished to the Badlands or some apostate is executed by the army, what do most decent Pakistani Muslims say?"

"What can they possibly do or say when —"

"They shrug and say, 'Well, what did you expect?' Just as you are."

"I never —"

"You're doing it right now, Red." The way my voice shakes annoys me. "You say I have a choice, a way out of this hell. But only if I stop being who I am. As if being gay or an apostate is a choice. There's a reason Sections 298 and 295 were around decades before the fucking sky burned away."

"You're twisting what I'm saying."

"Am I?"

"There are gay and lesbian Muslims in Pakistan. No one harms them."

"Yeah, celibate gays and celibate lesbians who're told Allah accepts them as long as they don't act on their desires. Is that a choice? Telling me to accept Islam regardless of how I feel about it. Is that a choice?"

"But you act like all Pakistani Muslims condone the violence. I don't."

"Then I wish more Pakistani Muslims were like you, Red. Because you're choosing compassion over scripture."

She presses her lips together so tightly they grow pale. "I get my compassion from scripture, mister."

"You think you do."

"You presume to know what I think better than me?"

I rip the paper tape from my wrist. "If you really followed scripture, you'd have turned me over to the army a long time ago, Red. You'd have stood by as they crucified me. You'd have justified your brothers chasing you out of the house."

"That's one interpretation."

"Fourteen hundred years of the same interpretation, Red? Come on."

"For me, there's beauty in Islam. I wish you could see that."

"I'm sure there is. But for all the beauty, people like us have suffered ugliness." I wait for a riposte. She doesn't have one. "You of all people should know."

Red takes a drag. "You remind me of that Baadal guy."

His name comes out of nowhere. A blind shot in the dark that hits home. "What about him?"

"He was armed, and he tried to kill soldiers. He's the one who started this fucking mess," she scoffs. "If it weren't for him, there might still be some peace between Old and New Pakistan."

"Peace? As before the Civil War?"

"Sure, things were always difficult. But he didn't help matters, did he? All those people who died in that shelter were so young. Their deaths are on him."

Three years ago, I'd never have guessed that this would be my little brother's legacy. A doomed child rebel. Something icy slides down my spine as I remember Inayah and the bomb in her hand.

It takes me a few seconds to reply. "He made his choice. Not all of us choose marble villas and fountains."

Her ears turn scarlet. She rolls another cigarette for herself, lights it, and takes a drag. There's a coldness to her as she exhales. She becomes unrecognizable in the smoke, a summoning ritual gone horribly wrong.

"Do you remember being in that house when you were shot?" she asks. "Do you remember those people there?"

"Yes."

"How did they look? Healthy? Sick? Did they look content with their fucking lives?"

"No."

"What about the house? Did you see — what was it you said — marble villas and fountains?"

"No."

"See, that's the thing: I've been in every single sector to help people suffering from Sky Sickness. Muslims, Christians, Hindus, atheists. Do you know what I think? I think I've never met a

Pakistani who isn't seeking solace in the past. It's all we ever think about because we're all hurting."

Looking away, into the light outside, I ignore the pins and needles prickling my eyes. "I didn't know Sky Sickness was so common in Sector 1."

"The snow isn't bigoted, Sal. Faith or no faith, green clothes or black, a Sunni seeks shelter from the snow as much as you do. It's the great equalizer."

"I didn't want to cause you any pain, Red. You saved my life. I'm grateful."

"You're still a real chuutya, though." Her lips a straight line, she glances at me. "I've saved your ass, what, twice now? Yet you've never asked me my real name. Which — surprise — isn't *Red*."

"Well, shit. What's your name, Red?"

"Jahan. Like Noor Jahan, you know? It's shortened from my birth name, Jahangir."

The past is a broken mirror. A reflection that cuts and bloodies. I sit up.

"What?" she asks, startled. "Is the name that bad?"

"You were Kanz's lover?"

Rage pulses across her face, then burns out quickly, pain rising from its ashes. "What did you say?"

"Kanz kept looking for you — he kept hoping that you'd —"

"What did you say?"

"You shot him. Why?"

Her voice is barely audible. "Get out."

"You ruined that poor bastard's life."

"Get out."

Slipping into the jeans and shirt, I tuck the .45 away, grab the plastic bag with the P38 in it, and head for the door. I stop. "You remember where I live?"

She doesn't answer.

"Kanz is my roommate. Or try Humayun's Diner. It's where —"

"Get out!" Her shoulders shudder as she watches the snow fall. "Get the fuck out."

Episode 16: Alone

Jahan

February 14, 2080

"You're being such a fucking chuut."

Kanz watched me, his jaw clenched. "Just using your real name, Jahangir."

"Stop calling me that name."

The more the Mullah-sahib told him to love Allah, the more Kanz had begun hating himself. And me. We were together for five lovely years. And for one year after that — a 365-day suffocation as we slipped down a dark hole.

"You make it sound like I kept my past a secret from you," I cried.

"You are a man." He poured more of that poison into himself. "I'm a homosexual. We both are."

"Kanz, I've loved you as a woman. As who I am in my heart, in my mind."

"It doesn't matter what you think. Allah made you a man. It doesn't matter how much you paint your face or the clothes you wear. It doesn't change what Allah willed, Jahangir."

"Stop calling me that."

He took another long swig, the golden-brown liquid sloshing in the bottle. He watched me pleadingly, his black eyes sorrowful as if apologizing for what the alcohol was making him say. For the things his hatred for himself was making him say.

———

August 20, 2080

"Kanz, where have you been getting all this money from? What do you do?"

"I work at Humayun's Diner."

"Who's Humayun?"

"He runs a diner."

"Don't patronize me."

"I'm not."

"Then answer my question."

"He's some guy. A Shiite who has a diner in Sector 3."

"How long have you been working there?"

"Couple of years. Maybe more."

"What work do you do?"

"Different things. Mainly cleaning."

"Cleaning? You can barely clean this room."

"Why are you asking me these questions?"

"Because you don't work there every day. You go once every few weeks, and when you come back, you drink and you don't talk."

"So?"

"What do you mean? Talk to me."

"I've told you: don't ask me about my work. You didn't before."

"I tried to."

"And I asked you to stop, and you'd stop."

"I want to know. I have the right."

"Why?"

"Because whatever you're doing, it's weighing down on you. Which can only mean one thing."

"And what's that?"

"You're doing something criminal."

"Something new in this city, is it?"

"I don't care. I don't want that kind of money in this house."

"We're all criminals to one degree or another."

"Don't give me that bullshit. I'm not a criminal."

"Oh yeah? You're a hijra living unmarried with a man for the last six years. Isn't that a crime in the eyes of Allah?"

"Don't you dare act like it's the same."

"You're a sinner just like me."

"I don't hurt people! Please. Tell me. What do you do for Humayun?"

"Why today? Why are you so fucking curious now?"

"Because it's changing you. The drinking, the secrecy, the lying. You're drifting away from me. You can blame yourself or you can blame me, but it's what you do that's doing this to you."

"I'm giving us a life. This life that we're lucky to have in Sector 2."

"It's not a life if it's based on lies."

"I got us out of the Badlands. Out of that stupid rooftop you called home. I'm the one who —"

"I was happy there. I could still be happy there."

"I got us this home, for you and me. I did that by working for Humayun. I did that."

"I didn't ask for this. I would've been happy anywhere. As long as there's us."

"There's always us. Always."

"Don't touch me."

"What do you want from me? Do you want to know what I do, Jahangir?"

"Don't call me that. Why do you keep calling me that?"

"Let me show you what I do."

"What are you doing? Kanz?"

"This is what I do."

"Where — where did you get that gun?"

"This is what I do."

"No, no —"

"This is how we have a home in Sector 2. This is how we escaped the Badlands."

"No, no —"

"This is who I am, Jahangir."

———

August 21, 2080
I shot Kanz.

I left Kanz.

———

August 1, 2083
What I hate about my apartment building is that the rooftop is locked. My pigeons have to cram onto my windowsill and bicker like crows when I feed them. When they fly to me for their lunch, as they have for nearly fifteen years, they often crash into the glass upon landing. I've spent many evenings putting these little creatures back together, healing broken wings and cracked beaks to the best of my ability.

J.J. would crash into the window frequently. My friend was getting up there in age, and his eyesight wasn't what it used to be. It's strange, and a little sad, how much these birds resemble old men when they age. He had become curmudgeonly, the first to peck at any bird that came near him, the last to arrive, the slowest to fly away.

One evening, J.J. didn't come at all.

I waited and waited, a cup of grains in hand. The other

pigeons had flown away, flapping toward the horizon. I pulled a chair next to the window, smoked, and waited, sleeping lightly. At one point, I heard a loud thump, like someone had struck the glass pane with an open hand. When I looked outside, there was nothing — no pigeon, no feathers.

The next morning, as I waited on the street below for Chacha and his pink rickshaw, I saw a white cat pawing and nibbling at a muddy, dirty clump. The more the cat played with it, the more I recognized the crusted feathers and dusty silver clouds around its talons.

That day, face after face looked into mine. So many men, women, and children spoke with me but didn't notice how I seemed distracted, or that I was speaking faster than normal or smoking too much. Or that I was drinking at work. Some noticed that I looked upset. I could tell that they'd noticed because they looked apologetic.

That day, no one asked me what's wrong. It's such a simple gesture. Just two simple words. So difficult to say. Because then you admit you've seen their pain and you'll have to hear about it. That you might have to do something about it.

No one asked me, no one stopped me. I kept drinking and smoking and speaking fast and looking distracted. Right up until a scarred, battered man held my hand to stop me from drinking and spoke two simple words.

———

August 2, 2083

"Have you seen those new flyers?" asked Chacha from the driver's seat.

The little pink rickshaw weaved and twisted through narrow roads, like a pebble rolling down a hill.

"Sure."

204 \ Saad T. Farooqi

Every time we swerved or screeched, I prayed for Allah's protection, tightening the green dupatta over my head.

"What do you think?"

"I don't know," I nearly squealed, covering my face as a pigeon
flew past the windshield. "Please be careful."

"How many times have you ridden in this rickshaw?" Chacha
laughed that laugh I found endearing. That sudden, breathless
gust of air, as if he'd just seen someone slip and fall on their bum.
He peeked at me in the rearview mirror. A golden crucifix dangled
from it. "This rickshaw is under the protection of God. No harm
will come to me or you."

"Please, Chacha, you should focus on the road."

"You still work at Blue Haven?"

"I've been working there since I was fourteen."

"You are a good woman, miss." He smiled, his droopy brown
eyes glowing. "People are lucky to have someone like you in this
city."

"I sense a 'but' coming." I smirked, watching Sector 3 go by
in a blur of rusting shutters and narrow homes and angry faces.
Even now, when they see my green kurta, I'm no longer a woman
but an idea to them. They see my green kurta and — in their
minds — I am the reason they have so little. As frustrating as it
gets at times, a part of me understands that they're right.

"But," Chacha sighed, "you should think seriously about
those flyers. Bad times are coming. Sooner or later, violence is
going to erupt in this city again."

"I don't know." I folded open the small, square flyer I'd kept
with me for days. "Are you staying?"

"No," he said. A big *no* that went on and on, as if he was
remembering something dreadful from his youth. "I'm an old
Christian man with no family."

"You never married?"

"I had a wife and two sons back in the Badlands. A long time ago."

"Where are they now?"

"Who knows. Haven't seen them in almost twenty years. That's my point. There's nothing for me here."

"There's nothing for me here," I echoed to myself.

"You are young and pretty and kind. Any man would die to be with a good woman like you."

I looked away from the rearview mirror. "Men always find a reason to leave me, Chacha."

I reread the flyer yet again, as I had been ever since I'd seen it posted on a streetlight three days back.

A NEW DREAM
And We had inspired to Moses, "Travel by night with My servants and strike for them a dry path through the sea; you will not fear being overtaken nor be afraid." Quran 20:77.
BLUE BUSES RIDE OUT OF PAKISTAN
Saturday, August 14, 2083, at sunset
Sector 3, Graveyard Station, King's Highway
Rs. 1,000,000 adults | Rs. 500,000 children

Episode 17: All or Nothing

Avaan

August 11, 2083

Doua's voice calls to me: *Wake up, Avaan.*

Somewhere far away, I hear footsteps coming. A door crashes open. Someone's yelling my name. I ignore it. I shouldn't ignore it. This is Old Pakistan. The footsteps grow louder.

Wake up!

A bottle shatters. My brain jump-starts with fifty thousand watts of adrenaline and terror.

Bang.

The Walther P38 shivers in my hand. Seven bullets.

A man slumps against the door, a bullet hole in his head. There's a P38 in his hand. He's not a soldier but a fellow paleet. No white armband around his arm either. Which means only one thing.

Humayun. He's finally making his move.

The gunshot still echoes in the room. My ears ring, but they haven't flatlined.

I frisk the dead hitman quickly and take his P38. Fifteen bullets.

Everything wobbles. My head grows heavy. There's hardly any light in the corridor. Fucking load-shedding. I'll need to double tap if I'm going to live through this.

Despite the *creee* in my ears, I hear the commotion downstairs. Someone's yelling.

"Kanz?"

I should've stayed away. I shouldn't have come back here.

A gun in each hand, I move into the tiny corridor. My left arm is killing me, a steady twinge going up and down its entire length. Adrenaline is a wonderful thing.

Heavy footsteps plod up the stairs. Two men. I can barely see anything in the dark.

A hazy shadow appears next to the stairs. *Bang, bang.* He goes down hard.

Thirteen bullets.

My eardrums are in tatters. I stay low against the wall, offering as small a target as possible.

"Kanz?" I call out again, his name echoing dully between my ears. "Kanz?"

Something cylindrical bounces a few steps away from me. A flash-bang. Military equipment. Humayun has Evergreen's blessing.

I punt it back down the steps.

The whole corridor throbs like an irregular heartbeat. Ignoring the pain, I rush down the steps, both P38s at the ready.

Two more assassins, both doubled over, clutching their heads. I shoot the first one in the torso. Then the head.

The second one tries to shoot wildly. Emphasis on tries. I blow him away.

Nine bullets.

"Kanz?" I call out again, his name a drowned sound inside my head.

No reply. I head down the steps slowly.

Four more of Humayun's assassins barge through the main entrance — right up until I empty both guns into them.

I collect two magazines off the dead hitmen and reload. Sixteen bullets.

Someone groans in all kinds of pain.

Running toward the sound, I find Kanz with a much larger assassin pinned under him. A P38 in hand, Kanz pistol-whips the poor bastard in the mouth again and again with his own gun.

Kanz looks behind him. At me.

He starts shooting, every bit the man from three years ago. I barely even twitch.

Behind me, two more rent-a-hitmans thud to the floor, 9mm holes in their faces.

Nothing happens for a while. My vision blurs again. Things feel off-kilter, making it difficult to focus.

I hand Kanz a couple of P38s and four magazines and take the same for myself. We both head back upstairs and take cover behind the door frames to our rooms — Kanz's to the right, mine to the left. Massaging my ears does little to get the sound back.

"More footsteps outside," Kanz says. "A dozen of them."

Humayun's throwing the kitchen sink at us.

"The fuck did you do this time, Sal?"

"I killed two soldiers. And shot Evergreen."

"You what?"

A large canister clacks on the floor between us. More military equipment. Purple gas wafts into the tiny corridor, stinging our eyes. Assassins creep up on either side of the stairs, a steady stream of 9mms pinning us behind our doors.

I fire blindly, unable to see through the slimy tears. Kanz does the same. Blood trickles out of reopened wounds in my left arm. I ignore it.

Bursts of 9mms chip away at the walls, splinters and plaster flying everywhere. The assassins dash up the last few steps, firing steadily, making sure we stay pinned.

They're closing the distance fast.

I've lost track of bullets. Everything begins to spin as I lean against the wall to steady myself.

Kanz makes his move.

"Kanz?"

P38 in each hand, Kanz dives into the corridor and shoots like no man I've seen before. In the purple smoke, in the muzzle flashes, in the deafening hail of blazing lead, I watch this beautiful, bite-sized Aaanold mow down one poor bastard after another.

By the time Kanz hits the floor, Humayun's assassins are reduced to inert mounds of flesh and bone.

When I help him to his feet, he cries out in pain. Blood spurts from a bullet hole a few inches below his right knee. A new one.

He winces as he puts weight on his leg. My left arm throbs, numb to the touch. My head rings loudly. The gunshot wound in my gut burns for a reason I don't want to know.

"Fuck." Kanz winces. "More footsteps. Counting six of them."

Another canister hisses purple gas throughout the corridor. Two more follow suit.

"I'm out," Kanz grunts, a bloody hand over his knee. "What're we going to do?"

I reload both P38s. Sixteen bullets. "Kill them."

I remind myself of it all. Of Humayun grinning at me. Of the day Mother walked out on Baadal. On me. Of Father's scalding gaze. Of that orange-haired Mullah and his wet lips. Of Evergreen. I remind myself how badly I want to see you, Doua, to tell you what happened that day. And how much I hate this world for making me do the things I've done.

I wait for everything to go red. It does.

As I jump down the stairs, the way the six assassins look up at me — I know this was the last thing they expected. Hell, some part of me can't believe it either.

Something in the air. All or nothing.

A hailstorm of 9mms shreds the six goons before my feet touch the floor. We crash down the steps, the seven of us. The world twists and thumps around me. Shreds of sight, aches of touch. A world that pokes and pierces.

I'm the first one to my feet, both P38s smoking.

Below me, there's an angled, tangled mass of unnatural contortions and steaming bullet holes. No new holes in me. Arms, legs, head — everything hurts but seems to bend the right way, scrapes and bruises notwithstanding.

I check the guns in my hand. Two bullets.

One of the assassins cries out. I shoot him.

One bullet.

My lungs feel like a house on fire.

I step past the abattoir. In the hallway, I feel the floor creak behind me.

Footsteps.

The hair at the back of my neck rises as I duck. A silver line glints near my face, missing me by an inch. My assailant is a pony-tailed chuutya in a navy blue button-up.

Slick Bastard.

I level the P38 at him, but I'm slower than I'd like, my hand numb and slippery with blood.

Knocking the gun out of my hand, he slashes at me again, going for the gut this time. He misses.

"You scared?" Slick Bastard mocks. His forehead glistens with sweat. "I thought you were this big hero."

The P38 glimmering by the wall might as well be across an ocean.

"I heard so much about you, man." He slashes horizontally at my chest. A move I avoid. A move I know well. Stumbling back, I gasp as a wall slams into my spine. "They kept telling me you were the best Humayun had, but you're just a fucking —"

A quick left hand stuns him — and probably hurt me more to throw. A knee to the jaw puts him on his ass. Need to stay on top of him, no matter what.

I slam his wrist to the ground. The knife slips out of his hand. I introduce Slick Bastard's jaw to my right elbow. Again and again.

Even on the ground, he has the edge. He's a relatively well-fed Shiite. Bigger, faster. Had the drop on me too. I'm a starving paleet from the Badlands, caught off guard, recently shot, and defenestrated. Barely a day into lucidity.

It was good while it lasted.

Slick Bastard kicks me off and is on his feet.

His turn to return the favour.

Two big haymakers leave me seeing double, his blows rattling my bones. Bhenchod has been eating his veggies.

There's a loud hum as the power comes back on in Sector 3.. Neon blues, pinks, and purples flood the hallway.

I swing a desperate man's swing and take another punch in the jaw. Ducking under a huge hook that would've torn my head off, I kick him in the balls. Hard. He sinks to the floor.

The knife. It shimmers in the billboard lights.

Scrambling for it, I grab the hilt and slash at him, but he tackles me to the ground. A second later, he wrenches the knife out of my grasp.

Pinned under him, I barely stop his blade from plunging into my right eye. I grab his hand. No matter what, I don't let it move an inch.

Sweat streams over his forehead, dripping into my face and mouth.

I try rolling him off me. He's too heavy, too strong.

My left arm fades. Something pops audibly in my shoulder. The blood makes it impossible to maintain my grip. Can't do much against gravity. Or pure hatred.

The blade starts to inch near my eye.

Doua is standing above us, her face hidden by the shadows.

Bang.

Slick Bastard slumps off me, his legs stretched and twitching. Took it in the spine.

Kanz leans against the wall, P38 in hand.

I breathe harshly, grasping my left shoulder.

"You okay?" Kanz asks, passing me the P38.

Instead of answering, I dig my foot into Slick Bastard's chest. "Is Humayun sending any more hitmen? Answer me and this ends quickly."

"N-no."

I twist my heel deeper. "Is Evergreen here?"

"No!"

I should be relieved. I'm not. "Does Humayun know where Doua is?"

Kanz looks at me, confused.

"No," Slick Bastard cries out, his breath gurgling. "Doua is no longer our priority."

"Why? Hey. Answer me. Where's Doua?"

He's dead.

————

Tearing off part of my shirt, I tie it around Kanz's leg. I've taken the bullet out and dressed the wound as best I could, but already his knee has swollen into a bulging mess. I will have to take him to Blue Haven. To Red. To Jahan.

Frisking Slick Bastard, I find a badly jammed P38. That probably explains why he came at me with a knife. Poor guy never caught a break.

I frisk the other corpses. Most guns are slick with gore. Collecting the halfway decent ones, I bring the lot to my room. Field stripping them, I check for rust and dirt, for blood and scratches, for twisted sights and grit in the triggers. No point taking some busted piece of shit that'll jam on me.

With great difficulty, Kanz hobbles into the room, bottle in hand.

"We can't live here anymore," I point out. I hand him the best P38 of the bunch and two spare magazines. Compensation for destroying his house, his life.

Kanz bites his lip. "Know what you're thinking, Sal. But no."

"I should've stayed away."

He punches me in the shoulder. The left shoulder. Fucking ouch. "Not your fault, okay?"

"I knew they were after me. If I had stayed away —"

"Then I'd be dead. You know that."

"I'll pack my things and leave."

I won't be leaving much behind here. Nothing but this broken man in a lonely place. Twenty years ago, a broken man left me in a lonely place. Father. Time is a spiral.

"Sal?" Kanz holds my arm, stopping me. "Who's Doua?"

———

It's been an hour since all hell broke loose. No more assassins came.

We're in Kanz's room, sitting on his beat-up sofa. It's the only place that doesn't reek of lead, blood, and shit. We've had time to kill. Kanz had many questions. Turns out I had some answers. Got him up to speed on Humayun. On Evergreen. On Doua. Stuck to the barest facts, left out some details. I told him my real name. He found it funny for some reason.

I feel lighter than I have in years.

"Had a strange dream today," Kanz says after a long swig. He's been drinking. A lot.

"About what?" Baadal's empty 1911 rests on the table before us, along with two fully loaded P38s and two spare magazines. My little armoury. My hearing is mostly back, despite the persistent *creee*. "Kanz?"

"Oh? Right." Hardballer in his lap, Kanz stares out into the obsidian night. "I'm sitting cross-legged in this huge grey metal plate that keeps shaking and wobbling, very unsteady. There's another plate, and in it, there's a body covered in a white shawl. Takes a while, but I finally understand that I'm sitting on a huge weigh scale in the middle of nowhere."

"Creepy."

"But I'm not scared. I'm excited. Around the scales, there's this endless lush cornfield with a green lake in the middle. The sky is grey. It's snowing. But it isn't cold. I'm sad when I realize this. I'm sad because it isn't our snow."

"Huh."

"I'm sitting there, really comfortable. Even the clothes I'm wearing — a white shalwar-kameez — it's unbelievably soft. Everything is soft and tranquil, except I'm holding a knife in my right hand. This large, mean-looking black knife. Then I hear this gong — or a gunshot — and the scale I'm on starts tipping lower. The other one keeps tipping higher until I can't see the body. And I — I just —"

I wait for him to continue. He doesn't. "Just what?"

"Can't tell you what it felt like. Like someone dug both hands inside my chest and was rummaging around. I'm sitting there crying, bawling, because I can't see the body anymore. So, I take the knife and I roll my sleeves back and I begin to cut myself."

"Hell on earth."

"But that's the thing — it didn't hurt. Felt like cutting off a crooked nail that's digging into the corner of your finger. Know what I mean? That relief even though the pain is still there?"

"And then?"

"I go on hacking away. Not just flesh but bone too. I cut my left hand off and toss it out of the weigh scale. I look up at the other scale and watch it sink lower. I cut up more of myself and start tossing it away. I'm freaking out, but I soon realize that there's no pain at all. It's just relief. I keep chopping. Forearm, arm, feet, legs, thighs, even my cock and balls."

"How did that feel?"

"More relieving than the others. Once the balls went, and I felt this huge, crooked nail gone from my life, it was ecstasy. I felt nothing there at all. I laughed and whimpered — this massive sense of relief."

What do you say to that?

"In the end, all that's left of me is my head, my right arm, and a triangle of torso. The scales are almost even. But there's a problem now: I'm all chopped up, and I can't turn or move to see a damn thing. I know the body is there, but I can't see it. I try to wriggle toward the edge to see it, but I can barely move."

"And?"

"I woke up. What do you think?"

"I think ..." We live so long running away from death, we can't bring ourselves to imagine it. Maybe it's lying inside a box, unable to move but feeling and hearing everything. Maybe it's hovering above loved ones, waiting for them to see us, hear us. Maybe it's becoming one more snowflake falling over this city, reminding us of all that's lost. "I think it's just a dream."

"Think it showed me what I deserve."

"Kanz ..."

He closes his eyes, his face sunken and pale. "I'm a homosexual. I'm a sinner."

"Or maybe the dream showed you things about yourself that you've never accepted."

He smothers his face in his pale hands. "But the scale. Was clear that I'm —"

"You're what? Unworthy?"

"I've sinned so much in my life. The drinking, the whitener. Jahangir. It's poisoned my soul."

That's religion for you. Century after century of women and men bloated with guilt and self-loathing. A madness we've inherited from the first ape as it gaped into the lonely night and wondered why none of this made any fucking sense.

"You know what's crazy, Kanz? You're more worried about the people you've fucked than the people you've killed."

That gives him pause. "Used to think Jahangir was the worst part of me. Guess it was Humayun all along."

"You loved Jahangir. If anything, that was the best part of you."

Jahangir. Jahan. Red. I've been wondering if I should tell Kanz. And if she would want that. I've been wondering if Kanz even realizes that they loved each other, and that's all that matters.

He rubs the Hardballer against his shirt, blows at it, and studies the slide. Satisfied, he presses it to his lips. "Think this is it."

"What?"

"I'm ready to do it." Kanz brings his face close to mine so that I can see the dappled light in his black eyes. He pulls his lower lip down. There, in the thin flesh, is a discoloured blue line. "I'm dying."

"Sky Sickness?"

"Been going on for a while now." He nods, staring at the bottle in his hands. He smashes it against the wall, the glass shards shivering over the floor like a disarrayed constellation. "One of the doctors at Blue Haven had a look at it. Told me what I already knew. Whatever the Sky Sickness spared, the drinking took care of."

"The liver?"

"The liver."

It's my turn to hold my face. "How long?"

"A few months. Maybe."

"Kanz, I —"

"All praise be for Allah." There's a smile on his lips. "Everything I was, everything I did, everything I could've been. I want to be at peace with it all."

"What's stopping you?" I'm asking myself as much as I'm asking him.

"Can't fix it all. But I can make sure the worst part of me doesn't live on, right?" He looks at me like he's waiting for me to figure it out.

I finally do. "Humayun."

"Isn't a better time to hit him than now. He's lost so many people already. But it all depends on you." Kanz thumps my shoulder. The left one. Again. "Is this what you want?"

"What I want." Ah, that unsung poem, that lost chapter in my life's story. That dream I'll inevitably wake up from. "I want to help you find peace."

———

"You fat madarchod!"

Everyone is staring at me and Humayun. I'm guessing it's because his collar is in my left hand. And because my Walther P38 is cocked under all three of his chins.

He smirks. "Didn't recognize you."

The absence of my long hair and beard. It's the only reason I wasn't shot to pieces at the door.

"You sent your goons to my house!" I yell in his face. "You destroyed my home."

The bhosdi-ka just smiles. "Yeah, I did."

A dozen waiters eye me with murderous intent. Three of them lurk by the kitchen, P38s sticking out of their sweaty shalwars. Another three appear a few paces to my left, weaving through the full tables where the patrons sit, frozen mid-bite.

One more waiter approaches me from the left. Some narrow-chinned, mousy creature I loathe instantly.

Four more stand to my right, watching my every movement.

Back at the entrance, I spot a waiter with a double-barreled 12-gauge.

Hell on earth.

"You're a liability," Humayun snarls at me. "I offered chances. You squandered them. Every fucking time."

"Chances?" I peek at Mousy Bastard, who's snuck forward to my left. "You gave me chances?"

Mousy Bastard shifts his weight, his right hand by his side.

Humayun grins. "You die tonight."

Bang.

Mousy Bastard takes a 9mm low in the gut.

It's here: the point of no return. A divine law broken. All or nothing.

No one moves.

A moment later, the spell breaks. Havoc reigns. The patrons — Sunnis, Shiites, kafirs, paleets — all scream and run out into the night, an all-too-animal instinct for self-preservation uniting them.

"Kill the bastard!" Humayun shouts, trying to duck behind the counter. I don't let him. Pulling him over the table, I use his fat ass as the world's largest human shield.

Hammers and safeties click. Tunnel vision takes over. Everything becomes clear and hazy at once.

It starts.

The gunshots seem constant, endless.

The three on my left drop instantly. Still holding on to

Humayun, I also drop the three by the kitchen who couldn't possibly risk shooting their boss.

The remaining patrons scream and scramble in all directions, jostling and shoving. Humayun breaks free from my grip and slinks behind the counter. I draw the other P38 in my left hand, all too unfamiliar.

The four bastards to my right start shooting. As I duck, a patron rushing past me collapses instantly.

Low against the ground, I dart behind the nearest table, past the bodies as they fall. Firing blindly, I flip the table over and use it as cover.

The 12-gauge blasts the table against my back, splinters and chunks of wood flying.

I've got no idea how many bullets I have.

Through the flailing limbs and crying faces, I spot the four bastards again. They're hiding behind tables too, scanning the crowd.

The shoulder, the reopened wounds — I can't properly level my left arm. I shoot anyway, fatally injuring the polished wood protecting them.

Click. Click. Click.

Humayun gets to his feet behind the counter, as smug as a toad in a cloud of flies.

"He's all out! Shoot him down."

I reload. Sixteen bullets.

"Cover!" I hear someone shout to my right. Two assassins.

Need to take them out. Fast.

I try to get a shot off, but the 12-gauge blows away another huge chunk of the table where my head was a split second ago. Table won't hold out forever. Not against this much artillery.

The 12-gauge — he's fired twice already. He's fresh out.

Feinting right, I pop out from the left, my P38 spitting fire and death.

The two bastards rushing me take a couple of 9mms in their chests and smack into the ground. The P38 roars as a 9mm implodes each of their heads.

Ten bullets.

I count my targets: three more chuuts left, including the guy with the 12-gauge. Plus Humayun.

The diner is mostly empty. Bodies and spilled food and beverages litter the area between the upturned tables. A few patrons cower under tables, pressing themselves to the floor.

Peeking over the table, I spot the bastard with the 12-gauge. He spots me. I get a few shots off before the 12-gauge blows a spray of splinters and debris into my eyes.

Wiping the tears that come instantly, I fire in his general direction with the left P38. I lose track of the bullets again and duck for cover.

A salvo of 9mms makes the table tremble against my back.

The 12-gauge blasts another chunk of wood away. He's fired twice again.

Snapping out from cover, splinters and tears be damned, I blast four holes in his chest and belly. Four holes that were meant for his head.

Click. I'm out again.

I reload the last set of magazines. Sixteen bullets.

The two remaining waiters open fire.

Shooting with both hands, I get one of them right in the torso. The other dives behind a table.

I do the same and check both P38s.

Not good.

Eight bullets. Three in the left P38; five in the right.

It's just us three now. Me, Humayun, and the bhenchod behind the table.

Bhenchod-behind-the-table peeks out from his cover.

Low on the ground, I shoot at the table shielding him. Once, twice, thrice.

Come on, panic, you piece of shit.

He does.

Jutting out from cover, his face twisted in fear, he trains his gun on me — and earns two 9mm punctures in his head.

Three bullets.

Shot or not, blurred vision or not, I stand up.

Humayun.

The way he looks at me, I know he's never been afraid before. "Avaan, just listen. We can talk."

"I'm done talking."

Grabbing him by the collar, I wind my fist back and throw it harder than I've thrown in my life. The feeling of my knuckle crunching into his nose? I'll cherish it forever.

He drops like a wad of putty, clutching his bloodied mouth and nose. Snivelling, he wriggles over the spilled booze and glass and plates and bullet shells toward a lone P38. He grabs hold and aims.

I don't flinch.

Click. Click. Click. Stubborn, quick trigger pulls; his denial and hubris crash into reality.

Slumping into the ground, he watches me as I drag a chair over to him.

My P38 pointed at Humayun's face, I lean back in the chair and exhale fully for the first time since all the shooting started.

For a moment, life is good.

The adrenaline subsides. I feel mangled. My lungs feel lined with crushed glass. Tears and dust cloud my vision. My left arm thumps sporadically, molten lava coursing through it.

I turn to the door, half-expecting Red to be standing there with a bag full of medicine.

She isn't.

I cock the hammer of the P38. "Doua. Start talking."

"I kn-know nothing. I swear it." He's on the ground, a blood-ied, beaten man. "She's a ghost."

"One of your goons squealed. Said Doua isn't your priority anymore. Why?"

Humayun tries to plug his bloodied nose. "Evergreen's gone mad. Wants Yaqzan badly."

"What do you know about Yaqzan, Humayun? Tell me, and I promise I won't kill you."

He shakes his head. "There's just rumuors. Connection with you. Connection with Ash."

"Ash? I've heard that name." From Red.

"She's his right hand. A fortune teller."

"What does she look like?"

"That's the problem." He shakes his head, breathing unevenly. "Names don't match. Descriptions don't match. Some say girl. A tea seller. Wears red sunglasses." He runs his finger diagonally across his face. "Others say woman. Ugly and scarred. Like some *dayan*."

I saw her: the woman with the scars. The one who gave Inayah that bomb. "Where can I find her?"

"In New Market. By the river. But it's pointless." He shakes his head slowly, a sullen child. "It doesn't matter. Evergreen's gone mad. You shot him. You maimed him. He's starting it."

"Starting what?"

There's true horror in his eyes. "Operation Searchlight III."

No Pakistani can forget those words. No Pakistani should. Pakistan didn't just lose East Pakistan in Operation Searchlight of 1971. It lost a piece of its soul. It lost another piece of its soul in Operation Searchlight II of 2043.

"He'll burn everything. The entire Badlands." He looks at me with true horror. "You did this. It's your fault."

"When is it happening?" I dig my P38 into his chins. "Don't tell me you don't know."

"I don't know. I swear it."

I believe him. Nothing appeals to a man's better nature like a gun pointed in his face.

P38 trained on him, I head over to the back room behind the counter and find the two legendary briefcases. The one with the hundred million rupees. And the golden Colt Python with a single .357 loaded.

"No, you can't," Humayun sniffles from the floor. "It's all mine."

Huh. For the first time in all that's happened, I realize the fat bastard never paid me for the Sector 1 hit. Or Rosa and Inayah.

I take the half-empty tray of dimpled hollow-points and load two magazines. Fourteen bullets. Taking out Baadal's .45, I pop one magazine in and rack the slide twice, catching the hollow-point that pops out. Thirteen bullets.

"You wouldn't dare," Humayun growls as I walk back to him, the Python in hand. "I'm fucking Humayun."

"Relax. I promised I'm not going to kill you, remember?"

I whistle at the entrance — or try to, blowing raspberries instead. Humayun shrugs in confusion. I try again, finger and thumb twisting my tongue. I whistle.

The Ashraf-ul-Makhlooqat sign jangles.

Kanz limps into the bar and stands next to me.

I hand him the Python. He marvels at it like any sane person should and then cocks the hammer back.

The look on Humayun's face is of a man meeting his maker a thousand years too soon. He holds up his hands. "Listen, Kanz, I —"

"Hasta la vista. Baby." Kanz shoots him dead.

———

At the counter, I pick up the last bottle left on the shelf. It's Huma-yun's new lassi. Kanz lines up two glasses before me as I begin pouring, but my hands are so bloody that the bottle slips and the lassi spills.

We laugh. It gushes out of us as our cackles ring in the diner.

He nods. "Thanks for —"

"Forget it. We're even now."

He surveys the diner. "Think there's more of his hitmen?"

"Yup. But without him, they're nothing. It's all over now."

He grins at me. "Ever thought it'd be us, Avaan? Popping the fat bastard himself?"

"You did that. This is your legacy, Kanz. Always will be."

"All praise be for Allah." Kanz, relapsing into an old madness, glances at the door. I know what he's hoping against hope for. But he doesn't find Red there. His eyes shimmer as they did back in the house. "Would be too good an ending, I suppose."

He takes out the Hardballer from his coat and passes it to me.

"You sure?" I load it with the one .45 ACP hollow-point I'd taken out earlier. No amount of chewing my lip or inhaling stops my breath from shaking. "Isn't this *haram*?"

He smiles sadly. "So is killing and drinking."

I love you, you dumb son of a bitch. "Kanz, I —"

"I know." Turning around, he faces the direction Muslims believe Mecca is in. His back to me, his shoulders bowed, he cups his hands before him and whispers a prayer to himself. Surah Al-Baqarah's last verses. "And if one of you entrusts another, then let him who is entrusted discharge his trust faithfully and let him fear Allah, his Lord." He continues reciting softly, his voice faint. "To Allah belongs whatever is in the heavens and whatever is in the earth. Whether you show what is within yourselves or conceal it, Allah will bring you to account for it."

Kanz's voice fails him.

Standing behind him, I recite the remaining words. "Allah does not burden a soul more than it can bear."

Kanz rediscovers his voice and joins me. "Pardon us and forgive us and have mercy upon us."

I leave out the last part, the one that asks for Allah's aid against disbelievers. "Ameen."

I press the Hardballer to the back of his head and pray to whatever is pure and holy in this world to bless me with the same dream as Kanz.

"Ameen," he whispers, soft and low.

Bang. The big full stop, just as the sign jangles.

She gasps.

Hands covering her mouth, Red can only gape in horror at the gun in my hand. A lone .45 ACP shell tings on the floor between us, the sound deafening for a reason I can never explain.

"It's too late," I whisper to myself or to her or maybe to no one. "It's all too goddamn late."

Episode 18: Chandramukhi

Jahan

August 11, 2083

"What did you do, Sal?"

I know this is the question I should ask. I should scream and howl in sorrow, beat my chest, tear at my hair. But I don't. Somehow, even before I opened the door to Humayun's Diner, I knew my Kanz was gone. I knew what I was doing was claiming the body of a man who had died years before.

"Red?" He watches me with his large golden eyes as I step over the bodies littered on the floor. All of them dead, all of them with the agony of their last moments frozen on their faces.

I stare at the corpse face down at his feet. "Is that him?"

Sal nods.

My voice is like a waning echo. "Did you …?"

Sal nods again. Smoke rises from the huge silver gun in his hand. The way it did three years ago, the night I shot Kanz so that he wouldn't follow me. So that he got a taste of what he did to other people. So that his blood money — our blood money — could go to Blue Haven.

Kneeling next to his body, I take off my dupatta and place it over what is left of my Kanz. I brush his soft, curly hair. Red stains cover my fingers.

I look up at Sal. "Did he suffer?"

Sal shakes his head. The whites of his eyes are pink at the edges.

"What are you going to do now?"

"Burn this place to the ground."

"What about Kanz?"

"We bury him."

"No, no. My Kanz was already dead." I take the gun out of his hand. "This is the only part of him that's left to bury."

Sal sets fire to the diner, leaving behind what's left of Kanz among the other bodies that will soon become one with the snow.

August 12, 2083

Morning appears, metallic cracks of light on the horizon.

Far, far away, his back to us, a grey-haired man stands before two graves. Even at this distance, the way his head hangs low and his shoulders stoop, I feel his sorrow. I wonder who he buried here and how long ago. I wonder how many times he's stood over those graves knowing there was nothing left for him in this city. I wonder why, now that Kanz is laid to rest, I still feel I am a hollow chasm where everything echoes.

Opposite me, leaning against the shovel, Sal stares at the small, square patch of dirt where we buried Kanz's gun. I pray in silence, but my eyes are drawn to the motionless old man in the distance. Sal feels just as motionless.

"Are you going to say something, R— Jahan?" he asks. It still takes an effort for him to say my real name. He prefers *Red*. There's something simplistic and casual about *Red* that I prefer too. Maybe because I've never had a nickname I liked.

"I don't know." I watch the grey-haired man place something on both graves. "You?"

"I don't know."

We pass the graveyard entrance, where a family of Christians marches behind a casket. Next to the entrance, several rickshaws honk at anyone who comes out. I look behind me one last time to see the old man still standing before the two graves, his hands cupped before him as he prays.

———

"Is your ride here, Jahan?" His voice is so much softer than you'd expect when you see him. Even back in Blue Haven, when he first spoke, I was surprised at how low and raspy his voice was. As if all his life he's been whispering with ghosts or talking to himself.

"Do you see a pink rickshaw?"

"Nope."

"Then no." We settle down on one of the cool cement benches. Those first few seconds when you place your bum on it are always the hardest. Then you just get used to it. Much like anything else. As we sit, his muscular thigh grazes against me. "What now? What do you want, Sal?"

His laugh is dry. "Why are you asking me that?"

"Here." Holding his hand in mine, I drop a set of keys in his palm. "Consider this not asking then."

"What's this?"

"You probably need a place to hang low, right? I've left most things as they were. Even your old clothes."

"What about you?"

I pull out the flyer I've kept with me. "Have you seen these?"

"You didn't write me a poem, did you?"

"Read it."

He unfolds the flyer and reads, his thin brows furrowed, his jaw clenched. "August fourteenth? That's a couple of days away."

"Sure."

"You're just going to leave? And go where?"

"Anywhere," I say. "There's nothing for me here, Sal. There never has been anything for people like me. Not before Allah burned the sky away. Not after."

"Red," he starts, then pauses. "Jahan, you can't go out in the world all on your own."

"Come with me then." I pat his thigh gently. "Why don't you come with me?"

If his eyes could speak, they'd talk about how much he wants to but can't. They'd speak of another life, of another world where our story could happen. If his eyes could speak, they'd whisper about another woman and how much he wishes he'd met me before her.

"See?" I smile, staring off into the horizon where all my pigeons have gone and left me behind. "There's nothing for me here."

Episode 19: What I Want

Avaan

August 12, 2083

The early morning hours stain the sky in dark blues. The freezing air scrapes against my cropped hair and jaw like a dull blade. I swaddle myself in a new shawl Red gave me. It's her parting gift. I won't see her again. On any other day, I'd be sad. I'd beg her to stay. But not today. Today, I can't think of anything else. I'm closer to finding Doua than I've been in three years. Closer to telling her what happened that day.

I'm getting ahead of myself.

New Market merchants arrange their paltry food stalls for the day. Their wooden carts jammed together, they shout their wares at me, herding me toward the cups of *haleem* and trays of samosas. Fishermen wave their rank catch of the day in my face; water boys with large pots mob me. A little girl brushes past me, and I twist her arm to snatch a roll of my rupees out of her hand. Etched on a forgotten wall to my right, a telltale message and handprint catch my attention.

Death to Avaan Maya. Death to all traitors.

I feel the .45's cold steel against my back. Two magazines. Thirteen bullets.

Finding a relatively emptier spot in this sea of poor bastards,

I breathe in deeply. I've been walking for hours. A tree of pain spreads its roots through my left side and down my leg. Every few steps, a maddening, numbing tremor shoots down my left arm. The world still wobbles, trembling at the edges of my vision.

"Oy, *chai waala*," I call out to a young boy pouring tea in a *dhaba*. It's a small, tented courtyard with three *charpaai* lined by the walls where women and men drink tea in silence. "How many tea shops are here?"

"Many, sahib. But this is the best one in Old Pakistan. Promise."

"I'm looking for a particular one," I say, pulling the brown shawl over my face. "It's owned by Ash. Do you know where it is?"

Some of the patrons get up and walk past me quickly.

The boy holds up his hands before him, palms touching. "I'm just a tea boy, sahib. I don't want any trouble."

Right.

The same thing happens at the next few shops I try. After being told to fuck off in a myriad of ways, I'm told to follow a wide street that leads to the river. Apparently, Ash's tea shop can't be missed from there.

Half an hour later, I'm at the pearly shores.

The river sparkles silver under the ink-stained sky, almost motionless as it glides along the white sand. A steamy cloud rises in the distance where the river spills into the Misty Wasteland, where no one goes and no one returns.

Two Hindu sisters sell bottles of filtered river water. I buy one and rest on the sand to soothe my cramped legs. The joints in my back and knees, in my ankles and hips, pop in sequence. The bombs, bullets, blades, and blows from the past few days are catching up to me.

The water cools my throat, soothes me.

A Christian girl fills a large earthen pot by the shore, coils a red dupatta over her head, and balances the container on it before walking away. A Sunni woman says *bismillah* before drinking a handful from her water pot. Farther down, close by the waterfall, a *paleet* family scatters ashes in colourful paper boats. The way we scattered Eksha's ashes. The way I scattered Baadal's ashes. The way I couldn't with Kanz's ashes.

"You're looking to buy tea, yes?" A young girl in an orange kurta and jeans stands to my right. Circular red sunglasses shield her eyes. The kurta stretches over her knobby shoulders and elbows. She sits next to me, closer than I care for. A smile wrinkles out of her surgical mask and twists around her nose and cheeks. "Who are you?"

"Martin Frost. Who are you, kid?"

"My name is Ash." She adjusts the many bracelets around her wrists. The scrapes and scratches over her sinewy forearms tell me, categorically, that she's not to be taken lightly. "What's your name?"

"Salaba."

"Where are you from?"

"Old Pakistan."

"I mean which sector."

"Old Pakistan."

"What do you want, Salaba from Old Pakistan?"

"I'm looking to buy tea."

"But what do you want? Is it love, yes? Redemption?"

I deserve neither. "I'm looking for someone from my past."

"Follow me."

Standing up, I spot several kids eyeballing us from the street corners or between groups of people. I pat the .45. Two magazines. Thirteen bullets.

I follow her into the busier part of New Market. Mostly young kids wherever I look, all of them glowering at me as they follow.

"Where are you taking me, Ash?" I ask, hand on the .45.

Her walk has no discernable movement in her shoulders and

arms. "To the woman you're looking for."

"I didn't say it was a woman."

"You didn't have to."

We stop before a cozy-looking dhaba. Large green-eyed flies buzz around as we enter. Kafir girls and boys pour tea for a menagerie of women and men from all sectors. Snug in a wooden chair, a white cat curls around itself in a ball, sleeping the world away.

"Why are we here, Ash?"

"Fortune telling." She removes her mask with the most minimal of movement. Without the mask, she's still impervious. "You may have cheated death more than once, Salaba from Old Pakistan, but even you cannot defy what's written."

I smirk. "Written?"

She shakes her head. "What is your name?"

Oh, for the love of ... "Salaba. How many times do I have to tell you?"

"In all the years I've known her, Doua has never mentioned anyone called Salaba."

"You know Doua? Who are you?"

"I am someone who is having trouble believing you."

"Look, it's complicated."

"I'm sure it is. I understand that you have come from far, but how can I possibly —?"

"Three teaspoons of sugar," I blurt out.

Ash tilts her head ever so slightly.

I continue. "Doua takes three teaspoons of sugar with her tea. And she holds the cup with both hands. Because her hands are always cold. Even if she wears gloves, even if you rub them in your hands. Her little hands are always cold."

A meditative hum hangs in the air as the kafir girls and boys talk among themselves. A sad smile spreads on Ash's lips. Seeing it, I know without a shadow of a doubt that she knows Doua.

Ash adjusts her shades. "Yaqzan will be here soon. But I need to read your fortune first."

"What does Yaqzan want with me?"

She ignores my question. "Do you know what you have in common with these people, yes?"

"That you're wasting their time too?"

"They're blind women and men trying to outrun the past by crawling into the future. All Pakistanis are like you. Always remembering the past. Except they'll end up where they started. Do you know why?"

"Why?"

"Because one of their eyes sees the past, and the other sees the future."

"I need to see Doua."

"Tell me, which one of your eyes seeks Doua?"

"What?"

"The right one, yes? You look to the future only because you're terrified of the past. Isn't that right? And more importantly, why?"

"Because I'm not a monster!"

Ash pours rich golden-brown tea into a plain ceramic cup. She's no longer smiling.

"Drink this with your left hand," she instructs, holding the cup close to her chest. The beads and bracelets circling her left wrist barely conceal two vertical, reddish scars.

"What's in the tea, Ash?"

"You'll find out."

I'm nailed to the ground. Invisible hands hold me in place for the sacrificial blade I can't see but can hear being sharpened. "How can I trust you?"

"If that's your concern, you wouldn't have come this far, yes?"

Thirteen bullets. "I could force you to talk. I don't want to.

But I could."

She nods slowly. "But you won't. Despite your penchant for hurting innocent women and children."

"I never hurt anyone by choice."

"But you did hurt them."

"Most men I killed were innocent too."

She has no response.

"I didn't have a choice, kid," I point out.

"How much choice can there be if I can tell your future with a cup of tea, yes?" She holds the steaming cup before me. "You followed me here when you knew you shouldn't have. You also know you shouldn't drink this tea. So, what will you do?"

Choices.

I think of Baadal's 1911 tucked at the back of my jeans. The Big Heat. Every time I chose to fire it, every time I blew away some poor bastard dumb enough to cross my path, I was making another circle around the drain. The more I pulled the trigger to stay alive, the faster I spun around this drain I've been circling for three years.

I take the cup.

"The saucer as well, Salaba from Old Pakistan."

I take the cup and the saucer.

"Sip slowly," she cautions. "After you finish, cover the cup with the saucer. Using your left hand. And don't peek inside your cup. It's a bad omen."

"Your name isn't Ash, is it?"

"Your name isn't Salaba, yes?"

"Where's the real Ash? Where's the woman with the scars?"

Given the lack of her body language and the red sunglasses, I've been observing her lips. The moment I mention the woman with the scars, the corner of Ash's lips twitch.

"Drink the tea. To the last drop."

I take a sip. And then another. The tea is silky and sweet, with a slightly bitter aftertaste. It's like no tea I've drunk before. I nearly ask for seconds.

Ash holds a chair forward for me. I sit.

"Good." Placing her hands over mine tightly, she helps me cover the cup using the saucer and flips it over. "Take three deep breaths. Focus on what you're searching for, Martin Frost."

Black eyes bubbling with something sneaky, something innocent. Small, cool hands brushing her collarbone, her ear, her neck. A sad smile. A ghost watching me from behind a mirror. A lady in white standing alone amidst the wreckage of my making. The one person who needs to hear my story, my side of things, so I can make sense of why I've become who — what — I am.

"This fortune will foretell only the next forty days." She's stalling, but I have no idea what for. She seems to have more answers than I have questions. She frowns at my cup instantly. "There are several drops of tea still left in the cup." After another few seconds of humming, she leans back and takes off her shades. Her grey-eyed stare is direct and emotionless, a bolt-action rifle. "I see a cat."

"That's good."

"No. Cats are treacherous little devils."

"I like cats."

The pain — the constant pain I've been in since I woke up in Red's room — is gone. I don't register it anymore. Numbness slithers from the pit of my stomach into my legs, an intravenous stream of ice that chills me.

"Cats are deceivers. You can't trust something that cheats death eight times." She frowns. Her voice sounds faint. "There are mostly incomprehensible shapes in your cup. Whatever shapes I do recognize — closed bags, clocks — are all bad omens. You have lived a difficult life, Salaba from Old Pakistan. You seek to escape your past, but in the end, there's nothing but death for you."

Murky darkness frames the whole world as I sink into the chair. "I already died once, Miss Whatever-the-fuck-your-name-is."

"I know." That half grin again. "When you wake up, you'll find only what you deserve."

Her voice echoes inside my head. I wince, pressing my fingers to my temples. As my head spins, I realize there's no one else in the shop.

"Where's Doua?" I ask.

Ash shushes me. Fragments of her face swim before me in doubles as I enter a world of shadows — shadows that bleed into me and I into them.

———

Doua.

There's a rich sweetness in the air, with just a strain of bitterness. It's what I'd smell every morning as I watched you drink tea by the bed, Doua. Always with a cup of tea in both hands, no matter how hot it was. You'd be so cranky if you didn't get your tea first thing in the morning.

Bright yellow light pierces my skull. First as a dot, then a line, and finally, painfully, it widens into a glorious golden morning. What a morning should look like.

I blink several times, trying to acclimatize myself to the richness of colour around me. Despite the pain, I feel a smile on my lips when I see her standing next to me, teacup in hand.

"Finally," Doua says, one arm crossed over her belly. Dressed in a black saree, she shields me from the intense sun. The light casts a halo around her. She's even more beautiful to me. I hate us both for who we've become. "I thought you were going to sleep forever."

"I can't —"

"You cannot move, right?"

I try to budge, try to peel myself off the tough mattress.

"Relax." She holds my hand, squeezing it lightly. "The drugs are still in your system. Give it time."

I inhale as much of the sweet tea scent as I can. There are so many questions bouncing around in my head, so many things I want to say.

"Where are we?" I ask. About the most unimportant question at this moment.

Doua takes a sip of her tea, chuckling, the faint acne scars scrunching her right cheek. She walks over to the luminous window and opens it fully. Kids laugh outside, their voices mingling with the gentle susurrus of the water.

"The river?" I ask.

"Yes. You always wanted that, remember? A home by the river."

"I want to see it."

"You will. Just as soon as you can move again." .

I'm blind in this moment of joy. "Describe it to me."

"It is —" she starts, but something makes her pause. "There are these colourful boats on the water. Just like we did for Eksha. How we went to the river and released the paper boats onto the water. All those bright colours. Do you remember?"

"The boats were full of her ashes."

"I choose to remember the paper boats. Not her ashes in them. Not what those monsters did to my little Eksha. To us all."

"Do you think she's at peace, Doua?"

She doesn't say anything as she looks outside, leaning over the windowsill. The dimples on her lower back are prominent, her skin a smooth, soft brown. Past her, the light is too bright for me to see much. My eyes return to her lower back, and I remember how her skin used to feel under my fingers. How I'd kiss those dimples.

I try to get off the mattress, but nothing happens. "Why are you with Yaqzan, Doua? Who is he? What does he want from me?"

She doesn't answer.

"Where were you?" I demand. "Where have you been? Three years, Doua. It's been three fucking years. I've looked everywhere for you." My voice breaks. I fight the tears.

"I know. I am so sorry. But I must do something."

"What? Tell me."

"Do you want tea?"

"What? No. Fuck tea."

"Here. I think the tea will make you feel better." She tilts the cup against my lips, and even though I want to spit it all out, even though I want to scream at the top of my lungs about why she isn't answering my questions, I don't. Because it does make me feel better.

I exhale slowly, calming myself.

"Better?" she inquires, wiping the drops away from my lips. Her touch — I hate how unfamiliar it feels. "You are pouting like a child." She squishes my mouth upward. "Stop being so impatient. I told you the drugs will take a while."

"What did she drug me for?"

"Ash was being cautious." She stands by the window again. The aureate light is still too much for my eyes, but I can make out patches of a crystal-blue sky. "She had no idea who you are. You were armed."

Who I am. Looking up at Doua, seeing her smile at me, who I am is a blemish over this entire moment. A rot at the heart of everything that's become my life.

She slips into bed with me, resting her cheek against my chest. I try to move my arms to embrace her, but nothing happens.

"Look." Doua uses her thumb to point behind her. "Not a single puff of snow. It is finally a clear, sunlit day in Old Pakistan, and here you are still miserable."

The song-like whispers of the river wash into the room. I hear no gunshots, no military jeeps, no screams, no *adhan*, no sirens, no bells. The sun is shining, and the sky is so blue it makes me want to cry.

There's no snow.

She runs a finger across my chest, across the horizontal scar. "Are you thinking about our first morning together?"

"Yeah."

She plants gentle kisses on the scar. "Do you think you deserve forgiveness for what you did to us? For what you did to Baadal?"

Something clutches my heart and squeezes. "Doua, please listen to —"

"When did you become a monster, my love?"

There's another voice in the room. Vaguely familiar. "Avaan?"

The light from outside grows brighter and brighter. Doua begins to fade away, no longer soft, no longer smiling. I try to stare at her face, to re-brand my eyes with every inch of her, but the blinding light snatches her away from me.

"Wake up, Avaan."

Something burns against my wrists and ankles.

"Doua?" She's gone. "Doua!"

————

Waking up feels like I've opened the door to another dream. After several blinks, the only thing I'm certain of is that I'm in a room with a barred window. The sky is a dull silver haze, the snow falling everywhere, heavier than before.

After a minute or two, I realize that I'm still in the dhaba. And that my arms and legs are tied to a chair. A dark shape draws the yellow-brown curtains together, leaving a square of whitish haze in the wall. Everything else is dark.

Someone flips the light on. An orange bulb whirs and groans a few inches above me. A few shadowy shapes stand at the circular edge of the light. It's a bunch of children. One of them steps forward, older than the rest.

Ash.

She takes off her red shades and presses down on my bound forearms, her face close to mine. Though drowsy, I notice the white rag tied around her right arm.

"You met Doua in your dreams, yes?"

"Where is she?"

Ash reaches into her pocket and places something inside my hand. An eye patch. I toss it to the floor.

"You're working for Evergreen, yes?" she inquires.

"Where's Doua?"

"Answer my question, Martin Frost."

"Answer mine."

She clocks me in the jaw. One of her many bracelets snaps on impact, the brown beads clattering across the floor. The little shit is stronger than I thought.

Jaw clenched, Ash gets in my face. "I saw you working with Evergreen. When you attacked Rosa and Inayah."

"Then you must've seen me let Inayah go. And the part where I pointed a gun to Evergreen's head."

She stands upright, arms crossed. "I saw you not shoot him when you had the chance."

"What about the part where he beat the shit out of me?" Something tells me to keep my mouth shut. I ignore it. "You got any other questions, kid? Because I've got many of my own."

"Okay." Ash pulls out a switchblade, the three-inch blade shining out of its ivory handle. She taps her finger against the tip of the blade. "Ask."

"If you're Ash, who's the woman with the scars?"

"That is also Ash. We're both Ash."

Straining against the bonds, I'm helpless. "Who the fuck are you?"

The bulb flickers. Her gun-metal eyes train on me like a firing squad. "Here I thought you could never forget me, bhaiyya."

I'm not looking at her anymore. It's the dark shapes in the dim light that have taken my attention. A black stain on everything, some inkblot test revealing the full spectrum of my madness. I see a teary-eyed Jahan getting into the pink rickshaw without looking back. I see Kanz dead at my feet. I see Inayah holding up the bomb. I see the female soldier as I choke the life out of her. I see Maseeh and the smoking gun in my hand. I see myself with the .45 jammed under my chin, praying for that dark courage. I see Baadal dead on the ground as the soldiers pin me against the floor and tape my hands behind my back. I see Doua, her back turned to me, sleeping on the mattress that last day at the library-shelter. Ground Zero. I see myself standing beside her, taking in the sight of her, memorizing every inch of her because I knew — some part of me knew — that this would be the last time I saw her. More than anything else, I see Eksha's gnarled hand, held over me like some divine indictment.

When I look at Ash, when I stare into those grey eyes, I know exactly where I've seen her before. "Asha."

"My name is Ash."

"I thought you — how? We looked everywhere for you."

"We? Really?"

"For weeks and months. We didn't rest until …" I try to stand. The ropes dig deeper into my wrists and ankles.

"I don't believe you. Not after what you did to Baadal-bhaiyya. To Doua-didi. To Eksha." Asha steps back. Back into the darkness that seems to hold her shoulders for support. "They killed her, bhaiyya."

"I'm so sorry."

She stares into my face. "You are, yes?"

"That pain you're feeling? That aimless rage? I know what it's like to lose someone you love."

"Are you telling me that you love anyone besides yourself? Who is it? Is it Jahan, yes?"

"Leave her out of this," I snap. "She's innocent."

"Eksha was innocent!" she screams, her voice a spear. "Do you think her innocence mattered when they cut her open, yes? When they dumped her in a garbage ditch?"

"Asha —"

"Ash." Her knife glimmers in the darkness. A thin, acidic cut opens across my cheek. The kids behind her whistle and hoot in unison. "My name is Ash."

"I tried so hard —"

She cuts me off. "Doua-didi told me that you barely left the library-shelter after Eksha's death."

"It wasn't like that. Losing Eksha was like —"

"Don't pretend that you cared about her!" she shouts. "Or me. Or anyone. You — the man who fed his own brother to the army."

"That's not what happened."

"Then why were you the only one who walked out that day, yes?"

"I would never —"

"Doua-didi saw it. She told me everything." Still holding the switchblade, she stands over me. "She saw what happened that day between you and Baadal-bhaiyya. The fight you two had, yes? She saw it all."

"No." I need to find Doua. I need to explain my side. "Where's Doua? Please tell me."

"Why? You want to apologize for what you did to her, yes?"

"What are you talking about?"

She kicks me, knocking me over. My back against the cold floor, my arms and legs still tied, I stare up at the swaying orange bulb. My heart flutters inside my chest.

"You want to hand her over to Evergreen, yes?" Ash towers over me.

"No!"

"Lies. More lies." She kicks me in the side. In the gunshot wound. "Why are you looking for Doua-didi? To hand her over to Evergreen? To finish what you started? To mutilate her some more, yes?"

"Mutilate her?" I can't think straight. "What are you —?"

She glares at me. It's not just her. It's all the children behind her. They loathe me.

"What?" I twist around on the floor, straining against the ropes. "What?"

"You still don't get it, yes?" Ash reaches down and squeezes my face. Like she's trying to crush my head. "Doua is the other Ash, you fucking monster."

———

Time is a spiral.

Whether it's Mother or Asha-Eksha, whether it's Kanz or Baadal, whether it's Red or Doua, everyone in my life is ensnared in the same story, bound in the stanzas of the same poem. From the moment I first touched them, I'd already begun to lose them, second by second, like sandcastles in a tide. All I can do is watch as they slip through my fingers.

———

"No." It's all I can say. I remember the woman sleeping on the mattress with her back to me. The last time I saw her. Ground Zero. I remember the blind, scarred woman who couldn't walk down the steps without help. "That's not Doua."

"It is." She kneels next to me, her face shining with sweat. Her voice is low as she speaks into my ear. "That's what she looks like now. Because you tipped off the army."

"No."

"Admit it."

"I didn't."

"You let them desecrate our home. You let them desecrate Doua-didi."

"I have no idea what —"

She stuffs my mouth with a ball of cloth. "Let me give you an idea then."

There's a glint of silver in the orange-tinged darkness. Everything happens in a single moment. A white-hot moment of piercing, bone-scraping anguish as Ash sinks her switchblade into my right eye.

Everything becomes black. Then silver and white.

I scream, but manage only a muffled gasp.

Everything is too loud, too staticky. I squeeze my eyes shut. Nothing happens. Nothing but the brightening light that bleeds off and scatters in odd lines and oblong patches.

In the electric darkness, Ash's voice echoes from all directions. "That's what you did to her, Avaan. Just half of it."

Episode 20: A Starless Night Sky

Doua

November 10, 2079

"What is the girl's name, madam?" the soldier asked me, sneaking a peek at my breasts now and then. He hitched his mask over his nose and tossed a handful of roasted *chana* in his mouth.

"They are twin sisters." I folded my arms. "They are turning fourteen next month."

I was repeating the story for the third time now. This time at the Sector 3 Precinct, because Asha-Eksha were Hindu girls, and their case fell under the Sector 3 Precinct. I had come here first, six hours earlier, but had been informed that since I was from the Badlands, Asha-Eksha's case fell under the Badlands Precinct's jurisdiction. Round and round I went.

"Are you their mother, madam?"

The way he attached *madam* to the end of his questions felt like contempt. Madam. Mad. Dumb. His glistening, rectangular moustache twitched every time he said it.

"No." I scowled, mirroring his contempt.

"Are you a relative?" He scratched his cheek, which was sprayed with blackheads. His gaze dropped to my breasts again. "Where are the parents, madam?"

"Their parents are not in the picture."

In the narrow jail cell behind him, two men sat together. They were alone and nervous, holding each other's hands as they stared at the floor.

"Why are they not reporting this case?" the soldier asked.

"Their father is a drunkard, and their mother is still in shock. I volunteered to help."

"Do you have rupees?" He began scribbling in a notebook.

I unfolded the knot at the edges of my dupatta and pulled out a small stack of rupees.

"What is this?" he asked, staring at the stack. "Do you want this girl found or what?"

"Girls," I snapped. "They are two sisters. This is all the money I can spare."

He stuffed the rupees in his breast pocket hurriedly. "How long have they been missing?"

"Three days."

"Three days?" The soldier shook his head. He tossed another handful of chana in his mouth. "Three days is far too early."

"Early? These girls are alone and scared."

"Let me show you something," he muttered, deflated. For the first time since I had sat in front of him to report my two missing girls, he seemed human. He stood up and waddled toward a cabinet that was as tall as me. He pulled out one of four sliding drawers. "Do you know what this is?"

I shook my head.

He slumped back down in his chair and poured himself a glass of water. "Missing children reports."

Oh no, I thought but did not utter a word.

He must have noticed the blood drain from my face. "A lot of children run away from home in Old Pakistan. Who can blame them? The good news is that such children usually come back."

"What happens to the ones who do not?"

He gulped down the water, a thin streak of it glazing down his chin.

"Madam, let me explain something to you." He poured another glass and placed it near me. I did not take it. "If you're lucky, Aisha and Ikra —"

"Asha and Eksha."

"— will come back to you mostly intact." He wiped his chin with the back of his gloved hand and rolled down his mask. He looked me in the eye. "And if you're really lucky, those poor girls didn't suffer too much."

———

June 13, 2080

"Why did you not come back home to me?" I held on to this tall metal rod of a woman who used to be one of my children. "Why?"

Earlier, after a long day of buying food and clothes in Old Market, I had been sitting by one of the stalls, dreading the journey back home. I had bought mutton in the hopes that it would stir everyone out of the gloom that had strangled us since Eksha's funeral. Hugging two large bags in my lap, I was drinking tea when this girl patted my shoulder. She wore red sunglasses and a surgical mask. As I squinted at her quizzically, she took off her sunglasses and pulled down her mask. The moment I saw her coin-grey eyes, I took her hand tightly and promised myself that I was not going to lose her again.

She remained as composed as ever, leading me somewhere through the clutter of New Market. Behind her red glasses, Asha was impervious, inaccessible.

"Why did you not come back home? Avaan has not been the same ever since. None of us have."

"Don't tell them."

"What? Why?"

"Because I'm not that same girl anymore," she said, pressing my hand gently in hers.

"Stop being silly. You are coming with me."

"No." She was vehement. "Everything would just remind me of Eksha, and then it wouldn't be home anymore."

"It is still your home, Asha."

"Ash."

She led me past the countless stalls in New Market until we stopped before a dhaba. Girls and boys of all ages were serving tea, and the moment they saw Asha, they nodded at her. Asha whistled, and within minutes, the girls and boys escorted the customers out. I stood where I was, confused and nervous, inching back to the door.

"What is this place, Asha?" I asked, rubbing my collarbone. "Who are these children?"

"Ash. This is why I didn't come back."

The children felt different from my own. It was not that they were mostly older. They were dirty and tough, more like chunks of wood than children. They had the same dark resolve as Ash had developed. The difference between these children and my own was the same as Asha and Eksha. Or Baadal and his brother. One was destined to survive, the other not.

Ash handed me a small paper bag. "Doua-didi, do you remember the things you used to tell Baadal-bhaiyya? About the war that's coming?"

The children formed a circle around me. Though their expressions were hardened and their hands scaly, they were still children.

I reached into the paper bag and found a large black handgun in it. "What is this, Ash?"

She took the handgun from me. "The same thing you gave Baadal-bhaiyya: a reason to fight."

Wave after wave of panic crashed into me. "Baadal nearly died. He can barely stand now."

Ash shook her head. "Baadal is just the beginning."

"Ash, stop it. This is madness." My collarbone felt hot from my rubbing it so vigorously. "You are children. You are too young to talk about war, to understand it."

"You always said you'd never forgive the army, yes? You said war is inevitable."

I felt like I was floating. The heat in my neck and ears was unbearable. "Yes, but I never said I wanted any of you to be a part of it."

Turning my back to Ash, to those children made of wood, I stepped outside. The snow against my face made me feel feverish; the cold air choked the life out of me. Everywhere I looked, I saw Old Pakistanis struggling, suffering. I saw them minced against a fence, begging soldiers for a chance to earn a living. I saw little children pulling carts like harrowing beasts, their childhood and innocence oozing out of them in drops of grimy sweat.

"Doua-didi," Ash whispered behind me.

"Please, Ash," I said. "I do not want to lose you again. I do not want what happened to Eksha to happen to you."

Ash took my hand. "What happened to Eksha happened to me. But I survived. She didn't."

"No," I snapped. "No."

"How many mangled girls do you need to find before you accept that we're already a part of this war, yes?"

———

August 14, 2080
Mama used to say that a woman always knows when her children are in pain. Like so many negative things she said over the years, she was correct about this one too. That last day — the day

everything turned to dust — the moment I woke up, my heart felt icy, my fingertips electric.

"Avaan?"

He was still asleep. I whispered to him, nudged him softly, but he did not answer.

While making breakfast, I cut my finger badly. The rest of the children took over. When we ate together, Baadal made jokes and tried to get everyone to laugh. It seemed like a tall order that day.

Still reeling with unease, I went up to Salaba's room to find him sitting on the windowsill. Though he smiled, the same unease seemed to strangle him.

I hid my hand from him, but he pulled it from behind my back. "What happened to your finger?"

"I cut it, Mr. Detective." As he kissed my bandaged finger, I noticed a dog-eared copy of *The Book of Illusions* next to him. "Are you still reading that? How long has it been?"

"I keep rereading passages over and over." He wrapped his arms around me, pressing his warm face against my stomach as I stood over him. "It's like I'm not meant to get to the end."

"Where are you now?"

He began kissing circles around my navel. "The bit where Zimmer is watching Hector's movie. The one where —"

"— Martin Frost is writing a story and as he does, he meets and falls in love with a woman."

"Yup. But the more he writes the story, the sicker the woman becomes. Until, finally, he burns the story to save the woman he loves."

"Such a strange, alluring bit." I cupped his cheeks. "You do not like it?"

"I don't get it." He stared at me with his large golden eyes, eyes that were even more luminous because of the morning light. "His story gave life to the woman he loved. But the more he wrote, the sicker she grew, and in the end, the only way to save her was to burn the story he'd been writing. I don't get what it means."

I sat down next to him on the windowsill, the cool glass tingling against my lower back. "You remember when I told you about Majnun? Or Orpheus, or Devdas?"

"Yeah."

"Do you know the one thing they all had in common?"

"Downer endings?"

I chuckled. "They are all tales of timeless love that end in death. In Sufi tradition, they believe in the seven stages of love: attraction, attachment, reverence, worship, obsession, madness, and then, finally, death. Is that not strange?"

"That's dark."

"Some days, I feel these stories are less about love and more about people who are young and beautiful who die so they remain young and beautiful."

"Aren't you romantic?"

"But it is all a mirage, right? In some way, maybe Majnun is the most realistic of them all: when he finally reunites with Layla, he rejects her. Because she is too old, and nothing like how he remembers her."

"What about Martin Frost?"

"That he falls in love with her when she is a story is typical, is it not? We fall in love with the story we tell ourselves about the other person."

"Then reality hits, like a sickness."

"Yes."

For the first time since I had woken up, the disquiet I had been feeling seemed to break like a fever.

"So, he's got to choose who he loves more." He turned to me. "The woman. Or the story he told himself."

"Yes."

———

Some days, I wonder what life would be like if I had told Salaba that I had found Ash. That she was alive and safe. Some days, I wonder if the old Asha is still buried behind this wall of stone who calls herself Ash. Some days, as much as I blame Salaba for what happened to my shelter, to my children and me, I cannot shake the feeling that I am to blame for it as much as he.

———

I woke up to loud footsteps plodding above me. They were heavy and rubbery. I did not recognize them.

"Avaan?" I called out, squinting in the afternoon light. Salaba was not in bed with me.

The footsteps grew louder, thumping against the floor like hooves.

I heard screams. It was the girls.

Lighter footsteps tapped against the floor. I heard voices. Loud, guttural.

"Avaan!" I cried out, louder. There was panic in my voice, as when I spoke to Mama. I ran to the door and tried to push it open. Someone was blocking it.

"Didi, stay quiet," whispered Mary from the other side. Uzma, Ujala, and Hameed stood behind her, shaking like terrified animals. "There are soldiers here."

"What? Why? Where are the others?"

"The soldiers are locking everyone inside their rooms. I snuck out and brought these three with me."

Mary pushed the other three inside. I grabbed Mary's arm and pulled her inside. She struggled, but I was not having any of it.

"I do not understand," I said. Was it because of what Baadal had done? But how would anyone know, unless — unless someone had tipped them off. But who? "Where is Avaan?"

"In his room. A lot of soldiers were there." Fear shone in her eyes. "I think they're going to kill Baadal, didi."

"Oh no." Closing the door behind me, I pressed my back into the frame. "Lock yourselves in. Do not open it unless you are sure it is me. Or Avaan."

I headed up the stairs. Something smelled awful. Caustic and repugnant. Diesel.

My ears, my neck, my shoulders felt hot. I could hear my children crying, shouting from their rooms. There was the sound of struggling. It came from Salaba's room.

"You did this!" someone shouted. It was Baadal. "You tipped them off."

I heard Salaba's voice. "Baadal, no! Don't fight them."

The sound of glass shattering.

Someone cried out, an animal in pain. It did not sound like anyone I knew. It did not sound human.

I ran up the stairs, my heart racing. Soldiers everywhere.

Salaba was on the ground, pinned under Baadal. There was something in Baadal's hand.

I tried to stop them, tried to scream. No sound came out of me.

A gunshot — so loud that I shuddered and covered my ears. That ugliness in the air, that foreboding miasma that had been weighing down on me, seemed heavier.

Before I could take another step, someone grabbed hold of me.

I cried for help, but he covered my mouth. A gloved hand that stunk of gunpowder and diesel.

In a daze, covered in blood, Salaba sat up with Baadal collapsed over him. Baadal was still, too still. I caught a glimpse of Salaba and the gun in his hand.

I tried to say his name, but more hands grabbed me and dragged me downstairs.

The soldiers tossed me at someone's feet.

"Do you know who I am?" asked the soldier standing over me. He was tall, very tall, with a gas mask that looked like a giant mantis head. Evergreen. The Colonel Evergreen. There was a small bottle of colourless liquid in his gloved hand.

I nodded, staring at the floor. "I know what you are."

A soldier crossed my hands behind my back and taped them together. He did the same to my ankles.

"Are you the leader?" Evergreen inquired. "Or are you receiving orders directly from Yaqzan?"

Mary, Uzma, Ujala, and Hameed kneeled on the floor to my left, their hands tied with the same thick grey coils of tape. Their eyes and lips were taped shut as well. I could hear their muffled cries. Soldiers stood behind them, rifles pointed at the back of their necks.

"Everything is going to be fine," I murmured. "Please, do not worry, children."

But the world was swimming around me. All my children, this monument I had built — everything was slipping away.

"Are you the leader?"

"Please let them go. They are innocent children."

"I asked you a question."

I stared at the floor, unable to look up. "I am no leader. This is a shelter."

"A shelter? The most impetuous terrorist in recent memory was just killed here."

"Killed?"

Baadal was stiff and pale. Salaba — how could he? Why?

Evergreen tapped the bottle in his hands again. "Do you have any idea what the punishments are for terrorism?"

"Terrorism?" Hot tears flowed down my face. Lying on the ground by his feet, my hands bound, all I had now were words. "You burn our homes. You jail us for wanting enough food for our families. You freeze us, banish us, torture us. You rape us. And we are the terrorists?"

Something changed inside him. Even behind the red circles of his mask, I could feel his eyes on me. What was hot and burning inside him turned to ice.

"He was just a boy." I gritted my teeth. "And you killed him."

"We didn't kill him." He bent down and grabbed my face. When I struggled, he forced me to look at him. "It was his brother who did that."

I saw it. I saw it. "Avaan would never —"

"Yes, he did." He poked his index finger under his chin. "Shot him right here."

"I do not believe you." I saw it. I saw it. "I do not believe you."

He nodded at someone behind me. Two soldiers pinned me flat to the ground.

"What are you doing?"

Evergreen held up his finger. Like a scolding mother. He opened the small bottle meticulously. "Do you know what this is?"

"No, please —"

"Answer me." He tilted the bottle slightly. Colourless drops fell from the bottle and hissed on the ground next to my face. "Are you the leader?"

"No."

"I'm going to ask you one last time: are you the leader?"

I was not looking at Evergreen anymore. The only thing I saw was the bottle in his gloved hand, the colourless liquid tilting toward the edge. I struggled. The hands pinning me to the floor seemed a hundred in number. A hundred black hands, a hundred faceless men.

Mary, Ujala, Uzma, Hameed — they were sobbing.

"Everything is going to be fine," I said.

The last thing I saw was four of my children kneeling on the floor, bound and gagged, their bodies shivering with fear.

———

August 15, 2080

When Papa died, I had stood over his emaciated, bluish body and imagined what he was feeling. I had imagined he was falling down an endless, starless night sky — and no matter how hard he tried, there was nothing to clutch, nothing to hear, nothing to smell, nothing to taste, nothing to see. There were no clouds, no celestial debris, no stars, no sun, no broken moon, not even snow, because death was an unending night that Papa was falling through.

When the acid burned into my face twenty years later, and everything turned from shiny blurs to this unforgiving blackness, one thought swam around with all the sorrow and rage: Papa falling in that night sky.

As time went by, I felt jettisoned in a new world overrun with countless hands that carried me and loud, panicked voices that implored me to stay calm. Despite the searing pain, I kept thinking of Papa and how scared — how utterly alone — he must have been in the night sky.

Alone on a Blue Haven bed with the scratchy bedsheet under me, I wanted to cry. I wanted hot tears to fill my eyes and soothe my itchy, flaky cheeks. I remember that numb, widening hole in my heart when I realized I would never fully cry again and that it was not just the colours but also the tears that had been stolen from me.

I never had to imagine what death felt like again.

———

November 9, 2080

I was alone and miserable. I wished Ash and her friends had not pulled me from the wreckage.

The dhaba might as well have been a tomb of brambly shadows. My only thoughts were of my dead children. Of Avaan, of what he had done to Baadal, his brother, of how much I missed him. I had to step outside.

I grabbed the knuckle-hard cane Ash had left by the mattress. Tapping it against the floor — a bony knock that helped me feel my way through this world — I headed up the steps. A faded glimmer of light widened in the coiled black seaweed that was my world. I was upstairs, out of the basement where I had been for the last three months.

Pushing the door's flat, mirror-smooth surface did nothing. I patted down its side, found the brass circle, and twisted it. I pushed again and the door gave. Tapping the floor under me, I stepped outside in the chilly, odorous air. Its sheer novelty — that it was not the basement air that I had been breathing for three straight months — almost made me smile. I breathed in deeply.

I should be miserable, I thought. *Why should I laugh or smile when so many bad things have happened? By what right do I smile when all my children are dead?*

The sounds. I focused on the near-constant rain of footsteps in New Market. A chewy, fleshy squish of a bare foot here, a crunchy poke in the pavement there, a rubbery squeak of a sandal elsewhere. As each footstep fell, the sound rose in the air and disappeared, only to be replaced by a hundred more.

I felt my way past the dhaba. The ground was muddy and uneven. It squelched under my feet. The bumps made me slip repeatedly. The voices, the sounds — women and men shouting, selling their wares, arguing, swearing; wooden beams creaking so that my teeth hurt; the rattling of heaving, rusty wheels — stormed me from all directions.

The smell of tea. It was my only reference point back to the dhaba.

"*Ya Allah!*" someone cried out. A child. "Look at her face."

I pressed the dupatta to the right side of my face and turned around quickly. I lost my bearings.

"Watch it," someone said, her breath blowing into my face, a cloud of tobacco.

"I am sorry," I whispered, tapping the ground that absorbed any sound my cane made. I waved the cane a little above the ground to feel where I was. It bounced off someone's leg.

"Hey!"

"Sorry." My voice was a feeble little yelp. "I am sorry."

"Is she blind?"

"I am sorry," I repeated, but something acrid and flaky settled on my tongue. Ashes. I coughed and spat them out, the bitter taste of death seeping down my throat. I kept my dupatta pressed against my face.

I turned around and was unmoored again.

The smell of tea. It was no longer there. I smelled only the mud and refuse. I tasted the bitter ashes.

Someone grazed past me. A man. I felt his sweaty, crusted kameez against my arm. He smelled of liquor. His hand, cool and clammy, touched my lower back. I recoiled from him, from his stench. The dupatta slipped away from my face.

Poking the ground rapidly, I hurried away. I kept walking until I could no longer smell the liquor.

"Excuse me," I croaked, as dark, inky shadows glided around me in hazy grey light. "Can you please …?"

No one answered.

"What happened to her face, Mama?" The voice sounded like a little child.

"I am sorry," I said.

I tapped the ground but heard nothing. The clammy sweat from the man's hand clung to my lower back.

Someone bumped into my cane. "Hey, what the hell?"

"I am sorry," I said.

I stumbled in the wobbly darkness. I felt something hard and unforgiving against my back. A wall. I pressed into it, feeling unsteady and uneasy. I was alone and adrift in the blackness, in this dense undergrowth of shadows and unfamiliar shapes.

The smell of tea was nowhere near.

"Avaan," I cried softly. "Avaan."

I was alone and miserable, just as Mama had said I would be. I could still hear her voice when she said it, the day I had returned home after my failed marriage. She'd refused to let me inside. I had shamed her, and she would never forgive me. We would not forgive each other. It was the last time I saw her, that wretched smirk following me as I walked and walked until I was in the Badlands.

My back pressed against the wall, I kept looking up and squeezing my only eye shut. The world was alien. It spun around me in sounds and smells that I failed to recognize. I should not have left the basement. I should not have come outside.

I was alone and miserable.

In this acid rain of thoughts, a fragrance reached me: tea. It reminded me of childhood evenings when Papa had come home from work smelling of tea because he wanted to end his shift with a strong cup so he could stay up and draw with me.

"Excuse me, are you okay?" asked a woman. Her voice was a little deep and breathless. As if running away from something. Someone. "Can I help you? Where are you going?"

"I am sorry for asking this," I said sheepishly. "But can you please show me to the river? I am feeling very claustrophobic."

"I don't blame you," the woman replied. She held my hand. "Here, take my arm."

She helped me weave through the people and obstacles with a wordless tug of her arm. Her hand felt gentle, comforting. She had done this before. I opened my mouth a few times to ask her name, but I did not.

"We're here now," she said after several obstacle-free minutes of walking.

"Thank you."

I took my sandals off and stood barefoot on the sand I knew was white. It was the first time I had come to the river in months. Not since the army had stolen my colours from me. At the back of my mind, I could hear Papa's voice telling me to be strong. He would have hated to see his daughter like this. Mama's voice told me to curl up in a ball and die. Because I deserved nothing better.

"I bet the river looks lovely right now," I said to the woman on my right.

"It sure does," she replied in a voice that was forlorn and angry. At someone? "Unfortunately, it doesn't always bring up the best memories for people like us."

"Are you from the Badlands as well?"

"No, no." I heard her walk over the sand. As she stood next to me, that smell of tea, of comfort, swam into my nose again. "I spent a few years here. I guess you could say I got luckier than most."

"Where were you before that?"

"Sector 1."

"Oh. I am sorry."

"Quite the fall, I know."

"Fall seems to be all everyone does nowadays."

"No arguments on that front." She pressed my forearm gently. "Is there something I can get you? Somewhere you need to be?"

"Can you …?" I did not know how to continue. I tried anyway. "Can you please describe the river?"

She took her time to form her thoughts. "You want to know what the river looks like?"

"Yes. I used to come here often before …"

She took a deep breath. "The water is green right now."

"What kind of green?"

She took some time to reply. "The light hits the river just right sometimes, and it looks like —"

"A gem. A liquid gem."

"Emeralds." She squeezed my arm gently. "I'm Jahan. You?"

I paused, reminding myself of what Ash and I had agreed on. "Ash."

"Are you — were you an artist?"

"I was."

"What was the first thing you drew?"

"A naked woman."

She chuckled loudly. "Pakistanis must've loved that."

"Pakistanis had a problem with it. They thought it was all too vulgar and indecent and filthy."

She made a sound like you do when you eat something disgusting. "I hate when people act that way. As if they're the ones who decide what is and isn't moral. But it's art, isn't it? If anything, I think art honours what He has created. Besides, even if He considers that blasphemy, you'll have to answer to Him. Not some unimaginative Mullah who doesn't know a paintbrush from his pubes."

I smiled for the first time in a long time. "Very eloquent."

"Thanks."

"Are you a Muslim?"

"Sure."

"And art does not offend you? Despite what the Mullahs say?"

"I practice my faith my way," she said and squeezed my hand again. "And in my heart of hearts, I know that a painting of a naked woman wouldn't offend Allah. He made breasts like he made everything else, right?"

I laughed, a quick expulsion of air that had felt trapped inside me. "It is rare for someone to make me feel good about my art." The way Salaba had.

She nudged me with her shoulder. "You made something beautiful. I don't see why something beautiful would offend Allah. He created all the beauty there is."

"It certainly offended the Mullahs."

"Everything offends them. Especially women. Our freedom, our laughter."

"Our breasts." I smiled, surprising myself.

"Definitely our breasts," she giggled. "But they don't own the soul of my religion. I wish there was a way I could show you that, Ash. Its true soul. There's love and patience, there's forgiveness and tolerance in Islam. All the things that make this world worth waking up for. There's so much beauty in Islam. I wouldn't believe in it if I didn't see that beauty."

For a while, we listened to the whispering river. I could not feel the scars on my face.

"I wish there were more Muslims like you, Jahan."

———

August 1, 2083

"We knew this day would come, my children." I felt the solemnity in the air. This was happening again. Although I believed that I would be ready, that I would not lose my children again, I felt as helpless as I had three years before.

Soldiers. They were coming for my children again.

"We always knew." Ash squeezed my hand in hers. This was her war as much as it was mine. It was hers long before it was ever mine. "This is why we did everything we have done for the last three years. The army finding our stronghold was inevitable. Our job now is to take advantage of it. We are going to make those bastards play into our hands."

"Keep your numbers small. Use only the narrowest passages as you move," I ordered, tapping my cane against the ground. "Avoid engaging the soldiers directly. Remember what our biggest advantage is: we know the Badlands better than they ever will. This is our home, our land."

"The military trucks will be our key." Ash kept my hand gripped in hers. I could feel her pulse quickening. Not with fear but with something else.

I tapped my cane into the ground again. "Some of you are accompanying Ash on a separate mission." The one involving Salaba. "You have been briefed already."

"The rest of you must ensure Doua-didi's safety." Ash, as she had for the last three years, followed what I said seamlessly. "We need to weather this storm. And we will."

Most of you will not survive, I nearly whispered but held my tongue. "Look for the red light in the sky. No matter what happens when the soldiers come —"

"— no matter how many of us fall," Ash said.

"The red light in the sky means our mission still lives."

In the darkness, the air felt hot, suffocating. But what I said next pushed it back.

"The snow falls over it all," I chanted, despite the waves of regret washing over me. I wished I could lay eyes on the children who were willing to die for me for a reason I hardly understood myself some days. Some days, even my war against New Pakistan was a war against Mama. That land where they say there is food and water, where no one has ever died from the cold or crime, where the snow does not fall. The land where Salaba wanted to go so badly that he betrayed us all.

"The snow falls over it all," my children echoed after me, their voices loud and proud.

———

August 12, 2083
Today is the most important day of my life. Today is the day everything Ash and I have worked for these last three years — the culmination of the mad gamble that Baadal made, of Yaqzan's vision for this country — pays off. Or comes crashing down.

Like all Pakistanis, I reminisce over what is lost. I have lost so much in my life, but it is the colours that I miss today. I miss the sunlit morning kisses of yellow; the fruity earthiness of orange; the symmetry and lifelong promise of red in a Hindu wife's parting line. I miss the sultry caresses of purple; the blushing cheeks of pink; the soothing rain that greys promised me, even if I knew they were lies. I miss the hopefulness of white with its tinge of naive optimism. I miss green with its lush silkiness, its gentleness, its opulence. I miss the saltiness of dark blue and the vast silence of light blue. I miss the lustrous blue of my father's kurta. It was a colour I once wore.

I miss brown the most. I miss the steaming, semi-lucid joy of morning tea; the gentle homeliness of brown eyes; the softness of brown hair as it caressed my cheeks. I miss naked breasts and nipples. I miss unpretentious lips.

They took all the colours from me and left me with black, the absence of colour.

It poured over my paintings, my pieces.

Some days I feel the jagged pain in my eyes. Even now, three years later, I wake up some nights with searing agony where my right eye used to be. I relive that moment when all the colours blurred, then gelled together in a teary haze, then turned bright, bright red. And then, blackness. The colours bled away, and I was adrift in a world of turbid shapes and featureless shadows.

Black.

That jaded over-ripeness of melancholy. Like rotten bananas. Like tumours. Like cracks. Like smoke from the tip of a red-hot knife. Like starving, mangy crows that caw. Like inert plastic sunglasses that always make the bridge of my nose itch. Like the hazy shadows that cover my vision almost entirely. Like soldiers and their guns. Like Mama's eyes.

Black.

Like whatever was left of my library-shelter. Like the charred bodies of my children. Like the hole that's left inside me now because of the actions of one man. One monster.

Today is the most important day of my life. Yet all I have is the memory of the things that I have lost. The memory of a man with delicate eyes and a lost sadness to him, like old postage stamps. The monster whose name I refuse to say, even though it once came as naturally to my lips as my own breath.

Today, all I have is a heart blackened with vengeance.

Episode 21: And All Our Yesterdays

Avaan

August 12, 2083

The truth. It's all I'm left with now.

Gagged and bound to the chair, I watch the morning light slice across the darkness. To my right, a viscous black circle stains everything I see. I blink hard, try to focus. Nothing. Everything to the right is a black nothing.

Ash stands over me. There's someone next to her. A curious little boy with brown eyes. The way he looks at Ash — the slightly wide-eyed stare as he watches her, the faintest blush in his cheeks, the hesitation when he tries to make eye contact with her — is all too familiar. Isn't it, Doua?

"Ash-didi, is the sad man dying?" he asks, pulling the rag out of my mouth. "Will he go to heaven?"

———

I was five, and I had a baby brother.

I didn't spend much time with Baadal in the beginning, preferring to look out the window. Mother, even as she began to speak less and less, became a somewhat attentive parent toward Baadal.

She kept me with her at all times when it came to raising him, demonstrating how to bathe him in water heated to just the right temperature, how she'd twist the head of a spoon so it could make feeding him easier. I never cared for any of it. Not until Mother placed Baadal's head in my lap one day and showed me how to hold a bottle of milk to his lips. Mother told me it was because she was too weak to feed him herself. She said it was because there wasn't enough milk in her. She said I had to protect him no matter what.

I didn't understand what she meant. But I did as I was told. Baadal's head would nestle in my lap, drinking the milk, cooing and giggling as he'd watch his big brother with large, loving brown eyes.

———

I was seven.

"I'm sorry." Mother's voice was breaking. "It was so long ago, and I thought —"

"You thought what?" Father asked in his deep voice. "That I'm stupid?"

Even behind closed doors, I knew Father was dousing her with his scalding gaze. I knew Mother's mouth was twisted and that hot tears were flowing down her cheeks. I have no idea what Happy Mother was like. Of Unhappy Mother, I know every version.

I covered Baadal's ears, swaddling him in a thick shawl. I heard everything.

"He's still your son."

"You lied to me."

"Please stay. At least for Baadal. He's still your son."

"You lied to me."

"I didn't. I wasn't sure, and I kept hoping and praying that Avaan was—"

"You lied to me."

"It wasn't my fault! It was that monster who —"

"Shut up!" Father screamed as I heard a glass break against the closed door. "Shut up."

———

I was eight.

Father had become more of a wound than an actual memory. Everything in our home reminded us of him, yet we wouldn't dare speak of him. Mother became both a father and a mother to me. She ignored me like she had all my life, but now whenever she looked at me, it was with Father's scalding gaze.

If she did speak to me, rare as it was, it'd be one of two things.

"Protect your brother," she'd say as I was feeding Baadal. "You're all he has now. Allah help him."

"I shouldn't be here, you know?" was the other thing she'd say, on days when cleaning work was scarce and we'd be down to a thin stack of rupees to last the month. "I could run away into Sector 3 and start over. Forget all this ever happened, you know? I'm still young. I was only twenty-four when you were born. But where will I find a good man now? What kind of a man will go for someone like me?"

There used to be a third thing she'd say, on really bad days when she wouldn't look at me at all. On those days, she'd talk and talk, her throat parched by the end, her amber eyes burning with rage, indignation. She'd speak of Father, who had ruined her life; she'd speak of the monster who had ruined her life. And long after the silence took hold of her again, she'd look at me with a twisted smile.

"You look just like him."

———

I was eight.

Mother's hands were rough, grainy. It was from the chemicals she'd use when cleaning and scrubbing. It was from the cold, which would get colder still when her wet hands were exposed to Pakistan's winter air. The kind of cold that needles into your bones. She was in her early thirties when arthritis caked her finger joints, making it impossible for her to open her hands fully at night. I'd break off morsels of food and leave them on a plate for her. Some evenings, she'd call me to her side and share the morsels with me.

Some evenings, enough of the broken moon would shine through the clouds and celestial debris to cast a milky-blue glaze over the buildings and half-sunken cars. Mother would drag a chair outside to watch the cracked white disk in the sky. I'd sit beside her and, mother and son, we'd spend hours in uninterrupted silence. She'd share half of whatever she was eating — a triangle of naan from the house she'd cleaned, a spiral of jalebi from across the street.

One such evening, long after Father had left us, I asked her why she was sitting outside in the dark, all alone. Instead of replying, she asked me why I was sitting with her in the freezing night.

"Because you're alone," I replied.

She didn't say anything.

Later that night, as I dozed off with Baadal in my arms, I felt Mother pet my cheek and brush my hair. Her hand was rough. As if Lut's wife had been granted one last miracle to say goodbye to her family. A family so precious to her that she had defied Allah in the first place. Mother brushed my hair, held my hand in hers, and patted my cheek. Wishing this moment would last forever, I drifted off to the only sunlit dream I ever had as a child.

When I woke up in the morning, Mother was gone.

———

I grit my teeth when I hear the sirens shattering the morning air. Unable to shield my ears, I slump in the chair miserably as the room becomes a glaring whirlpool of blues and reds. I keep my

eye open, endure the twisting lights. Tears blur my vision. Everything seems close and far at the same time. There's a searing pain
where my right eye used to be. The ropes sting my wrist.

"Are we doing it, didi?" More kids stand over me curiously,
nudging me. "Are we taking him to Doua-didi?"

"Leave him," Ash scoffs from near the window. "What's left
of him to show her, yes?"

———

I was thirteen and had no idea how much time had passed.

He was long gone. The orange-bearded driver.

A bulb flickered above me, swinging from the ceiling, and for
all it mattered, these were the last moments of my life. Baadal was
safe, I thought, and it was all that mattered.

Face down on the ground, the tepid, damp floor pressed
against my face and body, I knew vaguely that I was still at the
Laari Adda. When I tried to move, to peel myself off the floor, my
whole body ached as if crushed under a stone. Yet even this pain
was an echo. Alien and far away.

It was not me.

The pool of sweat and spit under me; the scratches from where
his fingers had dug into my hips and shoulders; the aftertaste of
blood as it dripped out of my busted lips; the scorching pain in
my asshole — some part of me noticed it all, felt it all. But as if
from behind a large window. As if I'd swapped places with my
reflection, and these moments — all the terrible things in my life
before then, and since — were on the other side.

———

I was fifteen.

A dark-haired woman came by our tent near Old Market. Cricket bat in hand, I listened to her talk about how she'd

obtained a permit from the army to repurpose the abandoned library. She was going to turn it into a shelter. Kids like me could live in a place with solid walls and a roof with food and clothes and books. She would teach us to read.

I gawked at her, dumbstruck.

She was older than me, her skin even darker than mine, with a few acne scars around her right cheek. Some Pakistanis wouldn't consider her pretty. But there was something about her. As if everything around her was foggy and unfocused, and only her face — her starry night eyes, her small thin lips, her little round nose, her long wavy hair — was lambent in this moment of harmony.

————

I was seventeen.

After weeks of scraping by, Doua found enough money to paint the inside of the library-shelter. She wanted the whole place painted white so that there'd be something for all of us to look at and call our own. Our own little New Pakistan. We all painted together, using brushes, scooping the paint with our hands and rubbing it over the walls.

Three days later, the last paint bucket ran dry. Only the bottom halves of the walls were painted. Doua spread her arms, her face and hands splotched with dried paint like the rest of us.

"See? Just like New Pakistan," she said, laughing as she stood next to me, her arm grazing mine.

We laughed and giggled in this ridiculous hall that was half grey, half white — a graveyard of forgotten books and broken furniture that we called home. And as we laughed, I reached down to hold her hand in mine.

————

I try to blink away the black cobwebs from my vision. The tight knots around my wrists have left my hands numb. I can't move. There's a confounding static at the centre of my skull; my mind is wrapped in tinfoil.

"He's still alive, Ash-didi," says the same curious little boy. He dangles something black and oval near my face. The eye patch. "I thought he died so he could go to heaven."

"No." Ash shrugs next to him, watching me nonchalantly. She wipes the blood off her blade with the front of her orange kurta. "He already died a long time ago."

———

I was twenty-five.

Once they found Eksha's body, I was no longer a reflection in the world. No longer a ghost. I was flesh and blood again because I was in the Badlands, where nothing was beautiful and everything hurt.

After her funeral, we placed Eksha's ashes in small paper boats made from her favourite storybook. Standing on the far shore, Doua held my hand as we watched Baadal and the others release the boats down the tranquil river. One by one, the paper boats took Eksha away into the Misty Wasteland, where no one goes and no one returns. As the last boat disappeared into the mist, Doua reached up and wiped away the tears rolling down my cheeks.

———

Baadal stood by the window, watching the streets. The snow fell over everything, snatching everything out of sight. I blew out the oil lamp and pulled the blanket over myself. After Eksha's funeral, I'd begun to sleep less and less.

"Avaan?" Baadal asked in the dark.

"What?"

"There's still no word on Asha. Doua keeps going out every other day, she keeps handing out those flyers, but —"

"Shocking."

I knew I was being unfair to him, to Doua, but I couldn't help myself.

"It's bad luck, you know. Misfortune." He was having trouble finding his voice, finding the words. He was twenty, and no matter how hard I'd tried, my brother had grown up too fast. "She was a Hindu. She came to the Badlands a lot. She was kidnapped. We searched for her. We were too few to do it. It's misfortune."

"I know."

"There's nothing you could've changed." He spoke again after a period of heavy silence. "I don't want you to blame yourself."

"I'm trying to sleep, Baadal."

———

"We cannot keep living like this," Doua said, her head pressed against my chest as the night refused to let us sleep. "We should not accept this life. We need to fight back."

A fleet of supply trucks rattled past the library-shelter, making the walls shake around us.

"Not this again." Massaging my temples, I sat up, forcing her to move away from me.

"You keep saying that. We have not talked. You do not listen. You just wait for me to stop talking."

"Okay." I rolled off the mattress, my feet tingling on the cold floor. I pulled on my jeans and stood up. "We can either die here, in this miserable place. Like Asha-Eksha. Or we can leave Pakistan."

"You cannot be serious. No one has gone outside Pakistan, and no one has ever come to it from outside. It has been decades since the sky burned, and even then —"

"Exactly."

"Exactly what?"

"Those are the options we have: we wait to die in this shithole, or we find an escape from Old Pakistan."

"Why do you keep saying that?" She ran her fingers along her neck and collarbone. "I refuse to accept those as the only options for my children. For us. Those are not choices."

"Then we go to New Pakistan."

"How can we? How is that an option for someone like us?"

"Fighting the army is?"

"I do not mean actually starting a gunfight with them, Avaan."

"Then what? Protests? Hunger strikes?"

"I do not know. I want them to answer for —"

"They will obliterate us."

"They are already obliterating us, Avaan. How many mangled girls do you need to find before you accept that?"

———

I was twenty-five. It was the only time I bothered to listen to a Friday sermon.

"And Hazrat Mohammad said to that vile human, 'Oh, Salaba, how can I forgive one whom even Allah can't forgive?'"

Lurking around the Blue Mosque's courtyard, I massaged my ears as the imam kept screaming into the microphone. He was reedy and goofy looking, with a beard that looked like something had squirmed over his face to die.

"So now, realizing that his actions had damned him for eternity," the imam shrieked, shaking, "Salaba returned every year to Hazrat Mohammad, and every year Hazrat Mohammad would send him away, saying the same thing: how can I forgive one whom even Allah cannot forgive? *Astaghfirullah, astaghfirullah.* May Allah forgive you and me, my children. May Allah save us from a sinner's hubris. From his lies. May Allah deliver us from the atheists and the apostates. Ameen. Ameen."

"Ameen. Ameen," muttered the mass.

"Ameen." His voice carried into the distance, where the snow fell on Muslims and non-Muslims alike. "A few years later, Hazrat Mohammad passed away, that noblest of men. As you know, Hazrat Abu Bakr became the first caliph. This is when Salaba came to him, begging for forgiveness, and Hazrat Abu Bakr sent him away, saying: how can I forgive one whom even Allah and His Messenger couldn't forgive? But Salaba came back the next year, and Hazrat Abu Bakr had the same answer. May Allah show us mercy. May He forgive us and guide us. Ameen. Ameen."

"Ameen. ameen," chanted the crowd.

"Then Hazrat Abu Bakr passed away, that greatest of friends to Hazrat Mohammad. Then came who? Who was the second caliph? Hazrat Umar. And then what happened? Salaba came to him too. See? The mind of a sinner? The arrogance? The entitlement to forgiveness? He came to Hazrat Umar begging for forgiveness, and what does Hazrat Umar say? He also sends him away, saying: how can I forgive one whom Allah and His Messenger and Abu Bakr couldn't forgive?"

"Astaghfirullah, astaghfirullah," the masses muttered, shaking their lowered heads.

"Salaba came back the next year and the next, until finally, death overtook him."

The imam allowed silence to settle over the masses.

"You see, my children?" he said, a sudden lull in an otherwise frenzied sermon. "Such is the fate of all sinners. Allah seals their hearts, their minds, and then — once it's too late — that, my children, is the moment Allah takes his revenge upon them. That's the moment their sealed hearts and minds lead them down a path from which they may never return to Allah's merciful light.

Don't be so lost, so arrogant, so wicked that Allah's mercy can no longer reach you, my children. Such was the fate of Salaba ibn Hatteb: to remain unforgiven for all of eternity. Astaghfirullah, astaghfirullah."

———

Sirens. More than I've ever heard.

Ash, the kids, they all rush to the barred window and pull the curtains apart. The flood of morning light stings my eye like a splash of acid.

"Is our mission a go, didi?" one of the kids asks.

"Yes," Ash replies.

"You're all going to die if you do," I say, remembering what Humayun told me. About a madman bent on destruction. "Evergreen doesn't know where your stronghold is. This is something else: Operation Searchlight III."

The air crackles with fear.

Bound to a chair, wincing in the light, I'm a mad prophet of doom. "Evergreen isn't going to the Badlands to arrest Doua. He's going to burn the whole place down. Like the army did before."

"Lies," Ash snarls. "More lies."

"No. Not anymore." There's a disquieting buzz in the room. "You need to get Doua and your people to safety, okay? Whatever your mission was, whatever you guys were planning —"

"We're ready to fight Evergreen."

"This won't be a fight. It'll be a massacre."

There's the slightest tremor in her hands as she holds the kids close.

"Ash. Please." I stare at her. "You need to listen to me. Not for my sake but Doua's. Please."

———

Two months before Ground Zero, I was reading an old copy of *The Book of Illusions* I'd found gathering dust in Doua's collection. There was a faded picture of a family of three from 1995 in the pages. The parents were faded slightly. The little girl's face was scratched over furiously like she'd wanted to erase herself. Doua would stare at the picture intently, as if it was another story from another world that somehow echoed.

"Figured you'd be here," Baadal said as he entered the room. He had grown his hair past his ears. "It was either here or, you know, the roof." He thrust his hips forward a few times. "With a certain lady."

Sitting on the windowsill, I barely glanced his way. "What do you want?"

"We did it." He grinned ear to ear. "My friends and I got these off a few guys."

Winking, Baadal reached into his shalwar and pulled out a nickel-plated Colt 1911, too large for his hand.

"Bang." He mock-fired. "I've given mine a name. *The Big Heat.*"

I tossed the book aside and stood up. "Where did you get that?"

"These scavengers stole a box of guns from Humayun. They sold it to us."

"Humayun from that diner? The Humayun?"

"Yeah."

"Are you fucking — Baadal, if anyone reports you to the army, they'll kill us all for this."

The light from a passing supply truck shone on my brother's face, illuminating how serious he was. Something sinister slithered inside my gut, and I knew he was going to die.

I lunged at him, trying to wrestle the gun out of his hands.

The vein in his temple bulged. Like Father. "What the hell is your problem, Avaan?"

"Give me that gun!" I was mad, yelling. "You're just a kid. Those are trained soldiers with rifles. You can't fight them."

He pushed me hard, knocking me over. So defiant.

"Don't do this, Avaan. You hear me? Don't."

I picked myself off the floor and leaned against the window. I wiped my hands over my face and cropped hair. Staring at the shanties and tents spread throughout the Badlands like entrails, I realized that I was going to die in this miserable place. Like Asha-Eksha.

"Have you told Doua?" I croaked. "That you're planning on getting killed for nothing?"

"Nothing? I'm doing this for us. All of us. We've got no food, no water. Electricity for a couple of hours. You sold your kidney to —" His voice cracked. "Is this what you want, Avaan?"

"I want us to be safe. I want us to live in peace, like before Eksha's death."

"These guns will keep us safe!" Baadal shouted. "We can fight. We can make a difference."

"The army will burn down this place and everyone in it."

"If we do nothing, they might as well burn it down now!"

"Shut up."

He points a finger downstairs. "Doua understands."

"What?"

"She knows we can't keep living like this. She knows we can't end up like Asha-Eksha."

"That's not what she means."

"I'm not watching another one of us get torn up. I'm no longer accepting that." There was a pause. I knew what he was going to say. "You're the only one who wants us to die." His words stabbed my heart right to the hilt. "Because you're a fucking coward. Just like Mother. Just like Father."

We came to blows. We would again, two months later.

_____

The Book of Illusions fluttered, lying torn where Baadal had stepped on it during our scuffle. Doua balled up her dupatta and dabbed at my bleeding lip and nose. My knuckles stung when she touched my hand.

"What happened? Where is Baadal?"

"We got into a fight."

"Why?"

"I was trying to stop him. But he had a gun."

"He what?"

"He pointed it at me. Then he took off."

"He had a gun?"

"Someone sold it to him. You filled his head with the idea of fighting back."

"Avaan, you are not making any sense. Where is Baadal?"

"You did this." I slapped her hands away and stood up. "All your bullshit about this not being a choice. About fighting back. About making New Pakistan answer. You got in his head."

"You are not making any —"

I wanted to punch a hole into her. "Why do you think he got a gun, Doua? He's going to attack the soldiers."

"Oh, no," she whispered, hand over her lips. "Oh, no."

_____

Baadal was rushed to Blue Haven by his friends who had survived his war-turned-massacre. He had been shot in the gut. The soldiers at the Badlands Precinct were armed with RPDs and hadn't wasted a second turning most of Baadal's little army into pulp.

Part of me still wishes Baadal had been one of them.

He was unconscious when we entered the tent where he was

being treated. As a nurse led us away, I caught a glimpse of the piles of bloody gauze and the almost plastic skin around the hideous wound in Baadal's abdomen.

Hours later, as we waited, I held Doua's hand and patted it. She smiled at me apologetically.

One of Baadal's friends was with us, a petrified boy wrapped in the smelly blankets they still give out in Blue Haven.

"Avaan?" the boy croaked, motioning me to join him. "Can I speak to you?"

Without warning, he snuck me Baadal's 1911.

"You need to hide this. Don't let anyone find it."

Still in a daze, I snuck the gun into the back of my jeans just as the nurse came out of the tent smiling.

"He'll live." She smiled wider. "He's very strong."

———

Baadal was convalescing. The large bullet hole in his gut was healing. We brought him more food than he had ever seen. He was weak and would likely walk with a limp for the rest of his life. I was sitting beside his mattress, which was stuffed with as many towels and pieces of foam as we could scavenge.

"Avaan? I'm sorry I pointed a gun at you."

"Just shut up and get better."

His lips white with pain, Baadal tried to sit up.

I eased him back onto the mattress. "Don't be an idiot. You need to rest."

"Listen." The urgency with which he held my arm made me look at him, at his brown eyes melting with pain. "I wasn't trying to be a hero, Avaan."

"I know."

I placed the thick blanket over him and sat on the floor next to him.

282 \ Saad T. Farooqi

He continued, "I was trying to choose for myself. Doua is right. You know that, don't you?"

"Doua says a lot of things, Baadal."

He didn't say anything for a while. "You still blame yourself for Eksha, don't you?"

"You need to rest."

"Doua told me you still think New Pakistan is our only option. Is that true?"

"Anywhere but here."

"Why? We're still together here, right?"

"Because I don't want to die here like Asha-Eksha. Not in this miserable place."

———

I'm alone. Ash, the kids, they are gone. I still hear the sirens. They're far off. Gagged and bound again, I watch the bulb sway above me, its orange hue fracturing the blackness of the room.

There were murmurs of some red light in the sky. Ash reminded the kids of it as she guided them all out of here, leaving without a glimpse at me. Why would she?

I'm alone. An affixed dot in time and space. The only motion around me is the flotsam of shadows and the jetsam of memories. Memories that make up so much of the present, even though they exist outside of it. What I remember, what I wonder about, what I wish had gone differently, what I wish I could forget — all of it is like the shadow that usurps the space I once occupied, to remind me that I don't anymore.

My shadow is tall and dark and riddled with three pairs of eyes that don't blink.

———

August 14, 2080

Pakistani Independence Day. Ground Zero.

The gun in my hand was the starting point to all the madness that became my life.

Baadal drank tea by the window. I searched for *The Book of Illusions*, through drawers and cupboards. I found the .45 peeking out from under a row of black shirts. I should've rid us of it. But I'd put it off, kept saying tomorrow. And tomorrow. And tomorrow.

"Is that mine?" Baadal asked, confused. "Where did you get it?"

Standing with the gun in my hand, I was wondering where to hide it — the basement? the roof? — when soldiers crashed through the door.

Someone had tipped them off about Baadal. Who? Why? I'd never know.

A soldier butted Baadal in the mouth and pinned him against the window. Six more soldiers stormed into the room.

The gun in my hand.

"Shoot them," Baadal begged, his face pressed into the glass. "Don't let them take me."

The way everything crystallized in time — me, Baadal, the soldiers, the scattered splinters, all of us immovable in this sphere of violence — I was inside a snow globe.

The gun in my hand. The soldiers trained their .303s on me. I didn't want to die in this miserable place.

I raised my hands.

Baadal understood what I'd chosen in that moment. Better than I did.

"You did this?" he cried. I'd never seen him roar like that. It was rage, indignation. It was disgust. "You tipped them off?"

"Baadal, no! Don't fight them."

Everything from that point onward happened too fast.

The window shattered.

Baadal shoved the soldiers away.

He grew larger and larger. I cowered. Like Father. Like Mother.

The last moments I shared with my little brother were of him ripping my chest open with a glass shard. Of him slamming me to the ground. Of him trying to plunge the shard into my eye, pressing down with all his might. The last words my little brother said to me were undecipherable screams from a face twisted in anger beyond recognition.

I didn't want to die in the Badlands. I didn't want to die.

The last sight of my little brother was his head jerking back violently as I shot him.

My world was snow and blood.

The sirens felt like a part of my world. My hands and mouth duct-taped, the soldiers dragged me past the dead bodies of my sisters and brothers. Past Baadal's dead body. My torso bleeding, I watched the library-shelter crumble to the ground as the soldiers taped my eyes, shoved me into a military jeep, and drove me far away from the only place I'd ever call home.

———

November 6, 2080

Each sound of this city registered on my nerves like drops in water torture. I had shaved off everything — my hair, my stubble, my eyebrows. I didn't want to be recognized. Especially by myself. Shivering in the air that suddenly felt like a frozen shroud, I kept myself hidden behind a shawl and a pair of dark sunglasses. My heart wringing in my chest, I stepped inside Humayun's Diner. A few icicles descended toward the ground, long and sharp and foreboding.

The man at the counter had flushed cheeks that had begun to bulge over his clean-shaven double chin. His pot belly and flabby triceps pushed against his blue kurta.

"*Salam*, I'm Humayun. First time here?"

Across from Humayun, slumped over the table with a pitcher of booze, was a short man in a long coat. There was a crutch next to him. He tilted the pitcher to his lips with his left hand, his right hand tucked inside his coat.

They both noticed my black jeans and exchanged a nod.

The overhead TV played a cartoon. A coyote ran after a bird only to rush past the precipice. He slowed down as defeat settled in. *Beep-beep*, gloated the bird. The coyote waved dejectedly before plummeting.

"Try sweet lassi." Humayun smiled a toothy smile that didn't make it to his eyes. He handed me a steel cup brimming with frothy white liquid. "It's a special."

Hand clutching the shawl, face hidden, I managed a sip. "Can you put some more sugar in it?"

Gingerly, he dropped three cubes of sugar into the drink and stirred. "You want something?"

Why are you here, Avaan?

I sprang up, knocked over the chair, and spilled lassi all over the counter.

Humayun glowered at me. "You want something? What is it?"

I heard it: the unmistakable click of a cocked hammer. The short man leaned over the table, a long silver gun shining in his lap.

What have you done?

"The special," I stammered, my face still hidden behind the shawl. "I want the DBE special, Mr. Humayun."

———

I stood shivering in front of New Pakistan's massive gate. That slice of heaven I'd wanted so badly for everyone I loved. Everyone who now was gone.

I held the golden Colt Python, shivering in the snowy night.

Evergreen stood a few paces before me, fingers waltzing over the pearl grips of his Peacemaker.

Only I could see Doua between us in a red saree. Her face was like that of dead lovers in old paintings, watching me.

I aimed the Colt Python, felt its steel in my hand.

Evergreen shot first.

———

My mind retreats to the one luminous moment when the world wasn't made of broken glass. The only solace I know. I don't hate her. I can't hate her.

———

I was eighteen.

Lying on the ground, my head in her lap, I watched Doua as she sang to me. Not very well, but I didn't care. That song would become ours. The pieces. The abrupt end.

"Doua?"

"What?"

"What comes after the last part?" I asked.

"I have no idea."

"Where did you hear it?"

"A long time ago. I was a little girl. A man was singing it by the river."

"Huh." I reached up, twisted a strand of her hair in my finger, then tucked it behind her ear. "What do you think the last part is?"

"Forgiveness, I think." Doua moved her face away from my fingers. "Is that not what love often entails?"

"Maybe it's about understanding."

"Understanding?"

"It's like Mother. At some point, it doesn't matter that what she did to us was horrible."

"It does matter. Your whole life has been shaped by it."

"But in that moment, the pain she must've felt when she left us — it must've felt like being torn apart. It had to. How terrible must've things been to make a mother abandon her children?"

"It did not stop her."

"No, it didn't. But all I can think of is how terrible, how miserable, her life must have been that she chose to leave her children behind rather than live one more day with us."

"Would you forgive her?"

"Maybe."

"I could never forgive her. I never forgave my mother."

"You don't forgive easily, huh?"

"Not betrayal. Not inhumanity." Doua ran her finger down my cheek. "What your mother did to you and to Baadal was monstrous."

"We're all monsters."

"You were an innocent child."

"How long do children remain innocent in Pakistan?"

"That is no excuse for what she did."

"It's not an excuse." I sat up. "It's saying, without forgiving you or forgetting what you did, I understand. I understand that guilt and sorrow must tear at you. I understand, and I'm sorry. I'm sorry that things were so bad that you had to choose a life where you'd hate yourself endlessly just to get away from it."

"You have nothing to be sorry for, Avaan. You have nothing to apologize for. Not to her."

"I know."

"Then why?"

"Because I loved her, Doua. Once upon a time. That must mean something, right? It has to."

PART III
THE LAND OF ASHES

Episode 22: Fairy-tale Endings

Avaan

August 12, 2083

The ropes gnaw into my wrists. I've managed to free my legs. The gag, too, hangs loose around my neck.

Twisting my hips and legs sharply, I roll to my side. Everything past the right side of my nose is a black mass. I twist as hard as I can, rolling onto my knees. The chair is still tied to my arms, but I've finally got my legs under me. Silver linings.

My Colt 1911 winks silver on a table. Maybe Ash is mocking me, leaving it behind. Or maybe she believes a single handgun isn't going to change anything.

Gritting my teeth, I run backward and lunge into a wall, slamming the chair into it as hard as I can. My spine creaks and pops as the backrest breaks.

Unsteadily, I pry the ropes off and stand under the swaying orange light bulb.

———

I walk through the rusting membrane of old cars surrounding the Badlands. I'm numb to it now: the screaming pain in my eye, the torn stitches, the gunshot wound, and the electric prodding in my left arm. It's only pain.

I check my 1911 and spare magazine. Thirteen bullets.

Despite the gunshots, despite the thick black smoke, a strange tranquility pervades the afternoon air. The few people I come across run in the opposite direction. Some flinch at the sight of me. Must be the eye patch. Or the trickle of blood I dab at with the shawl. Someone shouts in my face. Someone else steps on my foot. Deep-fried onions burn in an abandoned stall. The smell of gasoline, of burning rubber, of bloody clothes.

The gunshots grow louder. I walk toward them.

I follow a winding assortment of mud-and-wood steps, ridges on some monster's spine. The shanties and tents are colour indistinct; the browns, greens, and yellows are a residual collage of what is rusted, scraped, burned, decayed.

Evening glooms on the horizon as I make my way through cracked, graffiti-smeared walls that look like rotting fingernails. Passing by a large garbage ditch, I wonder how many other Ekshas lie silent and decaying in this trash. My dizzying vision gets the better of me. I lean against a wall, disoriented, discombobulated.

The sound of sirens comes from all around. A barrage of teeth-grating artillery.

People dash around me, terrified and screaming.

I run as well, twisting my neck left and right to get a full view of where I'm going.

More people spill into the dirt road. They stream from over walls, through narrow cracks and tiny passageways.

A black military truck plows into the crowd a few paces to my left. For a second, the screaming and running stops. The silent horror of broken bones, of broken bodies.

Soldiers jump out of the truck. The *clack* of AK-47s being locked and loaded.

A man plummets wordlessly in front of me. Blood spurts onto my face.

Then the sound comes — metallic rain and thunder. RPDs and AK-47s. The gunshots take away all other sound. I feel them shuddering inside my chest.

Everyone runs. Pushing, shoving, trampling. Twisting my way through the mass, focused solely on not slipping and falling, I lunge into a relatively empty pathway. The sirens are constant, a twin sister to the snow.

More screaming from behind me. Scores pour into the pathway, shouting, crying. Soldiers march behind them, one of them holding an RPD. I can't hear a word. I can't hear anything except the rumbling, coursing thunder of 7.62mms. Uninterrupted violence.

I keep running. I can't die. Not before I see Doua. Not before I tell my side of the story.

Racing into a corner to my left, I let the shards of memory guide my feet. Doua is here, I remind myself. Doua is here. Evergreen is here. I need to find her.

Three soldiers. A family of five lies at their feet.

Drawing my 1911 comes naturally. Aiming doesn't. The lack of clarity and depth perception infuriates me. The hole in my vision causes panic. The days of aiming, of shot placement and economic shooting, are gone.

The soldiers train their AK-47s on me.

I let fear and fury guide my hand.

Six hollow-points put them down before they can squeeze a trigger.

I reload. Seven bullets.

Gun in hand, I follow the huge black shroud of smoke spread overhead. On a bullet-ridden wall, there's a message and a handprint.

Death to Avaan Maya. Death to all traitors.

———

I run, cutting through a narrow passage between the old tailor shop and the tiny hut where Asha-Eksha sold their mother's pakoras.

A middle-aged couple kneels against a metal shutter, arms behind their heads. Sneaking behind a rusted generator, I watch two soldiers drag the couple's teenage daughter to a huge, eight-wheel military truck. A third soldier opens the back of the truck. It's full of girls like her, most of them younger. All are bound, gagged, blindfolded.

The girl pleads with the soldiers to spare her parents. They tape her eyes and mouth, push her into the truck. While the two soldiers shut the back of the truck, the other walks over to her parents and blows their brains over the metal shutter.

He thumps the door in three quick knocks, and the truck speeds off. Hopping into a nearby jeep, he follows.

They didn't spot me. That's all that matters now.

I run under the balcony of the deaf old woman who used to give me and Baadal delicious, sweet *laddu* whenever we brought her river water.

There's a scream. The sound of someone being dragged, of wet hands trying to hold on to the floor. Shattering glass makes me look up, and as I do, a body — an old woman? a man? — bounces off the pavement in a snap and pop that makes brine bubble up into my mouth.

I run. Turning a corner, I bolt into a dirt road.

Am I going the wrong way?

A jeep full of burning soldiers lights my way through a dark alley. A Molotov. The smell of alcohol and detergent and burning rubber congeals with the salty saliva I've been trying to swallow. The broken, ruptured bodies strewn in the streets let me know I'm heading in the right direction. Whatever doubt remains is quelled by screams and sirens.

Coughing into the shawl pressed against my mouth, I keep running.

Jumping over a wall and sprinting madly, I almost get run over by a truck to my right. Inertia works wonders, causing me to wobble before tumbling forward into an acrid sea of garbage, plastic bottles, and newspapers.

The truck screeches to a halt.

Footsteps. Loaded AK-47s. A whole platoon of them.

They approach the trash pit. Deliberate, deadly.

Grabbing on to whatever doesn't scrunch or splatter in my hands, I dive deeper into the trash pit, making sure to protect the remains of my right eye.

In the damp garbage, a woman's face appears. She places a bleeding, blackened finger on her lips. Clutched in her arms, his face pressed into her, is a toddler whimpering in a silence I thought impossible.

I nod. Pulling more bags of trash over them, over myself, I lie flat. We don't move. We don't breathe.

A light outlines the confined space around me, around the mother and child.

"Did you see where he went?"

"He's probably in the trash. Check it."

There's a pause. "You check it."

An exasperated grunt later, footsteps march toward us. A burst of 7.62mm explodes a trash bag next to my head.

The little boy yelps, like an injured mouse. The mother covers his mouth and her own.

We don't move.

Quietly, I cock the .45's hammer.

Another burst of 7.62mms goes off. There's a ringing clang of it hitting something metal close to the mother. She bites down on her hand, gripping her child tighter.

There are several more gunshots, all random.

"Anything?" asks one of the soldiers. More flashlights gleam in the darkness.

"No. Nothing."

"You probably got him. Let's move."

We wait in silence, not looking at each other. Not breathing.

The sound of tires seems far. I crawl away from the mother and kid, looking back once to watch her push the child out of the ditch and back onto the road.

"Stay off the roads," I say quietly. The woman nods and disappears into smoke and snow.

I crawl through the trash, through how many other decomposing Ekshas, before finding refuge under a rusting car.

Headlights. A truck squeezes through the narrow road.

My 1911 at the ready, I squeeze back into the shadows and filth. The smell of offal, rotten food, and refuse makes possible suicide by asphyxiation.

Headlights pass slowly. The loud growl of the engine and the smell of diesel dominate the air. Rubber boots thud against the floor in unison.

Hand covering my mouth, I watch dozens of people amble behind the truck, prodded by soldiers. All of them teenagers. Eyes and mouths and wrists taped.

I lie still, barely breathing.

Another truck rumbles by. More soldiers leading kids away. Low against the ground as I am, I notice something long and cylindrical stuck to the bottom of the truck. A dim red light blinks on it. I've seen something like it once before, when Inayah held it in her hand.

A bomb, only much bigger.

Several minutes go by before I drag myself out of all the filth.

I run into the lonely street no one went near. Kids said it was haunted. The one where Baadal found Doua pinned against the wall, her blouse open, her arms clasped around me as I kissed lower and lower down her neck.

A blood-curdling screech of tires and metal. A moment later, I find myself before a massive fire. The flames consume one structure after another, one garbage pile after another. Everything is ablaze — the tents, the shanties, the garbage, the people. The earth is red and black, a nightmare.

My eye stinging, my throat choking, I wrap the shawl around my mouth. I find myself in a wide crossroad with a swirling galaxy of empty bullet casings. A jeep lies on its side, wheels still spinning. One of the soldiers is an exploded mess, crushed under the jeep's mangled frame. The other two form a muddy, bloody skid mark several feet from the wreckage, tangled in ways the human body isn't meant to be.

The smoke and snow make it hard to keep my one eye open. But I see them: more than a dozen bodies lying in the mud, hands clutching Walther P38s. Almost all are kids wearing once-white rags on their right arms. The exit wounds in their torsos are the size of my fist.

I spot another jeep and scramble behind an overturned food cart. Two soldiers hop out on either side. Rifles trained, they survey the bodies.

"She's not here!" shouts one of them.

The third soldier remains at the back of the jeep, loading another box of sawtooth 7.62mms into a smoking RPD. A loud clack later, he whistles at the other two to hop back in.

As the engine hisses and crackles, there's a pained cry from one of the bloodied heaps on the ground. The jeep idles. The soldiers aim their rifles at one dead body after another.

A reanimated corpse stirs. She wipes the blood and dirt caked over her face. Then she rises, sitting up in the fire and mayhem, an ancient goddess of war made flesh again.

Doua.

As I watch this exhausted, battered creature surrounded by dead bodies, it reminds me how much lower in the ground we are. The world has spun for just three years, but in that time she and I have been ground into shreds of ourselves.

The soldiers shout at her. "Get on the ground!"

Seven bullets. I have seven bullets. Training the .45 on the soldier manning the RPD leaves me shaking for the first time. There's no guarantee I can get the other two before they riddle Doua full of 7.62mms.

Dazed, she wipes her face with her right hand, clearing grime and gore off. With her hair pasted in sweaty, dirty clumps over her scalp, I get a full glimpse. I see what she's been through. The left side of her face is unblemished, save for a curved, discoloured scar that cuts an inch into her forehead.

She turns her head, and I see the blotched X of scar tissue that streaks down her face and neck. Wounds that Ash said I carved into her myself.

"Hands behind your head, bitch!" barks a soldier, hopping off the jeep and stalking her. "Hands behind your head."

Doua's left hand clutches a paper bag. Something cylindrical and silver glimmers in the bag. The soldiers can't see it. Not from their angle. The bodies cover her lap where the bag rests.

"They were just children!" she cries out in a voice that's a faded memory of the one I knew. It takes everything out of her, leaving her shaking. "You monsters."

"Shut up!" shouts the soldier, his AK-47 levelled at her heart.

Seven bullets.

She swivels her head as if scanning everything around her. Her eye settles on me sheltered behind the food cart. It's an opaque black orb, no shine in it, none of that night sky lustre that would melt my heart in an instant.

She's not looking at me. She's listening. For what?

"The snow falls over it all," Doua says. No fear, no regret in her voice. Nothing like me. She holds the bag to her chest. "The snow falls over it all."

A shot rings out.

Doua shudders.

The soldier stalking her drops to his knees, clutching his shoulder. I was aiming for his head.

I shoot again, once, twice.

I don't know where the first one hit him. If it even hit him. The second one gets him in the torso, dropping him hard. Holding my gun with both hands, I leap over the food cart and charge the soldiers.

Two of them. Four bullets. No sense of distance. One eye.

I shoot twice, clipping the soldier manning the RPD in the side. He hangs on to the RPD. The other soldier ducks.

I tilt the gun so the sights alight with my left eye, the world skewed and warped.

The soldiers aim their guns at me, the RPD and AK-47 ready to blaze.

I freeze.

It's not fear.

It's Doua, who tosses what's inside the paper bag at the jeep. A small bomb. The soldiers scream.

The world convulses. Mud and dirt rain down on me as I press myself against the ground.

For a moment, the world is as quiet as it's ever going to be. That moment where everything slows down, where everything terrible seems like it won't last forever. Except time spirals lower and lower.

The air is saturated with the smell of burnt leather, hair, rubber, and flesh.

One soldier is reduced to a tattered, blackened slab of meat. The other rolls on the ground, the flames and shrapnel digesting him. He tries to tear his thick uniform with weak tugs before hunching over and collapsing on the dirt.

I hear sirens getting closer.

Doua.

Blackened with mud and soot, she stands with great difficulty, favouring her left leg. She says something, calling out to someone.

The sirens get closer.

The soldier with the RPD twitches. He isn't dead. He's a charred, smoking black heap. But he isn't dead. He shoulders the massive gun and aims it at Doua.

Another shot.

He drops dead. One bullet.

The sirens come from all around us now.

Hands crossed in front of her, Doua stands alone, so defenceless that it takes everything in me to stop myself from gathering her in my arms and kissing her a thousand times.

"Doua." My voice rasps as I hold her hand. "It's okay. You're safe."

"Who are you?" She struggles against my grip, panic in her voice.

I'm Majnun meeting Layla after years of separation, his mind still ablaze with the image of the woman she used to be. I'm Orpheus leading Eurydice out of the Underworld, doubt snaking its way at the back of his mind that she's no longer following. I'm Devdas riding the carriage to Paro's opulent mansion, seeing the gates that will never open for him.

"I found you," I say, squeezing her hand, transgressing as I kiss it. "I finally found you."

I transpose the woman before me over the one in my memory of her. The weariness, the pale skin, the weathered, bloodied frame, the worry lines, the scars, the grey streaks in her hair, the cracked lips, the shimmerless left eye. This is Doua now. When she pulls her hand from my grasp, I feel like it's already begun. The end.

Cold, blood-covered fingers touch my face. They feel and trace every inch of it; the forehead, the eyebrows — her fingers shrink away briefly at the leathery eye patch — the nose, the cheeks, the lips, the chin. She touches my lips again.

She takes a step back.

"No," she whispers. Her voice is the one I know. Only more tired and hollow. Her brow furled, her mouth open, she lets her arms dangle by her side. It's defeat. As if she first refused to believe in this dark fairy-tale ending but believes it now and hates me for making it come true. "Avaan?"

"Yes." In all my many faces, in all my half-truths. "It's me."

The sirens, the jeeps — the soldiers are almost here now. Grabbing the RPD off the dead soldier, I check its slide and trigger. Red and blue lights wash over us as two army trucks screech to a halt in the road, cornering us.

I cock the machine gun. One hundred bullets between Doua and the world.

Episode 23: The Archive

Avaan

August 13, 2083

Water sloshes in the tiny washroom. I pour another pot of hot water into the round bathtub and place a fresh disk of soap next to it. Tightening the towel around my waist, I speak the first words uttered in Red's white apartment since I brought Doua here.

"The water is ready." It takes me a moment too long to say her name — and then I don't. "You can clean up now."

I click my tongue. What a jackass I am.

Stepping out of the washroom, I find her on the white chair where she fell asleep minutes after we got here. She's awake now. Wrapped in my filthy shawl, she's about the only speck of colour in this white expanse of mirrors. The faint light from outside illuminates the orange-brown scars that twist down the right side of her face and neck.

She turns toward me as I approach. Other than that movement and her steady breathing, she's a defaced statue.

"You want to clean up, right?" I ask.

Doua presses her lips into a straight line, and her lightless black eye lingers in my direction.

"Okay." Holding her forearm, I help her to her feet, and again, like so many times before, the cool touch of her skin is like a half-stained memory. "You can walk, right?"

Facing away, her right arm extended against me, she nods once and starts walking.

"Take five more steps and turn left," I say at the washroom's threshold. "The soap is on the floor, next to the tub." I wince. "To your left."

She nods, her face turned away.

"Careful," I caution as she hobbles, clutching my arm. "It's slippery."

She drops my shawl on the ground. In her black blouse and skirt, she crosses her arms in front of her pale, sunken belly. As I collect the dirty shawl from the floor, I feel her discomfort.

I turn around. "I'm right outside ... in case you ..."

There's more silence as I leave the door ajar behind me.

———

Water continues to trickle inside the washroom.

Doua has said only my name and no other word to me since I found her. I tried to speak — monosyllables really. Sounds I made with my tongue and lips. The way I'd hum at night to keep myself from feeling alone as a child. Maybe that's how language was born: the first man, the first woman, huddled before a fire in the lonely, cold night. They stared at each other. They gestured. But they were still cold and alone. So, the first man made a sound with his lips. He said something he wasn't sure meant what he thought, and the first woman felt something she didn't mean to. And from that moment on, women and men have tried to archive their thoughts and feelings, like pinned butterflies. As if it's the only way to assure one another that these thoughts and feelings exist at all.

A military jeep rushes by in the street below, heading toward whatever is left of the Badlands.

I put on the clothes I was wearing when I shot Evergreen. When I fell. Red left them washed and folded. Sitting on the windowsill, I watch the snow fall under the hazy morning sky. It's heavier than before, a gyre of greyish-white ash whirling as people flock to the pale roads below. The colour of their clothes is difficult to make out.

The sky is burning again. Who will the Pakistanis blame this time?

Relapsing into an old madness, I hear Doua's voice. *What do you want?*

"Go away," I whisper.

She's wearing a green saree. Half of her face is hidden by her shoulder-length black hair. Everything else — the slight acne scars, the smooth curve of her belly, the pinch of her navel, the night-sky lustre in her exposed eye — pains me in ways that her three-year absence couldn't.

Closing my eye, I say the only thing worth saying. "Go away."

I'm alone.

I pull out my 1911. A solitary .45 ACP hollow-point glints golden in the chamber. The only reason we're alive is because of the RPD. Past the Badlands, there was no way I could've walked around with such a gun. It's just the Big Heat now. One bullet between Doua and the world.

Light footsteps patter across the ceiling, followed by heavier ones. A woman and a man. The faded sound of their voices.

Pressing my face against the windowpane, I see the orange flames flicker and fade on the black horizon. How many people made it out alive? Did Ash? And all the kids with her?

I touch the eye patch. The bleeding has stopped, and so far — despite bellyflopping into an ocean of garbage — it's not infected. The limited field of vision? The scorching pain in my left arm? The dull, prodding ache in my side? Nothing I can do about any of it.

I hear a slippery thud in the washroom.

"Is everything all right?" When no one answers, I almost call out her name. A name that feels alien on my tongue and lips. "Are you okay?"

No reply.

Rushing inside, I find her sitting in the bathtub, her arms and breasts glistening with suds. Her hand is extended at the edge of the tub. The chunky disk of soap is out of reach. Tearing my eye from the soft brown nipples I've kissed and licked so many times proves impossible.

As if feeling my gaze, she lowers herself back into the greyish water and crosses her arms before her. Numerous cuts and bruises line her forearms and hands.

Grabbing the soap from the floor, I place it in her outstretched hand. "I'll be outside. Let me know if you — you know."

I let my fingers linger over her palm, but she snatches her hand away.

Watching her curled up in the water, I'm reminded of how dainty and fragile Doua is. I catch a glimpse of the smouldering horizon, of the ashes raining down on us, and I'm reminded of the power she wields over Pakistan. Over me.

With the door ajar again, I sit on the floor beside it. Behind the wall, I hear the water dripping and Doua's gentle scrubbing. She's mere paces away. We breathe the same cigarette-infused air. Past this wall, it might as well be the edge of the world.

"Avaan?" Her voice is low. "Avaan?"

I rush inside the washroom. Wrapped in a towel, she has her arms crossed, a reminder of the distance between us.

"I do not have any —"

"Clothes," I fill in and head for the closet. "I'll get you some."

Green clothes. Green kurtas and sarees everywhere. I pick up white undergarments and head back to the washroom with a saree set and a kurta. "There's a saree. Or do you want kurta and jeans?"

"Saree."

"Here." I hold it against her hand. "It's probably too big for you."

She grabs the green clothes and the white undergarments. She faces me with tightly pressed lips. Her black eye looks no different than the barrel of my .45.

Okay.

Closing the door behind me, I return to my perch on the windowsill.

―――

I have no idea how much time has passed, but when I wake up, Doua is sitting on the pipe bed. She's in a green saree, her hair still slightly wet. She brushes her hair methodically. Parting her hair from the left, she brushes it over the right side of her face and neck.

You still look beautiful, I almost say. *You are as beautiful as ever. You'll always be the most beautiful woman in the world. You look terrible, and I'm the reason why.*

I approach her, stepping heavily. She recoils as I sit on the edge of the bed.

"You should sleep." I don't say her name. It would feel unnatural.

Silence.

I let my fingers venture toward her feet, but she pulls her legs close to her.

Standing up, I unfold the blanket and spread it over her feet, which I know are perpetually cold, as are her hands. She accepts the blanket. If ever a tiny detail could weigh more than the sum of all happiness over the last three years, this is it.

"This will keep you nice and warm. I was here a few days ago." I lean back against the foot of the bed. "It's been crazy the past few weeks. I was thrown out of a window by —"

"Evergreen." It's a shot fired straight at my heart.

She pulls the rest of the blanket over her.

I spring up. "Here, I'll —"

"No."

"Just let me —"

"No." It's final, said with an open-palm gesture that cuts the space between us.

Coiling the blanket over her, she curls up, her back to me.

Standing next to the bed in the same green saree, the Doua of memory smiles a sad smile.

Somewhere under this thick white blanket is the woman I love. The final victim of what my love does to people.

I finally say her name. "Doua?"

She stiffens but doesn't speak.

Three years later, I have no idea what to say to her. "I wanted to talk about —"

I hear her shallow breath. "Avaan?"

"Yeah?"

"If you try to tell me why you did the things you did, if you try to explain yourself or apologize ..." Her voice is muffled under the blanket. "I will fucking kill you."

Episode 24: The One Thing That Unites All Men

Avaan

August 13, 2083

I groan as the feedback from the PSA system scrunches the air. Sharp blades of red and blue light cut through the shielded windows.

"Return home and remain indoors," a female voice drones once the feedback subsides. "The curfew will soon be in effect."

My back pops audibly as I sit up from the floor. The thin layer of bedsheet has done little to cushion me. Sleeping without a blanket only ensured that the cold crept into my joints and bones. My left arm no longer hurts as much. Silver linings.

I stare at the white ceiling above me. There's a steady creaking of furniture and muffled moans from the floor above.

I almost utter her name, almost glance at the pipe bed.

Cracking the window open, I watch a sea of Pakistanis in the streets. They're covered in grey ash. Panic permeates the evening air. The celestial debris and the falling snow are one and the same.

More army jeeps skid toward the black hole on the right side of everything I see. They're headed for New Pakistan.

There's a loud whistle.

A crimson flare rises into the sky, illuminating the world

around me in reds before fading into nothingness.

I look at the bed. She's gone. I knew the moment I woke up. Creases and light impressions on the bedsheet are all that remain of the woman who spent the night here.

I don't call out for her. I don't run out into the snow. I won't make any deals with the devil. I won't rush headlong into the Badlands. I won't buy a gun and start a war.

I fold the blanket, make the bed, and head to the washroom. I take a piss in the chic Sector 2 hole in the floor, wash up with the freezing water from the pots. Using a white bedsheet as a makeshift shawl, I head downstairs and pause at the exit. I triple-check my .45.

The snow swirls around me like bad memories. It takes several minutes before I convince myself to mingle with the people in the streets.

"The curfew will soon be in effect," the PSA system blares again. "Return to your homes. The curfew will soon be in effect. This is for your own safety."

A military jeep honks, skidding and screeching past the Sunnis, Shiites, Christians, Hindus, and paleets. They're all here, rushing, scrambling, snow clinging to their clothes.

Another truck goes by with a soldier on loudspeaker.

"The curfew is now in effect. The curfew is now in effect. Return to your homes immediately. Anyone spotted will be shot. Return to your homes immediately."

In a quieter, calmer grove of buildings, I spot a young boy spray-painting on a wall. His misshapen head and the way he looks at me — it's gun-crazy Rumi.

"You're that man." He raises his hands, dropping the canister. "Salaba."

"Are you going to shoot me again, kid?"

"You're supposed to be dead," he whines, retreating.

Reading what he's painted on the wall makes me roll my eyes. The same drivel puked over this city in blues, pinks, and purples: *Quran 9:5* and PFM.

"Go home, kid. You're not safe here."

"I have no home. Everyone I know is dead. You people killed my family."

"I'm sorry."

"I don't care if you're sorry. They're all dead, and there's nothing you can do to bring them back."

"Painting this crap all over the city won't bring them back."

"It's a reminder."

"Of what?"

The little shit tries to dash, but I grab his arm.

"*Tchhh.* Let me go, you paleet. Don't touch me!"

Twisting his wrist makes him squeal. "I asked you a question."

"PFM! It's a reminder of who our real enemy is." Rumi struggles in vain against my grip. "Colonel Evergreen crushed you all. Just like he promised he would. We won. As long as there are warriors like him — a true *mujahid* — we'll always win."

Still twisting his arm, I hold up my 1911. "You saw me shoot Evergreen, didn't you?"

"He threw you out of the window."

"We both fell. But he's the one whose face was disfigured. I did that."

"Liar."

I let the miniature bigot go. "Go home before I shoot you too. Run."

He scrambles off into one of the countless nooks and crannies in the vast asphalt jungle that is Sector 2.

Purple canister in hand now, an idea creeps into my brain. I'll fight my own war against New Pakistan, against the Mullahs.

And what better weapon to defeat tyranny and bigotry than a canister full of paint and a mind full of juvenile humour?

I draw giant breasts over Rumi's drivel. I draw breasts all over another wall near me, covering more bigoted hogwash. And that's my new mission in life. Any mention of hateful scripture I find, any trace of divisive piss-on-the-wall, I will smear with breasts. Purple breasts will appear on the walls and doors of buildings and shops.

By the time the paint runs out, there won't be a word of bigotry left. Breasts will replace hateful scripture, as they always should have. Moses should've come down the mountain with tablet drawings of breasts, and the world would've been better for it.

I lean against a wall and snort and chuckle like a teenager until my cackles echo in the road that's suddenly empty.

A white cat crouches in a remote corner of the street. Her ears pointed back, her tail puffed, she shivers as we look at one another.

"All alone, huh?"

Choppy and distant, the PSA system crackles weakly. "Return to your homes immediately."

Home. The Badlands have been burning for almost the whole day. The library? Razed. Kanz's home? Kanz is dead. Hell, even Humayun's Diner is gone. Red? Gone. Baadal? Eksha? Mother? All lost forever.

Doua.

Here, in this moment, I'm an old, familiar tale. I'm Majnun running back into the wilderness because Layla is no longer the woman he knew. I'm Orpheus reaching madly as Eurydice fades away into nothing, mere inches from his fingertips. I'm Devdas, slumped against Paro's gate, the last gleaming of a fairy-tale ending snuffed away. I'm the story told a thousand times, in a hundred thousand words, across hundreds of nations.

The ground shakes. The cat hisses and runs away. The wall, the whole damn building I'm leaning against, creaks and heaves. Everything rattles under me, around me.

Static sputters from the PSA system. A voice is heard briefly — gasping, trembling — before more static drowns it out. Everything goes eerily silent.

More tremors come, one after the other. I felt these intermittent tremors yesterday when the Badlands burned to the ground.

Explosions.

The dim streetlights above me hum mechanically before fading out. Whatever power surged through these buildings has ceased. The bustling, the humming machines all flatline. People cry out in a collective drone, like a hive with no connection to their queen. They rush out into the streets, despite the curfew, to see the explosions light up the horizon.

New Pakistan is ablaze. Explosions light up the once-white skyline.

People call out for Allah, for Jesus, for Ram.

We watch the once-bright white lights fade. The only light now is the flash of yellow and orange from the explosions, contrasting against thick sinews of smoke that bind the earth to the dark sky. Another wave of explosions jolts the city. One of the white buildings topples against the rest, breaking in half before our eyes as huge plumes of smoke and falling debris veil that slice of heaven completely.

Everything goes black. All sectors.

There are a few gasps, a smattering of whimpers and sniffles. A stunned silence holds us all in place under the cold, black night.

New Pakistan has fallen.

Episode 25: Monsters

Avaan

August 13, 2083

The moment I step inside Red's apartment, I feel a knot in my stomach, tight and cruel.

Leaning against the open window, Doua faces the snow-eaten night where the moon is no longer visible. She remains motionless, as though in mockery of the dancing snow outside.

"Doua?" I can't seem to recognize my voice. I peel the white bedsheet off me and toss it to the floor. Instantly, the hairs on my arms bristle in the freezing air.

"I wish I was there." She turns around, arms folded. "I wish I could see it."

Something warm churns inside my heart. A kind of longing. A remnant of devotion.

I walk close to her. "What are you doing here? What do you want?"

She waves her hand to where New Pakistan once glowed. "It is over."

"You did it." I reach out to touch her but decide against it. "Your war is finally over."

"Is it?"

"New Pakistan is on fire."

"The Badlands are on fire too." She cups her face in her hands, her voice exhausted. "It will not bring anyone back. I do not know what I should do next."

I take a step forward. Then another, close enough that rogue strands of her hair brush against me. "What are you doing here?"

She doesn't answer.

"What do you want, Doua?" I ask, taking one more step so that I can feel her breath.

Hands smothering her face, she speaks. It's the same exhausted voice. "Avaan, I —"

I gather her in my arms, tightly. The softness of her skin, the feel of her breasts, the warmth of her body — they reignite a dream I thought I had woken up from.

"Doua," I whisper with an urgency that startles us both.

I kiss her.

Her small hands press into my chest, but I grab them in one hand and pin them above her. She moans something, but I don't care. I kiss her, deeper. The way we always kissed.

She whispers something, but a truck grinds by, drowning her out.

I'm far beyond caring.

My other hand slips up her blouse, feeling her breasts.

She tears her lips away from mine. "Avaan, stop."

I step back, dazed. She cowers against the window, arms crossed before her.

We both breathe heavily, hands touching our lips. Another truck goes by, and the trailing, alternating sequence of blue and red lights illuminate her face. Despite the dark shadows and her hair, I see it: the scars, the discolourations winding down the right side of her face.

It's her. Doua. My Doua.

"What are you doing, Avaan? What is wrong with you?"

What's wrong with me? I'm in love with a woman who's haunted me for three years. I'm seeing things, hallucinating, dreaming while awake, and I can't tell the difference. My world is on fire. There's nowhere for me to go. Everything keeps bringing me back to the hole in the world where she should be.

Above us, a woman yells something in anger. Someone shouts back. Heavy, lumbering steps traverse the entire length of the ceiling. A door slams shut.

I draw close to Doua, but she shrinks into the shadows.

Something has pierced the centre of my chest. "Doua, can you just — it's me, okay? You don't have to be afraid of me."

"I am afraid."

"Please don't —"

"You killed Rosa. You killed Maseeh. You killed Baadal." She pulls her hair away from the right side of her face. "You damn near killed me too."

"I didn't know they were working for you."

"That is your excuse?"

"That — that's not what I —"

"What exactly did you mean? That it would be okay to kill children if I did not know them?" Another large truck rattles by under the window, illuminating her in faint blue and red hues. Then the shadows return, sheltering her from me. She turns away. "What happened to you, Avaan? What have you become?"

I grab her arm. "What about you? If I'm a monster who kills kids, what does that make you?"

"Let go of my arm."

"You turned kids into suicide bombers. You filled Baadal's head with your ideas. How many people died yesterday because of your war? How are you better than me?"

"Let go of my arm, Avaan."

"What are you doing here, Doua? Why did you come back?"

"You are hurting me."

I let her go.

She turns her back to me, rubbing her arm.

I stare out into the burning night for what feels like three years. "When Evergreen attacked the library, I didn't —"

"Do not expect forgiveness. Not from me."

"I'm not asking for forgiveness."

"I do not want to hear it."

I massage my temples. "I know I don't deserve your forgiveness, but —"

"You murdered your brother."

"I deserve to be heard. There's enough history, enough something still between us, that you can do that. Can't you?"

"Avaan —"

"Tell me I don't deserve at least that much."

I take the silence that follows as her consent to speak.

I've imagined this moment on many sleepless nights. The moment when I'm reunited with the woman I've loved and wronged. It's when I finally explain it all. My reasons, my moment of weakness. My fears and regrets. Deep down, I thought this was the reason I fought as hard as I did — why I refused to die no matter what this city threw at me. Now, as she stands with her back to me, as her shoulders rise and fall, her head lowered, I realize that I've been lying to myself. What I say next doesn't matter. Not now, when so much sorrow has been sown in its wake. But I say it anyway. "I'm sorry, Doua. I'm so, so sorry. For everything."

Silence. It's our song now.

She turns to face me. "Do you remember that morning after we first —"

"Always."

"Do you remember what we talked about?"

"I do."

"Then why do you apologize?"

The lump in my throat is impossible to swallow. "I had to."

"You are right about one thing. Even back then. I am no one to judge you. I am the reason everything is on fire. I am the one who turned children into soldiers and human bombs. I am the reason so many people have died. I am no better than you." She exhales. "Look at what we have become, Avaan. What happened to us?"

"I lost you," I whisper, "and the world broke under my feet."

"Did you tell the army about Baadal?"

"I'd never."

"You are lying."

"I'm not. It wasn't me."

"Then who?"

"I don't know. Someone who wanted all this to happen. Someone who wanted revenge. Baadal's surviving friend who handed me the gun. Asha-Eksha's dad. Your ex-husband. My mother. Evergreen. Any one of the jilted men who Nargis refused to marry. Or simply any of the thousands of Pakistanis who loathe us for existing."

"Why?" she sobs. No tears form in her eye. "Why work for Humayun? After Baadal. Why him?"

"I deserved it." I hold her arm gently, like touching a wounded bird, and guide her fingers over the gun in my hand. My Colt 1911. "I told myself it was to find you, but it's because I deserved it."

"I do not understand," she says.

"It doesn't matter now."

I close the window and light the oil lamp. In the reborn flower of light, I watch Doua make her way toward the bed, impressed by how in her blindness she's quickly mapped out the room. I grab the blanket.

"Here," I say, wrapping it around her. "You must be freezing."

The bed creaks as she pulls her legs together and reclines against the headboard. Sitting opposite her, I feel — for the first time in so long — some kind of joy.

Above us, there are low voices. A woman and a man. Lighter footsteps walk away. The same low voice grows louder, choppier. The ceiling trembles as someone slams the door shut.

"I don't think I told you." I pat her foot lightly. "I met Asha. Ash."

"I know."

"You think she's safe?"

"Do you think anyone can kill that girl?"

I smirk. "She's like you."

"She is nothing like me. That is why she survived this city and not ..." Her voice trails off.

"You've survived this city."

"Some days, I think I have not. People who have seen my face would say that is true."

"Fuck those people."

"You have survived too. I used to fear that it would be Baadal who would endure and not you. But I was wrong. I was wrong about a lot of things."

"I died once already."

"And yet, here you are."

I place both hands on her feet. "Why did you come back, Doua? Why aren't you with Ash and the rest?"

She doesn't say anything for a while, her face lowered. "This war is bigger than one blind woman. Yaqzan's dream, his words, will carry on no matter who is leading the fight."

"Who is Yaqzan?"

Doua pauses, patting her hair down over her scars. "Yaqzan was a madman. A myth. A martyr."

"Martyr?"

"He died a long time ago, Avaan. Before the soldiers destroyed my shelter. Before Eksha. Before you and I. He died a long way outside this city, in the Misty Wasteland, where no one goes and no one returns."

Episode 26: A Short One Before the End

Avaan

August 14, 2083

Dawn is still a few hours away. Perched on the windowsill, I watch Doua seated on the bed, silent as a portrait. She reaches up to pat her hair down over the right side of her face.

"Let's leave this city," I say to Doua's reflection in the window. "Flyers talk about buses that will take us into the Misty Wasteland, where no one goes and no one returns."

"I have heard."

"It'll cost a lot of money. But I've got a decent amount stashed up in my old house." *Decent* being one hundred million rupees. Courtesy of one dead fat bastard. "It's risky, but I think I've got enough for —"

"Avaan —"

"There's nothing for you here, Doua." In the window's reflection, it's as if she's fading away. "Not anymore. Not for us."

She swallows audibly, like she's trying to cry but can't. "There is no us."

———

"Any idea when they'll be here?" These are the first words spoken in this room in hours.

"They will be here soon enough."

"You think they're okay?"

"Ash is with them. You have no idea how capable that girl is."

"Oh, I've got some idea. Still, it's Old Pakistan."

"You never were good at waiting."

"I waited three years for you, didn't I?"

She ignores me.

"When Ash was —" Torturing me. "She mentioned you people knew about this apartment. Is that true?"

"Yes." There's a pause. "We had been tracking Jahan for a while."

"Were you going to kill her? Or was it torture?"

"Neither. Jahan is an old friend."

"What?" It seems I know the least in any room I'm in.

"I was as surprised when you were first spotted with her."

"Why the fuck didn't she —"

"Relax." Doua holds up her hand. "She has no idea who I am. What I am. As far as she is concerned, I am a blind woman she helped out a long time ago. I am not exactly on anyone's list of suspected terrorists."

A woman who supposedly died three years ago, with a new name and a severely disfigured face. Two women who share the same name, yet have conflicting descriptions. And they fight a war on behalf of a man who died decades ago but is propped up as a mythic mastermind. Suddenly, I don't feel so bad about my detective skills.

I glance around the room. This temple of transience. "Red — Jahan — she's leaving Pakistan. Did you know that?"

"Good for her."

"You don't sound happy."

"I wish she would stay. I wish everyone who is leaving would stay in their own country. That is what a country is supposed to be: a home for its children. All its children."

"You can't blame people for wanting to leave."

"Are you leaving too?"

Don't think I didn't notice the hesitation in your voice, Doua. "Not as long as you're here."

She doesn't respond.

I keep talking. "Maybe leaving is the best thing we can do for these kids."

"What do you mean?"

"I don't think the Pakistan we know exists any longer."

"A good thing, is it not?"

"And maybe the best way to keep it that way is to remove ourselves. Clean the slate. Let the children decide which direction things go in."

"They will make mistakes. Like we did."

"They will. But they won't repeat ours."

"Some days, I think staying with them is the best way to make sure that does not happen."

"What about other days?"

Outside, there's an orange glow where New Pakistan used to be. She did this, I remind myself. Doua, Ash, and their army of children. They're not helpless. They're not alone. They're not staying silent.

"It's crazy, but a part of me is happy that the memory of the library-shelter lives on," I say.

"You mean Ash?"

"Yeah. Her being alive means something. Something about what you created."

Not a word.

"I wish it was Eksha."

"Why?"

"If Eksha had survived, it would mean something. Goodness and innocence prevail. A fairy-tale ending to all this horror."

"We make our fairy-tale endings where we can."

There's a knock at the door.

I turn to Doua and hold my finger to my lips. Then I remember that I'm a fucking moron. My 1911 cocked, I peer out into the hallway.

In the faint light, Ash's grey eyes match the colour of my gun. There are half a dozen kids.

"Martin Frost." She nods stiffly.

"Ash."

Bruised and covered in snow, they're the attendees from my recent torture session. Their contempt for me remains intact. The little boy with curious brown eyes is also there; most of his focus is on Ash. He smiles at me shyly. I wave at him.

I let them inside. "Is this all that's left of you?"

Ash pushes past me and melts into Doua's arms. "You're safe! I was so worried, didi."

The kids rush to the bed. Doua embraces them.

Gun in hand, I stand at the door and watch in silence.

"What's the plan, yes?" Ash asks with a sidelong glance at me.

"Avaan has something," Doua answers.

"Is it a miracle?" Ash pulls out a beat-up sawed-off .303. "Because I only have two bullets left, and no one else here can shoot straight." She nods at me. "Except for this guy."

This guy taps his eye patch. "My precision shooting days are done."

She shakes her head. "If you've got a stockpile of bullets or money lying around somewhere, now is the time to say."

I grin. "I've got a stockpile."

Episode 27: Independence Day

Avaan

August 14, 2083

A truck crawls past. Doua presses her hands against her mouth. The kids follow my lead. The 1911 glints in my hand, the hammer cocked. Ash grips her sawed-off sternly. Three bullets between us and the world.

The pavement shivers under our knees and fingertips as the truck goes by. I can't help playing out the horrible scenarios if they spot us, if the dumpster we're hiding behind in this little alley can't shield us all from view. Will they arrest us? Shoot us in half with the RPD? Will they arrest Doua and shoot the rest of us? Will the last thing I ever see in this world be Doua and the kids being snatched away as I'm shot dead?

The sawed-off .303 rattles in Ash's hands. She tries to peek from behind cover, but I hold her arm and shake my head.

"It's clear!" shouts a soldier. "Keep moving."

The truck rolls away. We exhale, almost laughing.

"Let's go," I say, holding Doua's small, cool hand in mine.

A deep, reddish-golden circle hangs at the interstice between the dark grey sky and the black edges of this city. Far ahead, past the bridges and Sector 3, whatever was left to burn in the Badlands has burned away. Behind us, past Sector 1, cradled between the five peaks, large black clouds of smoke churn where New Pakistan once stood.

Shadows. I keep seeing them where I shouldn't — behind a car, lingering in a pathway, or cast against a wall. As if we're being stalked.

The snow is constant, settling on everything. With shawls wrapped tightly around our faces, we press on in this snow that's equal parts Badlands and New Pakistan. I hold my .45 in my right hand. I hold Doua's hand in the other. I keep my pace steady as she toddles after me. The light tap of the children's feet makes my heart race.

———

Sector 3 is woefully unguarded and empty. There are no soldiers, no jeeps mounted with RPDs. The razor wire fences and barriers are unmanned. Whatever jeeps and trucks we come across are blazing their way toward New Pakistan. The shops are closed, metal shutters locked. The street vendors have abandoned their wares. Most of the gunshots we hear are echoes from New Pakistan.

On our way here, the kids giggled at the purple breasts I'd painted on a couple of Sector 2 walls. Doua asked Ash why they were laughing. When she found out, she shook her head and smiled for the first time since she came back into my life. Her smile hasn't changed. Silver linings.

We enter an isolated dirt road. There are bottles and newspapers and bullet shells scattered all over. Tepid sweat gathers at the back of my neck. I turn my head to stare after another shadow to my right. Before, I'd blitz right through, as certain in my shooting prowess as the falling snow. Now? I scan and re-scan every corner, every sound, every whisper with genuine terror.

"What do you see?" Doua asks. She's covered in a white bedsheet.

An overturned pink rickshaw blocks my view of the road. The driver lies stiff on the ground, a pool of blood cradling his head. The obscene smell of diesel permeates the air around us.

"There's a rickshaw about twenty steps from here. It's flipped over."

"What are we waiting for then, yes?" Ash asks, gripping her .303 tightly.

"I'm making sure the coast is clear."

"Is it?"

"Can't say for sure."

"We cannot stay here," Doua whispers.

I can't bear the thought of you getting hurt. Not now. "Walk right behind me."

Pressing the kids against the rickshaw, we walk past the old man's lifeless body. The sight of him breaks my heart for a reason I can't explain.

"How much farther?" Ash asks, biting her lip. She keeps a watchful eye on the kids.

"Not so far." Two miles. I squeeze Doua's hand. This breath-less blind woman holding on to my hand like a lost child. I don't want to lose her again. "Stay close."

Peeking around the rickshaw proves difficult. The dark circle that's my right field of vision is too large. Even though I keep my head on a swivel, there are too many shadows, too many corners. Too many sounds.

A gunshot several miles away. A scream.

Four soldiers march down the road from the opposite side, their masks and uniforms covered in ash. The female soldier sig-nals to the three males. Two of them join her. She takes point on the right. One of them sidles along to the left. They cock their Lee-Enfields.

Their rubbery footsteps grow louder.

"Avaan?" Doua's voice trembles.

"Stay low," I say, forcing Doua and the kids behind the heavier engine parts. I won't let them hurt you.

One bullet. Three bullets altogether. Four soldiers.

Don't know if Ash is a good shot. I'm half the shooter I used to be. Half will have to do.

"Ash, see if you can —" is all I manage to say before she darts out from behind the rickshaw and shoots the soldier on the left. She catches him in the chest, dropping him instantly.

A second later, a barrage of .303s punctures the rickshaw.

"Cover me." Ash whispers. That's the problem with a bolt-action gun. Manual ejection and loading.

One bullet. I lean past the edge of the rickshaw and let muscle memory do the rest. Except, now, everything feels out of sorts. Another salvo of .303s flies past my face and into the metal. I shrink back to cover.

"Why aren't you shooting?" Ash shouts.

It's not coming naturally. Things aren't where they seem, the dimensions of the world, the distance between things. It's a jumble. I used to shoot on instinct and muscle memory. Now, I need to tilt my 1911 at an angle and find the sights with my left eye. It takes a second, but in a gunfight with trained soldiers? Might as well be a lifetime.

Ash scrambles over to me and peeks from behind the cover. A .303 would've taken her head off if I hadn't yanked her back.

"Stay the fuck down," I snap. She nods, her eyelids fluttering nervously.

Every volley from the soldiers is concentrated, the bullet holes appearing an inch or two apart. They aren't fucking around. And they're getting closer. After every shot, while two of them fire and reload, the other takes point and fires. Their plodding shoes, the *click-clack* of their rifles grows uncomfortably, unnervingly louder.

Can't take them all on. Can't let them get the drop on us. On Doua. Whatever I do, it needs to be fast.

"Listen to me." Doua tears off a piece of her shawl. "This smell. It is diesel, right?"

"Yeah."

"Find me a bottle, quick."

Low against the ground, I slide over to the left side of the rickshaw and grab one of the many bottles littered around. Two bullets whiz past my face as I rush behind the rickshaw.

"Use the cloth to soak up the diesel and empty it into the bottle. Leave one end dry. Hurry."

I stuff the cloth down the bottle and pull the end out of the opening.

"Here." Doua holds up a lighter for me. My love, the demolition expert.

I light the Molotov. The rustling flames chew up the cloth rapidly. I dash out from behind the rickshaw and toss the Molotov at the trio mere paces away.

They weren't expecting the sheer audacity of it. They howl in terror.

I don't wait around to see what burning fuel does to a human being. The screams, the crackling of blistering skin, it's harrowing enough. Huddling over the kids, over Doua and Ash, I focus solely on not breathing in the unctuous, brackish smell that finds its way into my sinuses.

As if sensing my despair, Doua holds my hand and squeezes it gently. "We need to go."

We, huh?

———

The sombre brown walls, the single bulb, the barred window, the mattress that breathes out white puffs of foam; this room is a plundered shrine to the woman I love. A woman I have lost, I know now. Maybe it isn't a shrine to lost love but to loss itself.

"Careful. Don't step in just yet," I say, kicking away broken pieces of glass near the bloodstained door. Bullet casings litter the room, the hall, every inch of this house, where me and Kanz blasted through Humayun's goons.

A military jeep swerves down the street. Probably headed for New Pakistan, like every other vehicle we've encountered.

"Do you know where it is?" Doua asks, stepping inside.

"Yeah." I watch the crumpled sketches under the feet of the woman they meant to recreate. Sketches she can never see, sketches that no longer resemble her. Maybe it's meant to be.

Using a piece of glass, I cut down the length of the mattress where I re-stitched it. Ripping through the foam, I pull out the briefcase full of money. One hundred million rupees.

"How much do you have?" Doua asks as I grab her hand and step out of the room.

"Enough." I guide her down the stairs.

"How much?" she asks again, her voice sharper. Ash and the kids peek at us from the main entrance like we're their bickering parents.

"One hundred million rupees. I'm putting you and those kids on a bus. You're not staying here. Not in this fucking city." I place the briefcase in her hands. "I can't protect you anymore. None of you. Not in the state I'm in. This money is all you need to start fresh. Away from this place."

"We do not need you to protect us."

"You stay, you die. It's that simple." Holding her face in my hands, I'm touching my past and my present. "I can't lose you any more than I already have."

"What about you? Where will you go?"

"There's nothing for me here or out there." If it's without you, it doesn't matter where I am.

A jeep screeches outside.

"Am I supposed to be okay with that, Avaan?"

Time is a spiral. "I want you to be safe. That's all."

She reaches up and touches my face. Her hand, cool and soft, makes me forget the city is burning, ashes falling from the sky. "It does not matter if I live or die. Not anymore."

"Doua." I wrap her tightly in my arms and brush her hair. "New Pakistan is on fire. The only thing that soldiers want right now is —"

The main door swings open slowly, creaking the entire way. A tall, thin shadow blocks the bright light.

I hear that voice. Old and haunting, it's the call of a timeless bird of prey. Evergreen.

"Hello, Avaan."

Episode 28: Upon All the Living and the Dead

Avaan

August 14, 2083

Doua quivers in my arms when she hears Evergreen's voice. In an instant, her breath is hot and fast against my neck and chest. Ash gathers the kids behind her, a frightened mother bird.

Death has arrived.

He's in his uniform but without his gas mask. He looks greyer, his hair unkempt, his beard patchy and uneven. The left side of his face is badly disfigured, shredded with grisly cuts. From the fall.

With the Peacemaker in his left hand, he's here to make the obvious painful.

"You son of ..." Ash screams, drawing her .303. Before she can even raise her arm, Evergreen knocks her out with a quick, violent whip of the Peacemaker.

The rest of the kids rush to hide behind Doua.

Evergreen marches forward, but I stand in his way. "What are you doing here, Evergreen?"

"I did tell you. All wars begin and end inside a home." He studies the briefcase in Doua's hand. "That must be the one hundred million rupees you stole from Humayun. Hand it over."

I shield Doua and the kids. "Not happening."

Evergreen smirks when he notices my 1911. "Turns out you were right: New Pakistan didn't have enough bullets after all." His golden eyes pierce through me and into Doua. "You must be very proud of yourself, Ash. Even I wasn't prepared for your trump card."

The confused look on my face makes him snicker.

"Oh, you don't know?" he asks. "Explosives, Avaan. Your Loyalist Queen here has quite the fondness for them." He scowls at her again. "The terrorists wore suicide vests when we captured them. They rigged the trucks themselves. Once the trucks were inside New Pakistan — boom. The Iron Gate, the checkpoint, the perimeter guard — all of it, gone."

Hell on earth.

He continues, shaking his head. "Without the gate, without the guard, the whole thing lasted a few hours." A smile cuts across his mouth, thin as a razor. "It's over now. New Pakistan is reduced to this." He brushes the snow off his shoulder, sprinkling it in the air between us. "All order and structure, gone."

Some part of me feels sorry for him. He radiates the same strength he always has. That weary, desperate kind of strength that is as frightening as it is pitiful. As if he is the last beast of his kind.

My 1911 drawn, I don't take my eye off him. "Kids, run along upstairs," I say.

They scramble up the stairs behind us but freeze in place when Evergreen commands them. "No."

He trains his gun on them.

I hold Doua close with my other arm. "They're innocent."

"So were we! Once upon a bloody time."

"Let them go."

"No. They're a part of this war."

"The war is over, Evergreen," Doua states quietly, no longer afraid.

"And what did you achieve? The Badlands are razed. New Pakistan burns as we speak. Old Pakistan is covered in ashes. What exactly did you achieve?"

When Doua answers, her voice is low and soft. "Something new. For all of us."

"New?" Evergreen laughs. "A new New Pakistan?"

"No. One Pakistan." She breaks away from my embrace and stands against the tall black shadow looming in the corridor. "A Pakistan for all Pakistanis."

"Pakistan is for Muslims. It has been since 1947. It always will be." His voice is an echo in an icy cave. "The soul of this country is steeped in Islam. It's the reason it was born. It will never have room for people like you."

"And yet we are still here. We always will be," Doua says. "You cannot make us choose whom to love and what to worship. Our hearts belong to us."

"Your hearts are filled with sin and defiance," he snaps, startling Doua. "Your hearts are filled with hatred."

"I do not hate you," she says gently. "You hate us. You have hated us since 1947, and you have hated us for the last fourteen hundred years."

There's murder in his eyes. He clicks the Peacemaker's hammer back. The cylinder spins and clinks into place. It settles on Doua.

There's the gun in his left hand. There's a black hole in my vision.

Shots ring out.

A .45 ACP shell rolls on the floor.

Pure disbelief whitens Evergreen's face.

"You —" he growls, looking down at the gaping hole in his gut.

Evergreen stares through Doua, through me. He stares at something behind us that seems to disappoint him. A murmur escapes his lips, and he staggers back. Struggling to keep his legs under him, he fails and slumps to the floor.

A thin trail of smoke rises from the Peacemaker in his hand.

No.

"Avaan?" she whispers. With her small hand pressed to her chest, Doua says my name again as a dark red circle widens under her fingers.

No.

She sinks into my arms, and already it's like I'm holding an ice sculpture. The whiteness of her lips, the pallor of her skin, the longing with which she clutches my arms — she is everyone I've ever loved.

"Doua, please." I don't know what to say. I don't know what to say. "Please don't."

She shudders violently as I hold her close and beg her to stay.

Nothing happens. I pray for her to stay. I pray to whatever is pure and holy in this world. I wish for the world to end. I wait for the azure cracks in the burned sky, for the growling thunder under me as everything plunges into dust. I wait for my heart to burst inside my chest. I wait for a miracle.

Nothing happens. The world continues spinning, my heart goes on beating in my chest, and life bleeds out of her.

"Doua, please don't."

Evergreen winces as he stands, his scarred face twisted in pain. His arm drops limply, and the Peacemaker slips out of his hand. His long hair masking his face, he whispers our parting words.

"Goodbye, Avaan."

Limping out the door, he leaves behind a trail of blood.

Ash picks herself off the ground, wiping her bloodied mouth. She picks up the Peacemaker and prepares to follow Evergreen. The sight of Doua bleeding in my arms stops her.

"No," she murmurs. "Please do something, *bha*— Avaan."

I shake my head quietly.

She's Asha again, and I'm Avaan. The last three years have dissolved.

"No, didi, you can't leave us."

"This war," Doua says quietly, "is bigger than one blind woman, remember?"

Ash embraces the children.

"The briefcase that Avaan has," Doua says weakly. "That is all you need for the new world we wanted to build."

Doua can't see it, but Ash is holding Evergreen's Peacemaker. It's the missing piece of the puzzle Yaqzan was trying to build. In whatever world is going to grow back from this debris, Ash holds both keys for harnessing it. Money and power. These kids can build their own Pakistan — because the Pakistan that belonged to me, to Doua, to Red, to Kanz, to Humayun, and to Evergreen is in the ashes raining down from the sky.

"Avaan?" Doua whispers. She no longer shivers.

"Yes?"

"I want — I want to see it. I want to see this new Pakistan."

Squeezing my eye shut briefly, I scoop her in my arms. Ash and I look at one another, and without a word, we agree that she'll stay and console the kids while I take Doua outside.

Bloody footprints lead outside. I follow them.

The snowstorm is a dizzying spray of white that mutes the earth into an expanse as transient as the sky above.

Looking straight ahead, Evergreen slouches toward the fire and smoke in the distance. Toward New Pakistan. He's completely white now, his clothes, his hair. The red footsteps tell me it's him.

"There's nothing there, Father."

Steeling himself against the blizzard, he takes one more step toward the burning desolation before hesitating and looking back

336 \ Saad T. Farooqi

at me. A moment later, he collapses face down as the snow blots him out of my life.

Doua rests her head against my chest. "Please describe what you see. Paint it for me."

"The snow is falling so much that all shapes, all silhouettes look the same. The buildings and roads are white, the homes and shops are white. The snow is falling over everything."

A long, shaky breath rushes out of her. More follow suit, each shorter and more ragged than the one before.

"Every woman, man, and child is covered in whiteness. The whole world is white, Doua." I try to find my voice. "Everything is beautiful."

"Finally."

She is gone.

Episode 29: Epilogue

Jahan

August 14, 2083

"Are you coming, miss?" the bus conductor asks me impatiently. I don't blame him.

"I'm coming." I smile nervously, hugging my small backpack. My legs are weak and unsteady.

A flood of people are enclosed within this huge chain-link fence surrounding the buses. It's already evening. Several conductors do their best to maintain a semblance of order. The people shiver in the blinding greyish-white snow, suitcases and bags balanced on their heads. They inch closer and closer to the bright blue buses. They stare, they cry, they hug and console one another. This is the right thing to do. There is nothing left in Pakistan for them.

The conductor scratches his thick moustache as he looks at the rupees in my hand. "Are you waiting for someone, miss?"

"No, no." I search for what I've been searching for since I arrived: his big golden eyes; his tall, seemingly denuded frame. I see nothing but the steady sheet of snow that falls over everything. "I don't think he'll —"

"Miss, there's a lot of people behind you." The conductor exhales.

"There's nothing for me here," I say out loud, looking at the puzzled conductor. "Right?"

Head tilted, he shrugs. "Most people are leaving for that reason."

I scan the crowd behind me. I scan the chain-link fence for the face I've been longing to see.

I'm drowning. Voices and sounds grow faint, all motion slows down as I walk away from the bus and out into the whiteness collected over everything, over everyone.

———

Sitting alone by the river, I hug my backpack and rest my chin on it. Strangely comforting. The pearly white sand under me, the smoky evening mist hanging over the surface of the river, the ashes raining down. Everything else is ablaze and chaotic, but the harmony of this river abides.

Rummaging through my pockets, I take out a cigarette and light it. Through the falling ashes, I catch a glimpse of the Misty Wasteland, where no one goes and no one returns, and I remember my pigeons.

I sigh out a small cloud of smoke.

About a mile to my right, there's a fire. It's not the burning abyss that Pakistan is reduced to. It's gentler, like a bonfire. Shoes in my hand, I make my way toward it, shielding myself from the falling ashes.

As I approach, I realize it's a funeral pyre, surrounded by a gaggle of children holding hands. Standing among them is a tall man clad in black, wearing an eye patch.

I stand next to him. "Hey."

"Hey." He takes my hand, his golden eye even more luminous. "Still here?"

Behind us, Pakistan burns as it has for almost two days now.

I grasp his hand tightly. "Still here."

Glossary

Abaya: a full-length, loose-fitting outer garment worn by Muslim
    women, especially as a symbol of modesty and piety

Abbu: father

Adhan: Muslim call for prayer

Ahle Kitab: People of the Book, used by Muslims to refer to Jews and
    Christians

Ameen: Muslim version of amen

Ammi: mother

Ashraf-ul-makhlooqat: the noblest of creation, a title bestowed on
    human beings in Islam

Ankhon ko ankhon ne: a famous song by Pakistani singer, Junaid
    Jamshed

Astaghfirullah: said as a means to seek forgiveness from Allah

Bhaiyya: older brother

Bhenchod: sisterfucker

Bhosdi-ka: son of a bitch

Bibi: a polite way of referring to a woman

Bibi-ji: a polite way of referring to an older woman

Bidi: a cheap cigarette made of unprocessed tobacco that is wrapped in
    leaves

Bismillah: in the name of Allah

Chacha: (literally) paternal uncle; colloquially, a polite way of referring
    to an older man

Chai: tea

Chai waala: tea boy or tea server

Chana: chickpeas

Chandramukhi: (literally) moon-faced; in South Asian literature, a
pivotal figure in a famous Bengali novel, *Devdas*, who offers a
sympathetic shoulder to the titular character during his downward
spiral into alcoholism and depression

Charpaai: a bed with four wooden posts strung with ropes for bedding

Chuut/Chuutya/Chuutye: used the same way as *asshole* is in English.
The literal meaning involves the *c-word*.

Daal: lentils

Dayan: witch, especially one with a scary appearance

Dhaba: shack

Didi: (literally) elder sister; a polite way of addressing a woman who is
slightly older or higher in relationship status

Diya: oil lamps made of clay pots

Doua: (literally) a wish to God

Dupatta: a thin shawl

Dust-e-ilahi: (literally) the hand of God. The name is in reference to
Islamic eschatology, where on the Day of Judgment, Allah will hold
the entire earth in the palm of his hand and demand to know if
anyone has beheld a greater king

Gandu: faggot

Haleem: a stew made of meat, lentils and barley

Haram: forbidden

Hazrat: a highly honorific title used to address people, especially
religious figures

Hijra: a eunuch or transvestite

Howzat: in cricket, the phrase "How's that?" is shouted as an appeal to
an umpire

Imam: the person who leads prayers in a mosque

Maaro isko: hit him/kill him
Madarchod: motherfucker

Jalebi: a dessert made of deep-fried flour dipped in sugar syrup

Kaaba: a square stone building in Mecca, Saudi Arabia towards which
    Muslims face to pray
Kafir: infidel
Kajal: a black eyeliner
Kameez: a long shirt; *shalwar kameez* is the national attire of Pakistan
Karak chai: strong tea
Korma: a traditional spicy curry made of meat with yogurt and onion
    gravy
Kurta: a traditional loose-fitting shirt

Laari Adda: truck stop
Laddu: a sweet made from flour, ghee and sugar
Lassi: a drink made of yogurt or buttermilk

Majnun Layla: a legendary Arabic poem about two star-crossed lovers
    that Lord Byron described as the Romeo and Juliet of the East
Mashallah: Praise be to Allah
Miswak: a twig used to clean teeth
Mujahid: a soldier of God, a religious warrior

Naan: a thick leavened baked bread
Nirvan: (Sanskrit) the liberation from ego and the cycle of
    reincarnation; in the Hindu South Asian transgender community, it
    is the surgery that symbolizes their passage into a new identity

Paisay: money
Pakistan: (literally) the land of the pure
Pakora: a snack made of deep-fried chickpea batter
Paleet: Untouchable
Paratha: lightly-fried flatbread

Qeema: a spicy ground meat dish

Raksha Bandhan: the bond of protection; a celebration of the protective relationship between brothers and sisters in Hinduism
Roti: a thin bread

Saala: brother-in-law; pejoratively, calling someone Saala implies you are sleeping with his sister
Sahib: mister, can also be used as suffix when addressing a man of higher social/religious status
Samosa: a savoury, triangular pastry filled with a mixture of vegetables and/or meat
Shalwar: a loose-fitting trouser; *shalwar kameez* is the national attire of Pakistan
Sherwani: a knee-length coat buttoned up to the neck
Shraavana: the fifth month of the Hindu calendar
Surah Tawbah: the ninth chapter of the Quran

Tasbih: rosary
Taweez: a religious amulet worn around the neck for divine protection or fortune

Ya Allah: Oh Allah

Zabiba: a dark, scaly prayer bump on the forehead

Acknowledgements

Writing is not a solitary endeavor. Yes, you will spend countless hours alone in front of a screen or piece of paper battling doubt and despair. Yes, there will be endless days of secluded scribbling and endless nights of reclusive rumination. But, somewhere between the first draft and a published novel, you will discover genuine comradery with the people who've helped you reach the finish line. In the fifteen years it took to write and publish *White World*, I've had the privilege of working with some amazing, visionary people without whom this novel wouldn't exist as it does today.

Firstly, I would like to thank my agent, Sam Hiyate from The Rights Factory. By the time we met for coffee back in 2019, I had been rejected by around seventy publishers and literary agents from Canada, U.S., and the UK. Getting a one-on-one with Sam was a Hail Mary to make headway in my floundering "career." Sam was exactly the voice I needed in my ear: focused, pragmatic, and committed to quality. Above all, Sam believed in *White World*. Where others perhaps saw a dystopian novel set in Pakistan as a hindrance, Sam saw it as a new frontier. For three years, I'd send Sam new drafts and updates, and for three years, he'd send me quality feedback that enhanced not just *White World* but my writing in general.

I met Marc Côté from Cormorant Books on a rainy day in early 2022. No one knows this little detail but prior to the meeting, I had not slept in three days. I also had a gnarly migraine the whole time, and I had driven almost three hours in heavy traffic and rain to make the meeting. As pleasant as Marc was during our lunch, I couldn't help but think I'd made a horrible first impression. But two important things happened that day: Marc passed on the timeless wisdom that a writer should never pay for lunch, and just as importantly, he made the formal offer to publish *White World*. In the time since, his notes have been invaluable in helping me understand the macro world of publishing and marketing — to truly step back and see the novel from the reader's eyes. I always believed in *White World*, but it wasn't until I got to work with Marc that I truly believed in myself.

The same goes for the whole team at Cormorant Books — who, to me, are my team. Thank you, Sarah Cooper and Sarah Jensen, for putting this book out there, for arranging every event, and for cheering me on the whole way. Thank you, Andrea Waters, Matthew Poulakakis, and Fei Dong, for your laser-like edits and making me realize that I should never call myself a proofreader/ editor around you guys. Thank you, Marijke Friesen, for putting together such a great cover for *White World*. And thank you, Barry Jowett, for helping me navigate the many steps of copy edits and proofreads before the book made its way to the printer.

I'd also like to acknowledge the teachers who've been so generous with their guidance, knowledge, and — let's be honest — patience. I was tardy, easily distracted, and a sarcastic smartass to boot. A big thank you to the American poet, "Dr. Infidel" Nicholas Karavatos, who always challenged me to write about my experience as a closeted apostate in the Middle East. Your courage and passion for literature was so contagious, I'm still not over it fifteen years later. The Rancid Frog Collective lives on! The same goes for N. M. Browne, Jeremy Bendik-Keymer, William S. Haney II, Mohammad Zayani, and Nawar Golley for instilling a love for the written word that grows stronger with each day. Of course, it would be remiss of me to not mention my high school English teacher, Bernadine Pinto, who noticed my talent for storytelling even when I didn't. She worked with me for three years, assigning me novels to read and short-story topics to hone my talent. It was the birthplace of my dream to be a writer.

In writing, the only acceptable form of love is tough love. Before there were agents, publishers and professors, there was a tight group of friends who provided ruthless feedback bordering on mean. I want to thank Ali for poring over the many iterations of *White World*. Whether it's sage advice, a shoulder to cry on, or to crack a smile, our friendship for the last twenty-five years is one of my most treasured gifts in life. I am grateful to Tooba for designing the map for this novel's setting. And, if there is one person who always provided sapient critiques for years, it's Mo. Thanks, guys! With friends like you who needs editors, right? (Turns out you do.)

My brother, Jarjees, was my hero growing up. He encouraged me to think for myself and indulged my imagination when no one else would. Most importantly, when I decided to change majors from electrical engineering to English literature to pursue a dream (in my fourth year, no less), he went to war against anyone who tried to stop me. I also want to thank my parents for sponsoring my education, for sending me to the best colleges and schools they could and couldn't afford, and for always doing what they thought was right for me.

Finally, I owe everything to my wife and OG proofreader, Sana. Thirteen years ago, I was a broke 20-something writer who couldn't even afford to pay for our dates (massive red flag, what were you thinking?). Like Yeats, the only thing I had were my dreams — and you have treaded softly on those dreams every moment we've been together. You are and will forever be the highlight reel of my life.

P.S. I would thank my twin toddlers, but who am I kidding? You guys are the best thing to happen to me and the worst thing to happen to my writing schedule.

We acknowledge the sacred land on which Cormorant Books operates. It has been a site of human activity for 15,000 years. This land is the territory of the Huron-Wendat and Petun First Nations, the Seneca, and most recently, the Mississaugas of the Credit River. The territory was the subject of the Dish With One Spoon Wampum Belt Covenant, an agreement between the Iroquois Confederacy and Confederacy of the Ojibway and allied nations to peaceably share and steward the resources around the Great Lakes. Today, the meeting place of Toronto is still home to many Indigenous people from across Turtle Island. We are grateful to have the opportunity to work in the community, on this territory.

We are also mindful of broken covenants and the need to strive to make right with all our relations.